Three

Jane Blythe

Bear Spots Publications
Melbourne Australia

bearspotspublications@gmail.com

Paperback
ISBN: 0994538006
ISBN-13: 978-0-9945380-0-0

Cover designed by QDesigns

Also by Jane Blythe

Detective Parker Bell Series

A SECRET TO THE GRAVE
WINTER WONDERLAND
DEAD OR ALIVE
LITTLE GIRL LOST
FORGOTTEN

Count to Ten Series

ONE
TWO
THREE

Christmas Romantic Suspense Series

CHRISTMAS HOSTAGE

I'd like to thank everyone who played a part in bringing this story to life. Particularly my mom who is always there to share her thoughts and opinions with me. My awesome cover designer, Amy, who whips up covers for me so quickly and who patiently makes every change I ask for, and there are usually lots of them! And my lovely editor Mitzi Carroll, and proofreader Marisa Nichols, for all their encouragement and for all the hard work they put in to polishing my work.

JANUARY 8TH

He rolled his eyes.

This was getting ridiculous.

So, they were newlyweds. Did that mean they had to spend hours playing around in bed?

He loved sex, too. Especially with a hot girl. And Erica Landers was as hot as they came.

But, come on; he'd been waiting two hours already. And they'd started before he arrived.

Surely they must have tired themselves out by now.

He tried to wiggle himself into a more comfortable position without making a sound—not that they would have heard him anyway. The groans and moans coming from the bed were loud enough to stop traffic.

He stifled the urge to scream at them to hurry up.

He supposed he could go and put an end to things. That would come with risks, though. They would be two against his one; however, he was strong and fit, and Garton Landers was as skinny and wiry as they came. What kind of name was Garton anyway, he wondered? Erica was as skinny as her new husband, with breasts that had been enlarged a few too many times. It was a wonder she didn't topple over when she stood up, she was so top-heavy.

He chuckled at his joke; he had to do something to amuse himself as he passed away the time.

He was sure he could take the couple. But why risk it? It was much easier to wait until they fell asleep, and then deal with them individually.

For some reason the idea of killing newlyweds had appealed to him.

Why? He didn't know.

All he knew was, since he'd committed his first murder, his lust for blood had been insatiable.

He couldn't stop killing even if he wanted to.

And he didn't.

He would rather be dead himself than be unable to take the lives of others.

Speaking of which, he glanced at his watch, just able to make out the time by angling his arm in the thin strip of light that shone between the closet doors. He was getting annoyed now. Angry. And that would not bode well for the Landers.

Trying to stretch his cramped muscles, he was just about to go for it anyway, when he realized that—at last—the room had grown quiet.

Garton and Erica Landers had apparently worn themselves out and decided to call it a night.

At last.

It was time.

He glanced quickly at his watch. He'd give it ten more minutes, make sure they were asleep, and then he'd make his move.

The seconds ticked by excruciatingly slowly.

Finally, the ten minutes were over.

Stealthily he rose, slinking out of the closet, dragging his kill kit along with him, then set about making preparations. He had to be quick. The longer it took him to get ready, the greater the chances that one of his victims would wake before he was ready for them.

Not that he was worried.

He never got caught.

He had gotten away with his last murder spree and he would get away with this one, too.

He was invincible.

Collecting the chair from the desk in the corner of the room, he positioned it at the end of the bed. Then he pulled the small vial and needle from the side pocket of his bag. Filling the syringe, he quietly crept to a sleeping Garton Landers' side of the bed. Piercing the man's skin, Garton woke with a start, but the drug was fast acting, and before he could react, he was already passing out.

Fast as a rocket, he dragged Garton from the bed and tied him to the chair.

As well as being fast acting, the drug was also processed quickly through the body. Garton would wake up shortly, and he preferred to wait until the husband was awake before waking up the wife.

Within minutes, Garton was coming to. Groggy at first, but it didn't take him long to assess the situation and start fighting frantically against his bonds, trying to scream through his gag.

Ignoring Garton for the moment, he took hold of his axe and held the blade to Garton's neck.

"Wakey, wakey, Erica," he called.

The woman stirred sleepily. "Garton?" she murmured.

"No, not Garton," he corrected.

Erica's eyes snapped open at the sound of the strange voice in her bedroom in the middle of the night. When she caught sight of her husband tied to a chair, an axe to his neck, she opened her mouth to scream.

"I wouldn't do that if I were you," he cautioned, slicing the blade through Garton's neck, enough to draw a trickle of blood, but not enough to do any real damage. "Try anything stupid and your husband loses a hand and then a foot and then another hand..." He grinned at her, "Get the idea?"

Erica nodded slowly. Apparently, she was smarter than her oversized boobs suggested.

Garton, however, was not so smart.

He shook his head wildly and once again tried to brute force his way out of the ropes binding him. This, of course, was futile.

If he didn't know how to tie someone up, then his career as a murderer would have been pretty short-lived.

"It's okay, Garton," Erica's voice trembled, tears streamed down her cheeks. "Maybe if we do what he says, he won't kill us."

It was interesting, he mused, how different people reacted in these situations.

This was his sixth newlywed kill in eight months. At first he had gone slow. Making sure to space out the kills, making sure that he traveled the country so that no one connected the murders to the same killer.

Now he didn't care about that.

He was back home and he was going to keep killing here until he got bored.

"Alrighty then." He smiled again; it was time to get started. "I'm going to toss you some ropes. Please secure both your ankles to the bed."

Erica hesitated, knowing that once she was restrained, her chances of getting out of this alive dropped dramatically. Reluctantly, she picked up the ropes he'd thrown to her, removed the covers, and tied one end of each rope around her ankles. Another hesitation, but one glance at the axe still poised against her husband's neck and she secured the other end of the ropes to the bedposts.

"Very good," he nodded approvingly. He approached the bed with some more ropes, some duct tape, and the axe. Early on, one of his victims had almost gotten the jump on him. The woman had merely pretended to tie herself to the bed, and then when he got close enough, she tried to attack him. Her attack hadn't lasted long. He had quickly subdued her with a blow to the head and continued with his plan, but he had learned a valuable lesson. Now he always brought the axe with him—just to be safe.

Erica whimpered when he took hold of her wrist and firmly tied the rope around it, but she didn't fight back. With practiced efficiency, he did her other wrist, then went back around all four limbs and added duct tape. If for any reason one of his knots should come undone, as unlikely as this was, the tape would hold his victim firmly in place. Duct tape was virtually impossible to get off without something to cut it, and unluckily for his victims, they had no such tool at their disposal.

Once he was done, he took a moment to survey his handiwork.

He debated on whether to cover her mouth, but decided against it. Erica seemed to understand what would happen to her husband if she screamed for help, and he enjoyed the pitiful whimpers that his victims usually made.

Then it was on to the next step. After their sexy playtime earlier, the Landers had opted to go straight to sleep rather than putting on pajamas first. This saved him the trouble of having to cut clothing off her. Or maybe cutting it off was better, he pondered, as he took in Erica's naked body; it was kind of like his own personal strip show.

Stripping off his own clothes, he carefully folded them up and put them in a bag. He wouldn't be needing those again tonight. Climbing onto the bed, Garton struggled so violently that he wouldn't have been surprised if the man sent the chair toppling to the floor.

Paying Garton no mind, he positioned a knee on either side of Erica's hips.

"Please, please no," she hiccuped through her tears, eyes imploring. "Please. I'm begging you. Please don't."

Ignoring her desperate pleas, he held her still as she bucked her hips, trying to get him off her, and forced himself inside her. As he started to move, he watched her face. Erica had scrunched her eyes closed, and was chewing on her bottom lip to keep from screaming.

It mattered little to him if the woman was as into it as he was; his pleasure was the same either way. So, he barely heard Erica's stifled sobs as he pounded into her. Everything else faded away as the pleasure inside him slowly built. Higher and higher he climbed until the universe exploded into a wave of unimaginable bliss.

Aftershocks continued to rumble through him as he sagged against Erica, trying to catch his breath. When they eventually ceased, he climbed off her, ready for what would come next.

As good as the sex was, it wasn't his favorite part.

Nothing could compare to the killing.

To the sight of blood.

Blood was what excited him.

And he couldn't wait to shed some.

He slapped a piece of tape on Erica Landers' mouth. "Sorry, babe, but I can't have you accidentally letting out a scream."

He picked up his axe, taking just a moment to enjoy the feel of it in his hands. For some reason, the idea of being an actual axe murderer had always appealed to him. So, he had adopted it when he decided to start killing couples.

Noticing that Garton's frantic efforts to free himself from the ropes had indeed caused him and the chair to fall to the floor, he paused and heaved them back into an upright position. "Don't want you to miss all the fun," he said as he patted the man's shoulder.

With purposeful strides, he went to the bed, raised the axe high above his head, and with perfect precision brought it down on Erica's stomach.

Behind her gag, she choked and gurgled blood. Her eyes grew wide with shock and pain.

Behind him, Garton screamed through his gag. The muffled sound added to his excitement.

Bright red blood gushed from Erica's wound.

Mesmerized, he stood and stared at it.

It was so beautiful.

It virtually glowed in the moonlight that streamed through the window.

It was the most magnificent sight he had ever seen.

Raising the axe, he brought it down again and again, until blood streaked the floors, the walls, and the ceiling. It soaked the bed where Erica Landers now lay dead, her body in pieces.

Giddy. He was literally giddy.

Dropping the axe at his feet, he spun in circles around the room. The scene was magical. He looked down at his naked body and saw it, too, was covered in blood. He ran his fingers through the blood, then lifted them to the moonlight. They glistened prettier than water in the sunlight.

As much as he would have loved to stay in this room forever, he knew it was time to go. All good things must come to an end. But there would be more nights like this, more rooms just like this one.

Of that, Ricky Preston was certain.

* * * * *

3:33 A.M.

"Mango?"

She hated that name.

What kind of parent named their child Mango anyway?

Not that she was one to talk, she guessed. Her family was a nightmare. She was living, breathing proof of that. If the worst thing her parents ever did was give her a stupid name, then she never would have ended up in this position.

"In the bedroom," she called out, making sure that her voice perfectly mimicked Mango LeSeur's. She had spent *hours* practicing her imitation, making sure it was flawless. She needed him fooled long enough so she could get close enough to do what she came to do.

He all but came running through the hotel suite to the bedroom, his large frame filling the doorway.

The he who was staring at her, drooling, was one Roman Hitacheel.

Sixty-three, bordering on obese, bald on top, and with constant bad breath, it was a wonder he could find any woman willing to sleep with him. But she already knew what Mango LeSeur saw in Roman, and it had nothing to do with appearances. Roman Hitacheel was wealthy—mind-bogglingly so.

Even though he already had a wife and three grown children, Roman kept his mistress, Mango, very well. She had a generous living account as well as additional funds for clothes and accessories. So long as Mango kept up her appearance and made herself available to cater to Roman's every whim, then she would be well looked after.

Until, of course, she got too old; then Roman would move on to a newer model.

She knew all of this because she was good at listening—quietly and unseen—to others' conversations. And Roman had been a friend of her father's. She had overheard many a conversation on their hot, young girlfriends.

"You look amazing." Roman could barely get the words out past his panting. It seemed he was already in heat and ready to go.

A little work had had to go into her appearance for tonight, as well as all her impersonation of Mango's voice. She had gotten a spray tan, so her milky white skin now glowed a golden brown. She'd added a rinse to her hair to make it a deep dark brown. And she had gone a little overboard with the makeup. Not her choice, or preference, but tonight she was Mango LeSeur, and Mango LeSeur loved her makeup. She had carefully chosen some sexy lingerie that matched with the kind Mango had in her closet. All in all, she wasn't a dead ringer for Roman's young mistress, but she looked enough like her that in the dark room he would never know the difference.

At least not until it was too late.

"Aren't you going to come and join me?" she drawled

seductively. Sickened by having to let this repulsive man touch her, she had no intention of letting him sleep with her. She was a virgin. She was waiting for her Mr. Right before she gave that up. But she would be forced to let this man do some things to her. Let him think it was playtime as usual with Mango, and then, once he was good and distracted, she'd take him out.

In a flurry of activity that was all flabby arms and legs and blubbering belly, he ripped off his clothes and joined her on the bed, his weight making the mattress sag down toward him.

Before she could say another word, he was on her, his mouth practically devouring hers. Swallowing back her revulsion just a little longer, she had to focus on the bigger picture. She forced herself to play along and kiss him back, fighting the urge to bite him as his hand ran up between her legs and began to touch her.

"Kiss me all over, baby," she murmured in his ear.

Immediately, his hand withdrew, and his mouth began to rove over her body, hungrily licking and sucking at her. With Roman busy and focused on something else, her hands slipped beneath the pillows and retrieved the syringe. Roman was so consumed with his feeding frenzy that he didn't even feel the prick in his back as she pushed the needle through his skin. It wasn't until the drugs took effect that he finally slumped against her, his large frame practically crushing her.

Wiggling out from underneath him, she shuddered; Roman Hitacheel was a truly disgusting human being.

Setting to work, she tugged and dragged Roman's body into a sitting position, then with some duct tape, she secured his chest with his arms at his side so they were immobilized to the backboard of the bed. Next she tied a tourniquet around his arm and bent and examined the veins at his elbow. Choosing one, she gave it a couple of taps. No need to bother with an alcohol wipe to disinfect the area; Roman wouldn't be living long enough to develop any infections. Then with practiced efficiency, she inserted the needle, added the tube and collection bag, and once blood was flowing easily, she removed the tourniquet, then sat back and waited.

Roman came to with a jerk.

He tried to move, and his eyes grew wide when he found he couldn't.

Panic was written all over his face as he tried to comprehend what was happening.

Finally noticing his blood dripping into the bag, he tried to yank his arm up and down to dislodge the needle.

Of course, this was pointless.

"Ma...Mango?" he called into the darkness. Apparently, now that he wasn't all gung-ho about sex, he was struggling to see.

She switched on the light. "Not Mango, I'm afraid," she corrected him.

He blinked at the sudden light, or the aftereffects of the drugs, or that he was quickly losing blood. "Wh...who are you?"

Ignoring him for the moment, she removed the collection bag from the end of the tube and put another in its place.

"Pl...please," Roman sniffled, tears already streaking his face. "Don't hurt me. I'll give you whatever you want. Money—I can give you money—as much as you want."

Rolling her eyes at the pitiful display, not only was Roman a repugnant sex addict, he was also a crybaby. "Unfortunately for you, what I want can't be bought," she said simply.

"What are you going to do to me?"

She cocked her head to study him, trying to decide if he was stupid or if the question was shock-induced. "I'm going to kill you, of course."

Her brazen answer seemed to catch him off guard; he stuttered and stumbled over some words, opened his mouth to scream, changed his mind, and burst into noisy sobs instead.

"Why are you doing this to me?" he moaned.

"Because you're a cheater." Rage started to bubble inside her, and that didn't bode well for Roman Hitacheel. "And cheaters cause more damage than they could ever know." This was her new personal crusade. Her life—and her sister's—had been ruined because of adultery. Biting her lip to keep her anger in check, she removed the second full blood collection bag, and replaced it with another. "Last one," she assured Roman who was starting to grow woozy from the loss of blood. Three was realistically all the blood she could take and still make sure that her subject was with her. She had brought additional bags full of blood with her in case they were needed.

Finally deciding that he should scream for help, Roman opened his mouth and prepared to yell. She merely chuckled. And before his shock-jumbled brain could produce a sound, she had tape over his mouth. Petrified little squeaks still emerged, but the sound wouldn't have even carried to the bathroom let alone to the other hotel suites on this floor.

Tuning out Roman's muffled screams, she wondered again if she was doing the right thing.

She was conflicted.

He had told her that once she started killing, she wouldn't be able to stop and she hated to do anything that would prove him right.

But what else was she going to do with her life?

She needed a purpose. A goal. And this seemed like the best fit.

As the third bag filled, she removed it and proceeded with the final stage. "Sorry," she murmured to Roman, "this is going to hurt." She didn't like deliberately inflicting pain unless she was personally invested in her victim. And with Roman she wasn't. He disgusted her, but other than that she didn't burn with a specific hatred toward him. Standing on the bed, she spread his legs; she needed access to his genitals. His eyes grew wider than she would have thought a pair of eyes could go.

Roman mumbled something through the tape that she thought sounded like no, and wiggling desperately. Again, this was pointless. The fact that his top half was taped to a bed severely limited his maneuverability.

Raising her leg, she stomped her foot down as hard as she could against his groin. Dry retching, he began to cough and splutter and groan in agony, writhing pathetically. The pain and the blood loss should leave him incapacitated enough for her to move him without risk. So, moving quickly, she cut the tape, lay him down on his back, then wrapped more tape around his chest, arms still at his side, this time wrapping the tape around the base of the bed. She also removed his gag, as she would need access to his mouth.

Then she sat back and waited.

When Roman was back with her, now too out of it to question her motives or pepper her with pleas, she continued. Tipping the blood she had collected into a large jug, she kneeled on the mattress beside Roman's head. "You're a cheater," she reminded him matter-of-factly. "Cheaters cause devastation to their families, and sometimes this leads to bloodshed. Better that your own blood be shed than those who it is your job to protect."

With explanation out of the way, she held the jug above his mouth. Understanding what she was planning on doing, Roman clamped his lips together. She merely pinched his nose closed, waited till be had to open his mouth to take a gasping breath, and then begun to pour the blood down his throat. Immediately he choked, coughing and sending blood splattering out. She didn't stop, pouring quicker than he could swallow, so blood soon began to go down his windpipe rather than his esophagus.

In minutes, he had drowned in his own blood.

She thought it was a fair death.

His blood was shed so no one else in his family would have to shed their own.

As she dressed, Isabella Everette thought it was a night well spent.

THREE

* * * * *

10:11 A.M.

"We should celebrate."

Sofia Everette heard her boyfriend's words, but they didn't penetrate the jumble of thoughts in her head.

It had been almost five months since her life had been turned upside down, and as much as she had thought she was looking forward to this day, longing for it even, it had left her feeling oddly empty.

"Hey," his hand gently grasped her shoulder. "Did you hear me?"

Detective Ryan Xander was studying her with anxious blue eyes. They had met five months ago when someone was murdered on her family's estate, but she had known of him, and been attracted to him, long before then. Back before they had gotten to know each other, Sofia had thought he was adorably handsome. He had astonishingly bright blue eyes, an endearing smile that brought out his dimples, silky soft blond hair, and he was tall and muscled from hours spent working out. To sum it all up, he was heart-meltingly gorgeous. Now that she knew him, Sofia knew that his good looks didn't even come close to matching his good heart.

"I thought you'd be excited to finally have the cast off your leg," Ryan continued.

"I am," she replied, pasting a smile on her face to try and convince him. She *was* pleased to be free of the bulky cast she'd worn on her leg since her accident five months ago. It had been a long, slow recovery—all because of her sister Isabella. Thanks to the fact that Isabella had been poisoning her for months, her body had become weak. Meaning it had taken her longer than the average person to recover from the injuries she sustained in her fall down the stairs. She had spent several weeks in the hospital as

13

the doctors dealt with the poisoning, concussion, broken collarbone, dislocated shoulder, and badly broken leg that had required multiple surgeries and the insertion of a metal rod.

Even now, five long months later, she still wasn't completely better.

However, it wasn't her painstakingly lengthy recuperation that had her feeling drained and shaken this morning; it was because she felt like she had just lost her last connection to her sister, her only remaining family member. Her sixteen-year-old half-sister, Isabella, had completely lost touch with reality and embarked on a killing spree that left their grandfather, father, uncles, aunts, and both their mothers dead.

Sofia hated what Isabella had done, but she still loved her sister. She wanted to help her, but Isabella was gone. Ryan had been searching for her, using every resource he had at his disposal, but so far they hadn't managed to locate her. It scared her to know that Isabella was still out there, most likely still killing people. But now that her cast was off it was like the whole horrible nightmare was behind her. That should be a good thing, but now it was like Isabella was behind her, too—drifting farther and farther away. Sofia was scared her sister was too far away now to ever find again.

"What's wrong?" Ryan knew her well enough not to be fooled by a fake smile and slowed the car so he could focus more attention on her.

"Nothing," she lied. Ryan had worried about her enough the last five months; she didn't want to worry him further.

It had been a long road for him, too. It hadn't just been physical injuries that she had had to recover from; there were emotional ones, as well. Isabella had revealed to her that the man she had grown up thinking was her brother was, in fact, her father. Logan had been only fourteen when she was conceived. And he had raped her mother—Logan's stepmother.

Just thinking about it gave her a headache.

Everything had happened so fast. The murders, her whole family killed, learning that she was the product of a rape. It had felt so surreal at the time. And it had taken a while to sink in. When it finally did, it had hit her like a ton of bricks. Still weak and in pain, and basically stuck in bed because of her broken leg, she had fallen into a shell-shocked depression. She had stopped eating, barely slept, and she hadn't wanted to see anyone. Ryan had been right by her side the entire time supporting her, offering his unconditional love, and pushing her to start seeing a therapist to help her deal with things. She had started to heal and slowly she had begun to get better.

"What's wrong?" Ryan repeated. "The truth this time," he added with a raised blond eyebrow.

She didn't want to lie again. "It's just that...I just..." She tried to put the mess of emotions swirling inside her head into words. "I guess I'm just tired," she finished at last.

Ryan didn't buy that. "Sofia, what's bothering you?"

"I don't want to talk about it." She met his eyes. "Please."

"All right," he reluctantly conceded, the concern in his eyes obvious. "Later, though."

She nodded her agreement, since she knew Ryan wasn't going to take no for an answer, and he would push her until she opened up to him, just as he had many times before. As much as she fought it, she usually felt better after she and Ryan had talked things through. Right now, though, she just had to sort out her feelings before she could share them. Sofia wanted to focus on something else. "What were you saying about celebrating?"

"We should do something to celebrate you finally having your cast off. What about dinner tonight?"

"Restaurant or with your family?" Sofia absolutely loved Ryan's family. Every single one of them. His parents, Travis and Jacinta, reminded her of exactly what good parents should be. And she was already closer to Ryan's brothers than she'd been to her own: Jack was bossy and opinionated and a cop, and Mark was a doctor with four little kids.

"I was going to say romantic restaurant—just the two of us—but I can see from the look on your face that you want to have dinner with my family." He grinned at her.

"Your family is the best." Her smile faltered a little. "They're the family I always wished that I had. I wish they were my family," she said, with a tiny hint of desperation.

"Sofia," Ryan's voice turned firm, and he reached for her hand, "my family *is* your family now, and they always will be. They adore you, but not quite as much as *I* adore you," he teased gently.

She knew that what he'd said was true, and she allowed his words to soothe her. Sofia knew she and Ryan were going to get married one day, have a family of their own, and grow old together. And she knew that Ryan's family loved her as much as she loved them.

"Dinner with my family, it is," Ryan groaned melodramatically, pulling into the driveway at her house—more their house now. Ryan had moved in when she was released from the hospital. It had been both a personal and practical decision. She had limited movement and needed someone to help her with the basics, like showering, getting dressed, and cooking. She had also needed the emotional support. So as much as Ryan being there helped with all those things, they both also knew that it was what each of them wanted. It was the beginning of being a couple.

"Thanks," she smiled at Ryan.

"Anytime," he smiled back. "Wait for me to come and help you out," he ordered.

She rolled her eyes; she hated it when Ryan ordered her about, even though she knew he only ever did it when he thought it was in her best interests. Deciding to humor him, Sofia stayed put till he came around to her side of the car and opened her door.

"You ready?" Ryan asked.

She nodded slowly. She was a little tentative about walking on her own for the first time. Of course, her doctor had made sure she could walk before letting her leave, but that had been different. She'd been in the hospital, so if anything had gone wrong, there were doctors to help her. If she fell at home, she could hurt herself all over again. She still didn't have a lot of strength, and her leg hadn't been used properly in months, so it was extremely plausible that it could give out from underneath her.

"A little scared?" Ryan seemingly read her mind.

She nodded again.

"Take it nice and slow," he reminded her.

He handed her the walking stick the doctor had given her to use after graduating from both the wheelchair and crutches. Hopefully, she'd soon be down to nothing but her own two legs.

Wrapping his arm around her waist, Ryan eased her down to the ground, keeping his arm there until she was steady. Then he released her, pushed the car door shut, and headed for the house.

"Wait," she called after him, panicked, sure that she would fall if she tried to walk on her own.

He paused. "Sofia, you can do this. I *saw* you do it at the hospital. You're not going to fall."

"Ryan," she begged, tears tumbling down her cheeks.

"Come on, cupcake," he encouraged, "I'm waiting right here for you."

She whimpered, trying to catch her breath enough to try to take a step. Her body had let her down a lot over the last year. Being poisoned by mushrooms had led to nausea, vomiting, dizziness, dehydration, fatigue, and overall general exhaustion. She had been prone to frequent fainting spells and learned to distrust her own body.

"I can't do it," she protested.

"Yes, you can," Ryan contradicted, holding his arms out as one would ready to catch a toddler learning to walk. "Just come to me."

Gathering all her willpower, Sofia clutched the walking stick and forced her good leg to take a step. Then holding her breath, she cautiously dragged her bad leg up to meet it. Surprised when she remained upright, she looked to Ryan, who was watching her closely, ready to help her if she needed it, but wanting her to try it on her own. With renewed confidence, she took another step, and then another, and before she knew it, she was halfway down the path.

When she reached Ryan, he wrapped his arms around her waist and lifted her off the ground, spinning her in circles.

"I did it," she grinned, stupidly proud of her small accomplishment.

"I never doubted you for a moment," he grinned back. "Okay, now…" He paused as the phone in his pocket buzzed. He pulled it from his pocket, and his face grew instantly serious. "It's Paige," he told her setting her back down on the ground, but keeping her held against his chest, his arm around her waist.

"A case?" she asked when he hung up.

"Yes. Are you going to be okay here on your own?"

It must be a bad case judging from Ryan's distracted tone. "I'll be fine," she assured him.

"Okay, I gotta go. Call Edmund if you need anything because I might not be able to answer my phone," he reminded her.

"I know the drill." Ryan had taken a couple of months off work after her accident, but he had returned eight weeks ago. He'd worked several cases since then, so she knew that he wasn't always able to answer calls.

"All right." He released his hold on her and was almost to the car when he stopped and came back. "Sorry," he apologized, tipping her face up to kiss her. "I'll pick you up for dinner at eight."

Waving goodbye as he drove off, Sofia said a prayer for the family of the victim in Ryan's new case. She knew from firsthand experience what an overwhelming shock it was to be thrown totally unaware and unprepared into the middle of a nightmare from which there was no waking. She hoped the family had the strength to get through it.

* * * * *

12:00 P.M.

"Hey," Paige greeted him.

Ryan half heard his partner but was too lost in thought to reply. He hadn't wanted to leave Sofia alone; it had been a rough couple of months for her. She was still recovering both physically and emotionally. This morning she'd surprised him with her fears about walking on her leg without the cast. He hadn't realized just how much she had grown to distrust her body, as though it were an enemy that could turn on her at any second. Walking away from her had gone against his overwhelming instincts to protect her, but by coddling her in this, it wouldn't have helped her long term. She needed to regain trust in herself so she could keep moving forward. There were still things she needed to process, most notably her parentage. She hadn't opened up to him about that yet.

Still, Ryan was sure he could get her to eventually.

He wasn't good at knowing the right thing to say and do when someone was struggling emotionally. No, he corrected himself, that wasn't quite true. It was more like he wasn't *confident* enough in himself to do or say the right thing when someone he loved was suffering. Sofia had helped him a lot, probably more than she believed he had helped her. She understood that he felt guilty and responsible for his fiancée's suicide three years ago, even though his logical mind knew it wasn't his fault. But Katrina had been depressed, and he hadn't been able to help her. Sofia, on the other hand, reminded him on an almost daily basis that he helped her more than she could ever put into words.

Over the last five months they had both learned a lot about each other and themselves, and he was excited that their relationship continued to move forward…

"I said, hey!" Paige punched him in the shoulder, not soft but not too hard either.

He focused his attention on his partner. "Sorry, I was distracted. Hey."

Calm brown eyes studied him. "What's wrong with Sofia? I thought you'd be excited she was getting her cast off today. Did something go wrong? Is she okay?"

"She's fine," Ryan quickly assured Paige. His partner had grown close to Sofia the last five months.

"Then what's wrong?"

"I don't know," he answered honestly. "She freaked out about walking; she was scared she couldn't do it."

"Makes sense," Paige considered, "given what she's been through."

"There was more to it than that, though. She's upset about something else; I'll push her on it later." He then focused his mind on the reason for their presence here. "So, victim was sixty-three-year-old Roman Hitacheel. He drowned." Ryan strode toward the hotel elevators.

"Technically." Paige followed him into the lift.

He arched a questioning brow.

"He drowned in his own blood," Paige elaborated.

"Stab wound?"

"No." Paige raised a hand to smooth her already perfectly smooth brown hair; she always wore her curly hair pulled back out of her face.

The lift chimed as it reached their floor, the doors sliding open. "So how did he die?" Ryan asked his partner.

"Someone poured blood down his throat until he couldn't swallow it fast enough, and it went down his windpipe and filled up his lungs." Paige couldn't quite suppress a repulsed shiver.

"Oh." Ryan didn't quite know what else to say to that. It was certainly a unique way to kill someone. He wasn't sure he'd come across a similar case in the ten years since he became a police officer. "Sounds like Roman Hitacheel made someone mad."

"I agree." Paige snapped on a pair of gloves and rapped on the closed hotel room door they'd stopped in front of. "It seems personal. If you just want to kill someone, then there are tons of easier ways to go about it."

Ryan slipped his hands into gloves. "We need to interview his family ASAP, see who he hasn't been playing nicely with…" Ryan trailed off as the door opened to reveal Stephanie Cantini, his favorite crime scene tech. "Hi, Steph," he warmly greeted her. Ryan considered Stephanie a friend, not just someone he worked with from time to time. In fact, just a few weeks ago, they'd had a huge party to celebrate Stephanie's fortieth and Paige's thirtieth birthdays. Stephanie had become a good friend of Sofia's, as well, helping to support her through this difficult time. Ryan loved how smoothly Sofia had fit into his life and how well she had gelled with his friends and family.

"Hey, Ryan, Paige," Stephanie smiled back at them. Then her hazel eyes clouded over. "I don't like the feel of this one. Something feels…" She trailed off, seemingly thinking of a fitting way to express what she was feeling. At last she shook her head, a brown curl springing free of her messy ponytail. "I don't know. I just have a bad feeling about this case."

"Sounds like it could have been personal," Ryan offered, attempting to ease Stephanie's obviously jangled nerves.

"That doesn't make me feel any better," Stephanie shot back, then softened with, "How's Sofia? She got her cast off today, right?"

"Yes, and she's okay," he answered vaguely, shifting his gaze from the crime scene tech to the hotel room behind her.

"Okay like she's really okay or okay like you don't want to talk about it?"

He grinned at Stephanie's straightforwardness. "The second one."

"I'll call her as soon as I finish up here," Stephanie assured him.

"Thanks, I really appreciate it, and so will Sofia. So, you have anything for us?"

Opening the door wider, he and Paige followed her into the suite. "This place is a hotbed for fingerprints and fibers," Stephanie complained. "We have tons of samples, but most of the prints are partials. We have some good ones, though. We took exclusionary prints from the maids who cleaned the room, and chances are, we'll find some from our dead guy. Hopefully, we get lucky and our killer left some behind, too."

"Where's the body?" Paige asked.

"In the bedroom," Stephanie replied. "Doesn't look like anything much happened in here, nothing is disturbed. All the action seems to have taken place through here." She led them across the suite's lounge room toward the bedroom. "I'm going to see where we're at with the hotel's security footage. Frankie's in there with the body; she can probably give you more than I can at this point."

Ryan surveyed the room as he pulled open the bedroom door. Again, this room looked largely undisturbed, except for a pile of Roman's clothes on the floor halfway between the door and the bed. The majority of the activity focused around the bed.

"He came here willingly," Ryan observed.

"He knew whomever he was meeting; he wasn't threatened by them," Paige added. "Clothes don't look damaged, so they weren't cut or ripped off him. It appears he took them off himself. Girlfriend, maybe?" she suggested.

"A pretty angry girlfriend," Francesca Marks noted grimly.

"What have you got for us, Frankie?" Ryan focused on the medical examiner. Her usually jovial face was grim, her brown eyes serious, straight dark brown hair just brushing her shoulders.

Frankie had grown up in Japan, moving during her college years. Now in her mid-forties, she and her husband had finally added miracle baby, Tania, to their family eighteen months ago after years of trying to get pregnant.

"Well," Frankie took a deep breath, "as I'm sure Stephanie already told you, and you've probably already noted for yourselves, looks like he came here willingly. I found a small puncture wound on his back, so my theory would be that he came here for sex, only his partner had other plans. I'll do tests as soon as I get him back to the morgue, but I'd guess he was sedated so the killer could get him under control."

"You think the killer's a woman?" Ryan asked. If Roman Hitacheel was having an affair, then that could be motive for either his wife or his mistress to want him dead.

She shrugged. "I guess he could be gay. Or there was more than one killer—the woman to distract him and a partner to do the actual killing."

"Sedating him and then tying him up could point to a woman," Paige suggested. "Roman's a big guy, difficult for a woman to maneuver. She'd need something to give her an advantage. Pretending she was here for sex would get him on the bed and distracted enough for her to inject him without him noticing. Then once he's out, she uses the duct tape to keep him under control while she kills him."

"She moved him at some point." Frankie motioned them closer, then pointed to a red line on Roman's chest. "At first he was taped sitting up against the headboard."

"How do you figure that?" Ryan asked.

"Tape on the headboard." Frankie grinned at him.

He smiled back. "So did she—assuming the killer is a woman—have him taped sitting up first for a reason?"

"Easier to drain his blood." Frankie held up Roman's right arm and pointed to the needle marks at his elbow.

Ryan frowned. "She used his own blood to drown him?"

"I'm guessing so; we'll test it. It would certainly be easier than bringing some with her. Although, I guess she may have needed more than she was able to take from him assuming she wanted him awake when she poured it down his throat."

"That could be helpful in IDing her if she took blood from someone else. Maybe she works at a blood bank or a hospital." Paige jotted down some notes.

"He's lying down now. Again, he's a big guy, so how did she move him without him putting up a fight?" Ryan asked Frankie.

"He would have been faint from blood loss, and I think this helped." Frankie gestured at Roman Hitacheel's groin.

"Ohh." Ryan couldn't help but wince at the sight of the swollen and bruised genitals.

"He was probably in enough pain not to put up a fight long enough for her to lay him down and tape him up again."

"Are we sure he was alive when she poured the blood down his throat?" Paige asked. "Maybe he was already dead from blood loss."

"No, cause of death is drowning, not exsanguination," Frankie assured them. "See the blood splatters on the pillows around his face?" She gestured at them. "He coughed up blood as she was pouring it down his throat."

"Icky." Paige shivered.

Frankie chuckled. "Yeah icky," she agreed.

"So if he was conscious through all of this, he must have screamed, yelled out for help. No one reported hearing anything?" Ryan thought that seemed odd in a hotel this large.

"No other guests on this floor," Paige told him. "All the rooms were booked, but the guests never showed up."

"Well, that's suspicious." He was slowly starting to form a picture of this killer in his mind. "Speaks of premeditation."

"Hey, guys." Stephanie came barreling through the bedroom door. "We got video footage of the killer," she grinned.

"How are we sure it's the killer?" Paige asked the crime scene tech.

"Only two people came to this floor last night," Stephanie explained. "A tall, brunette female arrived at approximately two in the morning; victim arrived at three thirty. Then we see the killer leave around five."

Ryan was thrilled. Maybe they'd have this case wrapped up in a couple of hours, and he'd be able to grill Sofia on what was bothering her before they had dinner with his family.

Stephanie noticed his smile. "Don't get too excited," she cautioned. "We don't get a look at her face. She kept it covered the whole time. Still, at least you'll have something, and it seems to confirm the killer was a woman."

He was disappointed, but as Stephanie had said, it *was* better than nothing. "You find his phone, Steph?" Ryan asked.

"Yes. Why?"

"Fancy hotel, this was the place where he met up with his mistress, assuming he had one. Which I am, since I don't know who else he'd come running to meet in the middle of the night and take his clothes off for. So, let's say for the moment that's who he came to see. I want to know who it is, and chances are, it's the last person who called him before he died."

Stephanie went and retrieved the phone, handing it over. "Here you go."

Ryan took the phone and brought up the recent call history. "Last call came in at around two yesterday afternoon," he told the others. "Call came from a Mango LeSeur." He couldn't quite hide a grimace at the name. What kind of parent names their kid Mango?

"Mango?" Paige rolled her eyes, and Stephanie and Frankie snorted chuckles.

Scrolling through the call history for the past few weeks, there were dozens of calls from Mango's number—at least one every couple of days. Most calls lasted only a minute or two, probably just enough time to organize where and when they would meet up. "We should make a note of all the days Mango called Roman, so when we talk to the family we can confirm that he was out those nights," he said to Paige. "I'm going to call Mango, see if we can confirm she was his mistress." He dialed from Roman's phone in case Mango LeSeur was one of those people who only answered calls from known numbers.

"Hi, Roman," a low, sexy voice drawled in his ear.

"Mango LeSeur?"

"Oh, you're not Roman," Mango's surprised voice rose an octave higher than her seductive voice. "Who is this? Where's Roman?"

Mango's surprise that someone else was using Roman's phone seemed genuine; still, Ryan remained cautious. "When was the last time you spoke with Roman?"

"Three days ago," she answered after a brief pause.

"His call history shows you called him yesterday afternoon," he confronted her.

"I never called him yesterday," Mango protested. "Wait, yesterday afternoon?"

"Yes, why?"

"I never called Roman yesterday, but I lost my phone for a couple of hours."

"What time did you lose it and where?" If Mango LeSeur was telling the truth, then perhaps someone was trying to set her up.

"I met some friends for coffee at our favorite café; my phone must have fallen out of my bag, when I went to look for it later it wasn't there. I retraced my steps and found it at the café. Someone had found it and turned it in. But why would whoever found my phone call Roman? Maybe they just looked to see who I called the most and called that number looking for me? And you never told me who *you* are, and why you're asking me these questions. Is Roman okay? Did something happen to him?"

He ignored her questions for the time being. "What time was your phone out of your possession yesterday?"

26

Frustration edged into Mango's voice. "Maybe from around one till four or five. Now tell me what's going on or I'm hanging up."

"How do you know Roman Hitacheel?" Ryan asked instead.

"I'm hanging up now," Mango announced.

"Mr. Hitacheel is dead," Ryan told her before she disconnected.

"What?" Mango's voice became a shriek. "Dead? How?"

"I'm Detective Ryan Xander, we're investigating his death."

"Roman was murdered? And you think I did it?" Mango was bordering on hysterical.

"Yes, Roman was murdered, and no, you're not a suspect at the moment. We just need to speak with you, especially since the last phone call he received was from your phone, and he came to a hotel in the middle of the night to meet someone."

"I never called Roman yesterday. I swear." Mango began to cry.

"What's your relationship to Mr. Hitacheel?" He wanted confirmation of an affair; that gave them a possible motive.

"I was his mistress," she sobbed. "For almost two years now."

"Were you in love with him, Ms. LeSeur?" Ryan softened his tone.

"No," her tears intensified. "I didn't even like him. He was gross, but he paid me so well. I have a nice place to live, expensive clothes, trips to fancy hotels, and all I had to do was make sure I kept my looks and body perfect and be available for sex whenever he wanted it. I can't believe someone killed him. Who would do that? Who would kill Roman?"

"Can you think of anyone who'd want him dead?"

She seemed to consider this for a moment. "Maybe his wife, if she found out about us."

"When you meet up with Roman, where do you usually go?"

"Sometimes my place, but usually a hotel." Mango's voice had dropped to a whisper.

"Okay, Ms. LeSeur, we're going to make a time later today to come and talk to you," Ryan told her gently. Even though she said she wasn't in love with Roman, she was clearly shaken up by his death. "Is there someone you can call who can come and stay with you?"

"I'll call my sister," she assured him.

"I'll be in touch to let you know when we'll be by to talk with you," Ryan reminded her before hanging up. "I don't think she's the killer," he told the others. "She seemed genuinely shocked and distraught at the news of Roman's death. She said she lost her phone yesterday afternoon."

"Convenient," Paige inserted.

"Or it was deliberately taken from her bag so someone could use it to set up a meeting with Roman and set up Mango at the same time." Ryan felt in his gut that Mango LeSeur was not the killer.

"Well, we were thinking mistress or wife," Paige said. "If it's not Mango, then maybe it was the wife. What better way to get revenge on your husband for being unfaithful, than to kill him and set up his mistress?"

"Let's go talk to her and find out." Ryan wanted this case wrapped up ASAP. The longer it took to find the killer, the greater the chances she'd kill again. And the last thing he wanted to deal with right now was another serial killer case.

* * * * *

2:46 P.M.

"Hey, how was your day?"

Annabelle Englewood forced a smile to her lips as her boyfriend dropped the mail on their kitchen table, then wrapped an arm around her waist, pulled her against his chest, and kissed her.

"Fine," she replied, then quickly shifted the focus off herself. "How was court?" From the little she knew about the case, it was a particularly brutal one. Annabelle didn't like to know the details of what her boyfriend did for a living. What had happened to her and her family was still too fresh for her to hear about what other victims had suffered.

"It went well," Detective Xavier Montague replied. "I think my testimony was helpful in—hopefully—getting a guilty verdict."

"That's good." Annabelle attempted to keep her voice light as she tried to pull out of Xavier's embrace.

He maintained his hold of her. "What did you do today?"

"Nothing much." She shrugged.

"You baked?"

Of course, she had; it was what she did *every* day. Pretty much all she did. "Brownies and cupcakes."

"Did you go out?"

They had this same conversation every day when Xavier got home from work. And it always went the same way. Annabelle was tired of it, but it seemed Xavier was not. In fact, she couldn't figure out why Xavier wasn't completely tired of her already. It had been eight months since her family had been brutally murdered by a psychopath out for revenge. The psychopath had been her friend. At least she had thought Ricky Preston was her friend, before she learned he was just using her as part of his master plan for revenge against those he believed responsible for his mother's death. It had been eight long months since she and Xavier had met, and her world—however small it had been—had crumbled to pieces, and she wasn't getting any better.

"Belle?" Xavier took her chin in his hand and gently tipped it up. He opened his mouth as if to say more, then snapped it shut. His unusual eyes, one hazel and one green, studied her sadly. "I wish I knew how to help you," he said at last.

Tears welled up in her eyes. Annabelle wished she knew how to convince Xavier just how much he had and did help her. "You do," she whispered, resting her forehead against his strong chest, snuggling closer when his arms tightened around her. For a moment, she just let herself rest. She missed rest. *Real* rest. Her sleep was plagued with nightmares, and all day she was hyperaware of everything happening around her. It was completely draining.

"Why don't we go out for dinner tonight?" Xavier suggested at last as his hand stroked her hair.

Annabelle wanted to say no. She hated going out. Had hated it for the last eight months. Although ironically her life had been ruined while she was in her own bed, in her own home, fast asleep. That didn't seem to matter to her mind, though. Being around people terrified her. She'd been a kindergarten teacher before her assault, but she could no longer work. She went to her therapy appointments and the occasional trip to the store, but that was about it. Instead, she stayed home and baked until they had more food than they could eat in five lifetimes.

She wanted to get better, though.

She wanted to get her life back.

A life that would be so much better than the life she'd had before.

She couldn't hide in Xavier's house forever.

Annabelle knew this; yet, moving on was so hard.

"Okay," she said at last.

"Really?" Xavier sounded surprised.

She took a deep, steadying breath. "Really."

He kissed the top of her head. "You know I'm never giving up on you, right? However long it takes you to get better, I'm not going anywhere."

"I know," she assured him. "I don't know why you stay, but I love that you do."

"Annabelle," Xavier's voice had taken on a slightly reprimanding quality, and she knew he was about to tell her all the reasons why he wanted to stay with her.

"It's okay, Xavier." She reached up on her tiptoes to press a quick kiss to his lips, then gently extracted herself from his arms and went to sort through the mail. There were a few bills and then a letter addressed to both her and Xavier.

That should have tipped her off right away that something was off. They never received anything other than bills and a few magazines in the mail. Everyone they knew, or rather everyone Xavier knew, would text or email or call them. However, Annabelle was distracted, and she was already opening the letter before she even thought about it.

Sliding out a single sheet of paper, Annabelle could feel the color drain from her face as she skimmed it.

This couldn't be happening.

And yet she'd known this day was coming.

It had always been only a matter of time. Not that that fact made this any easier.

Her knees went weak.

Her head began to spin.

Her vision began to go cloudy.

"Belle?" Xavier suddenly appeared before her, face screaming alarm, arms outstretched as if to catch something.

To catch her, it turned out.

"Whoa," his arms came around her as her legs buckled. "Belle? What's wrong? What happened?"

Annabelle couldn't answer. Her lungs weren't working properly; her chest was heaving in short, sharp gasps.

He lowered her into a chair. "Head down, deep breaths." Xavier's hand on her back bent her over, then he began to rub soothing circles on her back.

Clearing her head of everything else, Annabelle focused on getting her breathing back under control. Luckily, her therapist had giving her several techniques to calm herself. She forced herself to take as deep a breath as she could manage, hold it to the count of five before blowing it out and then repeating the process. She repeated this several times, and after a few minutes her eyesight cleared and she could draw a near normal breath.

Xavier sat her back up, then crouched in front of her, and asked, "Belle, what upset you?"

"It was him," she whispered.

"Him?" Xavier looked confused.

"*Him*," she repeated. "He's back."

Understanding flashed in his eyes, quickly followed by fear and anger. "Ricky Preston? Back where?"

She reached her trembling hand toward the letter on the table. "He sent us this." She handed it to Xavier.

Face hard, he took the letter and read it. Then for a long moment he just sat there. "Arrgghhh," Xavier growled at last, slamming a fist onto the table. "I wish there had been a way for me to kill him, or at least arrest him, when I had the chance."

"But there wasn't," Annabelle reminded him. "He didn't give you a choice. It was me or him."

"And you know I would never have done anything differently," he said fiercely, grabbing her shoulders in a death grip.

"I know," she assured him, gently placing her hands over his and tugging till he loosened his grip.

"You were my priority," Xavier continued, as though he needed to justify his decision. "If I hadn't chosen you, you would have died."

She shuddered at the memory of how close she had come to death. Annabelle wished, too, that there had been a way for Xavier to kill Ricky Preston and still find her in time to save her life. She knew that Xavier was eaten alive with guilt some days about allowing a vicious psychopath to walk free, even if he'd had to do it. They both knew that Ricky would never stop killing. Before he'd disappeared, Ricky had told them that he'd be back. And apparently now he was.

He embraced her. "I won't let him hurt you again," he

murmured in her ear.

"What if you can't stop him?" Annabelle half whimpered. Ricky had already hurt her twice. There was no guarantee that Xavier could stop him if he came at her again, no matter how much he wanted to protect her.

"I'm going to upgrade the security system." Xavier released her and began to make a list. Xavier's house, into which she had moved after being released from the hospital eight months ago, already had a fabulous security system, but apparently, it wasn't good enough now that Ricky was back. "I'm also going to ask to have a patrol car pass by the house regularly. And maybe we should consider getting a guard dog. I always wanted a dog." He shot her a strained smile. "Both my mom and dad were allergic, and once I became a cop I was never home enough."

"I like dogs." She tried to smile back but it was weak.

"I'll do whatever I have to, to keep you safe," he promised, sounding so sincere and confident that Annabelle believed him despite herself.

She moved back into Xavier's arms. "I changed my mind, I don't want to go out to dinner tonight."

"I guessed that." He tucked her shoulder-length brown hair behind her ear.

Closing her eyes, Annabelle wrapped her arms around Xavier's waist and pressed her ear against his chest above his heart. The rhythmic thumping helped to soothe her a little. "Hold me," she begged, desperate to lose herself and try to feel safe and normal. "Don't ever let me go."

"Never." Xavier drew her closer. "I'll never let you go, Belle. Never."

* * * * *

4:26 P.M.

"Please take a seat," Peter Hitacheel gestured to a white leather three-seater couch.

Paige Hood took a seat beside Ryan in the Hitacheel living room. It appeared as if Roman Hitacheel's entire family had gathered at his home in support of his widow. It had taken quite a bit of persuasion on her and Ryan's part, to convince the many friends and extended family members to remain in another room while she and Ryan spoke with Roman's widow, Eve, and their three grown children: Peter, Cindy, and James.

A quick survey of the room revealed minimal decoration. A large screen TV that took up most of one wall, three white, leather couches grouped in front of it, and a glass coffee table were the only pieces of furniture. The walls were painted white with a couple of bright abstract paintings breaking the monotonous whiteness of the room. There were no family portraits and no personal accents. All in all, the room was too white and glary for Paige's liking.

She turned her attention back to Eve Hitacheel. The woman was perfectly attired in a pale pink skirt suit. Gold earrings dripped from her ears, and she wore a large diamond pendant on a gold chain around her neck. Her eyes were appropriately red rimmed, but Paige didn't get the sense that the woman was particularly disturbed by her husband's murder.

"We're very sorry for your loss," she told the family once again. You could never say that too many times at a time like this, especially when one of the family members was a potential suspect.

"Thank you," Peter Hitacheel nodded. Apparently, he was the designated family spokesman. Roman's eldest son looked exactly like him, minus around two hundred pounds.

"We'll need one of you to come and do an official identification later today," Ryan announced.

"I'll do it," Peter volunteered immediately; no one else in the family offered.

Exchanging glances with Ryan, her partner gave her a slight nod, indication that she should lead the interview. "I know this is a difficult time for you," she began, "but it's important that we ask you these questions now, so we can find the person who killed your husband and father."

"Someone really killed him?" Cindy asked, disbelievingly. Of all of Roman's immediate family members, middle child Cindy seemed to be the only one truly upset about his death. Paige wondered whether she had been a daddy's little princess. If she had, she was probably the least likely to know anything about his affair.

"Yes, I'm afraid someone did," Paige answered gently. "Have any of you noticed anyone or anything suspicious over the last several days or weeks?"

"I wouldn't know," Peter replied. "Birthdays and Christmas are the only times I see my father."

Paige wondered about the reason for the estrangement between father and son, but now wasn't the time to ask about it. Tucking it away for later, she turned to the others. "What about the rest of you?"

Youngest son James shrugged and looked away. Widow Eve fiddled with the clasp of her diamond bracelet, refusing to make eye contact.

"Mrs. Hitacheel?" Ryan prodded.

"No," she answered briefly. "Nothing suspicious."

"Are you sure?" Paige wasn't sure whether the woman was being truthful or just didn't care.

"Of course, I'm sure," Eve snapped. "Nothing unusual has happened. No one suspicious has been hanging around here. No strange phone calls or emails. Roman never mentioned anything out of the ordinary."

"James," Ryan turned back to the youngest son, "are you sure you haven't seen anything?"

"Like Peter, birthdays and Christmas is it for my family time,"

James replied. "I would be the last person to know if anything was going on with him."

Wondering what had caused such a rift in the family, Paige made a mental note to call her parents and siblings tonight and make a time for all of them to catch up. Paige loved her parents and her brothers and sister, but for all of them, life was so busy that they rarely had a chance to spend time together outside family celebrations. But looking at the broken Hitacheel family, if anything happened to someone in her family, she didn't want to be sitting there telling the detectives that she didn't know what was going on in the lives of her loved ones because she only saw them for birthdays and Christmas.

Her partner, on the other hand, saw his family all the time. They were close; they made the effort to set aside time to spend together. Paige wondered whether the fact that Ryan's nephew, seven-year-old Brian, who had successfully fought and won a long battle with leukemia, had pushed the family to realize just how important the people you loved really were, and that seeing them regularly was worth making the effort to do so.

"Cindy?" Paige turned to Roman's daughter. "What about you? Do you see your dad regularly?"

Brushing at tears, Cindy gave a shaky nod.

"When was the last time you saw him?" Paige pressed.

"Yesterday." Cindy clasped her trembling hands tightly in her lap. "We had an early breakfast."

"And did your dad mention anything unusual, anyone suspicious, or anything that was worrying him?"

"No," Cindy whispered.

"What about you? Did you see anything that seemed odd?"

Cindy shook her head.

"All right, is there anyone you can think of who might want to hurt Roman? Anyone with a grudge against him, or anyone who might stand to gain something if Roman were dead?" Paige moved on to the next question in her mental checklist.

"My father didn't have any enemies," Peter answered for everyone.

When Paige glanced at the others, they all nodded their heads in agreement. *For people who had just had a loved one murdered, they weren't very forthcoming with information,* Paige thought irritably, but kept her face calm and neutral. "Any ideas why Roman might have been out at a hotel in the middle of the night?" She watched each family member closely for signs that they were aware of Roman's affair.

Cindy shook her head, but all the others averted their gazes. They knew. Paige was sure they knew. All three of them.

"It was too late for a business meeting," Paige continued innocently. "And Peter and James, you both said that you don't have much to do with your father, so I'm guessing he wasn't meeting you."

Peter and James both gave reluctant nods when she paused and fixed them both in a stare.

"Cindy, were you meeting up with your father last night?" Paige asked.

"No, Dad would never ask to meet me so late. I have a newborn at home, but even if it was an emergency, it would never be at a hotel; he'd come to my house," Cindy rambled.

"Mrs. Hitacheel, did you and your husband have plans last night?"

Eve simply glared.

"Could he have been meeting a friend?" Paige pressed on.

More glares from Eve, Peter, and James.

"Or maybe…"

"He was meeting his girlfriend," James finally snapped.

"What? No!" Cindy shook her head vehemently. "Dad doesn't have a girlfriend!"

"Yes, he does." Peter frowned at his sister. "For years now. Lots of them. The current one is Mango LeSeur."

Cindy stood and begun to pace frantically. "That's a lie!" she shrieked. "Dad would never cheat; he would never do that to Mom. I know you don't like Dad, Peter, but that's no reason to say that about him. He's dead, he can't defend himself. Someone murdered him and you're accusing him of having affairs."

Eve stood, the first flash of real emotion crossing her face, and went to her daughter, taking Cindy's arms and stilling her.

"Dad wouldn't cheat on you, Mom," Cindy stated adamantly.

"Yes, honey, he would, and he did. He has been for years," Eve told her daughter. "I'm sorry. I know you love him, but he's been unfaithful our entire marriage."

"No," Cindy whispered, tugging herself free from her mother's grip and dropping down onto the sofa, her face a mask of disbelieving shock.

"You knew?" Peter was staring at his mother in surprise.

She nodded. "For years." Tears streamed down her cheeks. "I didn't know that you knew." Turning to James, she said, "I didn't know you knew, either."

"I'm sorry, Mom." James went to his mother and hugged her tightly.

Eventually, Eve lifted her head from her son's shoulder. "He would go to hotels at least once a week," she told them. "At first he used to get prostitutes or women he picked up in bars for one-night stands," she explained. "Then he moved on to mistresses. I know of at least three; but there could have been more. The older he got, the younger he liked his women. I think Mango LeSeur is only nineteen."

Eve's blue eyes seemed to darken as she spoke of her husband's unfaithfulness, and Paige could feel the anger rolling off her. She knew about the affairs. Had she finally had enough and just snapped? Then again, both sons knew about their father, and neither seemed to care much about him. Perhaps one of them had decided to kill him.

"We're going to need alibis for each..." Ryan started to say when Cindy bounced to her feet.

"Alibis?" Cindy repeated incredulously. "You want alibis from *us*? Why would one of us kill him? How dare you even suggest that!" she yelled. "He was my father. I loved him." She shrugged off the hand Peter placed on her shoulder. "Get away from me," she screeched at her older brother. "You never loved him. But he was a good dad. He used to take me to the ballet. He used to come to my room and have tea parties with me and my dolls, and he came to every one of my music recitals," she broke off into hysterical sobs.

James went to her, wrapping his arms around her, and Cindy buried her face against his chest. "Shh," he soothed, "it'll be okay." Cindy continued to cry, and after a few more minutes, James turned to the rest of them. "I'm going to take her upstairs and give her a tranquilizer."

"All right," Paige nodded. Her gut said Cindy and James weren't involved in their father's murder. She was leaning toward Eve, but anger and disdain toward his father was rolling off Peter in almost tangible waves. She wasn't sure where this intense hatred seemed to come from, but Paige was going to find out, and having the over-emotional Cindy out of the room might help.

"I'll come see you when we're done here." Eve gave her daughter a quick kiss.

Once James had led a still-crying Cindy from the room, Peter immediately offered apologies for his sister's tears. "Sorry about Cindy. She's always been a daddy's girl. I think she's probably the only one of us who really loved my father."

"Why don't you love your father, Peter?" Paige asked quietly.

He shrugged fitfully. "Let down too many times, I guess," he finally answered.

"How did he let you down?" Ryan asked.

Another shrug. Peter was trying too hard to appear nonchalant about his relationship with his father, but Paige had seen the genuine pain and regret in his eyes and knew that Peter didn't so much hate his father as he felt hurt by him.

"Peter?" Paige prompted gently.

"He was obsessed with younger women," Peter snarled. "*Much* younger women."

"How much younger?" Ryan asked.

"Illegally younger," Peter answered.

Eve opened her mouth as if to protest, then snapped it shut again. Apparently, she was aware of this.

"I caught him with my girlfriends several times when I was a teenager," Peter glowered. "I swear he would have slept with anything in a skirt. I wouldn't be surprised if he'd done Cindy."

"Peter," Eve reprimanded sharply. "Your father would never do that."

He huffed unapologetically. "If you say so."

In her mind, Paige dismissed Peter as a suspect. He was too angry. If he'd killed his father, he would have stabbed him or shot him or maybe beaten him. Something wild and anger-fueled. Not the calm, cool, and collected method that their killer had used. She could see why Cindy didn't like her brother. Peter took his anger at his father too far, taking it out on everyone around him. Eve, on the other hand, was completely calm and in control. She hadn't seemed rattled throughout their entire interview.

Paige wasn't sure what she thought about Cindy now, though. She wasn't sure if Peter was simply spouting off out of anger, or whether his accusation had some basis in fact. If Cindy had been sexually abused as a child by her father, perhaps her traumatized and shocked brain had tried to make sense out of what had happened to her by deluding itself into thinking that she and her father were in love and in a committed relationship. Maybe she had killed him out of jealousy. They needed to talk to Cindy again once she'd calmed down.

"We need your alibis," Ryan reminded them.

"Cindy and James would have been at home with their partners. Peter, too," Eve added.

Peter nodded his assent. "My wife is in the other room, as well as James' wife and Cindy's husband."

"Mrs. Hitacheel?"

"Home alone," she replied.

"Anyone who can verify that?"

"No one," she answered. "Even Roman wouldn't have been able to; we sleep in different bedrooms. I'm going to go check on my daughter now, and then I'm going back to my family and friends," Eve announced, standing and leaving the room.

"I know you have a job to do, but I don't think any of us— other than Cindy—really care if you find who killed my father or not," Peter told them before following his mother from the room.

Once they were alone, Paige glanced at her partner, who nodded that they were on the same page. "I don't think James was involved, but Peter is so full of anger toward his father, I don't think we can count him out just yet. And we need to find out whether Cindy was abused; if she was, it could speak for motive. But Eve knew about the affairs, including the ones with their children's underage girlfriends. She had no alibi for last night. She's too calm about the whole thing. I think for now she's our number one suspect."

* * * * *

6:11 P.M.

Detective Xavier Montague arrived at the Landers house just as the ambulance pulled away. He would talk to Garton Landers as soon as the doctors said the man was strong enough to be interviewed. Per his Lieutenant, Robert Hollow, who had called him an hour ago to give him the case, Garton had sustained only minor injuries, but the man was in shock, able to cry only that the 'blood man' had killed his wife.

Slipping on booties over his shoes and a pair of latex gloves before entering the Landers house, Xavier headed straight for the master bedroom but stopped short at the door.

The room was literally covered in blood.

It streaked the walls and the ceiling.

It drenched the carpet.

It soaked the bed.

And it left Xavier with a horrible sense of déjà vu.

He had seen this level of violence once before.

His mind flashed back in time eight months.

Another house. Another family. Blood everywhere. Mutilated bodies.

It was the first time he'd met Annabelle. She had been unconscious and bleeding, then she had opened her eyes, such a pale blue they appeared white, and looked at him. A part of him had immediately known there was something between them that wouldn't go away.

A hand on his shoulder startled him.

"Xavier? You okay?"

Slowly his vision cleared and he was back in the present.

"Xavier?"

"Yeah, I'm okay." He had to force the words out past the fear choking him.

Ricky Preston had sent them a letter.

He'd said he was back.

And this crime scene had Ricky's name scrawled all over it.

She seemed to read Xavier's mind. "I know. I thought the same thing the second I walked in here."

He considered the brown eyes that looked back at him anxiously. "So I'm not crazy?"

She offered up a faint smile. "Maybe you're a little crazy, but on this we agree," Diane Jolly assured him.

Xavier had known Diane for years. In fact, he'd met the crime scene tech on his first day as a cop. He respected and trusted Diane, and the fact that she, too, sensed Ricky Preston's presence here was reassuring.

"We can't jump to conclusions, though," Diane continued. "We don't know for sure that it's him. We don't want to miss something important because we're fixated on Ricky."

"He sent me and Annabelle a letter today," he confessed.

"Oh no." Diane's face creased with concern. "How's Annabelle?"

"Not good." The familiar rush of fear washed over him as he thought of the trauma Annabelle had suffered at Ricky's hand. She rarely slept through the night; she rarely left the house. Knowing that Ricky was still out there was slowly killing her. And her fear was killing him.

Xavier wanted to see Annabelle relax; he wanted to see her enjoy life in a way he knew she never had—even before Ricky killed her family. She was beginning to trust him, though. Beginning to believe that he was truly over his first wife, Julia. Beginning to believe that he was serious about and committed to their relationship and future together. Beginning to believe that there was more to life than shutting yourself off from everyone because you were afraid of being hurt.

There was still so much more he had to teach her. He wanted her to start seeing herself as others saw her. Annabelle was beautiful, with her unusual white eyes, delicate features, and silky brown hair, but she didn't see it. He wanted her to learn to stand up for herself. Annabelle hated confrontation so much she would do or say anything to make sure everyone around her was happy with her. Xavier wanted to see her be truly happy.

However, he knew the reality was that as long as Ricky Preston was out there, Annabelle would be forever paralyzed by fear. And he couldn't let that happen.

"Poor thing, she's been through so much. What did Ricky say in the letter?"

"That he was back," Xavier took in the blood-splattered room. "And this certainly looks like he's back."

Setting aside thoughts of Ricky Preston for the moment, he

took in the scene before him. Diane was right. They couldn't get sidetracked just because the blood-soaked room reminded them of Ricky's previous murderous rampage. Garton Landers and his deceased wife Erica were the priority here, not Ricky Preston. But if it turned out that Ricky was responsible, then Xavier would stop at nothing to make sure he didn't get away this time.

A chair lay on its side by a bureau, shorn ropes scattered around it.

A sheet, blanket, and quilt lay in a tangle on the floor on one side of the bed.

Bloody footprints crisscrossed the room.

Xavier walked slowly toward the bed, around which most of the blood activity was focused. Medical examiner, Billy Newton, looked up at him grimly, then back down at the body—if it could still be called that. Erica Landers had been struck so many times that her body was barely recognizable as a body. One arm had nearly been severed at the shoulder. A leg had been severed at the knee. Her torso had been cut open, exposing more internal organs than Xavier wanted to see.

"Approximate time of death?" Xavier asked Billy.

Billy stifled a yawn. He had seven kids including three sets of twins; the man was always tired. "Sometime early this morning."

"So it took Garton Landers a long time to work himself free from the ropes," Xavier pondered aloud. "The killer came prepared with rope and duct tape." He gestured to the ropes on the floor by the chair, and the rope and tape still binding Erica's wrists and ankles to the bedposts. "He probably waited for them to fall asleep before he made his move." He spun in a circle to scan the room, searching for the perfect hiding place. The closet. Heading for it, he opened the doors, noting immediately that the shoes on the floor at one side were messed up while the shoes on the other side were perfectly aligned. "Diane, check out the closet; I think this is where he waited."

Diane came over and immediately began to search for

fingerprints on the door handles and shoes. "I printed the bloody footprints, too," she told him. "When you get your guy, the prints will tie him to this conclusively."

He nodded absently; his mind still working on how this had played out. It helped to talk things through with someone, and this was when Xavier missed his old partner the most. Kate had been gone on maternity leave for four months now; her baby boy was almost three months old. Xavier knew that Kate was toying with the idea of not returning to work when her maternity leave was over, and he was torn between desperately wanting her to return and hoping she stayed home with her little boy because he knew how much she loved it. Xavier knew he'd end up with a new partner any time now. He'd already gone through two since Kate had left, but both had fallen through for various reasons.

"You think he went after the husband or wife first?" Diane asked.

"Husband," Xavier replied immediately. It made sense that the killer would neutralize the biggest threat first. "Once he had the husband tied up he had a way to keep the wife under control. Garton Landers had a cut on his neck, right?"

Diane nodded.

"He probably threatened to hurt her husband unless she did as he said. Then once he had her tied up he was free to kill her. He wanted the husband to watch. Probably had the chair set up behind the bed while he killed the wife. He wanted the husband to suffer, wanted him to be left all alone." Again, Xavier couldn't help but think of Ricky Preston's killing spree. His MO was to always leave one family member alive.

"Then it looks like he spent some time enjoying his handiwork." Billy gestured at the bloody footprints circling the bed.

"Not just enjoying his handiwork, enjoying the blood, too." Xavier went back to the bed. "He was naked while he did this."

"Could have been a forensic countermeasure," Diane

suggested. "No bloody clothes to tie him to the crimes. Or maybe he just wore no shoes. We don't have any evidence to suggest he was completely naked."

He shook his head. "Then why walk around and around the bed? It was the blood. He was obsessed with it. He would have been covered in it. He enjoyed that. He loved it. I'm sure he did."

Now all Xavier had to be sure about was whether Ricky had committed this crime.

He couldn't afford to get it wrong.

If he focused all his attention on proving Ricky Preston was the killer and he was wrong, then the real killer would be free to keep on killing.

And he couldn't deal with more guilt.

Some days his guilt over letting Ricky Preston go free nearly crushed him. What he'd told Annabelle earlier today was true. She had been his priority. She would have died if he hadn't chosen her, and he would do it again. But that didn't mean he didn't blame himself for Ricky Preston still being on the loose. At the time, he'd known Ricky would keep killing, but he hadn't expected the next kill to come so soon. Annabelle had merely been a distraction while Ricky killed the final family in his revenge plan. By the time he and Kate had arrived at the Adams' residence, Ricky had already killed four more people—only Barney Adams and his seventeen-year-old daughter Vanessa had still been alive.

Again, Ricky had fled, using the teenager as a human shield, outmaneuvering him once more by giving him another choice. Go after Ricky or try to save Vanessa's life after Ricky cut her throat. He had stayed with the girl and Vanessa had survived, but Ricky had gone free.

Every person that Ricky killed after that was on his head.

Xavier wasn't going to make the same mistake again.

He was going to keep his mind open to all possibilities on this case no matter how much his heart pushed him toward believing Ricky was the killer.

THREE

9:39 P.M.

This was fun.

Ricky loved watching the people he was soon going to kill. It added an extra layer of excitement—and power—to know that there were people walking around, going about their everyday lives, not knowing that they were about to die. That he was about to kill them. That he and he alone would determine the exact second at which their lives would end.

It was completely exhilarating.

It made him feel like God.

With a chuckle, he thought of Annabelle.

She would have gotten her letter by now.

She would be freaking out. Probably having panic attacks and refusing to leave her house. That girl was so high maintenance Ricky didn't know how Xavier Montague put up with her.

Boy oh boy, was that girl messed up.

Despite what Annabelle might claim, it was *not* Ricky's fault that she was messed up.

She had been messed up long before Ricky met her.

He knew from personal experience. He had spent hours sitting and listening to her drone on and on about everything that she was afraid of. And there were a lot of things that Annabelle Englewood was afraid of. She was weak and pathetic and useless. Well, he debated with himself, maybe she wasn't *entirely* useless. He had managed to use her pretty darn perfectly.

Annabelle had been the perfect distraction to help him eliminate all the people who needed to pay for his mother's death. Barney Adams had been last on his list because he had been the person most responsible. In the end, the man had survived, but he had lost his parents, his wife, and his young son. The girl,

Vanessa, had survived, as well. But she was no longer on speaking terms with her father. She had blamed him for the events that led to her family's slaughter and very nearly her own death.

It was a fitting punishment for Barney, so Ricky was satisfied.

He liked to cause suffering.

It soothed him somehow. Made him feel better.

And knowing that he still held the power to bring Annabelle to her knees was a high that never let him down. He would come back for her soon. He wasn't quite sure when that would be. But he knew he would.

Maybe once he got tired of killing newlyweds.

The fun of that couldn't last forever. Sometimes Ricky wondered whether he had ADD. Attention deficit disorder sufferers struggled to focus on any one thing for a length of time, and that definition certainly fit Ricky.

However, there was something about Annabelle that intrigued him. Something that he couldn't get out of his head, that he couldn't let go of.

Maybe it was because they had spent so much time together.

Ricky was sure he knew more about her than any other person on the planet. He was sure he knew things that she hadn't even told that new boyfriend of hers. Xavier Montague thought that he knew Annabelle. Thought that he could help her change. But he was mistaken. Annabelle would always be weak and pathetic.

The more he thought about her, the more Ricky wanted to run straight to her house and grab Annabelle immediately.

But he wouldn't.

When he took her, he wanted to be able to spend a little time alone with her before he killed her. And right now, he had other things to take care of.

He signaled for the check as the Mendlesons exited the restaurant. He didn't need to follow them home. He already knew where they lived and more about their routines than he needed to, to kill them. But he liked to follow his prey. It made him feel like an invincible hunter.

The Mendlesons would be easy kills.

They were older—both in their late fifties—and neither seemed to take great care about their appearance, so they were not physically fit. Both had been widowed young, while they still had small children to raise. But now, with their kids grown and moved on with their lives, they had found love again. The fact that their later-in-life love story sounded like something one may read in a sappy romantic novel frustrated Ricky.

He didn't like love. Or rather, more accurately, he didn't believe in love.

Maybe that was why he had found the idea of killing newlyweds so appealing.

Whatever, he shrugged, as he followed the laughing, canoodling couple as they strolled down the street, blissfully unaware of their fate.

Soon the Mendlesons would be dead.

And then, if he chose, he would move on to Annabelle.

JANUARY 9TH

8:00 A.M.

"Good morning, everyone," Lieutenant Belinda Jersey announced. Everyone's conversations faded away as they focused on their morning meeting. "Okay, the Hitacheel case, where are we?" Her black eyes glowed enthusiastically; Belinda was always enthusiastic in the first days of a case.

Ryan looked to Paige, who nodded that he could detail what they knew so far. His partner looked tired. There were dark circles under her eyes, and her long curly chestnut brown hair, which she always wore in a neat and tidy bun, was hanging loose around her shoulders. He was sure something was bothering her, but when he'd asked her about it earlier, she had brushed him off.

He inwardly uttered a weary sigh. The women in his life were going to age him prematurely with all this worrying. Ryan hadn't had a chance to talk to Sofia about what was bothering her yet. Last night he had barely made it home in time to pick her up for dinner with his family. Sofia must have been exhausted because she fell asleep in the car on the ride home. She hadn't even woken up when he'd carried her inside and up to bed.

He would have to make a point of making time to talk to both Sofia and Paige, but both would have to wait.

"Alibis checked out for the sons," Ryan began. "Peter and James Hitacheel were at their homes, in bed with their respective wives, when their father was murdered. No real motives either. James doesn't like his father but no real animosity that would lead him to kill him. Peter is plenty full of anger toward Roman, but I can't see him being controlled enough to kill in such a methodical manner."

"Any chance they may have paid someone to do it?" Belinda asked.

He shook his head. "I can't see a hit man killing someone in such an unusual way. We'll go through their financials just in case, but I doubt we'll come up with anything."

"What about the daughter?"

He exchanged a glance with Paige. "Peter claimed that his father would sleep with any woman, including his own daughter."

Dark eyes grew wide in surprise. "Cindy Hitacheel was sexually abused as a child?"

"She says no," Ryan replied. "But she was kind of out of it when we talked to her. She became hysterical when we talked with her and her brothers and mother. James took her and gave her a tranquilizer. When we went back later to ask her about Peter's claims, she was still doped up."

"She was adamant though," Paige piped up. "Said her father never laid an inappropriate hand on her and was angry that Peter would suggest such a thing. She said her brothers were jealous because she was closer with their father than they were. Said Roman preferred daughters and couldn't connect with his sons."

Belinda raised a suspicious brow. "So we don't know for sure that Roman didn't abuse her?"

"I guess not," Ryan confirmed. "Although Eve also said that Roman never touched Cindy."

"Either way, Cindy's alibi checked out, too. She was home with her husband and their newborn son," Paige explained.

"So the kids are out. At least for now," Belinda added. "What about the wife and the girlfriend?"

"Well, Mango has an alibi," Ryan replied. "Apparently, she has a boyfriend."

"She has two boyfriends?" Belinda again looked shocked. "Roman Hitacheel and another guy?"

"Yep," Ryan nodded. "The other guy, Calvin Reed, is her age.

Apparently, they've known each other since high school; they'd wanted to marry but they're young and broke. When Mango met Roman and he became smitten with her, she and Calvin looked at it as a win-win situation. Mango gets a fancy apartment, a generous living allowance, extra money for clothes and accessories, and all she has to do is keep up her looks and be available for sex whenever Roman wants."

"The boyfriend thought that was a win-win?" Belinda looked doubtful. She'd never been married, and her job took up most of her time, but she had lots of hobbies to keep from burning herself out.

He shrugged. "Seemingly so. When we spoke with him, he said he wasn't pleased with Mango having to sleep with Roman, but they both knew Roman would tire of her once she aged a little more, and then they thought they'd be financially set for life. To be honest, he seemed less upset about the fact that his girlfriend was prostituting herself, than their having to keep their relationship a secret."

"So Mango was with Calvin Reed when Roman was murdered?" Belinda asked.

"Yes, they were hanging out at his apartment," Paige nodded.

"Maybe they killed Roman together?"

She shook her head. "No, they ordered takeout that placed them there during the time of the murder."

"That just leaves the widow? She have an alibi, too?" Belinda queried.

"Nope, she's the only one without one," Paige answered.

"Do we like her as the killer?"

"She's a plausible candidate," Ryan confirmed. "She was home alone at the time Roman was killed. She knew about her husband's affairs and has for years. And she was too calm when Paige and I interviewed her and her kids."

"Maybe she was in shock," Belinda suggested.

"She didn't seem too shaken up by her husband's death," Paige contradicted.

"So far we haven't come up with any enemies or people with a grudge against Roman. Right now, we're going with either the wife killing him for revenge, or a stranger," Ryan told their boss. "But it looks like he was lured there so it seems less likely that it was a stranger. Maybe Roman had another girlfriend—or even a boyfriend—that we don't know about it. Paige and I will keep interviewing friends, maybe someone knew something."

"We think someone stole Mango LeSeur's cell phone for a couple of hours on the afternoon before Roman was killed," Paige explained. "Seems she lost it at a café, but since there was a call to Roman's phone during the time it was missing, it seems likely that someone stole it to call Roman and set up a meeting, then returned the phone to café staff. Eve and Peter Hitacheel both knew Mango's name, so it's plausible that one of them set him up."

"What we need are some forensics," Belinda announced. "Steph?"

"We're working on the hotel security footage, but right now we don't have anything more than we did before. A tall brunette. That could be Mrs. Hitacheel, or it could be any number of women," Stephanie replied. "We're running all the fingerprints; hopefully, that will be helpful."

"Ask Eve Hitacheel to provide you with a set; if she agrees, it could help count her out as a suspect," Belinda told them. "Anything else, Stephanie?"

"Not yet," the CSU tech shook her head.

"Frankie?" Belinda turned her attention to the ME.

"I did blood tests and found faint traces of sodium thiopental in his system," Frankie replied.

Belinda waved her hand at Frankie in a 'please explain' gesture.

"Sodium thiopental is a rapid-onset, short-acting, barbiturate general anesthetic. It causes unconsciousness usually within 30-45 seconds, and you would usually start to wake up within five to ten minutes," Frankie summarized. "Seems perfect for what your killer wanted. Got Roman Hitacheel distracted in bed, injected him, he would have passed out quickly, and given them enough time to get him secured without having to wait long for him to wake up. Assuming they wanted him awake before he or she drained his blood and then drowned him in it."

"Supports the theory that it was someone who knew him," Ryan thought aloud. "Whoever killed him wanted him to know what was going to happen and why they were doing it."

"Where would you find this sodium thiopental?" Belinda asked.

"It's used in general anesthesia in hospitals and veterinary clinics, although it's largely been replaced with propofol these days," Frankie replied. "Plus, you can find most things online. So, your killer might have stolen it from a hospital or a vet clinic or ordered it over the internet. Who knows, maybe he made it himself."

"The fact that the killer had the tools to draw blood might suggest that they stole it from somewhere. Or maybe they work in a hospital or at a vet." Ryan sighed, "Or maybe they ordered the whole lot online."

"We're interviewing the hotel employees today that were working that night," Paige announced. "Maybe we'll get lucky and someone will be able to ID the woman from the video."

"Then we'll talk to more of Roman's friends and colleagues and see if anyone knows of another girlfriend or any enemies," Ryan added.

"All right then people, let's get moving and wrap this case up ASAP." Belinda shooed them all from the room.

* * * * *

10:31 A.M.

She stood silently at the window looking in.

Isabella watched the woman inside.

Her sister, Sofia, moved slowly around the kitchen, favoring one leg. Isabella had kept tabs on her sister's slow recovery. She'd been there the night Sofia fell. It had been at their old house. Sofia had been afraid of her. It had broken Isabella's heart to think that she scared her own sister. She had wanted Sofia to know that everything she had done was done for them.

Perhaps she had been a little naïve at the time.

Sofia had been through a lot. And then on top of that, Isabella had sprung some enormous surprises on her.

Of course, Sofia had been in shock.

When she'd seen Isabella walking toward her, she had panicked, stepped back, and tumbled down a flight of stairs.

Isabella blamed herself. So, she had been making sure to keep tabs on how her sister was doing. Not that that had been easy. Isabella was a wanted criminal. Wanted for multiple counts of murder. Plus, kidnapping and assault. And Sofia lived with a cop.

But Isabella couldn't just let her sister go.

And so she made regular trips to Sofia and Ryan's house, always when Ryan wasn't home, so she could stand in the shadows and watch through the windows to make sure her sister was okay.

What she wanted was to go running indoors, throw her arms around Sofia, and let her sister make everything bad in the world fade away. Sofia had helped her so many times before. Her sister's sparkling silvery gray eyes and warm smile were such a contrast to the rest of their family that Sofia was the only one that Isabella felt connected to.

Unfortunately, there was nothing her sister could do to make all Isabella's problems go away. Still Isabella would love nothing more than to just lie in her sister's arms and know that someone loved her.

However, her sister was so vulnerable right now. Isabella didn't know how Sofia would react if she saw her again. For the moment, this had to be the extent of their relationship. But maybe one day things could be different. Maybe one day they could go back to the way they had been before. Maybe. But Isabella wasn't pinning all her hopes on that ever happening.

As Sofia limped from the kitchen, Isabella debated moving to another window to keep watching, but decided against it.

As much as she loved being close to her sister, she had other pressing matters she had to take care of.

Slipping quietly from the yard, she walked down the block then climbed into her car. She had another kill coming up. Soon. Maybe within the next day or so.

Killing was all that was sustaining her now. It was the sole purpose for her being.

But how long could that last?

The police could catch her and lock her up, then what would she do? She didn't think Sofia would visit her in prison. And she wouldn't be able to keep killing in jail.

Even if the police never caught her, could she keep killing forever?

She honestly wasn't sure.

Right now, it gave her a reason to get up each morning, but maybe that would change in time.

Isabella hated that there were so many maybes in her life these days.

What she wanted was what Sofia had found.

She wanted someone to love her. She wanted someone who looked at her the way Ryan looked at Sofia. She wanted someone who thought she was the most precious thing on the planet and who would do anything for her. Ryan had walked inside a burning building to save Sofia, but there was no one who would do that for her.

Life just wasn't fair.

Although if she were being truly fair, then as bad as her life might be right now, it couldn't top Arthur Bentley's. The thirty-year-old had no idea that his life would be over in just a day or so. He had no idea that his cheating ways were going to come back to haunt him.

It was the way the world worked, though.

There were always consequences for your actions.

Sometimes the consequences were good and sometimes they weren't.

But no matter which, there were *always* consequences.

And soon it would be time for Arthur Bentley to face his.

As she headed for his workplace, Isabella wondered when it would be time for her to face the consequences of her own actions. And just what those consequences would be.

* * * * *

11:21 A.M.

"Mr. Landers?" Xavier opened the car door and leaned inside.

Garton Landers turned dead, empty, green eyes in his direction.

"Are you sure you should be here?" He had been searching for Garton for the last couple of hours. The man had already left the hospital by the time Xavier arrived to interview him. Supposedly he had gone to his parents' house, but when Xavier got there, his parents informed him that Garton had been restless and said he needed to go out. Instinct convinced him that the man was back at the house where his wife had been killed. When Annabelle had been abducted, Xavier had wanted to feel close to her and gone to the one place that he felt most connected to her. It had made sense to him that Garton would do the same thing. Luckily, he was correct. However, sitting in his car outside his marital home was probably not the best place for Garton to be, psychologically speaking.

Garton offered a disinterested shrug and returned his gaze to the house.

"I'm Detective Montague. How about we go somewhere else to talk?" Xavier suggested.

"No." Garton spoke for the first time, his voice surprisingly strong. "I need to be here."

Xavier didn't necessarily agree that this was the best place for the grieving husband right now, but he didn't protest. "May I sit?" he asked instead.

Garton nodded.

Xavier slid into the passenger seat and closed the door. The car was ice cold and he couldn't help but shiver; Garton didn't seem to notice the cold. "I know the timing sucks," Xavier began sympathetically, "but we really need to talk while things are still fresh so we can find the person who killed your wife."

Garton didn't acknowledge him, but his hands, clutched tightly on the steering wheel, began to tremble.

"When did you meet Erica?" Xavier asked, deciding it would be best to start with something easy and then ease into the hard stuff.

"Middle school," Garton answered softly.

Xavier was surprised. "You two were a couple since middle school?"

Giving a slight shake of his head. "We dated in seventh grade, then broke up. We went to the same high school but we weren't friends. Then I bumped into her in a café one day after we'd both graduated from college. I spilled coffee all over her. I was so embarrassed, but she just laughed it off." A small smile turned his lips up as he drifted off into his recollection. "We started dating again, and I proposed a couple of months later. Our families wanted a huge wedding, so we were going to have a long engagement while Erica planned everything. But one day we both realized that *we* didn't want the big wedding our parents did, so we eloped. Our families were so angry with us, even though we promised to do another ceremony with all of them present. We've only been married a month. One month. And now she's gone," Garton broke off with a sob.

Xavier counted his lucky stars that he had been spared what Garton was currently going through. He had found Annabelle in time, although she'd been barely clinging to life. His heart still thumped painfully in his chest whenever he thought about it. "I'm sorry," he said softly, the words feeling completely inadequate to put even a dent in the man's pain.

Pressing his hands to his eyes, Garton drew in several deep breaths, then raked his fingers down his face. "I want whoever killed Erica to pay." His face went fierce, his eyes dark. "What do you need to know?"

"Why don't you tell me what you did last night, and I'll ask you any questions I need to as we go," Xavier suggested.

Steeling himself, Garton fixed his gaze on the house and began. "It had been a month since the wedding. We wanted to celebrate. We went out to a restaurant for dinner. Then we stopped at the park where I proposed on our way home. We used to play at the park when we were kids." His forlorn eyes met Xavier's for a moment before returning to stare once more at the house.

"What time did you get home?" Xavier asked.

"Around eleven," Garton replied.

"Did you notice anything off when you arrived home?" Xavier asked. "Were there any signs that someone had broken into the house?"

Garton thought for a moment, then slowly shook his head. "Everything looked the same as usual. Erica had been bugging me," he hesitated, "to get a security system installed, but I kept putting it off. I was trying to save money for the wedding ceremony our families wanted," he finished bleakly.

And that would play on his mind for the rest of his life. Guilt was like that. "Did you put your clothes away in the closet when you got home?" Xavier didn't want him dwelling on the security system. There was no way Garton could have predicted that all of this would happen.

"I think so. Why?" Garton's blond brows furrowed in confusion.

"It's possible that's where he was hiding," Xavier replied gently.

"We put our things away; he wasn't there," Garton said more emphatically this time.

"Did you check the rest of the house?" Xavier continued.

He shook his head slowly. "We went straight to bed."

Garton didn't need to say more. They were newlyweds; Xavier got the picture. "Do you remember hearing anything unusual while you were in bed?"

Garton shook his head again. "I doubt we would have, though; we were kind of preoccupied. Someone probably could have come stomping through playing a trumpet and we wouldn't have noticed."

"What time did you go to sleep?"

His cheeks tinted pink with embarrassment, lending a little color to his virtually colorless face. "Maybe around three o'clock."

"What's the first thing you remember after falling asleep?"

The color faded from Garton's face, and it was back to pure white. "Something sharp in my back. I tried to see what it was, but I couldn't move, and then my vision started to go black."

"What next?" Xavier prompted.

"I woke up," he answered tightly. "I was tied to a chair. I tried to get free, but I couldn't. I tried to scream but there was tape on my mouth."

"Was there anyone else in the room with you, besides Erica?"

He bobbed his head up and down jerkily. "There was a man."

"What did he look like?" Xavier tried not to hold his breath as he waited to see if the description of Garton and Erica Landers' attacker matched Ricky Preston.

"Tall, dark hair, blue eyes I think," Garton replied. "I'm sorry, I wasn't paying much attention to him."

The description matched Ricky. "What did the man do?" Xavier prodded.

"He held something sharp to my neck, and he woke up Erica. When she saw me tied up she went to scream, but he told her he'd hurt me if she did. He cut my neck to prove his point." Garton's hand strayed to his neck where a white bandage had been taped.

Xavier waited silently for the man to continue.

"I wanted Erica to run," Garton spoke at last. "I didn't care about me; I just didn't want him to hurt her. I tried to break free, but I couldn't. She told me it would be okay, that maybe if we did what he wanted he wouldn't hurt us. But we both knew it was a lie. We both knew he was going to kill us. He threw her some ropes and told her to tie herself up. Once she'd tied up her ankles, he went to her and tied her wrists, then added some duct tape."

Garton's pause was longer this time. "And then?" Xavier finally prompted when it became clear Garton didn't want to say more.

Devastated green eyes looked over at him. "He took off his clothes and raped her. I totally lost it. I just saw red. I tried so desperately to get free, but all I could do was tip the chair to the floor." One hand absently rubbed his head where a large lump had formed, the other rubbed his shoulder. "Erica was crying, begging him not to do it. I can still hear her voice in my head. When will that go away?" The man's voice bloomed with childlike vulnerability.

"I don't know," Xavier answered honestly. "I know this is hard, Garton, but I need you to keep going."

Garton sucked in a shuddering breath, then continued. "When he was done, he sat my chair back up and picked up an axe. He hit Erica. Over and over and over again. There was blood everywhere."

"Did the man do anything in the blood?" Xavier asked.

"He looked at it like it fascinated him, and he walked around and around the room for ages after."

That sounded exactly like Ricky Preston. "What happened next?"

"He left," Garton said flatly. "I tried for hours to get free. When I did I wanted to hold her, but...but I couldn't." He had that faraway look in his eyes. "I called for help, but what was the point? Erica was beyond help."

He needed to keep Garton engaged just a little longer, so he asked, "Had you ever seen the man anywhere before?"

Garton gave a slight shake of his head.

"Is there anyone you can think of who would want to hurt you or Erica?"

"No, of course not." Garton looked horrified that he should even suggest such a thing.

"Why don't you go back to your parents' house?" Xavier suggested. The broken man shouldn't be alone right now. "They want to help you."

"But they can't," Garton murmured distractedly. "I need to be here. I need to be close to Erica."

"Do you want me to stay with you for a while?" Xavier offered. He was meant to meet with the Landers' next-door neighbor in a few minutes, but he could postpone.

"Thanks," Garton shot him a weak smile, "but I need to be alone."

"All right," Xavier agreed reluctantly. "Here's my card." He pulled one of his cards from his pocket and jotted his cell phone number on the back. "My number is on here; please call me if you need anything...anything at all."

Garton took the card with a shaking hand, then resumed his silent study of the house. Xavier climbed out of the car, and with a last look at the lost man inside, he headed for the house to the left of the Landers.

Rapping on the front door, it was opened almost immediately by a short lady, leaning heavily on a cane, who looked to be in her late eighties. "Mrs. Ruffus?"

"Yes," she nodded. "Detective Montague?"

"Yes," he nodded back. "May I come in?"

She nodded absently, her gaze on Garton Landers' car. "Is he all right?"

He followed her gaze, then answered, "As well as can be expected."

"Should we leave him there alone?"

"I think he needs some time to himself. I'll check on him before I leave," Xavier assured the old lady.

"All right." Mrs. Ruffus took a step back and held the door open wider. "Please come in."

Xavier walked behind her down a dark, dusty hallway and into a large, cluttered lounge room. The elderly lady sunk into an overstuffed armchair with a sigh, propping one leg up on an ottoman.

"Arthritis," she explained. "I was laid up yesterday when an officer came to the door. Besides, I wanted to talk with the detective who'd be working the case. I didn't realize they'd send me a cute one," she winked.

He smiled back. "Did you know the Landers well?" Xavier asked.

"Not really." Mrs. Ruffus picked up a pair of glasses from a small table beside her chair and fiddled with them. "They'd only moved in a few months ago; last August, I think. I'd talk to Erica sometimes while I was out getting the mail. She was a teacher, so she was home sometimes in the afternoon. And Garton would occasionally mow my lawns for me when my grandsons were too busy to do it. They were both so sweet." Tears misted her eyes. "When we had that big snowstorm a few weeks ago, Erica sent Garton over to check on me to make sure I was okay."

Xavier gave her an encouraging smile. "Did you see anything

that night, Mrs. Ruffus?"

"Yes, I did." She gave him a firm nod.

He perked up; he was beginning to think the old lady had asked for him to come merely to give her some much-needed company. "What did you see?"

"I saw a man," she told him. "He was tall, with dark hair, and he looked like he was wet."

Confused, he asked, "How could you tell he was wet?"

"There was a bright moon that night. His skin was too..." She seemed to search for the right word. "Too shiny," she finished.

"His skin?"

"He was naked," she said matter-of-factly.

"In January?" Xavier couldn't help but shudder. It was ice cold out during the day, let alone at night.

She chuckled. "Only telling you what I saw, sonny."

"What time did you see him?"

"Mmm, around four," she replied. "I couldn't sleep. Insomnia. I was in the kitchen making some warm milk. I was staring out the window while I waited for the kettle to boil. Gave me a shock when I saw that man walking through Erica and Garton Landers' backyard."

"Why didn't you call the police?"

She hesitated, and her wrinkled face turned bright red. "I thought he was an invited guest."

"An invited guest?" he repeated, puzzled.

She avoided making eye contact. "They like...sex, those two. I hear them sometimes. Our houses are close together, and sometimes they leave the window open. I thought maybe they were into something kinky." Her devastated brown eyes met his. "It was the killer though, wasn't it?"

He was unable to lie to her even though he was desperate to ease the old woman's guilt. "Yes, I think it was, Mrs. Ruffus. Do you think you could work with a sketch artist and give us a better description of him?"

"I don't see too good these days, and it was night." She looked doubtful. Then she straightened her spine, "But I'll do my best."

"Was the man carrying anything with him?"

She thought for a moment. "A bag, I think."

"Did you see him get into a car?"

She shook her head. "He disappeared into the garage, but I didn't see him leave. The kettle boiled and I made my milk and took it up to bed. I assumed he'd parked in there so no one would see him leave."

He probably had, only not for the reason Mrs. Ruffus had assumed. "Had you seen this man, or anyone else, hanging around the Landers' house recently?"

"No, nothing unusual, and I'm always here. Too old to go out these days," she added ruefully.

"I'm going to have an officer come and pick you up and take you to the station to work with a sketch artist. Is that all right?"

"If he's as good-looking as you are, then it's fine by me." Her grin was back.

"Can I get you anything before I go, Mrs. Ruffus?"

"No, thank you, dear; I'll be fine. I'm just going to take a nap while I wait for your officer to come and get me."

He passed her his card. "Please call me if you think of anything else."

"Of course." Her hand lingered on his. "When you find this man..." She trailed off. When she looked back at him, her eyes were fierce. "He doesn't deserve to live."

Xavier couldn't agree more.

* * * * *

2:57 P.M.

Annabelle left the bathroom light on as she walked back into the bedroom. The bedroom light was on, too. Practically every light in the house was on even though it was only three o'clock in the afternoon. And despite the fact that she hadn't left the bedroom since Xavier went to work.

As soon as Xavier had gotten a call about a case and left her, albeit extremely reluctantly, she had headed straight for bed. Xavier had wanted to call someone to come and stay with her, but there was no one to call. She didn't have any friends, only acquaintances, and none that she'd spent time with since her family was killed.

Xavier had tried hard to slot her into his life, encouraging her to spend time with his friends; in particular, his ex-partner Kate. But Annabelle wasn't comfortable with Kate. She liked Kate and her husband and their adorable baby, even if she'd only met the baby once. But being around people was too hard right now. She'd never been good with anyone over the age of five before she'd been assaulted and nearly killed; but now, even just the thought of being around people brought on a panic attack.

What was wrong with her?

Was she ever going to get better?

Could she ever learn how to trust people?

Xavier was positive that she could. But that was probably just wishful thinking on his part.

Annabelle didn't think she'd ever trusted anyone. At least she hadn't since she was four years old. Something had happened to her when she was four. She couldn't quite remember what it was. She knew she'd been hurt, but all she remembered was a dark room, screaming, and a man with a scary face.

After the police had taken her home, everything had been different.

Her parents had been different.

They'd become cold and distant, and she'd thought it was her fault—her fault that they didn't love her anymore.

Xavier kept telling her that it was probably because they felt so guilty about her being hurt that they hadn't known how to deal with it and emotionally pulled away.

Annabelle didn't believe him, though.

And there was no way for him to prove it to her by getting her parents to say it because her parents were dead now.

Some days Annabelle wished she was dead, too.

Some days she wished that Ricky had killed her along with the rest of her family. And some days she wished that Xavier hadn't found her in time and she'd died in the basement.

It was so hard. Moving on. Moving forward. Continuing with life. Making herself climb out of bed each morning. Making herself go through the motions. While all the while she was waiting. Waiting for the fear to recede to a manageable level. Waiting for her nightmares to stop plaguing her sleep each night. Waiting for panic to stop plaguing her every waking second. Waiting for her life to get better.

Sometimes she thought of killing herself.

She didn't really want to, but it seemed like the easier option.

Surely death would be better than this living nightmare she was trapped in.

She'd nearly attempted it once.

About a month after she had moved in to Xavier's house, he'd been out at a counseling session and she had been home alone. She was so tired of jumping at every tiny noise—so tired in general. All she wanted was to curl up in bed and sleep. But sleep was no good, either. It was just reliving everything Ricky had done to her repeatedly. She had taken out her bottle of sleeping pills and contemplated swallowing the entire lot. She had even taken them out and held them in her hand. She had been about to start taking them when Xavier had arrived home.

It terrified Annabelle that she didn't know what she would have done if Xavier hadn't come home when he did.

There had been no more attempts since that day.

But Annabelle knew she couldn't guarantee that she wouldn't be tempted to try it again.

If it wasn't for Xavier, she would probably have done it already.

Xavier was her lifeline.

He was literally the only thing that kept her sane.

She loved him so much.

She just wished she could be sure that he loved her the same way.

It wasn't Xavier's fault that she couldn't truly believe that he could love her forever. It was hers. She believed he loved her. It was just that she was sure that he would have to get tired of her eventually. She doubted him because of his complicated relationship with his ex-wife, Julia. And that niggling little bit of doubt annoyed her.

Annabelle hated herself for doubting Xavier when he had done nothing but help and support her every step of the way. He had opened up about himself and talked about how his childhood had left him feeling alone. Xavier's parents had both been married to other people when he was conceived. And while they had shared custody and he had had two families to shower him with love, he had still always felt alone. Knowing that she was self-conscious about her unusual eyes, he had stopped wearing the hazel contact lens over his green eye, so that his heterochromia was now obvious to everyone who met him. And he'd admitted to her that his real name was Romeo Montague, and that he'd started going by his middle name Xavier around the time he entered high school because he hated all the Romeo and Juliet jokes. He talked to her about himself to try and make her feel more comfortable about opening up about herself. And yet she still held back.

She knew Xavier's love for her was unconditional, so why couldn't she shake that niggling doubt?

Xavier kept telling her that there was no timeline for recovering from trauma. However, that wasn't what Annabelle wanted to hear. She wanted Xavier to give her a date—a date when she would magically recover and be able to live her life like a normal person. She could deal with anything if she knew it wasn't forever. If she knew, she just had to hold on until a certain date, and then all her pain and fear and lingering doubts would all just disappear as though they'd never existed in the first place.

Because what Annabelle was most afraid of was that this would be how she would live the rest of her life—stuck in an endless nightmare with no escape route.

She wasn't sure she could do it.

* * * * *

4:08 P.M.

Xavier couldn't take his eyes off the picture he held in his hands.

It was Garton and Erica Landers on their wedding day. Erica was dressed in a simple white cotton dress; Garton in a white shirt and black pants. Their arms were entwined around each other's necks, their beaming smiles aimed directly at the camera. They were young and in love with their whole lives ahead of them. Until someone had decided to cut those bright futures short.

The smiling couple in the picture contrasted so violently with the couple now. Visions of Erica's destroyed body ran through his mind. The unnaturally white skin, the vacant eyes, the tape over her mouth, the limp blonde hair stained dark red with blood. There was no resemblance between the dead woman at the Landers' house and the beautiful woman in the photo. If Xavier hadn't known they were one and the same, he would never have believed it.

Garton, too, looked nothing like the grinning man holding his new wife on his wedding day. He had grown old in the last forty-eight hours. Old and drawn. The man Xavier had sat with in the car hours earlier seemed thinner; his skin more wrinkled. His eyes, which had once shone with life and excitement, were now extinguished. They were lifeless. Just like his wife's. Garton may have survived the attack, but he would never recover from it. He would always bear the scars. And emotional scars ran so much deeper than physical ones.

Unfortunately, Xavier knew all about that.

Annabelle still bore the scars of what she'd been through.

The physical scars from whatever happened to her as a child, and the new one on her shoulder from Ricky's attack eight months ago, had faded. But her psychological scars were still bright red and angry. It was rare for Annabelle to sleep through the night. She still jumped at every little noise during the day. She lived in constant fear that Ricky would return for her.

What hurt Xavier the most, though, was that she still didn't completely trust him. She trusted him to keep her safe. She trusted him to look after her. She trusted that he loved her. But try as she might, or try as he might to convince her, she couldn't trust that he would never leave her.

He knew that, in part, it was his fault. Admitting that part of him would always love his ex-wife, Julia, had allowed Annabelle to believe that his feelings might return if Julia were ever to come to him needing his help. It still hurt, though. He had been right beside her, holding her hand, every step of the way. He so desperately wanted her to believe in him. To be able to let go of the doubts that she had. To just clear her mind and allow it to trust him. To allow him to help her carry the load of emotional baggage that she seemed determined to shoulder alone.

Annabelle's parents had messed her up. He was sure he was right when he kept telling Annabelle that the distance they'd created between them and her after her childhood abduction had more to do with them and their guilt than it did anything to do with her. Unfortunately, there was no way for him to convince her of this, since her parents were dead. Maybe it would help if Annabelle could remember what had happened to her. But she had locked the memories away so tightly it was like they didn't even exist anymore.

Some days he just didn't know what to do.

Xavier had to keep reminding himself—and Annabelle—that it would take time. Time for her to recover. Time for her to see for herself that everything he kept telling her was true. But he wished that time was now.

"Xavier."

He blinked and the conference room floated back into view. His Lieutenant, Robert Hollow, crime scene tech, Diane Jolly, and medical examiner, Billy Newton, were all staring at him expectantly. He realized he'd zoned out. "Sorry, I got a little distracted. What were you saying?"

Rob's sympathetic gray eyes studied him. "Diane said that you and Annabelle got a letter from Ricky Preston earlier today saying that he was back. That must have been a shock for both of you. How's Annabelle handling it?"

She isn't, Xavier wanted to answer. She was withdrawing again, and any progress that she'd made the last few months was fading away. They had to end this. They had to find Ricky Preston whether he was Erica Landers' killer or not. If they didn't, Annabelle would never be able to move on.

Rob's sympathetic eyes turned concerned. "Is she still seeing her therapist?"

"Yes." He had made it clear from the beginning that Annabelle needed to seek help for the trauma she'd suffered. Julia hadn't and it had eaten her alive. He wasn't going to get involved with Annabelle only to watch her go down the same path as his ex.

"Good, make sure she keeps going."

Xavier nodded. "What were you saying?"

Robert gestured at the ME. "Billy was just saying cause of death was exsanguination, not that that comes as a surprise to any of us."

"Looks like he used an axe," Billy added.

"Fits with what Garton Landers said." Xavier nodded.

"Who kills with an axe?" Billy looked baffled. "It's not the most practical of tools. And whatever happened to a good old-fashioned knife or gun?"

Xavier knew exactly what kind of killer used an axe. The kind who was completely unbalanced, loved the sight of blood, and who probably thought being a real live axe murderer was hilarious. Ricky Preston. But he kept his mouth shut. "Any forensics so far, Diane?"

She shook her head. "I have the footprints, but there's no database for that, so it'll only help you with your comparison once you find this guy."

"What about the closet? Any fingerprints there?"

"No; he must have worn gloves."

"Fingerprints anywhere else?"

Another shake of her head. "Must have kept his gloves on the whole time. He came prepared, though. No duct tape in the house; he brought his own. This was completely planned and premeditated."

"Garton Landers said there were no signs of break-in when they returned home, and that they put their clothes away in the closet before going to bed. So, the killer was either hiding out in another room or he came in after they were already home," Xavier explained.

"Pretty cocky if he did." Diane raised an eyebrow. "Especially if he did sneak in and hide in the closet."

Xavier nodded his agreement. Again, this fit with Ricky Preston. The man was arrogant and had more confidence than any killer should have.

"Garton give you anything else?" Rob asked.

"Description was vague: a tall guy with dark hair who maybe had blue eyes. He said that he'd never seen him before," Xavier replied. "Neighbor gave the same description, minus the eye color. She also said she saw a naked man leaving the house around the time the murder was committed, heading through the

Landers' backyard toward the garage. If he knew their routine, he'd know they never park their cars in the garage, so it would be the perfect place to park and remain unseen."

Taking a deep breath, Rob asked, "All right, well the big question we have is, do we think that this is the work of Ricky Preston? I don't like coincidences, but the fact that Ricky sent you that letter and on the same day you receive it we get a crime scene that all but screams his name is a pretty big coincidence."

"I don't want to get sidetracked," Xavier told his boss. "I feel like it's Ricky, but what if I'm wrong? I don't want more bodies on my conscience because I was obsessed with Ricky."

Rob frowned slightly. "There shouldn't be any bodies on your conscience," he reprimanded gently. "You're a cop, you're only human, you're not God. Ricky is responsible for every person that he killed. And so is this killer if it's not Ricky."

He didn't believe his boss, but he was not in the mood to argue. "I'm going to speak with family and friends of the Landers, see if there's anyone with a grudge against them. But this doesn't feel personal."

"I have a possible avenue that may help," Billy announced. "Blood tests on Garton Landers show that he was injected with sodium thiopental."

"Which is?" Rob prompted.

"It's a rapid-onset, short-acting barbiturate general anesthetic," Billy explained. "It knocks you out for maybe five to ten minutes and starts acting almost immediately upon injection. You'd be out cold within maybe forty-five seconds."

"Is it hard to come by?" Xavier asked.

"It used to be commonly used for general anesthesia, although it's largely been replaced by propofol," Billy replied.

"So that could help us." Xavier was pleased they had an avenue to pursue. If they could track down where the killer sourced the drug, it could lead them right to him.

"Okay," Rob stood, "we meet back here tomorrow morning;

hopefully, we've made some progress by then."

* * * * *

5:16 P.M.

Her leg was aching.

Aching badly.

Sofia knew she'd overdone it, but once she'd taken those first terrifying few steps, she hadn't been able to stop. It felt so wonderful to be able to walk almost normally again that she just kept going.

Now she was paying the price for it.

She should go and sit down, prop her leg up and let it rest for a while, but she wasn't sure if Ryan was going to be home for dinner, and if he was, then she should make something.

Sofia couldn't wait until she could go back to work. Before she'd gotten sick, she had run a charity—a women's shelter—that had been financed by her family's money. Now that her entire family, bar Isabella, were deceased, she had inherited everything. Money, businesses, properties—they were all hers now. She didn't care about being rich, though; she just wanted to decide how best to use the expansive resources now at her disposal to help as many people as she could.

As soon as she was well enough, she was going to put that money to work. Right now, though, she had to focus on her recovery and regaining her strength—both physically and emotionally.

Yawning loudly, Sofia glanced at the clock; it was only five in the afternoon. Even if Ryan came home for dinner, it wouldn't be for a few hours yet. Maybe she should take a nap. She was exhausted; good sleep had been something that she hadn't had since Isabella's murderous rampage.

Limping toward the living room, she caught sight of a delivery truck pulling out of the driveway. It had to be the package she'd been waiting for. Something special for Ryan's nephew, Brian. Sofia empathized with the child in a way no one else in his family could. Brian had faced, and beaten, leukemia. The seven-year-old knew what it was like to think that you were going to die. And so did Sofia. She had quickly grown close to the little boy and was guilty of spoiling him.

Deciding that she would get the parcel and then take a nap in the living room, she made the slow trek to the mailbox. Retrieving the parcel, Sofia had to pause halfway back up the path to the door, taking a moment to just enjoy the fresh air. It was chilly, and she wasn't dressed properly for outdoors, but Sofia didn't mind. After weeks of being cooped up in the hospital and then in her house, it was such a blessing to simply stand in the waning sunshine and enjoy the winter afternoon.

She couldn't wait until she was strong enough to go back to doing all the things she'd loved doing before: hiking, camping, skiing, and rowing. Sofia had loved everything about being outdoors, and she knew Ryan did, too. As soon as she was able, they were going to do all those things together.

When she'd recovered a little strength, she resumed her walk back indoors. The hammering pain in her leg was too much for her to bear right now, so she hobbled for the kitchen where painkillers were waiting.

A sigh of relief was just escaping her lips as she stepped into the kitchen, when she froze.

Something was wrong.

The kitchen was cold.

Colder than it should be.

The back door was open.

Sofia *always* kept the doors and windows closed and locked.

Her gaze fell on the table.

A bouquet of flowers sat there.

A small envelope was propped up against them.

Her name was written on it in an all too familiar script.

On shaking legs, she walked to the table. With hands that shook just as much, she picked up the envelope and slid out the card. And her worst nightmare was confirmed.

Yanking her phone from her pocket, she dialed Ryan.

"Sofia?"

At the sound of his voice she felt a calm rush through her.

"Sofia?" Ryan repeated, alarm inching into his voice. "What's wrong?"

"He's back," she answered softly.

He was confused. "Who's back, cupcake?"

"My stalker." Her calm was beginning to crack. Ryan's voice wasn't enough. She was scared; she wanted him here with her.

"What?" Ryan demanded, panicked now. "How do you know?"

"He was here, in the house, while I was outside getting the mail. He left me flowers and a note that says not to worry, he's back." It all came tumbling out in a rush, her calm was quickly turning to blinding panic.

"Is he still there?" Ryan was frantic.

"I don't think so, the back door is open," she assured him.

"I want you to leave immediately. I want you to go next door to the Barretts' and wait for..."

Sofia stopped listening to Ryan when the doorbell rang. "Someone's at the door," she whispered into the phone.

"Stay on the line with me, Sofia," Ryan ordered.

Her heart was hammering painfully in her chest as she supported herself with the wall as she headed for the door.

"Sofia? I mean it, don't hang up," Ryan insisted. "Stay on the line."

Pain in her leg forgotten, she was shaking so badly she could hardly slide the deadbolt undone. "I'm about to open the door," she informed Ryan.

"Just don't hang up," Ryan commanded again. "Whatever

happens, stay on the line."

Barely breathing, she pulled the door open and gasped, her knees going weak, she pitched forward.

"Sofia? Sofia?" Ryan's voice screamed from the phone. "What happened? Who is it? Sofia? Answer me!"

Unable to answer Ryan, she was too breathless to speak. Strong arms caught her as she started to collapse.

"Sofia? Honey, what's wrong?" Jack Xander, Ryan's older brother, asked her, his concerned blue eyes darting from her to the hall behind her.

"Sofia? Answer me," Ryan continued to yell. "Come on, talk to me."

She leaned heavily on Jack. "It's okay," she told Ryan. "It was just Jack at the door."

Ryan's breath whooshed out in relief. "Let me talk to him."

Sofia handed Jack her phone. He took it but didn't raise it to his ear; instead, he kept his attention focused on her.

"What happened? What freaked you out?" Jack asked.

"My stalker, he's back, he left me flowers and a note," she gaspingly related to Jack.

He held her up with one arm, and with his other he pulled out his gun. "Is he gone?"

"I think so." Tears began to trickle down her cheeks and she shivered violently.

"Okay, let's get you inside." Jack guided her gently away from the door and closed and locked it behind them. Without Jack's supporting arm, Sofia knew she couldn't remain upright. As it was, her trembling legs gave out halfway down the corridor and Jack picked her up and carried her the rest of the way to the kitchen, depositing her on a chair and setting his gun and the phone on the table.

"Jack? Jack? Come on, talk to me," Ryan's panicked voice floated from the phone.

He snatched the phone back up. "I'll talk to you in a moment,"

Jack calmly told his younger brother. "Right now Sofia is my priority."

"Is she hurt?" Ryan's panic ratcheted up a notch.

"She's in shock," Jack told Ryan. "You don't sound so good either, so try to calm down. I'll be back in a sec."

Once more setting the phone down, Jack crouched in front of her, his gaze appraising. "Did you see him?"

"No," she hiccuped through her tears.

"All right, I'll be right back, okay? You're shaking, I'm just going to grab a blanket." He stood, closed the backdoor, and briefly left the room. He returned moments later with a thick woolen afghan which he wrapped around her shoulders. Then he rummaged through the cupboards and pulled out a glass, which he filled with water, then grabbed the bottle of painkillers from the counter, handing her both.

When she'd swallowed the pills, Jack knelt in front of her again, perching the phone between his shoulder and ear, he took her freezing hands in his warm ones and began to rub them. "Did you calm down?" he asked Ryan.

"Of course not," Ryan snapped, although from what she could hear he did sound a little calmer. "Don't leave her alone, Jack," Ryan begged.

"I'll be all right," Sofia assured Jack, trying desperately to calm her ragged breathing. "He's never tried to hurt me before."

"Head down, deep breaths," was all Jack said, his hand on her shoulder bending her over. "Of course I won't leave her alone. Don't worry, I'll stay with her until you get here."

"I don't know when that will be," Ryan sounded desperate.

"I can't get warm," she told Jack, her teeth chattering relentlessly. Try as she might, she couldn't control the tremors racking her body.

"You're in shock, sweetheart," Jack reminded her gently, pulling the blanket tighter around her shoulders.

"Jack?" Ryan prompted.

"Don't stress, Ry." Jack remained calm. "I'm not going anywhere. I'll get her to eat and then rest, and I'll make sure CSU comes, and I'll make sure she gives her statement to whomever worked her stalker case before. Really, Ryan, I've got her."

Sofia wanted to protest that no one needed to 'get' her, that she would be perfectly okay on her own. But the truth was, she wouldn't. She was terrified. She didn't want to deal with her stalker all over again. And didn't stalkers sometimes escalate to violence? It had been a year since he had last left her anything. Who was he? Why would he come back now? And what did he want from her?

Tears starting all over again, she rested her head against Jack's shoulder and let him take care of her until Ryan came home.

* * * * *

6:45 P.M.

"Did you hear from Jack?"

"Uh huh," Ryan confirmed. "Jack knows that if I don't hear from him every ten minutes I'm jumping in my car and driving home. I just got a text; Jack called Edmund and got the name of the detective who worked her case before and Sofia gave him her statement. Then he called Stephanie to come and collect the flowers and card and check for fingerprints, because he thought someone Sofia knew would be less stressful for her right now. Jack made Sofia eat, and he's given her a sleeping pill so she can get some rest."

"Knowing all that's not enough, though, is it?" Paige asked sympathetically.

He sighed deeply. "Not even close. I'm not going to feel better about this until I see that Sofia's okay with my own eyes and I'm holding her in my arms. Scratch that, I'm not going to feel better about this until we find out who the stalker is and he's in jail," he amended.

"Jack sounds like he has everything under control," Paige attempted to console him.

"I know," Ryan couldn't agree more. "If I can't be with Sofia, then the people I'd trust her with the most would be Jack and you. I know Jack won't let anything happen to her. And I'm not even sure if her stalker is a threat to her yet—at least a physical threat. But she has enough to deal with without having him pop back up in her life."

"You're going to have to come to terms with the fact that someone can't be with Sofia twenty-four hours a day," Paige reminded him gently. "You work, I work, Jack works, Edmund works, and as soon as she can, Sofia intends to go back to work. And even if you could work something out so one of us can be with her all the time, I don't think she'd like that. She wants to get her life back; she's not going to let you lock her up like some sort of prisoner until we can find her stalker."

Ryan didn't want to think about that right now. He wanted to believe that they could find her stalker before there were any more incidents. Why would he leave for a year and then suddenly return now? The possibility that he had been in jail on unrelated charges seemed the most likely. And the most terrifying.

"Ryan, how's the situation at your house?" Belinda entered the room.

"Jack has everything under control," he replied tightly.

"Of course he does," Belinda smiled.

"Did the warrant for Eve Hitacheel's arrest come through yet?" Ryan asked.

"Should be any second now," Belinda answered. "Are we sure it's her?"

"We spoke with every family member, friend, and colleague of Roman that we could find, and when pressed, several of them admitted that they knew that Eve was aware of Roman's affairs," Paige explained, rubbing tiredly at her eyes.

Concern for Sofia was briefly inched aside as worry for his partner took over. Paige looked terrible—tired and drawn. Ryan needed to get her to tell him what was going on with her. "We spoke with Eve's sister," Ryan expanded. "She was reluctant at first to tell us anything, but after we threatened to arrest her with obstruction of justice, she finally opened up. She said that Eve found out less than a year after their marriage. She got suspicious of Roman being gone so regularly at night, so she followed him. Found him at a hotel with a prostitute. Ever since, she kept track of his mistresses."

"If she's known for over thirty-five years, then why would she kill him now?" Belinda looked puzzled.

"According to her sister, Eve has recently been diagnosed with cervical cancer. The human papillomavirus causes most types of cervical cancer. It's sexually transmitted; she blamed Roman," Ryan explained.

"Her stressor," Belinda nodded understandingly.

"To make things worse," Ryan added, "the sister said Roman forced Eve to have sex with him. Said Eve didn't want to sleep with Roman anymore, was okay with remaining married so she could have the benefits of Roman's money, but she didn't want to be intimate anymore. Roman had other ideas."

"Marital rape is hard to prove," Belinda pointed out. "If it's true, though, she may use it as part of her defense. It could make her sympathetic to a jury, especially with her medical diagnosis. Anyone you talk to give you any other suspects?"

"No one could think of anyone who would want to hurt Roman," Ryan replied. "And," anticipating his boss' next question, "no one knew of any other girlfriends or boyfriends. Roman's closest friend said two women were all he could deal with at any one time." He cast a concerned glance at Paige as she looked at her phone, and then stood and began to pace. "Everything okay?"

"Fine," Paige replied, stopping abruptly and turning back to the table. Partway back, she began to sway.

Darting to her side, Ryan wrapped a hand around Paige's arm to steady her. "Easy, I got you. Are you okay?"

"A little light-headed," Paige murmured, pressing her eyes closed.

Belinda pushed a chair over, and Ryan lowered his partner down into it, then crouched at her side, reaching for her wrist to check her pulse. With Eve Hitacheel's medical diagnosis in mind, he was conjuring up all sorts of reasons for Paige's faintness—none of them good.

"Should I call an ambulance?" Belinda asked, phone already in hand.

"No," Paige opened her eyes. "I'm fine. Really. I've been a little distracted today and haven't eaten anything. I'm sure that's why I was a little faint."

Raising a doubtful eyebrow, Belinda looked to him, "How's her pulse?"

"Too fast for my liking," Ryan replied. "What's going on with you?" he asked Paige.

Before his partner could reply, the door swung open and Stephanie bustled in, her gaze immediately going to Paige. Her hazel eyes narrowed in concern, "What's wrong with Paige?"

"Nothing," Paige insisted.

"She nearly passed out," Ryan supplied with a small frown at his partner. He didn't understand why Paige wouldn't just tell him what was wrong. Usually she talked to him about everything. He remembered back when Paige and Elias had just started dating, and she was upset because she thought he was cheating on her; it had taken him all of two minutes to get that out of her. Why was she shutting him out now when something was obviously upsetting her to the point where it was affecting her physically?

Setting her papers on the table, Stephanie took Paige's other wrist.

"Ryan already did that," Paige murmured.

Ignoring her, Stephanie turned to him and Belinda, "Her pulse is racing. Why is she still here? I'll call an ambulance."

"I don't need an ambulance," Paige insisted. "Really, I probably just need to eat something and get a good night's sleep."

"All right," Ryan reluctantly agreed. "But I'm calling Elias to come and pick you up." Paige merely nodded her assent, which did nothing to ease his concern. Standing, he pushed the chair—with Paige still in it—closer to the table. "Put your head down," he gently pressed on Paige's shoulders. Folding her arms on the table, Paige rested her forehead on them.

"I'll call Elias," Belinda dialed Paige's husband and walked to a corner of the room.

"How was Sofia when you saw her?" Ryan asked Stephanie.

She shifted her worried gaze from Paige to him. "She was pretty upset, but Jack was doing a good job at calming her down. She didn't want to take the sleeping pills, but Jack managed to convince her that you would worry less about her if she was getting some rest. He'd set her up on the couch in the living room so he could keep an eye on her while she slept. When I left, she was just drifting off."

That made Ryan feel better. If Sofia was asleep, then she wasn't driving herself crazy with worry. Typically, she wasn't a big worrier, but her nerves had taken a battering lately. "Did you find anything in the house? Or any fingerprints on the card or flowers?"

She shook her head. "Sadly, it doesn't look like I'm going to find anything useful. We know in the past he's never left fingerprints, and it seems like he's been just as careful this time. I'll keep looking, though. Maybe I'll get lucky."

"Elias is on his way," Belinda announced. "I'll go with you, Ryan, to arrest Eve Hitacheel."

"That's what I came to talk to you guys about," Stephanie's hazel eyes were grave.

A sinking feeling in his gut hinted that he wasn't going to like what Stephanie was about to say. "What did you find?"

"There were some useable prints from the hotel room," Stephanie began.

His mood lightened. "Well, that's a good thing, right?"

"Yes," Stephanie nodded.

"They weren't Eve Hitacheel's?" Belinda asked.

"No."

Stephanie's one-word answers were disconcerting. "Did you get a hit in AFIS?" If their killer was in the Automated Fingerprint Identification System, then they could go and pick her up immediately. Ryan didn't see why Stephanie was acting as though this were a bad thing.

"Yes."

"And?" Paige prompted, lifting her head.

"Head back down," he and Stephanie said simultaneously, each pushing softly on her shoulders. Paige rolled her eyes but complied.

"And?" Ryan turned back to Stephanie. "What're they wanted for?"

"Murder. Several counts of murder," Stephanie replied.

"Well that's no surprise, given how coldly calculated Roman's murder was." His brows furrowed in confusion. "What's up, Steph? Why are you being so evasive? Whose fingerprints were they?"

Anxious hazel eyes looked back at him. "They're Isabella's."

Shocked and disbelieving, "Sofia's Isabella?"

"Yes, I'm sorry, Ryan. Isabella was in that hotel room. It doesn't prove that she's the killer, but she was there, and given what she did to her family, it's logical that she was the one who murdered Roman Hitacheel."

* * * * *

9:41 P.M.

She was giddy.

Could a fifty-eight-year-old woman be giddy?

Helena Mendleson wasn't sure, but what she felt whenever she was with Tyler certainly felt like giddiness. That feeling hadn't left her since she first met Tyler almost eighteen months ago.

She had thought things were over for her in the love department. And they had been for a *long* time. The love of her life had died just three years after they were married, leaving her with eight-month-old twins to raise on her own. It had been hard—and lonely—work, but she had managed. Sometimes just by the skin of her teeth. Her son and daughter were all grown up now, in their thirties, and both were happily married with kids of their own. Helena loved being a grandmother but she had known that something was missing in her life.

While raising her kids, she had been too busy to even think about dating anyone else. And her love for her deceased husband was still so strong that even the idea of dating had felt like she'd be cheating on him. But once she was all alone she had realized just how lonely she was.

After a few awful dates, she had met Tyler Mendleson. Her life had changed from that second on. Her kids and Tyler's three daughters had all been happy to see their parents find happiness with someone after so many years alone. And her second wedding ceremony had been as small and intimate as her first one had been a huge, over-the-top celebration.

Now, it was like all those sad years had been wiped away. She still loved her first husband with all her heart, but she had found a way to love someone else, too. And even thought it would never take away what she and Jacob had had, and their two beautiful children, she was glad that she had met Tyler.

"Ready to go?"

She looked up at Tyler, at the love shining from his sparkling brown eyes. Helena nodded.

Taking her hand, he led her out of the restaurant and into the cold night. As the initial slap of icy air faded, Helena suddenly had the feeling that someone was watching them. Turning her head, she scanned the parking lot. There were a reasonable number of cars parked there, but it was too dark for her to see if anyone sat inside one of them watching. The park was across the street, full of trees and places to hide. Helena shivered.

"Cold?" Tyler asked, wrapping an arm around her shoulders.

Helena leaned into him, but his warm body did nothing to ease the feeling of watchful eyes following her every move.

JANUARY 10TH

1:24 A.M.

"Sofia."

Her name barely penetrated her haze. She was running. As fast as she could. But she wasn't getting anywhere. Isabella and a faceless man were chasing her.

"I'm sorry, Sofia; you shouldn't exist," Isabella told her calmly, a knife clutched tightly in one hand.

"Sofia."

She tried to get away from her crazy sister but suddenly Isabella was standing beside her. "I don't want to. I must. You shouldn't exist. I'm sorry," Isabella pleaded.

"Sofia. Wake up."

Now she was lying on a bed in a small room. Isabella standing above her. The knife blade glinted as it came toward her. Her sister stabbed her repeatedly.

Sofia thrashed. Desperately trying to avoid the knife

"Sofia, it's Ryan. It's just a nightmare."

Gasping, she raised a hand to her sweat-streaked forehead, and her eyes popped open to see Ryan kneeling in front of her. As she'd fought Isabella in her dreams she had backed herself up against the headboard. "It was just a dream?" she asked Ryan. It had felt so real that she couldn't quite believe it wasn't.

"Just a dream, cupcake," Ryan assured her, lifting a hand from her shoulder to brush her sweat-dampened hair from her face. "Are you okay?" his worried blue eyes were assessing her.

Sniffing, she gave a small nod. Memories from the previous evening flooded her mind. Her stalker was back, and she had no idea how to make him leave her alone because she didn't even know who he was. Glancing at the window, it was dark outside. "What time did you come home?"

"It was close to midnight." Ryan gently slid her down so she was lying on her back, pulled the covers over her, then settled beside her. "You were completely out cold, didn't even stir when I carried you up."

Pressing her trembling body closer to Ryan's, Jack had convinced her to take some sleeping pills only because he had insisted that Ryan would feel better about being stuck at work if he knew she was resting, and by promising he'd keep watch over her in case her stalker returned. Thinking of Jack, she wouldn't have been surprised if Ryan's older brother was keeping watch downstairs. "Jack still here?"

"Yes, he thought I'd sleep better if he stayed. I hate that that man broke in while you were here alone." Ryan's voice was fierce.

Catching on to where this was heading, she said, "I won't be a prisoner, Ryan. You can't be with me all the time. And neither can Jack or Paige," she added. "I don't think I'm in any physical danger; my stalker has never tried to hurt me before."

"Doesn't mean he won't," Ryan sounded terrified.

"I know that," a shudder racked through her.

He gripped her tighter. "I know I can't lock you up somewhere so he can't get you, but it doesn't mean I don't worry about you."

Whether it was the emotional turmoil of the last few months wearing her down, her stalker's visit, or the lingering effects of the sleeping pills, Sofia was finding herself feeling weepy and self-pitying, and tears sprang to her eyes. "I'm sorry; you've worried about me enough lately. And you have a new case. I'm sorry my dramas keep distracting you."

Beside her Ryan stiffened. "Don't talk like that," he said darkly. Sitting up, he pulled her up with him. "I love you, and it isn't your fault that someone is stalking you or that Isabella went off the deep end."

Sofia's head knew that but her heart refused to believe it. She was Isabella's sister. If anyone should have seen how unstable she was, it was her.

"I have to tell you something."

The trepidation in Ryan's blue eyes scared her. "What is it?" her voice trembled.

Reaching for her hands, he clutched them tightly, his thumbs absently brushing backward and forward across her knuckles. "This new case. There was a development yesterday. Stephanie found something at the crime scene. She, uh…she found some fingerprints…"

"Just tell me, Ryan." The longer Ryan delayed, the more her mind was conjuring up all sorts of terrifying scenarios. Because of Ryan's history with his fiancée's suicide, he had a fear of saying or doing the wrong thing with her. This often led to him putting off telling her anything he thought would upset her. She understood his fear, but right now, she just needed to know.

"I'm so sorry, cupcake, the fingerprints were Isabella's."

The bed seemed to tilt beneath her, the sound of blood rushing in her ears drowned out everything else, and white spots began to dance in front of her eyes. What Ryan had just told her couldn't be true. Isabella was gone. She wasn't still killing people. There was no reason for her fingerprints to turn up at a crime scene.

"Sofia? Honey, don't pass out on me," Ryan's voice penetrated her haze.

Slumping against Ryan's hard chest, fresh tears filled her eyes, and spilled out in noisy sobs. "No, I don't believe you," she clawed desperately at denial. "Isabella has no reason to keep killing. Our whole family is already dead."

Technically that wasn't quite true, as well as herself and Isabella, there were their father's other two young daughters, and their grandfather's baby daughter. However, the only two legitimate children her father had had lived in Europe with their maternal grandparents. And Isabella had taken the baby—who was both Isabella's sister and aunt—with her when she ran off—leaving Sofia, for all intents and purposes, all alone in the world. At least alone in terms of biological family. She had Ryan, and he meant the world to her.

"Shh," Ryan soothed, his hand stroking up and down her spine. "I'm sorry, but it is true. Isabella's fingerprints were found at a murder scene, but that doesn't mean she's the killer."

They both knew that wasn't true. If her fingerprints were there, then she had done it. As much as Sofia hated knowing that Isabella was still killing, the knowledge that her sister was still close by was oddly comforting. "I thought she was slipping away," she whispered against Ryan's chest. "I thought we'd never find her. I want her caught. I want her someplace where she can't hurt anyone else, where she can't hurt herself. I want to be able to go and visit her. I hate what she did, but I still love her, and I miss her." More tears came tumbling out, and she clung to Ryan, sagging against him with a heaving sigh when her tears were spent.

"We'll find her; I promise." Ryan pressed a kiss to the top of her head. "Is that why you were upset earlier? You felt like with every bit of progress you made getting better, your sister was slipping farther and farther away from you?"

She should be amazed that Ryan knew her well enough to figure out what was going on inside her head, but she wasn't. That Ryan was so good at reading her was just one of the many things she loved about him. "It's stupid, I know," she murmured, embarrassed.

He pressed her tighter against him. "It's not stupid. You lost a lot. Including your own identity."

Stiffening, Sofia didn't want to discuss her true parentage. She tried to pull away. "I'm tired. I think I'll go back to sleep."

Ryan refused to release her. "We'll sleep soon. Talk to me, Sofia."

"I don't . . ." she began to protest.

"Please," Ryan interrupted.

The single nicety spurred her into acquiescing. Letting out a shuddering breath, she confessed what had been bothering her the most the last eight months. "I shouldn't exist."

He pulled her back so he could look her in the eye, perplexed outrage on his face. "What are you talking about?"

"Logan forced himself on Gloria. He raped her. She didn't willingly sleep with him. He was her fourteen-year-old stepson. She didn't want to get pregnant. She didn't want me. She didn't treat me any different than Logan, Lewis, Lincoln or Isabella. She knew I shouldn't exist," she finished on a hiccupping sob.

He grabbed her chin so she had to keep looking at him. "Sofia, that is *not* true."

She yanked her face free. "Of course it is." She heard the hysteria creeping into her voice. "Gloria never acted like a mother to me. How could she? Every time she looked at me she remembered how I was conceived. She hated me. She hated having to see me every day. She hated that I existed. She wished I didn't. She knew I shouldn't. She knew she should have aborted me while she had the chance . . ."

"Stop, baby. Shh," Ryan pressed a finger to her lips to silence her.

Another wave of crying wracked through her. Her chest ached as it heaved, her eyes burned, and she felt drained. Physically and emotionally. She didn't want to cry anymore. She didn't want to feel like she shouldn't be alive. And yet, she didn't know how to stop feeling that way.

"Shh, cupcake," Ryan was holding her, stroking her hair, rubbing her back, trying to calm her down. "Stop crying, baby. Please. Don't cry anymore. Shh."

But Sofia couldn't stop crying. Her emotions were controlling her right now, not the other way around. At last Ryan tilted her face up, his mouth taking hers, his hand threading through her hair. Ryan's kisses smothered her tears, and soothed her jangled nerves. Slowly, she felt herself start to relax.

Sensing the tension inside her subsiding, Ryan eased her down against the mattress and settled her under the covers once more. "You want some sleeping pills?" Ryan asked.

Shaking her head, Sofia curled herself against Ryan's warm, hard body. Her mind was exhausted enough that sleep was already edging in.

"Need some painkillers?"

"No," she whispered, resting her head on Ryan's shoulder. "All I need is for you to find Isabella."

* * * * *

3:17 A.M.

Sliding back into bed after a bathroom stop, Tyler Mendleson gave a contented sigh. His wife Helena, still asleep, curled her body toward him and snuggled her head on his shoulder.

Could life get any better than this?

Tyler didn't think so.

The last eighteen months had been pure bliss.

Tyler had never thought he'd find love again. In fact, he thought he'd been lucky to find it once in the first place. His parents' marriage had been one screaming match after another before they finally divorced. And Tyler hadn't held high hopes of faring any better.

Until he'd met Joy.

Joy was just that, the joy of his life. And the three beautiful daughters she had given him before her death had brought him just as much joy as their mother had. Raising three girls on his own had been tough. And many a night he had laid in bed unsure how to help his daughters on their journey to womanhood. He must have done okay, though. All three were wonderful young women.

And now he had another wonderful woman in his life.

Helena was a breath of fresh air in a life that had become stale and musty. He had his girls and his job, but he was just going through the motions. There had been no real enjoyment in his life, nothing that made him excited to get out of bed in the morning. Helena had changed all of that.

Tyler had known from the moment he laid eyes on her that she was the one for him. She was the woman who would make it feel like his life was starting all over again. It had taken his daughters a little longer to adjust to the fact that he was in a relationship with someone other than their mother. To them it had felt like he was betraying their mother's memory. But over time they had come to understand that he wasn't trying to replace Joy. No one could ever replace her, he had simply been lucky enough to find another woman to love. Now they were one big happy family, him and Helena, his daughters, her two children. One big happy family.

Kissing the top of his wife's head, Tyler was just about to close his eyes and try to get a little more sleep before he had to get up for work when he felt something sharp pinch his leg. He was reaching a hand down to find out what it was, hoping it wasn't a spider—he hated arachnids—when his vision began to tunnel, fading in and out before everything went black.

Something was squirming beside him.

That was odd, Tyler thought.

He and Helena were in bed. Perhaps she was having a nightmare?

He tried to move toward her, but he couldn't.

Panic shot through him.

A spider had bitten him. It must have been a poisonous one. He was paralyzed.

"For goodness' sake, hold still," a voice snapped above him. "You're the wriggliest woman I've had to deal with."

Everything clicked, and Tyler knew a spider hadn't bitten him.

His eyes snapped open. The light was on in the bedroom. A man was standing on the other side of the bed, wrapping duct tape around Helena's wrists. His wife was wiggling and squirming frantically, trying in vain to get away from the binds that tied her to the bed.

On instinct Tyler tried to move toward the man. No one hurt his wife and got away with it. Of course, he couldn't move. That didn't stop him from trying, though. He yanked on his restraints so violently, it felt like he was about to rip his joints out of their sockets.

The man glanced his way and chuckled. "I think that's a little pointless, tough guy. Although I hear ladies love a knight in shining armor," the man chuckled again as though that were the funniest thing he'd ever heard.

Tyler tried to yell at him, but all that came out were muffled grunts. There was duct tape over his mouth. This was a nightmare. It had to be. It couldn't be happening.

Turning his head, his eyes met his wife's, and suddenly he was fighting back tears. Tyler knew he couldn't cry. Crying would stuff up his nose and with his mouth taped closed he wouldn't be able to breathe. Still, knowing all of that didn't seem to help. The tears were coming whether he wanted them to or not.

Then a hand touched his. Gentle fingers caressed his palm.

The man had tied his right wrist to the right top corner of the bed, and Helena's left wrist to the top left corner of the bed, but he had tied their other hands together.

Helena's strength calmed him enough that he could hold back his tears.

"Holding hands; that's sweet," the man grinned at them. "Usually I do things a little differently, but unfortunately tonight I'm running late. Thanks to that stupid manager," he added in a mutter.

Usually, Tyler thought. What did he mean by 'usually'? Had this man done this before? Broken into people's homes in the middle of the night and tied them up in their beds? And just what was he planning on doing next? This seemed a little elaborate for a plain robbery. Was this man going to kill them?

Tyler had a horrible feeling in his stomach that that was exactly what this man intended on doing.

What was he thinking? Of course, the man was going to kill them. Why else would he be doing this?

The little piece of calm he'd drawn from Helena evaporated, and he began to yank wildly at his bindings. He wiggled and squirmed violently until his muscles ached in protest and then, drained, he went still against the mattress.

"Finished?" the man rolled his eyes.

With a defeated nod, Tyler accepted his fate. What else could he do? As far as he could see there were no means of escape.

"Good," the man nodded approvingly. "I don't have all night." A pair of scissors appeared in his hand and he moved closer to the bed.

Tyler tried, pointlessly, to shy away from him. Beside him Helena did the same thing.

Another eye roll. "Don't bother, I'm not going to cut you, just removing your clothes. They get in the way," he added.

The man's explanation did nothing to ease his terror. Which started to crescendo as the cold metal of the scissors brushed his skin as the man begun to cut off his pajamas. Once Tyler was naked, the man turned his attention to Helena, quickly removing her clothing as well.

Brushing his thumb across Helena's lips, then tracing a fingertip down her chest, circling her breasts before moving down her stomach, stopping just above a line of pubic hair. He shot them both a grin. "Don't worry, I'll have to skip that step today. No time."

Stepping away from the bed, the man returned a moment later with an axe in his hand. Tyler's fear became so strong it was like a living thing inside him. Pulsing up and down his body so that every limb trembled. His stomach rumbled till it heaved and it was all he could do not to throw up. His head pounded till the whole room started to tilt and spin.

The axe blade caught the light and glinted. The man's smile was borderline manic.

Muffled screams filled the room.

His.

Helena's.

The man's eyes gleamed with excitement.

The axe came hurtling toward the bed.

* * * * *

5:51 A.M.

Hands on her shoulders made her jump a mile.

"Sorry," a voice rumbled behind her. "Didn't mean to scare you."

Heart hammering in her chest, Paige drew in a shaky breath and turned from her mindless staring out the window to stare at her husband's bare chest. She had been so lost in thought that she hadn't even heard him enter the room. Even after food and sleep, she was still feeling a little wobbly.

"What time is it?" she asked, trying to suppress a shiver. She was ice cold, even though she was wrapped up in flannel pajamas and a fleece robe and wearing fluffy slippers.

"Nearly six," Elias replied, frowning slightly as he rubbed her arms. "Are you cold?"

Her husband seemed to be throwing off heat like a furnace this morning, even though he was dressed only in a pair of sweat pants. Paige had been burning hot when she'd awakened from the grips of a nightmare a couple of hours ago. She had woken up thrashing desperately against the sheets and blankets, in which she was tightly tangled. She had been soaked in sweat, but as soon as she'd dragged herself out of bed she'd been unable to get warm.

Elias hadn't stirred; he slept like a log and nothing short of a meteor shower would wake him up. Too restless to attempt sleep again, she had come down to the kitchen, made a pot of tea, of which she hadn't drunk even a sip, and stared out at the black night.

"Paige?" Elias hooked a finger under her chin and tipped her face up.

The concerned frown he was shooting at her as he searched her face reminded her of the way Ryan had looked at her yesterday evening. She knew her partner couldn't understand why she wasn't just telling him what was going on with her. Usually she told Ryan everything. She trusted Ryan implicitly. Whenever she needed help, she went to him. Despite all that, she wasn't ready to share this with Ryan yet.

"Honey, you're shaking," Elias' concern had grown.

She rested against her husband's chest, his arms wrapping tightly around her. Elias' warmth only managed to heat her skin, but couldn't seem to penetrate deeper. "I'm a little cold," she murmured.

"Let's go back to bed; after yesterday you should be resting," he tried to tug her towards the door.

"I'm fine," she said restlessly, moving out of his arms. She liked to be on the move when she was on edge.

"Come on," Elias persisted. "Let's go back to bed. You need sleep."

They had been married only a little over a year, and usually Elias was more into sex than sleep whenever they were in bed. So, the fact that he wanted to go to bed for just sleep must mean she looked as bad as she felt. "No, I don't want to." Instead she began to pace the kitchen.

He let out a frustrated breath. "All right. I'll make you some tea."

Elias bustled about the kitchen and Paige resumed her staring out the window. She needed to pull it together. Now was not the best time to be falling apart. She just needed to forget about it for the moment, and focus on her husband and her cases. It was probably nothing, anyway—at least nothing to be getting so upset over.

"Babe?"

Again, she jumped as hands closed over her shoulders.

"Honey, you are so on edge; you need to rest." Elias turned her around to face him.

"I can't." She leaned against her husband and let him hold her up.

"You had nightmares." He sounded grim. Hands on her upper arms, he pulled her back so he could see her better. "It's been a long time since you've dreamed about it." He studied her face with his dark brown eyes. Paige presumed he was searching for signs that she was going to lose it. "I think you should tell Ryan what's going on."

Slipping her arms around Elias' waist, she rested her head against his smooth, muscled chest and gave it a small shake. "He has enough going on right now. With Sofia's recovery, and her stalker reappearing, and then Isabella's fingerprints turning up at a crime scene—I don't want to worry him."

"He'd want to know," Elias reminded her.

Paige knew that, but still, she wasn't about to burden him with her problems when he had enough of his own.

Elias sighed when she didn't respond, and he tugged her toward the table. "If you won't go back to bed, then at least sit down and have some tea." Elias sat and drew her down onto his lap. "You come up with anything?" He gestured at the kitchen table, which was covered with papers and reports.

Taking a sip from the cup in front of her, she eyed her case notes from Roman Hitacheel's murder. After the nightmare, she'd known that more sleep was out of the question, so she'd studied her notes until her tired eyes had started to water. She shrugged fitfully. "I don't know. I've been trying to come up with a reason for Isabella Everette's fingerprints to be in that room."

"Drink some more tea," Elias urged. "You have a theory?"

The hot liquid was slowly warming her up as she swallowed a few more mouthfuls. "I was wondering about how she got the drugs. She came from a wealthy family. She didn't hang on the streets, she didn't have friends—let alone friends who got into trouble or had criminal records. I'm not sure she could find a drug dealer to buy the drugs she used to knock him out. I was thinking that she...uh...she..." Paige trailed off, her mind seemed to be growing sluggish.

"Paige?" Elias prompted.

Finishing the tea in her cup, she tried to gather her thoughts but couldn't seem to manage this usually simple task. "Sorry, I'm feeling a little confused; what was I saying?" Paige pressed a hand to her head as though that could help her focus her jumbled mind.

"You were telling me about how you think Isabella got the drugs," Elias reminded her.

"Oh, yeah, I think..." She trailed off; her eyes were heavy and she was feeling drowsy. The cup in her hand began to shake, and suddenly, it clicked. "You drugged me," she accused Elias, trying to pull free from her husband's grip, but her limbs were clumsy and sluggish.

"Sorry, honey, but you need rest, and if you won't take care of yourself, then you leave me no choice."

"No choice?" she wished she sounded as outraged as she felt, but her voice was weak and slurred. Again, Paige tried to get free of Elias, but it was too late. The sleeping pills her husband had crushed and put in her tea were taking affect and she was falling asleep whether she wanted to or not.

He lifted her into his arms. "You'll feel better once you sleep," Elias told her as he carried her back upstairs.

Head drooping against his shoulder, the last thing Paige

thought before she fell asleep was that never in her life had she been as angry at anyone as she was right now with her husband.

* * * * *

7:06 A.M.

The street was quiet as Xavier pulled his car to the curb.

The morning was cold but clear. There hadn't been a lot of snow so far this winter, but Xavier knew that wouldn't last. They weren't that lucky. The sky was the palest of pale blues as the sun slowly began to rise. There was no one about. No dog walkers, no parents bustling kids into cars for the morning school run, no weary workers dragging themselves off to start another day. Everyone wanted to delay leaving their warm and cozy homes to face another dreary winter day until the very last second.

He was quite obviously the first one to arrive.

The Mendleson house was only minutes away from his and Annabelle's. As soon as the call had come in, it had been linked to the Landers' case, and a call had gone to Robert, who had promptly called him.

Racing to the house, Xavier hadn't been quite sure what he would find upon arrival. Obviously, there was one surviving victim. But how many were dead? Had the killer stuck with another couple, or had he escalated to a family? If Ricky Preston was the killer then he had deescalated, which was unusual for a serial killer. But Ricky was smart; he killed for a reason. Before it had been for revenge. If he was doing this, then he had to be choosing these victims for a particular reason. If Xavier could only figure out how he was doing that, then he was positive it would lead him straight to the killer.

He jumped from his car and sprinted down the flower-edged path to the front door. Drawing his gun, Xavier thought that there was little to no chance that the killer was still lurking about the property, but it was better to be safe than sorry.

He knocked on the front door. "Police," he identified himself. "Open up."

He waited a moment; there was no sound from within the house, and he could see no movement through the frosted glass door.

"It's the police," he repeated. "Open the door."

Another pause. Still nothing. Maybe the house was empty. Maybe, too traumatized to remain inside the house until help arrived, the killer's surviving victim had fled to a neighbor's for solace.

Xavier would check the house out first, and then move on to the neighboring houses.

Hammering on the door one last time, he prepared himself for the scene that would inevitably meet him inside. There was no doubt in his mind that this was the work of the same killer who had killer Erica Landers. That scene had been bloody, and this one would, no doubt, be the same. Or worse. "Police. I'm coming in."

Breaking in turned out to be unnecessary. When he tried the doorknob, it turned and he swung the door quietly open.

A trail of bloody footprints was the first thing he saw.

Xavier would bet a year's salary that they would match those from the Landers house.

Bypassing the living room to his left and the kitchen and dining room to his right, he followed the trail down the hall. He paused cautiously at the door to a study, and a spare bedroom, both of which appeared to be empty, before coming upon the master bedroom.

Just as he had expected, the room was a bloody mess.

The sense of déjà vu was so strong, he may as well have been standing in the Landers bedroom. Streaks of blood splatter crisscrossed the ceiling and walls. Blood pooled both on and beneath the bed—upon which lay a mangled body.

Not wanting to contaminate the crime scene, Xavier turned and was about to head back to the front door to go and see which house the remaining Mendleson had fled to, when he heard muffled breathing.

Scanning the room, his eyes settled on a door on the far side of the room. He picked his way carefully across the floor, carefully avoiding the bloody footprints that dotted the carpet. Opening the door to the en suite bathroom, he surveyed the white tiled room. The shower curtain was fully drawn. Taking a step toward it, Xavier was just about to reach a hand to pull it back when something suddenly flew at him.

More like a someone.

Screeching and screaming and moaning, the person kicked and clawed and swung at him.

It didn't take Xavier long to subdue them, though.

The person was older than him and nowhere near as fit and strong. Within seconds, he'd wrapped an arm around the squirming form.

"Shh, Mrs. Mendleson," he murmured in the woman's ear. "It's all right. I'm a police officer. Detective Montague. You're safe now."

The woman in his arms suddenly went limp. Tightening his grip on her, he eased Helena Mendleson down to the floor, propping her up against the side of the bath.

"I...I...th...thought you...you...were him," she gasped, her eyes squeezed closed. "I thought he came back. I heard...heard footsteps. Then...then the door...door started to open. I pa...panicked."

He scanned the woman from head to toe. She was naked and drenched in blood. The skin beneath was snow pale. Her teeth chattered and she was trembling. Clearly, she was in shock. Hopefully beyond that she wasn't injured.

"Mrs. Mendleson?" He hooked a finger under her chin and tilted her face up. Ever so slowly the woman's eyes opened, glassy with shock, and struggled to focus on him. "Are you hurt?"

"I...I...I don't...I'm not..." she stammered helplessly.

Giving her a reassuring smile, Xavier began to quickly run his hands up and down her body, coming to a stop on her right arm where he found a nasty looking gash. Standing quickly, he grabbed a towel from the rack on the back of the bathroom door, and a washcloth from the side of the sink. Wrapping the towel around the shaking woman's shoulders, he took her injured arm and pressed the washcloth to the wound.

She stared in disbelief at her arm. "I didn't even feel that," she murmured. Then her tear-filled brown eyes lifted to meet his. "Tyler's dead."

"I know; I'm sorry." He tried to keep his voice gentle when he was mentally beating himself up because he was responsible. If he hadn't let Ricky Preston go, then this woman wouldn't be suffering right now.

"He killed him," Helena continued. "He hit him over and over again. I didn't think he'd ever stop. Over and over again. Tyler wasn't moving. He just laid there. There was so much blood," she babbled.

"Can you describe the man?" Xavier asked.

Her head bobbed up and down so violently that Xavier put a hand on the back of her neck to stop it. "He was tall. Really tall. And he had dark hair. He was so excited by the blood. He kept staring at it. And after...after...after Tyler stopped moving, he rubbed blood all over himself. Then he kind of danced around the room." Words were tumbling out of her mouth so quickly he could barely follow what she was saying.

"How did you get free?"

"He must have cut the tape binding me while he was cutting Tyler. At first I didn't realize. I was lying so still. I thought he was going to kill me, too. He injected us with something. Knocked us out and tied us up. He cut our clothes off with scissors. He said he would have raped me, but he didn't have time. Then he started swinging the axe. So many times. I just laid still. I thought maybe he'd think I was dead, too. But he never even looked at me. Once I thought he was gone I reached for Tyler and realized I could move one hand. It took me a while but I got the rest of the tape off. Then I called the police, and I was so scared he'd come back, so I hid. I can't believe this is happening. It must be a dream." She looked at him desperately, pleading for him to confirm this.

"Okay, shh, it's all right; you're safe now," Xavier soothed.

Sobbing, she collapsed forward against his chest, clawing at his shirt with her good hand and clinging to him. "I have to call Tyler's daughters and my children," she continued to ramble.

"I'll call them," he assured her. He decided it was best to get her out of the house, hoping that might calm her down a little. Clearly Helena was in no shape to walk out on her own steam, so he fastened the washcloth around her arm and scooped her off the ground.

An ambulance and several cop cars pulled up in front of the house as he walked out the front door, and he deposited Helena on a gurney, and with another assurance that he'd call her family, left her in the capable hands of the EMTs. Then he headed for Diane Jolly's car as he noticed the CSU tech pull up to the curb.

"You're okay, right?" she said as soon as she climbed out of her car, her eyes focused on his blood-streaked shirt.

"Yeah, it's the victim's blood," he assured her, making a mental note to change ASAP. He didn't want to get distracted and arrive home tonight covered in blood. That would completely freak Annabelle out, and she was strung out enough as it was right now. "This is Ricky. I know it is," he told Diane. "I feel it."

"We need proof, though," she reminded him. "And, so far, we have nothing on him."

"Helena Mendleson just told me that the killer said he didn't have time to rape her. Ricky Preston plans everything out to the tiniest detail. He's meticulous. He wore gloves last time. But he loves blood. I'm sure he couldn't have resisted touching it. What if he took the gloves off at the Landers, but put them back on before he touched anything other than the blood on himself?"

She narrowed her brown eyes at him. "Where are you going with this?"

"He picked these victims for a reason. He met them somewhere. When we find the link, we'll find him. Something messed him up for tonight's kill. He was running late, worried about having enough time to finish up. What if he forgot to put his gloves back on after he touched the blood? He could have left prints somewhere."

Diane's eyes sparked with hope. "On it." She grabbed her kit and hurried toward the house. She paused briefly at the door to throw on gloves and booties before disappearing inside.

Xavier stood, watching officers bustle about, the paramedics tend to Helena, and neighbors slowly start to trickle out of their houses to brave the cold now that they realized something exciting was happening in their sleepy little street. He was so sure that this was the work of Ricky; he just had to prove it. Then they just had to find Ricky so they could arrest him. Once he was in custody, things would finally be over for Annabelle, and they could finally have a life.

"Xavier."

He looked over his shoulder to see Diane waving wildly at him from just inside the Mendlesons' front door. He jogged over to her, hardly daring to hope. "Did you get something?"

She grinned broadly up at him. "I got a bloody fingerprint on the door handle."

* * * * *

2:45 P.M.

"Why are you here?" Ryan looked up, surprised to see his partner walking toward him.

She frowned at him like he was an idiot. "I work here."

"I know that," he replied patiently. He was on edge; he hadn't slept after his talk with Sofia last night, just laid there and held her sleeping body in his arms and promised her that he would somehow make everything better for her. However, despite his edginess, he was worried enough about Paige to remain calm with her. If he wanted to drag out of her what was bothering her, then he had no choice.

"So were you a co-conspirator?" she demanded, dropping down into the chair at the table that was furthest away from where he sat.

Raising a querying brow, he asked, "What?"

"I would have been here earlier this morning, only my husband drugged me," Paige ground out.

"What?" Ryan really and truly had no idea what she was talking about.

"Elias decided that I wasn't looking after myself up to his standards, so he had no choice but to crush up sleeping pills and put them in my tea." She was clearly still stewing about that. She glared at him. "So, were you in on it?"

Ryan winced at what had been a mistake on Elias' part, but he completely understood the desire to protect someone you cared about. Ryan wondered how long Elias was going to pay for it. "I had nothing to do with that," Ryan assured her. "But I do think you should have stayed home today. You nearly passed out in my arms not even twenty-four hours ago."

"I'm fine," Paige said tightly. "Elias took me home yesterday just like you wanted. He made me eat and then he put me to bed—where I slept just fine," she added.

"No, you didn't," he contradicted. "I texted Elias several times last night to check on you, and he said you were up half the night."

That earned him a frown. "Look, I'm okay now. I don't want to hear any more about it." With that she picked up some papers and began to read, effectively shutting him out.

He breathed deeply to squash all traces of irritation. The fact that Paige looked tired and drawn and had black smudges under her eyes made it easier. He'd wait until she had calmed down before bringing up whatever was upsetting her. For now, he'd focus on the case. After letting Paige read in silence for a few minutes, he began cautiously, "I was thinking about Isabella."

"What about her?" Paige didn't look up from whatever she was reading.

"Before, with her family, she was mission oriented," Ryan explained. "She was killing them because she blamed them for not stepping in and stopping Logan from murdering those girls. She thought that she—and Sofia—would be better off if their family no longer existed. It was all about achieving that goal. She didn't deviate from her plan. She didn't stop until her self-appointed mission was completed."

Finally looking up at him, Paige nodded. "So, you think she has a new mission?"

"She believed before that what she was doing was for the good of others. I'm sure she thinks the same thing now. Roman Hitacheel was a habitual adulterer. Logan senior paid women to get pregnant with his children since his wife struggled to get pregnant and carry to term. I don't think that it's too much of a stretch to say that she thinks her grandfather's adultery was the start of her family's problems, and therefore she has a thing against cheaters. I was wondering whether she knows Roman Hitacheel; he could have been a friend of the family."

Paige considered it. "We can ask Sofia if she knows the Hitacheels. If Isabella did know him, it wasn't up close and personal."

"Agreed. She didn't make him suffer. Everything she did was simply to serve her purpose; there was no unnecessary cruelty. Totally unlike what she did to her family. Logan senior, Logan junior, Brooke, Gloria, Lewis and Lincoln: she was angry with them and it came out in what she inflicted on them. She wanted them to know just how angry she was. But with Roman, she just killed him—albeit not in a very pleasant manner, but it wasn't in the same league as her other murders." Ryan shivered at the memory of some of the horror Isabella had inflicted. "We should talk to Sofia and find out if we're right and her family knows the Hitacheels, and then if she knows of any other family friends where the husband was cheating, maybe we can get ahead of Isabella. Predict who she's going after next and preempt it."

He paused when Paige lifted her phone. She turned pale and her expression was one of fear. She shoved the phone back into her bag and bounded for the door.

Jumping up after her, he was closer to the door and managed to block her path. He stopped her with a hand on her arm, "Paige, wait. What's going on?"

"It's nothing," she murmured, refusing to meet his gaze.

He gave her a gentle shake. "You don't really expect me to believe that, do you? What is going on?"

Her eyes rose slowly to meet his. "I don't want to worry you."

"Too late," he informed her. "I'm already plenty worried." Guiding her back to the table, he eased her down into a seat, pleased when she didn't make a move to resist. Taking the chair beside her, he implored, "Talk to me."

She let out a deep shuddering breath. "I've been getting these text messages."

Not liking the sound of that, he asked, "From whom?"

"I'm not sure exactly."

Clearly Paige wasn't going to make this easy for him. "Who do you *think* they're from?"

She began to fidget with her hands, which were coiled tightly in her lap. "While you were taking time off to help Sofia recover, I arrested this guy. He broke in to someone's house to rob them, only they came home early and he panicked and beat them to death. His fingerprints were all over the house. We found him the next day, but he kind of…"

"Kind of what?" he prodded when Paige didn't continue.

"He kind of latched on to me, and not in a good way. Not that there is a good way, I guess. I mean, he's a criminal. A murderer. So there really wouldn't be…"

"Paige," he interrupted her rambling and put a hand over hers to still them. "Did he threaten you?"

Bleak eyes looked back at him and she nodded.

"And now you think he's harassing you?"

Another dismal nod.

"But he's locked up, right?"

"Yes, his lawyer convinced him to take a plea. But I'm sure he must have friends on the outside, and I keep getting these texts from someone saying that they're watching me, and I should be careful, and…"

"And it has you freaked out," he finished for her. "Let's trace the number and find out who's harassing you and we'll go pick them up."

"Can't. It's never the same number, just the same message."

He was perplexed; it was plain to see that Paige was shaken up by this, so why hadn't she come to him? "I don't understand why you didn't just tell me."

"I'm sorry. I'm sorry for freaking out, and I'm sorry I didn't tell you. I've been threatened by criminals I've arrested before; I don't know why this one upset me so much."

"Nice try," he said wryly. He could read his partner like a book, and she most definitely knew why this had upset her so much. "You can tell me; you know that, right? Whatever it is, I'm here for you."

Indecision was battling in her eyes, she looked like she just needed a tiny bit more of a push.

"Come on, Paige, talk to me. Please." The 'please' always worked with Sofia when she was debating opening up to him or not.

"I'm a little sensitive about stalkers." She was looking at him anxiously. "I know what Sofia is going through with hers. I know because my mom had a stalker when I was a kid. She didn't even know him. He dropped some groceries in the rain one afternoon and she stopped to help him pick them up. That was all it took. He became obsessed with her. He wrote letters, he called her, he would turn up at our house. She kept telling him that she was happily married but that only made him angry. And then one night…"

"One night what, Paige?" he pressed gently.

Tears were glittering in her eyes. "One night he turned violent. Broke in while my dad was at work. He tied up my mom and my brothers and little sister, and then he, uh, he…" She drew in a ragged breath as tears began to spill down her cheeks. "Then he was going to rape me. He already had my clothes off when my dad arrived home and shot him. He died instantly. Collapsed on top of me. I… I had his blood all over me. I just screamed and screamed."

Wrapping his arms around her, he held Paige while she cried. She remained stiff in his arms but didn't resist his comfort. "Shh," he soothed, "it's all right now. Shh."

"I was fourteen, I was so scared, I kind of shut down after it happened. I couldn't sleep. I couldn't eat. I couldn't stay in that house. I couldn't go to school. I couldn't do anything. My parents put me in a hospital for a while. Eventually I got better, went on with my life, but being harassed by this guy has kind of brought it all back up."

"I'm sorry, honey." He wished Paige had told him this earlier. "Elias knows about all of this, right? Is that why he drugged you?"

She nodded against his shoulder. "He didn't like that I had nightmares last night; he's worried I'm going to fall apart again."

"Why didn't you tell me?" Right now, Ryan was hating stalkers. The hell that Paige and her family had been put through and the hell that Sofia was now suffering, all because of people who thought there was more to a relationship than what there really was.

"It's embarrassing." She tugged herself out of his arms and brushed at her red-rimmed eyes. "I'm a cop, I don't like people knowing that I had a nervous breakdown."

"You were fourteen," he reminded her. "You were traumatized, there's absolutely nothing for you to feel embarrassed about."

She shrugged uncomfortably. "So, now you know it all. That's why I was a little preoccupied yesterday and forgot to eat."

"We'll look into who's stalking you. We'll go talk to this guy you arrested and get him to tell his friends to back off. We'll sort this out, Paige, but until we do, I don't think it's safe for you to go anywhere alone."

"Ryan," she protested immediately. "I'm a cop. I can take care of myself. Right now, let's just focus on finding Isabella. And speaking of which, when I couldn't go back to sleep last night I was thinking about her, about how she may have gotten her hands on the drugs."

Obviously, both the topic of what she'd been through as a kid, and her current situation, were now closed. "You got a theory?"

"Actually, yes." She shot him a shaky smile as she brushed away the last of her tears. "As far as we know, Isabella doesn't have access to money anymore. And I'm not sure she had the connections to know where to go to buy the drugs she used. What if she's working at a hospital? She planned her entire killing spree down to the last detail, so she could easily have made sure she got false papers and a new identity while she still had access to money. If she has been working in a hospital, she would have access to drugs and the medical supplies she used."

Paige's theory made a lot of sense. "Isabella looks a lot older than seventeen, and she's certainly not squeamish, plus she's very intelligent. She could probably pull off working as a nurse."

"We should hit up the hospitals, show her picture around, see if anyone recognizes her." Paige stood and headed for the door.

"Paige."

She paused. "Yeah?"

"I'm glad you trusted me enough to tell me all of that, but next time, come to me right away, so I can be there for you. And Paige, please promise me you'll be careful."

* * * * *

5:33 P.M.

Isabella watched from her car as Arthur Bentley ducked out of the pharmacy door, pulling his scarf and jacket collar tighter around his neck to try and ward off the chilly winter wind. He hurried toward the car parked beside hers, flung open the back door, tossed the bag from the pharmacy containing his wife's medications inside, and then jumped into the driver's seat.

As Arthur's car pulled out of the parking lot, Isabella followed. She didn't need to bother to keep close. She already knew where he lived, so she kept her distance, not that she thought Arthur would notice anything other than himself anyway, but it was better to play it safe and not get too close.

A motto that Arthur Bentley himself seemed to live by.

He wasn't close to anyone. He wasn't close to his parents or his brother or even his wife. Especially his wife.

Maddie Bentley was drop-dead gorgeous—an ex-model. She was sexy and playful and vivacious, everything that Arthur had been looking for in a wife. At least, she had been.

Tragically, just weeks after their wedding, Maddie Bentley had been permanently brain damaged in a car accident. Now the formerly effervescent model couldn't talk, couldn't move, couldn't feed herself, or take care of herself. Forbidden—under threat of being disinherited—from divorcing his disabled wife, Arthur had sought an escape route from the nightmare he now found himself trapped in. Hiring a full-time nurse, from Arthur's point of view no doubt one of the times he was most happy to be filthy rich, he had dedicated his time to his many affairs.

First off, he had worked through all of Maddie's model friends. Not one to want more than casual sex, his relationships never lasted more than a couple of weeks, and then he was on to the next woman. Other than sex, all he had to offer was expensive gifts, which he showered on his woman of the moment. Until he got bored with them.

Isabella couldn't fathom why these women would demean themselves by allowing Arthur to make them just another notch on his belt. Sure, Arthur was probably what most women would call drop-dead gorgeous. He had big green eyes, dimples, and chestnut brown hair which he wore kind of long so that it hung in his eyes and gave him a sort of little boy look. He was tall, had broad shoulders, and well-developed muscles from hours spent working out. None of that appealed to Isabella. She didn't understand why women could be sucked in by a pretty but vacuous package.

Still, she had to do what she had to do. So she had followed him to his favorite bar, some fancy place where he now went to pick up his women, and gotten his number. He hadn't tried to pick her up, of course. She wasn't pretty like her sister, Sofia. She was tall, and most guys didn't like a woman taller than them. She was only seventeen, but she looked years older than her age. She wasn't overweight, but she wasn't thin either. Her hair was too red; lacking the golden tints that made her sister's hair so beautiful. Her eyes were too serious, and she never smiled. All in all, there was nothing attractive about her that would appeal to someone like Arthur Bentley.

She had—accurately—zeroed in on the woman in the bar she thought would be most likely to draw in Arthur, and she sat close by. When Arthur had left the woman his number, written on a napkin, she had surreptitiously swiped it so the woman was unable to call and set up a date.

Instead, Isabella intended to call in her place.

Right now, in fact, she thought, as she pulled to a stop in front of Arthur's house, watching him drag his feet as he headed toward the front door of his own personal prison. She dialed the number, then folded the napkin and placed it in her bag. She watched as Arthur's face lit up as he pulled his phone from his pocket.

"Hello?" his eager voice filled her car a moment later.

"Arthur?" she replied, perfectly mimicking the blonde from the bar.

"Yes," his eagerness morphed into fervent desperation.

"It's Vanessa. From the bar," she added.

"Hi, Vanessa from the bar," he drawled in a voice Isabella was sure he thought made women swoon. Which it probably did. Luckily, she wasn't most women.

"I was wondering if you wanted to meet up later tonight," she asked, keeping her tone low and seductive.

"Oh, yeah," a greedy quality inched into his voice and Isabella suppressed a shiver. There was no way she was letting this man touch her. Arthur rattled off a time and address, which Isabella knew was an apartment he kept to entertain his women. "Can't wait, babe," he all but sang at her, then hung up.

Arthur danced down the path and up to his front door. The man was obviously a sex addict, Isabella decided. She didn't see the point of sex if it wasn't with someone you genuinely loved and cared about. And Arthur certainly didn't care about her or Vanessa or any of the other women he slept with.

Oh, well, she shrugged. She had given up a long time ago trying to understand how most of the world saw things. It was pointless. She was different. She just didn't get it.

There was one thing she *did* get, though.

And that was consequences.

And Arthur was about to suffer his.

As she pulled away from the curb, Isabella knew that one day she too would have to suffer the consequences of her actions.

* * * * *

6:28 P.M.

Xavier should be home by now, Annabelle decided.

She was worried.

Which annoyed her.

Mainly because Xavier wasn't even at work right now; he was visiting with his ex-partner, Kate, and her three-month-old baby boy. He had asked her to go with him, of course. Begged her was probably a more accurate description. But she had turned him down. She couldn't face leaving the house right now.

So here she was in the bedroom, curled up on the bed with the TV on but having no idea what was playing, with every light in the house blazing, worrying about him.

What was worrying her was the overwhelming fear that Ricky Preston had gotten to Xavier.

Ricky wanted to toy with her. He wanted to make her suffer. And there was no greater way to make her suffer than to take away the only good thing she had in her life: Xavier.

Annabelle had no doubt that given enough time, Ricky would come for her.

It was a given.

He had made it abundantly clear that he wasn't finished with her.

And the longer he waited to finish her off, the worse it was.

Which she suspected was the point.

With each day, with each hour that passed, she was beginning to feel more and more like she would never be able to climb out of the black hole Ricky had flung her into. She just wasn't sure that she had it in her to get better. And if this was going to be her life, for the rest of her life, then she just plain wasn't sure she could do it.

She was starting to think about alternatives.

One of the things that worried her the most about her present emotional state was Xavier. He had already been through this before with Julia. He had already had to suffer watching the woman he loved be eaten alive by trauma. Julia had imploded with it. And Annabelle was sure that she was on the same track.

She knew her emotional demise would crush Xavier.

She just couldn't bear to put him through that again.

Therefore, she was thinking about simply disappearing. Not that she knew where she would go. She didn't have any family. And she didn't have any friends. Nor was she capable of working right now. It wasn't the best look for a kindergarten teacher to jump at every little noise, or to shriek as flashbacks plagued her, or to come to work in a fog because she didn't sleep. All of that made her totally unsuitable to be around young children right now. Since she couldn't work, she couldn't support herself financially.

Maybe she could just disappear into the woods some place. Some place quiet—though that wasn't a realistic proposition either. She hated the woods. She hated the bugs, and the mud, and basically everything to do with the outdoors. Still, the idea of living in a little log cabin in the middle of nowhere held a certain appeal. Although Annabelle didn't think she could live without running water and electricity and a toilet. Nor could she catch or grow her own food. So, that plan was essentially useless.

There was an overall problem with her disappearing anyway, even if she could figure out a way to make it work. And that was Xavier.

Annabelle knew there was no chance that he would simply let her disappear. He would do whatever it took to find her. He would quit his job, leave behind his family, and he would search the entire world until he found her.

Which meant that disappearing probably wasn't going to work.

In fact, it was only going to do the exact opposite of what she would have been trying to achieve. Instead of sparing Xavier the stress and worry of watching her fall completely apart, she would only be causing him stress and worry of a different sort.

There was another way she could spare Xavier pain and that was simply to end her life. Annabelle knew, of course, that killing herself would indeed cause Xavier pain, but at least it would be over and done with. He wouldn't have to watch her die slowly, a little piece at a time; she would just simply be gone.

Suicide could be the answer to all her problems.

That's why it kept coming back into her mind each time she banished it.

If she were dead, then she wouldn't have to be afraid anymore. And Xavier wouldn't have to stand by and witness her demise.

With a shaking hand, she reached into the pocket of her fluffy pink robe and pulled out the bottle of sleeping pills. For some reason, she carried them with her most of the time. Maybe because suicide was always at the back of her mind.

She studied the small bottle.

Could she do this?

Could she swallow an entire bottle of pills knowing it would kill her?

What if it didn't?

What if she survived?

Xavier would be so disappointed in her.

That hurt.

She didn't want him to be disappointed in her. And yet, by living the way she was right now, she was making him disappointed anyway.

Slowly, she unscrewed the lid.

Giving the bottle a shake, she watched the pills bounce inside—almost mesmerized.

Taking a long, slow, deep breath, she tipped a few out into her hand.

This was it.

It was time to decide.

Was she going to do this?

"Annabelle?"

With a strangled squawk, she spun around, managing to slip the pills back into the bottle before Xavier saw what she'd been about to do. She forced a smile to her lips. "I didn't hear you come in."

"Yeah, I got that." His eyes were searching her face, clearly aware that something was up.

She tried to surreptitiously sneak the bottle of sleeping pills back into her pocket before Xavier saw it. "Did you have a nice time at Kate's?" She hoped her attempt at making her voice sound bright and bubbly was working.

"What was in your hand?" Xavier asked instead, his gaze zeroing in on her pocket.

"Uh, nothing." Annabelle made a move to breeze past him, but he grabbed her arm, holding it in a vice like grip.

"What's going on?"

Tears were brimming in her eyes, and she was already ashamed of what she had nearly done. How could she have even contemplated killing herself? If she did it, if she committed suicide, she couldn't take it back. Regret wouldn't be an option. Giving a sharp shake of her head, she tried to tug her arm free.

Apparently, Xavier wasn't buying that. He held her with one hand, and with his other, he reached into her pocket and pulled out the bottle. His face grew pale and his eyes were wide. "What were you going to do with these?" he demanded.

"I...I...I..." she stammered, unable to come up with a quick lie.

"How many did you take?" he sounded panicked.

"I...I..." She couldn't seem to form a coherent sentence.

"Belle? How many did you take? Do I need to call an ambulance?"

"None." She managed to force the word out only because Xavier was looking so scared.

He let out a relieved sigh. "Belle?" He held her chin and made her look at him. Xavier's eyes were turbulent, but his voice was impossibly gentle. "Were you thinking about killing yourself?"

The tears that had been welling up in her eyes overflowed, streaming down her cheeks, and she let herself fall against Xavier's sturdy chest. She didn't want to admit that she had been. She didn't want to let him down. She wanted to pretend that she had never even contemplated suicide. And yet, at the same time, the need to tell him everything was almost overwhelming. She was tired, upset, and more than anything else, she just needed to be in Xavier's arms right now.

He wrapped his arms around her, cradling her against him. "Belle?" he prompted. "Honey? Have you been thinking about suicide? You can tell me if you have; we can work through it together."

Everything came tumbling out in a rush. "I don't really want to," she sobbed. "But I'm so tired, I don't know what to do. I don't want to be afraid anymore. I don't want to remember what happened. I don't want to think about what Ricky might do to me in the future. I don't want to die; I just don't want to live like this. I just want to be normal. What if I'm not? What if I won't ever be normal? Xavier..." The last was a desperate whimper.

Instead of replying, he picked her up, carried her back to the bed and laid down with her snuggled at his side. He held her until her tears were spent, stroking her hair and murmuring to her that he loved her and he was never going to leave her. When she finished crying, she felt drained—completely exhausted. She could barely lift her head from Xavier's shoulder. Her eyes wouldn't open, no matter how much she tried.

"Relax," Xavier whispered in her ear. "Just rest. We'll talk in the morning. We'll get you more help. We'll do whatever we must, to get you through this. But right now, just sleep. I love you,

Belle."

Annabelle wanted to return the sentiment, but she was quickly fading toward sleep. Instead she just pressed closer against Xavier's warm, hard body, and prayed that he was right. That there was a way to get her through this.

* * * * *

10:16 P.M.

Behind him, Annabelle sighed in the bed and rolled over.

Xavier watched her intently. She was terrifying him. He hadn't realized just how much she was struggling. Again, he'd been oblivious. This couldn't be Julia all over again.

He had known that Annabelle was having a hard time. Especially now that Ricky Preston had reappeared. However, he hadn't known that she was suicidal. When he'd walked into their bedroom to see her holding a bottle of sleeping pills in her hand his heart had almost stopped. He hadn't seen whether she'd swallowed any, just seen that the bottle was open and she already had some in her hand. When he'd asked how many she'd taken and she didn't answer him, he had been about ready to call an ambulance and have her taken to the hospital to get her stomach pumped.

Thankfully, he had arrived home before she'd swallowed any of the pills. But what if he'd been just a little later? What if Kate had been a little slower cooking dinner and they'd eaten later? What if he'd given the baby one last cuddle before he left to go home? What if he'd gotten stuck at an extra red light on the drive home? What if traffic had been a little worse? If he had been just minutes later, then Annabelle could have decided to go ahead and take the pills and already taken enough to kill her before he got home.

It could have been just a matter of minutes between life and death.

This nightmare just kept getting worse and worse.

He rubbed his tired eyes. One thing at a time. As soon as Annabelle had fallen asleep in his arms, he'd carefully eased out from underneath her and collected all the medications in the house, locking them away in his gun safe. If Annabelle was being tempted to take her own life, then at least he could make it more difficult for her. He'd also called her therapist and insisted that she see Annabelle in the morning. Whatever it took, he was going to get her back on track. If he had to put her in a hospital for a while, he'd do it. If he had to take more time off work so he could be here with her twenty-four/seven, then he would do it.

It had been a mistake to leave her alone tonight.

He realized that now.

It was just that he had needed some normal time. He's wanted Annabelle to come with him to Kate's; he'd practically begged her. But, as usual, she had refused. Xavier was sure that was one of the contributing factors to her struggling so much. She shut herself away from everyone and everything else so that all she did all day was think about Ricky Preston and what he'd done to her. She needed something else to focus on—something or someone. She needed to go back to work, or some variation of work since he knew she was concerned that her emotional instability would be a danger to the children she would be working with. Or she needed a good friend. Someone that she trusted, someone she felt comfortable with, someone who could help ease her back into the real world.

Xavier was glad Annabelle had opened up to him. Admitting that she was thinking about taking her own life had to be a step in the right direction. And yet he kept thinking about Julia. Julia hadn't trusted him enough to open up to him. She hadn't taken any steps in getting herself the help that she clearly needed. And it had destroyed not only herself, but nearly destroyed him, too. But Annabelle wasn't shutting him out, and she was trying her very best to get herself well.

What was worrying him was the niggling doubt that he was wrong.

That Annabelle wasn't strong enough to work her way through this.

No, that isn't quite true, he corrected himself. He was worried that Annabelle might not have it in her to climb out of this hole she found herself in. But what worried him more was that he might not have as much strength as he thought he did. Could he stand by and watch as Annabelle shrank and withered away until she was nothing more than a shell of a person? Was he strong enough to stand by her if she never improved, if she never got better?

Xavier wanted to believe that he was. He had no intention of deliberately abandoning Annabelle. But what if it came down to a choice between her mental health and his? Was he strong enough to potentially lose Annabelle like he'd lost Julia?

He decided he'd cross those bridges if he came to them. For now, what he would focus on was the fact that he loved Annabelle and she loved him. That had to be enough.

Right now, since he was way too wired for sleep, he should go through the Landers and Mendleson case files. He may as well put his time to good use.

All right, he focused himself. Neither the Landers or the Mendlesons had any known enemies. And the chances of them both having upset the same person to the extent that that person wanted them dead and suffering was beyond unlikely. Therefore, both couples had to have met the killer somewhere along the way. This killer was meticulous and organized; he wasn't choosing these people randomly. He didn't just feel the urge to kill and pick a house; he came to the house to seek out his intended victims with the tools he needed to complete the task.

He had spotted them before and something about them had appealed to him.

Xavier had been going through the Landers' and Mendlesons' lives looking for anything that they had in common. Unfortunately, he wasn't having much luck; so far, he had come up with nothing.

They didn't live in the same area. They didn't shop at the same grocery store, they didn't use the same car garage, they didn't go to the same hairdressers, they didn't use the same doctors or dentists. They hadn't attended the same churches, or had the same hobbies. The Mendlesons' kids or grandkids didn't connect with the Landers either. As best as he could see, they didn't have a single commonality in their lives.

His cell phone began to buzz on the table beside him. Thankfully, he'd left it on silent so it didn't disturb Annabelle. He glanced at it and saw the text was from Diane. Heart beating faster with excitement, he picked it up, hoping she was giving him confirmation that the bloody fingerprint she had found at the Mendleson house matched the prints they had on file for Ricky Preston.

He let out a sigh of relief as he read the text.

He'd been right all along.

Ricky Preston was the killer.

Far from feeling scared, Xavier found himself feeling rejuvenated, energized. Ricky was back—and this time he wasn't getting away.

Now all he needed to do was figure out how he had chosen his victims and it would lead him straight to Ricky.

Helena Mendleson had mentioned that the man who killed her husband had said something about being held up at work. The call from the Mendleson house had come in a little before seven in the morning, and Helena had estimated that it had taken her a couple of hours to get herself free and call for help—putting the attack at approximately four am.

If Ricky had been held up at work before heading to the Mendleson house, then he had to be working somewhere that was still open in the middle of the night. Obviously, he wasn't still working as a carpenter; so what was he doing now?

Hospitals were open twenty-four hours a day, but he couldn't see Ricky working in a hospital. Maybe an all-night restaurant or store? Cleaners weren't usually still working at four in the morning. Emergency services were out of the question for obvious reasons.

And then it hit him.

Both the Landers and the Mendlesons were newlyweds.

Both presumably had honeymoons.

Hotels also never closed.

If both couples had honeymooned at the same hotel, it was a connection

If Ricky Preston was working at a hotel, then it was how he met them.

First thing in the morning, Xavier was going to take Annabelle to see her therapist, and then he was going to find out if the Landers and Mendlesons had indeed honeymooned at the same hotel. Once he had confirmation, he was going to go and pick Ricky Preston up and end this.

Right now, though, he needed some sleep.

He needed to be completely on his game when he went to arrest Ricky; he wasn't going to risk getting played again.

Throwing off his clothes, he slid under the covers, and Annabelle immediately curled into him. With the lightest heart he'd had in months, Xavier drifted quickly off into a deep and dreamless sleep.

JANUARY 11TH

12:43 A.M.

Isabella couldn't deny that she was a little excited.

She had always maintained that she only killed to serve a purpose. But if she was honest, she was looking forward to killing Arthur Bentley tonight.

That made her mad, though.

She didn't want to prove her father right.

Although she'd been raised as the daughter of her grandfather and his wife, she was, in fact, the daughter of his oldest son and a woman that both her father and grandfather had been having an affair with. Her biological father had been a monster. He had committed his first rape at the age of just fourteen. He had raped his stepmother, which had led to her getting pregnant with Sofia.

Her father, Logan Everette IV, hadn't stopped there.

For years, he had abducted vulnerable young women, tied them up in a secret room in the basement, where he had tortured, raped, and killed them. Her grandfather, Judge Logan Everette, had known what his son was doing and helped to conceal his crimes. The judge's wife, Gloria, had known, too—as had Logan's brothers, Lewis and Lincoln.

Sofia had also known. But she hadn't known that she'd known.

Sofia had sleepwalked as a child and stumbled upon the horrors in the family basement. The judge had convinced her it was nothing more than a dream and she had believed that up until five months ago.

Now she knew the truth about their family.

Isabella had seen no other option than to wipe her despicable family off the face of the planet.

Sofia wanted to believe that Isabella had gone off the deep end following an incident at her school. Four classmates had tied Isabella up and sexually assaulted her before simply leaving her there. It had taken her almost twelve hours to get herself free. No one had believed her when she'd told them what had happened to her. And so she had taken it upon herself to exact her own revenge.

Just like she had exacted her own revenge on her family for allowing all those poor girls to be assaulted and murdered by Logan.

But this was different.

Isabella couldn't deny it.

Killing Roman Hitacheel had been fun. And anticipation over tonight's murder had been buzzing in her veins all day.

She was beginning to think her father was right.

Before she'd killed him, Isabella had tied Logan IV up in a secret room in the attic of her family's home. She had wanted a little alone time with him before she killed him. Plus, she had intended to frame him for the murders.

While the two of them were alone together, he had told her that she was delusional. That she would never be able to stop killing. That even though she claimed she had killed her family because of what he had done, that she had killed them simply because she wanted to.

He was wrong, of course.

At least about why she had killed their family.

But he was right on one count—killing her biological mother had been personal. She had hated Brooke Mariano. Hated her for sleeping with both Logans. Hated Brooke for giving her up for money. Hated that she thought only of herself.

And so, she had killed her.

And now here she was killing all over again.

Just for the fun of it, it seemed.

With a start, she realized that it *was* fun. She *did* enjoy it. Logan was right. She was her father's daughter, after all. Only she was better at killing than he'd ever been.

Thinking of that, she checked her supplies to make sure everything was in order, then readied the syringe. She would need it handy this time around. There wasn't a lot she could do to make herself look like Vanessa. She had dyed her hair blonde, but Vanessa was short and skinny, and there was no way Isabella could lose weight quickly enough to pass for Vanessa.

She was going to have to do things different with Arthur.

Instead of letting him find her on the bed, she was going to have to take him as he came through the door.

She would have to be quick. Not just in injecting him, but in moving him, as well. She was strong, but Arthur was big and well-muscled; no doubt he would be heavy and awkward to maneuver. Still, she would rather take her chances in moving him than risk letting him get close to her and discovering she wasn't Vanessa before she could jab him with the syringe.

From outside she heard the rev of an engine and headlights flashed through the windows.

Arthur was here.

She took a steadying breath, more to keep her excitement under control than because she was nervous.

She positioned herself where the door would hide her once Arthur opened it; that seemed to be the best place. Arthur would enter and head for the bedroom, where he expected to find his latest fling awaiting him. He had no reason to be suspicious, so he wouldn't even think to check that there was no one else in the apartment.

Footsteps sounded and Isabella tensed, syringe in hand, ready to pounce as soon as Arthur closed the front door.

The door opened.

Arthur took a step inside.

The door closed.

"Vanessa?" Arthur called, taking a step toward the bedroom where Isabella had left a light on.

She moved quickly.

Arthur turned at the last second, but it was too late. She already had the needle plunging into his shoulder.

His eyes widened. Then his face creased with an angry frown and he swung at her.

Isabella quickly dodged out of the way.

"What the—?" Arthur looked surprised as he made a second attempt to grab her only to have his body refuse to cooperate.

Then he dropped.

Isabella sprang into action. As she had anticipated, it wasn't easy to maneuver the large man into the bedroom and onto the bed, but somehow she managed it. Probably because adrenalin was coursing through her system, giving her extra strength.

She wasn't stupid; she wasn't going to even attempt to move Arthur once she had him secured. This wasn't an obese guy in his sixties—this was a fit guy in his thirties, who could easily take her down if given the opportunity. Therefore, she took extra care to make sure she had him properly fastened to the bed frame, adding extra layers of duct tape.

Next she added tape to his mouth. She had been confident that Roman Hitacheel would not scream for help. He was at heart a weak, pathetic, wimp. But Arthur Bentley was not. When he realized that he couldn't brute force his way off the bed, he would most certainly start yelling.

And yelling would inevitably bring people.

She could kill anyone who tried to respond, but she didn't want to.

More than anything they would be more of a bother than a real hindrance.

Especially if they called the police.

Not to worry, though; the duct tape over his mouth would prevent Arthur from uttering more than stifled yelps. She would be the only one to hear him. And she was not going to be offering him any help.

She tapped her foot impatiently as she waited for Arthur to regain consciousness. Isabella was aware of movement behind her a split second before something slammed into the side of her head and everything exploded into a screaming black hole of pain.

* * * * *

1:16 A.M.

Sofia knew the second she woke up that something was off.

It was just a feeling.

As she looked around her and Ryan's bedroom, lit by the dim glow of a lamp beside the bed, nothing looked out of place. The fluffy bright yellow teddy bear Ryan had given her on their first official date—he'd chosen it specifically because yellow was both of their favorite color—was still lying beside her. She often slept with it when Ryan was working late. The shades were half-drawn; Sofia liked to be able to see the sky if she awakened during the night. Ryan's clothes were still thrown over the back of an overstuffed armchair in the corner of the room. No matter how many times she told him to put his clean clothes in the closet and his dirty clothes in the hamper in the laundry room, he never did either.

She climbed out of bed. It didn't matter that everything looked the same, because she felt that something was off. And the last five months had told her to trust her instincts.

Her leg had stiffened up while she'd been sleeping, but with adrenalin coursing through her veins, she didn't feel more than a distant throb as she hurried to Ryan's gun safe. Punching in the code, she grabbed a gun, thankful for the first time that she had let Ryan and Jack teach her to shoot. Between her stalker and Isabella's crime spree, plus the fact that her sister was still on the loose, Ryan had thought it was important for her to know how to protect herself if the need arose.

Which it seemed it had.

Scanning the bedside table, Sofia realized that she'd left her phone downstairs on the kitchen table. She cursed her stupidity. She *always* remembered to bring it up with her. Even before her stalker had reappeared, she always made sure she had her cell phone with her in case—given her shaky health lately—she needed to call Ryan, on the rare nights he didn't come home.

As she slowly and cautiously made her way downstairs, she wished that she had let Jack spend the night, as both he and Ryan had wanted. But she had to go and be all stubborn. She'd slept in her house alone after her stalker had first appeared in her life, and she didn't want to give up her independence. She was also wishing that she and Ryan had had a security system installed. They had talked about it but never gotten around to doing anything about it. Isabella hadn't seemed like she was going to be a physical threat to them, and Ryan was a cop, so they had felt safe enough. Until now.

Plus, she hadn't believed that the stalker was a threat to her.

At least, not yet.

But what if she was wrong?

Someone was here in her house, or had been, in the middle of the night.

If Jack had been here, then there would be no chance of anyone even getting through the door. But he wasn't here. No one was. Just her.

Keeping the gun clutched in one hand, Sofia needed to use her other to help steady herself as she went down the stairs.

Nothing seemed out of place, but she couldn't shake the feeling that she wasn't alone.

She was a little breathless now as she headed for the kitchen. She knew she was pushing her leg too far, and she was going to pay for it later. Sinking down into a chair at the kitchen table, she was pleased to see that the backdoor was still closed.

Perhaps she had overreacted.

She was tired and in pain. She'd learned Isabella was killing again, even though she had known it was likely, but having it confirmed was still a shock. Maybe it had all just been too much. She just wanted to move forward with her life and not remain stuck in this awful sort of limbo. She wanted Isabella and her stalker caught. She wanted her and Ryan to be able to be a normal couple, to focus on their future.

She fingered her phone, unsure whether to call Ryan or not. She wanted him to come home. Even if she had imagined the whole thing, she was still shaken up and wanted him here with her. However, she also didn't want to worry him unnecessarily. And he'd probably he home soon anyway. He hadn't called to say he wasn't coming home, so he'd probably just got held up with work.

Deciding against calling and upsetting him over what was most likely nothing, Sofia decided she'd take some painkillers and then go sleep on the couch, unable to summon enough energy to drag herself back up to bed. She was just standing up when she became aware of a presence behind her.

"You don't have to be afraid. I won't hurt you," a deep voice declared.

Sofia tried to scream, but her voice seemed to have stopped working.

"I only want to help you."

Clutching the gun in her hand, she didn't want to have to use it but she would if it was her only option. "I don't need help," she managed to force the words out through a throat that felt like it was quickly closing up as fear gripped her tightly.

"You do," the voice was earnest. "I'll stop her for you. I won't let her hurt you."

"Who?" Maybe she could keep him talking long enough for Ryan to get here. "Isabella?"

"I won't let her hurt you," the voice repeated. "I won't let anyone hurt you." His voice turned tender and Sofia shivered.

"Who are you?" she demanded in as strong a voice as she could muster.

There was no answer.

"I said, who are you?" she repeated.

"Someone who cares about you," the voice replied softly. "Someone who loves you. Someone whose whole life revolves around you."

Sensing the change in his demeanor as his tone went wildly possessive, Sofia tensed. She had misread him. Maybe he wasn't going to hurt her, but he was never going to let her go. She could read the obsession in his voice. Even without looking, she knew when he took a step toward her. Letting out a small scream, she turned quickly, gun in hand and fired off a shot at the man dressed all in black.

Grunting in surprise, he stumbled toward her. Ignoring her injured leg, Sofia jumped up, realizing too late that she had let the gun clatter to the floor. As the man recovered, she had no choice but to bolt from the room. Frightened tears were streaming down her cheeks now, and she was shaking so badly that she could hardly keep her balance. Blindly, she ran up the stairs, pausing at the top. Where could she hide?

There was nowhere to go where he couldn't find her if he wanted to.

And if he hadn't been armed before, he certainly was now.

Was he following her?

Had she hit him when she got off a shot?

She didn't know the answer to either of those questions and she didn't want to wait to find out.

Feeling like an extra in a low budget horror movie, she fled to the closet in hers and Ryan's bedroom. Burrowing herself inside, she almost certainly pointlessly covered herself with the extra quilts they stored in here.

She attempted to hold her breath, so that her ragged breathing wouldn't attract the man's attention. Realizing that she had managed to keep hold of her cell phone when she'd dropped the gun, she quickly dialed Ryan.

"Sorry, honey," Ryan's voice came through the phone seconds later. "I got held up, but I'm almost home."

Relief at both hearing his voice and knowing he would soon be here, left her momentarily speechless.

"Sofia?" anxiety inched into his tone.

"He's back," she whispered into the phone.

"What?" anxiety changed swiftly into panic. "The stalker?"

Footsteps approached. He had found her. "I have to go," she told Ryan, hanging up before he had a chance to say more.

Beneath the closet door, she could see a shadow.

This was it.

He was going to kill her.

Sofia couldn't believe she was going to die like this.

"I'm here to help," a calm voice told her. "I'll take care of her for you. Don't worry."

Curling herself up into a little ball, ignoring the burning protesting pain in her leg as she yanked it up against her chest, she began to whimper. Why hadn't she insisted they get a security system? Why hadn't she agreed to let Jack stay with her? Why hadn't she gone and spent the night at Edmund's like he'd asked her to? Why did she always have to be so stubborn?

Huddled on the floor of the closet, waiting for her stalker to rape her or kill her or both, she let out a petrified screech as the quilt she was hiding under was ripped off her. She thrashed wildly as hands grasped her shoulders. She wasn't going to go down without a fight.

"Sofia. Sofia," a voice slowly penetrated her terrified haze. "It's okay. It's me. It's Ryan. You're safe now. He's gone. Sofia."

Opening her eyes, it was indeed Ryan kneeling before her. Collapsing against his chest, she started grabbing huge handfuls of his sweater and clinging tightly.

He wrapped his arms around her. "Are you all right? Did he hurt you?"

Sofia shook her head; she could feel the adrenalin rushing out of her system, leaving her drained and shaky.

"What happened?" Ryan demanded, fear making his voice fierce.

"I woke up, and…and something was…something was wrong. He was…in the kitchen…I shot at him," she babbled. Her teeth were chattering so badly, it was making talking difficult.

"You shot at him?" Ryan sounded incredulous.

Only this time, Sofia couldn't answer. Her body was trembling so violently that she couldn't hold a coherent thought in her head. Someone had broken into her home. Again. She had fired a gun at someone. Possibly hit them. She had been sure that she was going to die. It was too much for her to deal with.

Sensing her distress, Ryan grabbed the quilt he'd pulled off her and now wrapped it around her. "You're safe, cupcake." He had deliberately gentled his voice. Picking her up, he walked with her back downstairs, going into the living room and settling in a corner of the couch with her on his lap.

While Ryan held her, stroked her hair, and murmured soothingly in her ear, Sofia concentrated on stilling the tremors racking her body. She thought that she was doing a good job at calming herself until she jumped a mile when the doorbell rang.

"It's just Jack," Ryan reassured her. "It's open," he yelled.

Moments later, Jack and a tall redheaded woman entered the room. "I knew I should have stayed," Jack muttered, shooting her a half-frustrated, half-concerned frown.

"Sofia said she shot at him," Ryan informed the pair.

"Did you hit him?" Jack asked, eyebrows raised in surprise.

"I'm not sure," she answered, pleased when there was only a small wobble in her voice.

"Where?" Jack asked.

"Kitchen." That time she couldn't stop the wobble that rocketed through her body.

Ryan exchanged glances with Jack above her head. "Are you going to be okay in here with Rose for a few minutes?" Ryan asked her.

When she nodded, he eased her off his lap, tucked the blanket tighter around her shoulders, and kissed the top of her head. "I'll be back in a minute."

Once they were alone, Detective Rose Lace, Jack's partner, joined her on the couch. "You doing okay?" Rose asked, green eyes studying her carefully.

"Yeah." She tried to summon a smile. Even though Rose was Jack's partner, she had gotten to know the woman more through Paige. Paige and Rose had been friends for years, and often when Sofia hung out with Paige, Rose would tag along. She liked Rose. The woman was outspoken, smart, and tough. She and Paige had promised to teach Sofia everything they knew about self-defense as soon as Sofia's body could handle it.

"I can't believe you shot at him," Rose marveled.

Sofia shrugged. "I thought he was going to kill me."

"Did he say anything to you?" Rose questioned.

"He said he wasn't going to hurt me, that he wanted to help me. Then he kept saying he'd take care of *her* for me. I think he meant Isabella," she explained. "He...he said that his whole world revolves around me." Of the whole horrible night, that had been the most terrifying thing. To think that a man who was stalking her thought she was the most important thing in his life couldn't be anything but bad.

"Did he tell you who he was?" Rose asked.

"No," she whispered. "I asked him, but all he said was that he loved me."

"Did you see him?" Ryan asked from the doorway. He looked tense and a tad bit possessive himself, so Sofia knew he'd overheard what she'd told Rose.

"Not well," Sofia tried to put herself back in the moment so she could make sure she remembered every possible detail. "He was behind me at first. Then I felt him move toward me. I got scared," she took a deliberately slow breath to calm herself. "I turned and shot at him. He stumbled toward me and I panicked. I dropped the gun and ran."

"When you turned, did you see him?" Jack asked gently.

"It was dark," she put in first. "All I know is that he was dressed all in black. He was wearing a hoodie so I couldn't see his face."

"What about his voice?" Rose asked. "Did you recognize it? Do you think you've heard it before?"

Considering this, Sofia honestly couldn't be sure. She had been too scared and everything had happened too quickly. "I don't know."

"All right," Ryan came back over to join her on the couch, perching on the arm beside her. "Steph's on her way over, and you can give your statement in the morning."

She suddenly realized that Paige wasn't here, which was odd. Ryan was scared, seemingly rightly so as her stalker continued to escalate things. Usually when Ryan was scared, he called in the troops. Jack and Rose had come, but not Paige. It was totally unlike Ryan not to call his partner in unless there was a good reason. Plus, she hadn't heard from her friend in a couple of days. "Where's Paige?" she asked Ryan.

"I sent her home to bed," he replied. Then when he read her confused expression, he added, "It's a long story; I'll tell you about it later." Catching Rose's concerned frown, Ryan said, "You should call her later, get her to tell you what's going on."

"We'll stay and wait for Stephanie, then lock up," Jack offered. "You two go and get some rest."

When Ryan made a move to pick her back up, she made an abortive effort to stand. "I can walk."

"I need to hold you," Ryan told her as he lifted her into his arms.

Understanding that Ryan needed to touch her right now to convince himself that she was okay, she allowed him to carry her back upstairs. Sinking down into his strong arms, Sofia was beyond glad Ryan was here. What would have happened if he hadn't arrived when he had? He had probably scared her stalker off. If he hadn't, would she be dead right now? And what happened if next time he couldn't get here in time to save her? The stalker had come to their home twice in two days. His visits were escalating. And that couldn't be a good thing.

* * * * *

2:04 A.M.

Hmmm…this was quite an interesting turn of events.

Not what he had expected.

Ricky Preston had been following his next kill, Arthur Bentley, when the man had suddenly driven to an apartment in the middle of the night. Wondering what Arthur was up to, he had waited a few minutes then followed him inside.

To his surprise, the scene that had met him was one he couldn't have dreamed up in a million years.

A young woman was dragging Arthur Bentley's unconscious body across the floor toward the bedroom. As he'd watched quietly in the shadows, she had pushed and shoved and heaved the body up onto the bed, where she had promptly secured him with layer after layer of duct tape.

Intrigued, Ricky had wanted to know what the woman was up to.

She didn't look like Arthur Bentley's wife. Maybe the guy was having some sort of kinky affair. Maybe he was into that rough stuff where people role-played and tied each other up for sex.

Or maybe this woman was here to kill Arthur.

That was totally unacceptable.

No one got in the way of his plans.

Not even a beautiful woman.

And Ricky thought the woman was beautiful. Not in a classic way, he supposed, but she appealed to him. She was tall and solid, with long red hair and sharp features. She was wearing a bright orange sweater that should clash with her bright red hair but somehow didn't. But it was her eyes that had him. They were gray and serious, and lurking in their depths, he saw something that stirred him.

He wanted to know more about her.

He didn't want to just approach her. If she was here to kill Arthur Bentley, then she had to be armed. Ricky couldn't see a gun or knife, but there was a bag on the table, into which she had put her roll of duct tape and scissors, perhaps whatever she intended to use on Arthur was in there.

Instead, it was safer to take her by surprise.

Ricky hadn't come prepared for a confrontation. He had simply come to watch Arthur, make sure he knew the man's movements and routines down to the tiniest detail, so he wasn't armed.

Giving a quick search of the living room, he found a heavy paperweight that would do the job. With years of practice under his belt, he moved stealthily toward the woman, who didn't notice him until he was already swinging the paperweight at her head.

As it connected, she dropped like a rock. He checked quickly to make sure she was still breathing, even though Ricky knew he was an expert at delivering incapacitating yet non-lethal blows. When his fingers found her pulse beating strongly, he grabbed a chair and the woman's duct tape, then balanced her in the chair and quickly secured her in place.

Once he had the woman taken care of, he went to Arthur Bentley on the bed. The man was lying flat on his back. Tape crossed his chest, his shoulders, and his legs—both at the knees and ankles, circling all the way under the bed. The woman had made sure to add multiple layers of tape, obviously concerned that the well-muscled and obviously strong Arthur might be able to get himself free if given the opportunity.

One of Arthur's arms was positioned out straight, away from the rest of his body. She had used rope to tie his wrist to the headboard, then added more duct tape around his wrist, to make sure the rope held. Arthur appeared to still be out cold from whatever the woman had done to him.

Interested to see what she intended to do to Arthur, Ricky decided to check out her bag while he waited for the woman to regain consciousness. Rifling through it, he was surprised to find medical supplies. Tubes and syringes and IV/blood collection bags. Now he was *really* curious about what exactly the woman had planned for Arthur Bentley.

Turning back to check on the woman, he found serious gray eyes studying him. "You're awake," he smiled and took a step toward her. He expected to see fear flash through her, but instead she remained completely calm. It had to be an act.

"Who're you?" she asked.

"Who're *you?*" he asked back, moving closer so he was right beside her chair, hoping their proximity would force her to lose the act and show how scared she must be feeling.

Instead, she simply shot him a small smile. "I asked you first."

He was impressed by her spunk, but determined not to let it show, he'd never met someone he couldn't intimidate and the thought that perhaps this woman couldn't be frightened by him was as exciting as it was annoying. Putting his face just inches from hers, he murmured, "I'm the man who's going to kill you." He pressed one hand to her chest and his other to her neck, expecting to feel her heart hammering and her pulse thumping. Instead they continued to beat rhythmically; she truly wasn't afraid of him.

She raised an eyebrow, "How?"

"How, what?" he couldn't focus on anything other than the fact that this woman wasn't even a little bit scared of him. Or death, apparently.

"How are you going to kill me?" she asked patiently.

The question left him stumped. And Ricky Preston had never been stumped before in his life. Fascinated by her, he asked instead, "Why aren't you afraid of me? Why aren't you afraid to die?"

Her brow furrowed as though perplexed. "I'm a bad person. A killer. Death is what I deserve. If you're here to do it, then why should I be afraid of you?"

Her answer was not what he had been expecting. "You're here to kill Arthur Bentley?"

The look she shot him suggested she thought as well as being here to kill her, he was also an idiot. "Of course."

"Why?"

"What does it matter why?"

"I want to know," he replied honestly. He had never in his life met anyone like her.

Considering this, then apparently taking him at his word, she explained. "He's been cheating on his wife. I don't like cheaters."

He was surprised to hear this. "Arthur Bentley is cheating on his wife? Already? He just got married. And not to you, by the way; you weren't the woman with him at the hotel."

She shook her head. "No, Arthur had been married for years now. His wife is disabled. If you saw him at a hotel, then it was with one of his mistresses."

He wondered if this was a lover's quarrel taken to the extreme. "Are you another of his mistresses?"

Repulsion crossed her face. "Of course not," she said indignantly.

"Then why do you care if he's a cheater?"

"Because cheating destroyed my family, and besides, if I don't kill people who deserve it, what else am I going to do with my life?" She looked up at him as though she truly didn't know the answer to that.

This was weird. Really weird. This woman appeared to be just like him. How was that even possible? He hadn't thought that there was anyone in the world like him. This was almost too weird to be true. What if it wasn't? What if this was some weird police sting, and this woman was here to set him up? "You said you're a killer; who have you killed?"

She studied him for a moment. "Have you ever heard of the Everette family?"

He was shocked; he had indeed heard of the Everette family, and the killer who had systematically worked their way through killing them a few months ago. "You're Isabella Everette?"

She nodded. "I killed them because they deserved it, but now I can't seem to stop. I kind of like it," she admitted.

He smiled at her, "Honey, I know the feeling."

Her gray eyes turned curious. "You know Arthur Bentley. You're not here to kill me, are you? You're here to kill him."

Lying to her never even occurred to him. "Yes."

"Why?"

He shrugged. "I like to kill. Arthur and I crossed paths and he appealed to me."

She was seemingly enthralled by his answer. "So, you don't have to have a reason for killing someone? You just pick someone and do it?"

"Uh huh," he confirmed. "At least these days. Why? Do you feel like you need a reason?"

She mulled that over. "I don't know. I thought I did. I thought I had to justify it, but maybe I don't."

"Maybe," he said slowly, moving to the table where she had her bag of tricks and retrieving the scissors, then moving back to stand in front of her. "Maybe you're not alone anymore."

* * * * *

3:11 A.M.

Maybe you're not alone anymore.

Those were the words that the man standing before her, with a pair of scissors in his hand, had just uttered.

Was he going to kill her?

No, Isabella didn't think that he was. She wasn't afraid of him. Hadn't been since the second she had awakened to find herself taped to a chair and a strange man going through her bag.

At first he had tried to scare her, and he'd been surprised when he couldn't.

But what was there to be afraid of?

Certainly not death.

Obviously, Isabella knew that death was the end for everyone; she also knew that the consequences of her actions were that she would most likely die young—probably violently.

Meeting and locking her gaze with his dark blue eyes, the man knelt before her, and cut the tape binding her. When he had her free, he reached for her hand, taking it gently in his, and pulled her to her feet. Then before she knew it, he had threaded a hand through her hair and was tilting her face up and bringing his lips toward hers.

She froze, but didn't flinch, as their lips touched. For a man who had admitted to her that he was a killer, his kiss was surprisingly soft. Not that Isabella had anything to compare it to. She had never been kissed before.

Perhaps the knowledge that her first kiss was by a man who had knocked her unconscious and tied her up should concern her. But it didn't. This man understood. He understood her. He was what she'd been dreaming of all her life. She knew that for absolute certain. And she didn't even know his name.

Maybe it helped that he was gorgeous. Although he had to be in his forties and she was only seventeen. Dark hair, blue eyes, tall and well built—she never dreamed that someone as good looking as he was could ever be interested in her. And yet he certainly seemed interested. From the moment he had realized that he couldn't intimidate her, he had been looking at her with captivated reverence.

Suddenly, as if he could read her mind, he deepened the kiss.

No longer was it soft and gentle.

Now it was fiery and hot.

Before she knew it, he had her up against the wall. His tongue pushed between her lips and roamed her mouth. His hips pressed against hers and pinned her in place. His hands left her head and began to roam her body; one went to her breasts and the other traced up her leg. She could feel his erection pressed against her. Was he physically attracted to her? Did she turn him on? Did he want to have sex with her?

Startled, she pulled away.

Breathing heavily, he raised a questioning eyebrow at her.

"I'm sorry," she murmured, feeling her cheeks heat in embarrassment. "I'm a virgin. Well, not technically because I've been..." She couldn't say the word. "But I've never been with a guy before. Never even dated. Never even thought that anyone could be interested in me. I'm not pretty. I'm not the kind of girl who attracts guys. And you're hot. And I don't even know your name," she blathered pathetically. She was so out of her element.

"Ricky." His eyes were twinkling in amusement.

"Wh...what?" she stammered, still totally shocked that a hot guy seemed to be into her; the knowledge seemed to be making her brain go all flaky.

"My name," he elaborated. "Ricky Preston."

For some reason that name seemed familiar to her, and Isabella tried to place where she had heard it before.

Once again he seemed to read her thoughts. "The family murders about eight months ago. Five families, killed in their homes, I always left one alive."

She nodded as she recalled the case, she had always loved reading about murder cases. "I remember those. That was you?" Isabella had to admit she was a little awed.

"Uh huh," he nodded, still smiling.

She was still feeling self-conscious. "I'm sorry I couldn't...you know...do it."

He shrugged indifferently. "No big deal. There'll be other opportunities."

She wasn't sure she was hearing him correctly. Did he want more from her than one night of sex? Was he interested in a relationship? Was she?

"We have a lot in common." There he went again, knowing what she was thinking without her even opening her mouth.

That couldn't be more true.

"There aren't a lot of people like us," Ricky continued.

Again, that couldn't be more true. She had opened up to him, explained why she killed, told him that she had been sexually assaulted. She needed to know if he could open up to her, too. "Why did you kill them? I mean, I know you said now you just kill because you want to, but you also said that it wasn't always the case. Those families—you killed them for a reason. What was it?"

Searching her face, he turned serious, his smile disappearing, replaced by a bleakness she recognized. "My mother was murdered. They said it was an accident, but she was murdered. She died in a fire. She was trapped in our house. She was screaming for help because she couldn't get out. No one helped her. They just stood there and watched her die. Our neighbors, they may as well have set her on fire themselves."

"So you killed them—your neighbors."

"They deserved it," Ricky said fiercely.

Isabella didn't disagree. In fact, her heart broke for him. Obviously, he had loved his mother very much. That must be nice. She wished that she had had that kind of a relationship with her mother. She couldn't imagine losing someone you loved in such a horrendous way. Burning alive was a horrible way to die. And for Ricky to know that it could have been prevented if his neighbors had just done something to help her. No wonder he had killed them. Sofia was the only person that Isabella loved, and if anyone hurt her, then she would stop at nothing to make sure that person paid for what they did—painfully.

Suddenly, she remembered that they weren't alone. Arthur Bentley was still here. "He's conscious, you know," she gestured at the bed behind them.

All traces of despair wiped off his face as his easy smile returned. "I know."

"We can't let him go," she reminded him. "He's heard everything." At that, Arthur sprung to life on the bed, shaking his head from side to side and thrashing as violently as he could manage against his restraints. Mumbling through the tape on his mouth, presumably trying to tell them that he hadn't heard anything and even if he had he'd never tell. She ignored him. "I gave him sodium thiopental; he was only out for a few minutes."

Amusement lit his eyes again. "Sodium thiopental? I use that, too. See, a lot in common."

Smiling back at him, Isabella wasn't used to being around someone that understood her so well. She felt both shy and liberated at the same time. She could get used to this. Maybe this was the man who would love her unconditionally. Maybe she was going to get a chance to have her own happily ever after. She hardly dared to hope it was true. "We were both planning on killing him, so which one of us gets to do the honors?"

"We could do it together," Ricky suggested.

"Really?" she stared at him longingly. She was falling hard and fast for Ricky Preston.

"How were you going to do it?" Ricky asked. "I've been using an axe. For some reason, the thought of being an axe murderer appealed to me." He grinned, making him even more gorgeous.

His grin made her grin—something she didn't normally do.

"Drain his blood and then pour it down his throat till he drowned in it," she replied.

Ricky chuckled. "Neat," he nodded approvingly.

Wanting, almost needing, more of his approval, she continued. "I've tried lots of other ways before, too. Strangling, shooting, stabbing, carbon monoxide; I like to be creative."

"Creative, huh? Okeydokey, well, let's see what we can come up with." He strode toward the bed where Arthur Bentley was now staring back at them with tear filled green eyes.

Isabella could tell, even though what he was saying wasn't discernible, that he was pleading, begging for his life. Too bad for Arthur Bentley that neither she nor Ricky were going to feel remorse for killing him. They just weren't built that way. And after a lifetime of thinking that she was all alone in the world, that no one understood her, although her sister tried, she had concluded that she was just too different. That she was one of a kind.

Now she knew it wasn't true.

Ricky Preston was just like her. He was her other half. Now she would be able to have the best of both worlds. She could have a friend, a lover, maybe even a husband and family. And she could do it all while being who she truly was. This kill together would cement their connection. It was the beginning of their lives together.

"Got it. Got the perfect way to kill him."

* * * * *

9:42 A.M.

It wasn't even ten in the morning and already it had been a long day.

Xavier was in the car on the way to the hotel where both Erica and Garton Landers, and Helena and Tyler Mendleson had honeymooned. He had called Garton and then Helena as soon as he and Annabelle had left her therapist earlier this morning. His hunch had been correct. The hotel was where the two couples overlapped. Therefore, the hotel had to be the place where Ricky had seen them.

It was a huge hotel with thousands of rooms, a conference center, restaurants and bars, a gym, pool, and a shopping center. That meant thousands of workers. And Ricky Preston could be any one of them.

Still, so far, his luck had been more good than bad.

The fingerprint in Tyler's blood on the doorknob of the Mendlesons' front door was proof Ricky was in the house at the time of the murders, finally finding a link between the couples. Both were strikes of good luck. He just needed his luck to last a little longer.

If he was lucky, Ricky would be at work right now and he'd be able to pick him up. There would be too many people about for Ricky to play games. And, hopefully, he wasn't armed—not that he had any reason to be. He didn't know they had his prints, and he didn't know they had the link, so he would have no reason to think anything other than it was another normal day at work.

If he was only a little lucky, he would be able to confirm that Ricky Preston worked there, more than likely under a false identity, but not at work that day. Furthermore, he hoped whatever address he had listed on his file was correct. At least confirming that he worked there would mean they could get proof that he had been working on the nights the Landers and Mendlesons honeymooned. And they could get his work schedule so they would know when he would next turn up if his address turned out to be a fake.

If he was unlucky, then it would turn out that Ricky Preston didn't work at the hotel at all. It was possible that he had simply been a guest at the hotel at the time the Landers and Mendlesons were there. In that case, it would be virtually impossible to identify him. Even though they had the dates of the two couples' honeymoons, Ricky could have been anything from a patron at one of the eateries to a guest staying at the hotel to a shopper at the mall. There was no way they could find every person who had been present at the hotel complex.

He had his fingers crossed he was going to be lucky.

Xavier was also hoping a little of that luck was going to spill over into his personal life.

Annabelle had been quiet and distant all morning. From the moment he'd woken her up, it was like she had been in a fog. She had blindly followed him to the kitchen for breakfast. He'd had to remind her several times to eat her food. Then he'd virtually had to wash her in the shower. She'd just stood there under the water spray, staring through him as though he wasn't even there.

On the drive to her therapist, he had attempted to engage her in conversation, but the most he could get out of her was one word answers delivered in a monotone voice. Still, from what he could tell, her session had gone well. She seemed to have perked up a little. However, he wasn't pleased with her decision to remain home alone. So he had asked Kate to go over there and stick like glue to Annabelle until he got home tonight. Xavier was sure that Annabelle wasn't going to be pleased about that, but that was just too bad. He couldn't do his job if he was worried about her hurting herself. And, hopefully, the distraction would do her some good.

Pulling into the main parking lot of the hotel complex, Xavier grabbed some paperwork from the trunk before heading for the main check-in desk, which seemed as good a place as any to begin.

He flashed his badge at the first attendant he came across. "I'm Detective Montague. I'm looking for this guy," he held up a picture of Ricky Preston. "Do you know him?"

The young woman threw a quick glance at the photo and shook her head.

Ignoring his irritation, Xavier kept his voice calm. "I really need you to look more closely. His name is Ricky Preston, but he may be going by a different name. I believe that he works here, and it's very important that I find him. *Very* important," he repeated.

Frowning at him, but obediently giving the photo another look, she said, "Sorry, I've never seen him before, but I'm new, only been here a few days. Maybe you should speak to human resources."

Xavier intended to, but it would probably be quicker to identify if Ricky was an employee by someone he worked directly with. In such a large establishment, human resources probably weren't going to recognize every single worker. "Is there someone who's worked here longer that I could ask?" he persisted.

Gesturing at the concierge desk, she said, "Frank has been here longer than anyone I know; you could try him."

Doing just that, Xavier headed straight for Frank, a short, skinny, balding man who looked to be in his early fifties. "Frank?" The man turned to look at him. "I'm Detective Montague." He held up his badge in one hand and the picture of Ricky in the other. "I'm looking for this man; do you know him?"

Glancing briefly at the picture Xavier held up, he said, "Oh, sure. That's Rick. Rick Palmer. He works here." Then the man's gaze grew wary, "Why? Did something happen to him?"

"Not that I'm aware of. Is he working today?"

"No, he works nights, but tonight is his night off. Did he do something? Is that why you're looking for him?" The man's brown eyes were wide with repulsed fascination, like he almost hoped his co-worker was indeed guilty of some horrible crime.

"Yes, he did," Xavier confirmed. "Could you please point me in the direction of human resources?"

Looking a little disappointed that he wasn't going to be given all the gory details, Frank pointed to a door marked staff only, then reluctantly returned to his work.

Xavier hurried through the door, down a hall, and into the human resources room. Now that he had confirmation that Ricky was working here, he wanted an address ASAP. A surprised receptionist looked up as he came through the door. From the frown on her face she was clearly about to tell him that he shouldn't be in there. Pre-empting her, he held up his badge. "I'm Detective Montague. I need to talk to someone about a hotel employee going by the name of Rick Palmer."

Before the receptionist could comment, an office door opened. "Did Mr. Palmer do something?" a middle-aged lady asked.

"Yes, ma'am, he did," Xavier replied. "And it's extremely important that I locate him. I understand that he won't be working tonight, so I'm going to need his home address. I have a warrant for his contact information." Thankfully, he had thought to sort that out before he turned up at the hotel. Given that Ricky Preston matched the description of the killer given by both Garton Landers and Helena Mendleson, his prints were found at the scene, and both couples had honeymooned at this hotel, it hadn't been hard to get the warrant.

She looked doubtful. "Okay," the woman agreed slowly, returning to her office and pulling out a file.

Minutes later, Xavier was back in his car, speeding toward the address Ricky Preston had given his employer, and hoping that his lucky streak continued.

* * * * *

2:33 P.M.

"I can't believe you didn't call me last night." Paige glared at him as they climbed back into the car.

Ryan had been wondering when his partner was going to bring that up. So far they had been run off their feet all morning. They were hitting up hospitals, hoping their hypothesis that Isabella was working as a nurse would turn out to be true and one of the hospitals would recognize her. So far they were two for two and heading for the third.

"You were tired," he told Paige. "You needed the rest."

She stared at him incredulously as he pulled out into traffic. "You thought me sleeping was more important than Sofia's stalker breaking into your home while she was there alone and she shot at him?"

He tried not to let his terror over last night consume him. He hadn't been the one to tell Paige about last night; Rose had. Apparently, his brother's partner had followed his advice and called Paige. Ryan wasn't sure if Rose and Paige had talked about Paige's stalker, but they had certainly talked about Sofia and last night's events. And now his partner was mad at him for not calling her.

"No, not more important." He tried to make his voice soothing, which apparently had the opposite effect than what he was going for because Paige's voice went frosty.

"Don't try and placate me," she snapped. "You should have called me. Sofia is my friend, not just your girlfriend."

"I'm sorry. I should have called; I just didn't want to worry you, given…" He trailed off and shot her a concerned glance.

"Don't make me regret telling you, Ryan," Paige was deadly serious now. "That's why I haven't before. I don't want you looking at me differently. What happened with my mom was a long time ago. I'm not going to fall apart again over what's happening now. If you don't trust me anymore, then I'm going to ask for a new partner."

"What?" he asked, alarmed. He did *not* want a new partner. "You don't really want a new partner, do you?"

Paige exhaled deeply. "No. But we need to trust that we have each other's back, and if you don't, now that you know…"

"I do," he cut her off. "Paige, I do trust you. And I am sorry that I didn't call you. I was busy panicking and I didn't think things through properly."

Softening, she asked, "How's Sofia?"

"She's okay. She's scared, but she's tough. The stalker is apparently making threats about taking care of Isabella, and I'm thinking that him taking her out could be a good thing, although Sofia would probably end up blaming herself. It's just, I don't see this thing with Isabella ending well." In fact, Ryan had a feeling in his gut that the whole thing was going to end terribly.

"If we luck out and Isabella is working as a nurse at one of these hospitals, then we could have her in custody by the end of the day. Maybe even within the hour if this one is the hospital where she works and she's on duty," Paige declared optimistically.

Ryan hoped so, but he wasn't feeling particularly optimistic this morning. Two nights back to back of virtually no sleep, plus the stress of the last few days, were taking their toll on him. If he hadn't gotten home when he had last night, then Sofia's stalker could have done more than just scare her.

The fact that Sofia had felt so scared and vulnerable that she had felt the need to arm herself left him feeling icy cold with fear. This guy just wasn't letting up. After a year or so of no contact, he was clearly ready not just to engage Sofia again, but also to take things up a level.

And that terrified him.

Just what was this guy's end game?

Did he want Sofia for himself? Did he want her dead? Would he turn out to be a threat to the people around Sofia if he thought they were getting in between them?

Unfortunately, once again, Stephanie had come up empty when she had come to check out the house last night. This guy was good. He never left a single print or fiber or hair or any piece of himself behind.

Ryan had only been about ten minutes away from their house when Sofia had called him but it had seemed like hours. The terror in her voice, and then when she had hung up on him after whispering that he was back, had left him feeling more helpless than he ever had in his life. Not knowing what had happened to her, whether she was dead, alive, or injured, while he was powerless to help her, was not an experience he wished to repeat.

Seemingly reading his mind, Paige asked, "So what are you going to do to stop this guy from getting back into your house?"

"I have a security firm coming out tomorrow to install the best security system they have. And I don't want her alone in the house after dark. If I'm held up and not home in time, then Edmund's going to go and pick her up and take her to his place. Sofia's also interested in a protection dog. And she's itching to get better so you and Rose can start training her in self-defense."

"And she didn't recognize him at all?"

"She said she didn't really get a good look at him," Ryan replied. "He spoke to her, but she said the voice wasn't familiar. He also told her he loves her and that she's the center of his world."

She winced. "He sounds totally obsessed."

"Have you had any more text messages?" With Sofia's stalker upping the ante, he was hoping Paige's wasn't going to as well.

"No. And don't go getting distracted by that; let's focus on Isabella, and Sofia's stalker," she said firmly.

Yeah, right, he wanted to say, *as if that was happening.* Ryan had already asked Jack and Rose to investigate whoever was sending Paige texts.

"You're not going to let it go, are you?" Paige asked.

"Did you really expect me to?" he asked as he pulled into an empty space in the hospital's parking lot.

"No, I guess not. You've got Rose and Jack working on it, don't you?"

He smiled at her; he and Paige knew each other so well he couldn't imagine having anyone else as his partner. "Yep."

She rubbed her tired eyes. "They have better things to be working on," she grumbled.

He eyed her carefully as they headed for the hospital's front door. "Tired?"

"Yes, and yes," she answered his unasked question. "I did have nightmares, but it's no big deal. I'm used to them."

Before he could ask her anything else, she had walked ahead of him to the main reception desk. Hurrying to catch up, he pulled out a picture of Isabella. "Hi," he announced to the woman at the desk, "I'm Detective Xander, and this is my partner, Detective Hood. We wanted to find out if this woman works here at the hospital," he explained, and he passed her the photo.

The woman studied it for a moment. "She looks a little familiar, but I'm not sure."

Xander exchanged hopeful glances with Paige. "She's tall; she wouldn't have been working here for more than five months."

The woman nodded along as he spoke. "You're right. She started here about four months ago; she works in the geriatric ward. I think her name is Isobel." She glanced around conspiratorially. "I remember her because she never talks to anyone. She's a little odd, and there's lots of gossip going around the hospital about her. But she does her work well, she's polite to the patients, she's always on time, and she's efficient. She's only called in sick once since she started here, and that was because her baby was ill."

So, Isabella still had Brooke's baby. "Is she working today?"

"I'm not sure, sorry; I can call and check, if you like." The woman picked up the phone in front of her and dialed a number. A few quick questions later she hung up. "No, today's her day off. She won't be back until tomorrow."

"We're going to need her address," Paige informed the woman.

The woman's eyes grew wide with surprise. "Is she wanted for something?"

"We need to talk with her; she may have information on a case we're working," Ryan answered vaguely. A moment later, he was holding a sheet of paper with the name Isobel Evans and an address on it. He was anxious to drive out to the house and pick Isabella up, but there was one other thing he needed to know first. "Have you had any thefts here recently? Any medical supplies and drugs gone missing, specifically sodium thiopental?"

"Actually we have. How did you know that?" Realization dawning, the woman asked, "Is that why you want Isobel? Did she steal drugs from here?"

"Thanks, ma'am, you've been extremely helpful," Ryan told her instead.

He was buzzing with excitement by the time they got back into the car, driving toward Isabella's house where they would hopefully end this once and for all. "Are you and Elias okay?" he asked Paige as he drove off.

Paige just shrugged.

"Look, what he did was wrong; but you know he loves you and he was just doing what he thought was best for you."

She just shrugged again.

"Come on, Paige. You two love each other, don't let one stupid mistake ruin that."

For a moment, she was quiet. "It's not that he gave me the sleeping pills, it's that he thinks I'm going to lose it like I did when I was a kid. I don't know that I want to be married to someone who thinks I'm weak and an emotional wreck."

"You know he doesn't think that," Ryan gently rebuked her. "Sometimes I worry about Sofia having a breakdown," he admitted.

"But she's so strong," Paige protested.

"I know, but she's been through a lot and I worry about her. I love her," he added. "Same way Elias loves you. We worry about the people we love; sometimes it makes us a little crazy. I know you're hurt, but try to give him a break."

"I'll think about it," Paige told him, but he could hear in her voice that she was letting herself let it go.

"We're here," he announced. Both of them set aside their personal issues and readied themselves. Ryan didn't think that Isabella would try anything, especially given the fact that he was dating her sister, but they still needed to be careful.

They approached the small house cautiously. It had a neatly mowed front lawn and two leafless trees in the yard. The house was single story and painted a fresh white. There was no car in the drive and no lights on inside.

Rapping on the front door, Ryan thought it was best not to identify himself until Isabella opened the door. No one answered his knock. He rapped again. After waiting a full minute, there was still no response.

"She's not here," he admitted at last.

"Excuse me," a voice came from the sidewalk. "Are you looking for Isobel?"

His head snapped toward the elderly woman staring at them inquisitively. "Do you know Isobel Evans?" he asked, as he and Paige walked toward her.

"She used to live there, but she moved last week," the lady told them.

His heart dropped; they had been so close to arresting her. Now they'd have to hope that no one from the hospital tipped her off and she turned up for her shift tomorrow. "Okay, thanks." He started for the car.

"I have her new address," the lady called after him.

He froze. "You do?"

"I used to babysit Sophie. Isobel gave me her new address so I can still watch her sometimes. She's a cutie and such a good baby, I couldn't bear not to be able to see her again," the old woman gushed.

Sophie must be Brooke's baby. At least Isabella seemed to be taking good care of the child, who was both her half-sister on her mother's side, and aunt on her father's side. And it seemed she had named the baby after Sofia. If Isabella had only moved to her new address last week, then she was most likely still there. "We're going to need that address."

* * * * *

5:28 P.M.

Xavier was desperate.

The address the hotel had for Ricky Preston had turned out to be an abandoned warehouse. Clearly, Ricky was not living there.

The day hadn't been a complete loss, though.

A call had come through about a house where drugs and medications stolen from a hospital were reportedly being sold. Given that sodium thiopental was among them, Xavier was going to check it out. Perhaps he'd get lucky again and Ricky Preston had been a customer.

Or if he was *really* lucky, maybe it was Ricky who had stolen the drugs and this was where he was living. If he was dealing stolen drugs, that would certainly be a reason to give his employer a fake address; plus the fake address gave Ricky the additional benefit of covering his tracks in the event the police were ever on to him.

After Xavier checked this out, he was going to head home.

Annabelle had been steadfastly refusing to answer his calls and texts all day. Presumably, she was unhappy with him for sending Kate to babysit her. Right now, though, Xavier couldn't care less if Annabelle was angry with him. She'd scared the life out of him with her admission that she was contemplating suicide; there was no way he was leaving her alone any time soon—not until he was convinced that all thoughts of taking her own life were gone for good.

Annabelle may have been uncooperative about returning his calls, but thankfully Kate had not. He'd already texted her a couple of dozen times, plus called her at least five. So, he knew that Annabelle was doing okay. While she hadn't been overly enthusiastic about Kate's presence, she had allowed Kate to keep her company without complaint. Most importantly, though, Xavier knew she was safe. And that was all that mattered.

Pulling into a street, he checked the address he had jotted down on a scrap of paper to confirm he had the right place and then stopped in front of a house. The house looked completely innocuous. It was brick, two stories, a neat and well-maintained yard that Xavier guessed would be full of flowers in the spring. It was not the kind of house where one would expect to purchase stolen drugs.

There was a white van parked in the drive, and a blue sedan on the curb out front. As he passed the car, he saw a baby seat in the back. That wasn't good. Hopefully, there wasn't going to be a child inside. Although, potentially, that could make whoever was in there less likely to try anything stupid.

Xavier was feeling like it was less and less likely he was going to find Ricky Preston here. Ricky had no children, and he couldn't see the guy settling down with a woman who had a child while he was on the run from the police.

Maybe the car belonged to one of the other houses on the street. He glanced up and down the road. That seemed unlikely. There were no other cars, bar his own, that were parked out on the street instead of in driveways, so there would be no reason for the car's owner to park in front of someone else's house instead of their own, or the home of whomever they were visiting.

Maybe this wasn't even the right house.

It certainly didn't look like a drug house.

And he'd been to plenty.

He checked out the house as he approached. The blinds were drawn, but he could see light emanating from around the edges. Someone was obviously at home.

After rapping on the door, Xavier thought he heard movements and muffled voices from inside but couldn't be sure.

He knocked again. "Police, open up, please."

At his announcement, the house went suddenly dark.

A feeling of foreboding began in his gut. "Police, open up."

The house had gone deadly silent.

Trying the doorknob, it turned, and he pushed the door open, pulled out his gun and stepped inside.

It took a moment for his eyes to adjust to the near complete darkness in the house. Outside it had been dark, but there had been the streetlights, car headlights, and a porch light above the door.

Once Xavier could see enough to make out shadows he found himself in a large living room. Couches, lamps, an entertainment cabinet with a large screen TV, a couple of small tables, but Xavier couldn't see any people.

"My name is Detective Montague; come out with your hands up," Xavier yelled into the empty room.

Somewhere in the house, someone chuckled.

Confused, his bad feeling was growing. "You need to identify yourself. I need to ask you some questions."

When there was no response, he moved cautiously forward, checking out the room to confirm it was empty. Xavier was halfway toward the nearest door when he heard the chuckle again. Before he could give another order for the house's inhabitants to come out, a familiar voice spoke.

"Detective Montague, my all-time favorite cop."

The blood in his veins felt like it had turned to ice. "Ricky."

"Long time, no see," Ricky singsonged.

Focusing every cell in his body, Xavier knew he needed to play this right. There was no way he was letting Ricky get away again. However, he also knew that Ricky was intent on torturing Annabelle. And the best way to do that would be for Ricky to kill him. Xavier was sure that Annabelle would not survive that. If she didn't outright commit suicide, she would simply let herself waste away.

"How's Annabelle?" Ricky's tone was mockingly polite.

Wanting to keep Ricky's attention on himself and as far away from Annabelle as he could, he responded, "Ricky, it's time to give up. Let me take you in. End this now. You knew at some point you'd get caught."

Ricky merely chuckled and ignored him. "Been missing me?" he asked instead. "I've been missing Annabelle. I think about her *all* the time. I bet she thinks about me all the time, too."

Xavier could hear the grin in Ricky's voice, he was obviously loving this. Xavier forced his own voice to remain calm. "Ricky, it's over. This time you don't have a stunt to pull to coerce me into letting you go. Don't bother dragging it out." As he spoke, Xavier continued to slowly cross the room. He was sure that wherever Ricky was hiding, he couldn't see him. If he could find Ricky first, he'd have the element of surprise on his side.

"Oh, I don't know," Ricky drawled. "So far I'm two for two; I bet I can make it three for three."

Xavier remembered that he had heard voices from inside the house while he was out on the porch. It was conceivable that Ricky had a hostage. So far, he had made sure that if the police stumbled upon him he always had an escape plan. The car outside had a baby seat. Ricky could be dating a woman with a child so he would have the perfect leverage to get away again should the need arise. As much as he wanted Ricky arrested and safely locked away in jail, he wouldn't risk harming an innocent child to do it.

"Do you have someone in here with you, Ricky?" Xavier asked. "I saw a car outside. It had a child's car seat in it. Is there a baby here? Do you have a hostage? I don't want you to hurt anyone else, Ricky. If there's someone here with you, then let them go."

"I can't wait to see Annabelle again," Ricky continued as though Xavier hadn't spoken. "You got my letter, right? I remember last time Annabelle and I were together, and I just can't wait to go at it again."

Xavier chewed on his lip to keep himself from speaking. Ricky was just trying to antagonize him. There was no need to play into it. His priority right now was to arrest Ricky. Besides, there was no chance in hell that Ricky Preston was going to get his hands on Annabelle ever again. Xavier was in the next room now—a huge kitchen with a large dining table; on the table he could just make out the shape of bottles. Most likely a baby was indeed here.

"Have you and Annabelle…how should I put this?" Ricky paused dramatically. "Have the two of you been intimate yet? Or did I make such an impact that she hasn't been able to do it yet?"

Xavier could taste blood in his mouth and realized that he'd bitten his lips hard enough to break the skin. Annabelle had been a virgin before Ricky raped her, and she was still too traumatized to do more with him than kissing and a little touching. Not that Xavier minded. He loved Annabelle and he was in this with her for the long haul; he didn't mind waiting until she was ready.

"I'll take that as a no," Ricky laughed.

Xavier hated that sound. Hated that Ricky took such pleasure in Annabelle's pain. Pain that he had caused. The man was pure evil. The kitchen looked empty, but he could still hear Ricky, so the man had to be close by.

He turned to head back to the living room when Ricky Preston suddenly appeared before him. Before Xavier could react, Ricky fired a gun and his chest exploded in agony. His gun clattered from his hands and fell uselessly to the floor. His hands clutched at his chest, coming away covered in warm, sticky blood. Suddenly woozy, he swayed, staggered backwards and collapsed to the floor.

"One down, one to go. Can't wait to do Annabelle." Ricky's sneering face hovered above him, and then he was gone.

* * * * *

6:32 P.M.

"Ryan, that was shots coming from Isabella's house." Paige's wide brown eyes turned to him as they pulled to a stop outside the address the old woman had given them. Grabbing the radio, she called for backup and an ambulance.

Ryan had heard them, too, and his heart had almost stopped.

He was almost positive that Isabella was living here, and he was terrified that the gunshot was Sofia's sister killing herself. Isabella was unbalanced. She'd already had a bad temper, and a sexual assault at the hands of some kids at her school had pushed her completely over the edge. While he personally couldn't care less if Isabella died, he could never forgive her for poisoning Sofia and making her think she was dying or for causing her to fall down the stairs. He knew Sofia would be devastated if her sister committed suicide.

If it wasn't a suicide, then it could also be a drug buy gone wrong. They already knew that Isabella was proficient with a gun—she'd shot her grandfather, so she was more than likely armed. Especially if she were selling drugs she'd stolen from the hospital.

Both he and Paige grabbed their guns as they jumped from the car and ran toward the front door of the dark brick house. The door was ajar and the house appeared empty as they stepped inside. Covering each other, they checked out the living room— which turned out to be empty.

They headed toward the door on the far side of the room. Paige pushed it open and then turned back to him. "There's a body," she murmured.

He scanned the room as Paige knelt beside the tall, brown haired man lying on the floor and pressed her fingers to his neck. "Dead?" he asked.

"No, I got a pulse," she replied. "And a gun." She gestured at a weapon lying about a foot away from the man.

He retrieved the gun. "Cuff him, and I'll finish checking the house."

Ryan was about to leave the room, when the man on the floor suddenly sat bolt upright, one hand snapping around Paige's wrist.

Ryan trained his gun at the man's head. "Police. You're under arrest. Let my partner go."

The man let out a sigh that seemed to be one of relief. "You're cops?"

"Yes," Ryan reconfirmed, wondering whether perhaps this guy had unwittingly gotten himself caught up in Isabella's games.

"Me too. Detective Xavier Montague. My ID is in my pocket." He gestured with one hand at his coat's front pocket, his other hand was still clamped around Paige's wrist.

With her free hand, Paige reached into his pocket and pulled out what looked like an ID. "He's telling the truth," Paige said to him, then turned to Detective Montague. "Want to let go of me now?"

"Oh, sorry." He released his grip on Paige, who flexed her hand and rotated her wrist, wincing. "Let me look at that." Detective Montague grasped her hand again, gently this time, and examined her wrist. "You should ice that. Again, I'm sorry, I didn't mean to hurt you. I just woke up and you were there, leaning over me, and I thought you were..."

Ryan exchanged glances with Paige when the man didn't continue. "You thought we were...?" Ryan prompted, finally lowering his gun so it no longer pointed at the man's head.

"I thought you were Ricky Preston," Detective Montague replied.

"Who's Ricky Preston?" Paige tugged her hand free from Detective Montague's grip and pushed to her feet.

"A serial killer I was forced to let go free," he explained. Noting the surprise on his and Paige's faces he added, "It's a long story."

Wondering how this Ricky Preston connected to Isabella, Ryan was about to ask when the other detective attempted to stand.

"Whoa," Ryan put a hand on Detective Montague's shoulder and held him down. "You got shot, you're bleeding, maybe you ought to stay still till paramedics get here."

He shook his head. "It's only a flesh wound, just skimmed me."

"You were unconscious when we came in." Paige looked skeptical.

"I don't like the sight of my own blood." Detective Montague looked embarrassed as he stood up. "I'm fine with other people's, but mine makes me woozy; I just fainted. Were you here looking for Ricky?"

"No, Isabella Everette," Ryan answered.

The detective's eyes grew wide, and Ryan realized for the first time that the man had different colored eyes; one was hazel and one was green. "The rich girl who killed her family?" he asked.

"The very one," Ryan told him. "This is her house, but I have no idea what she's doing with your serial killer." Paige was still cradling the arm Detective Montague had grabbed, and Ryan could already see bruises forming and the joint swelling. "You should go grab an ice pack from the first aid kit in the car," he told her.

Paige looked like she was going to argue, but then reluctantly nodded her agreement. "I'll be right back."

"Did you see Ricky leaving when you got here?" Detective Montague asked as Paige left the room.

"We arrived just as we heard shots; no one's left," Ryan replied.

"Then he's still here somewhere, probably your Isabella Everette, too. I heard voices when I first arrived."

Without a word, the two of them moved back into the living room, scanned it and then headed for the stairs. They had cleared the bathroom and one bedroom when they heard Paige's voice.

"Ryan?"

It sounded like his partner was still outside, so he went to a window to look out. Paige was standing in the middle of the yard. A man, Ryan presumed it was Ricky Preston, was standing behind her, his gun aimed at her head. Beside them stood Isabella.

"Don't let Ricky know I'm still alive," Detective Montague whispered as he darted out of the room.

"Hello, Ryan," Isabella looked up at him, her face white in the thin moonlight.

He ignored the man for the moment. "Isabella, Sofia misses you. She wants to see you. Let me take you to her."

"You mean let you arrest me?" Isabella's voice was serious, yet he detected a hint of sadness.

"You miss her, too," he continued. "Don't you want to see her? She's so sad that you've been gone. She worries about you. She wants to know that you're okay. She's doing better now; she's recovering well from the fall. She got her cast off a couple of days ago. Isabella, her stalker came back. He broke into our house two nights in a row. Sofia was there on her own. She's scared, Isabella. Seeing you will make her feel better. You want to see her, don't you?"

"Yes," Isabella acknowledged hesitantly.

"Then get your friend to let Paige go; Sofia would be devastated if anything happened to her." Ryan was praying that Isabella loved Sofia enough to convince Ricky Preston to let Paige go and to turn herself in.

"Ricky," Isabella turned to him, laying a hand on his arm, "let her go, she's my sister's friend."

"I'm not going to jail," he growled.

"Oh, yes, you are." Detective Montague suddenly appeared in the yard.

In a flurry of activity, Ricky Preston slammed his gun into Paige's temple and then threw her at Detective Montague. Stunned from the blow to her head, Paige stumbled, Detective Montague caught her before she hit the ground. Using that as a distraction, Ricky Preston grabbed Isabella and darted toward the white van parked in the drive. Balancing Paige with one arm, Detective Montague fired off a shot at the van as it rocketed out into the street. The rear window exploded, but the van didn't stop. Seconds later, it was out of sight.

Darting from the window, Ryan bounded down the stairs and out into the front yard just as Detective Montague was lowering Paige to sit on the grass.

"I can't believe he got away again," Detective Montague roared, stalking between his car and the house as though deciding whether he should try and chase Ricky and Isabella, even though he knew it was pointless. They were long gone.

He kneeled in front of Paige. "Are you okay?" Ryan asked her. She nodded, but blood was trickling from a wound on her temple and she appeared dazed. Paige made a feeble attempt at standing, but he easily held her in place. "Hey, I don't think that's a good idea. You need to stay still right now. Paramedics will be here any second."

"I'm fine," Paige protested weakly, pressing her good hand to her head, the one Detective Montague had injured earlier was resting limply in her lap.

"She okay?" Detective Montague squatted beside him.

"She's a little out of it, but I think she'll be fine." He gave the other man an appraising look. "You should sit down, too; you're still bleeding pretty badly."

He sunk to the ground next to Paige. "You never told me your names," Detective Montague murmured.

He kept a hand on his partner's shoulder to steady her. "Ryan Xander and Paige Hood," he filled in.

Sirens filled the air and Ryan let out a relieved breath; Paige and Detective Montague both needed to be checked out. And he wanted Isabella found ASAP. If Ricky Preston hadn't been there, Ryan was sure he could have talked Isabella into turning herself in. As it was, he'd nearly had her convinced. But now she was on the run again. Only this time with a killer. Sure, Isabella was one, too, but he had a bad feeling about Ricky Preston. Sofia's sister wasn't safe with him. And as much as he didn't want to, he cared because Sofia did. They needed to find Isabella before it was too late.

JANUARY 12TH

Xavier couldn't believe that Ricky Preston had slipped through his fingers again.

Once again, Ricky had managed to make sure that he had a hostage between him and the police. There had been no way for Xavier to get a shot at Ricky without hitting Paige Hood.

And, once again, Ricky had managed to use a distraction to make sure he could get away. When Ricky had hit Paige over the head and thrown her at him, Xavier had no choice but to catch the woman before she hit the ground and caused herself more injuries.

By the time he'd maneuvered Paige so he could keep a hold of her with one arm and keep her on her feet, Ricky had already been in the van. He'd still fired off a shot, hoping that he might be able to take Ricky out, or at the very least take out the van so Ricky lost his getaway vehicle. Unfortunately, he'd missed out on both. The van had disappeared before he had a chance to jump in his car and follow it.

Ryan had insisted that his partner go immediately in an ambulance to the hospital to get checked out. Paige had been too woozy to do more than offer a few weak protests, and had been quickly bundled into an ambulance by some paramedics and taken away. He had refused to come to the hospital until he'd had a chance to confer with Ryan about Isabella Everette and what possible reason there could be for her and Ricky Preston to team up.

When he'd finally agreed to climb into an ambulance himself a couple of hours had passed by. As he had predicted, the gunshot wound was little more than a flesh wound from where the bullet had grazed his shoulder. Obviously, Ricky Preston was not a good shot, or maybe the dark had messed with his aim. Or perhaps he was simply playing another game—toying with Annabelle to cause her maximum terror and pain.

First thing he'd done after the gash had been stitched was to go and check on Paige. He felt awful for hurting her, and was hoping he had not broken her wrist. When he'd come to and seen a body hovering over him his immediate reaction had been to assume it was Ricky.

He'd found Paige dozing in a bed, waiting to be released since she had refused to spend the night, with her anxious husband hovering at her bedside. Thankfully, her wrist was not broken, just badly bruised, and he had apologized a few more times, until she'd cut him off with a tired smile. The doctors had also determined that she did not have a concussion, just a bad bump to the head. They'd given her a couple of stitches to close the gash and some painkillers and told her to take it easy for the next few days. Xavier highly doubted that Paige intended to follow that directive.

Now he was sitting waiting for Kate and Annabelle to come and pick him up and take him home. When he'd called Kate back at Isabella Everette's house after the paramedics and officers had arrived, he'd asked her not to tell Annabelle that he'd been shot until he could do it in person. He was concerned that Annabelle would work herself into hysteria about it if she couldn't see for herself that he was okay. However, it seemed that Annabelle had convinced herself that something had happened to him when he didn't come home by nightfall and hadn't called to tell her why, and Kate had had no choice but to let her know what had happened.

A sharp gasp sent him spinning toward the door.

Annabelle was standing there. Her near white eyes were wide

with shock. Even from across the room he could see that her whole body was shaking.

"Belle, I'm fine, really." He walked toward her. "Look," he grasped her chin and tilted her face toward his shoulder; he'd deliberately left off his shirt so she could see that his wound was small and superficial.

Annabelle didn't move or utter a sound. It was like she was frozen.

"Belle, I'm really okay." He took her gently by the arm and led her to the bed, sitting her down on it. "Honey, there's nothing for you to worry about. I'm completely fine, it barely even hurts," he told her, not just to reassure her but because it was true.

Annabelle just stared blankly into space. She was barely even blinking.

Starting to get a little alarmed, he took her face in both hands and leaned over, trying to force her to meet his gaze. "Belle, look at me. Annabelle," he repeated more forcefully when she didn't react. "Come on, honey, you're scaring me." He had expected her to be upset, but not this upset once she saw that he was all right. When she still didn't move, he kissed her—softly and gently. At first she didn't respond but then ever so faintly she kissed him back.

When he broke away from her, he could see her eyes had cleared a little. She whispered something, but her voice was too quiet for him to hear what she'd said.

"What was that, honey?" he asked, brushing her hair back from her face and tucking it behind her ear.

Her eyes finally sought his, and in them he could see tears shimmering. "It's my fault," she murmured.

He was confused. "What's your fault?"

"That Ricky shot you." Like a switch had been flicked, she suddenly turned frantic, her hands all but clawing at his body. "I'm sorry," she babbled. "Are you okay? There's blood. And you have stitches. I'm sorry. I'm sorry."

"Hey, hey," he soothed, catching her hands and pinning them against his chest. "What do you mean, it's your fault?"

"It's because of me that he's still out there." Tears began to spill down her cheeks.

"Why would you think that?" He cupped her face in his hand and brushed his thumb across her cheekbone, tracing the pale pink scar that Ricky had given her eight months ago.

"That's what he told me." She was crying now. "He used me to get away, and it worked. You came running to find me and he got away. And now he's still out there. Killing people. Hurting people. He could have killed you. He could have taken you away from me. What would I have done then? What would I do without you?" The last was a hiccupping gulp as she began to sob in earnest.

Drawing her against his chest, Xavier wrapped his arms around her and stroked her hair, attempting to calm her. "Shh," he whispered, "it's not true, baby. It is not your fault. And I'm not going anywhere. I'm right here and I'm fine. No one is going to take me away from you. Not Ricky and not anyone else."

Annabelle continued to cry, so he sat on the bed beside her and pulled her into his lap, rocking her gently. He had been so caught up in blaming himself for the fact that Ricky Preston was still on the run that he hadn't realized just how much Annabelle blamed herself. She had told him in the hospital after he'd found her, close to death in her parents' airtight wine cellar where Ricky had locked her, that it was her fault, but she hadn't mentioned it since.

Ricky had abducted her with the express purpose of using her as an insurance policy. If the police had been on to him then he had her locked away where she had a limited air supply so that they had no choice but to let him go to save her life. It had worked perfectly. While he had her tied up Ricky had explained to her his plan to use her as a distraction. His betrayal had been like a sharp knife in Annabelle's heart. He had been her only friend—

at least she had believed they were friends—and she had opened up to him in a way she hadn't with any other person.

He was furious with himself for being so distracted with his own guilt that he had been oblivious to Annabelle's. He was determined not to make that mistake again. With Annabelle so vulnerable and fragile right now, he had to make her his absolute priority. "Baby, don't cry anymore," he implored her. He hated to see Annabelle a quivering mess in his arms; it broke his heart.

But Annabelle continued to sob, her arms wrapped so tightly around his neck as she clung to him that it was pulling painfully on his stitches. Not that he was going to tell her that. If Annabelle needed to be in his arms right now, then that was where she was going to be.

"Is everything okay in here?" The doctor who had stitched his shoulder earlier suddenly appeared in the doorway.

"She's a little upset," Xavier replied, thinking that had to be the understatement of the century.

"She looks more than a little upset." The doctor smiled and crossed to the bed. "Let me take a look at her."

Annabelle didn't protest as he slid her off his lap and onto the bed. She just squeezed her eyes closed and clutched at his hand. "I'm not going anywhere," he assured her.

The doctor checked Annabelle's vitals while he watched anxiously. This was exactly why he hadn't wanted Annabelle to find out about the shooting until he could be the one to tell her.

"Is it unusual for her to become this hysterical?" the doctor asked.

"No, she suffered a severe trauma a few months ago. She has a Xanax prescription, but I don't have any on me," he explained.

"Okay," the doctor nodded. "I assume she's seeing a psychiatrist?"

"Yes," Xavier confirmed, intending to call Dr. Hastings again first thing in the morning.

"She needs rest; do you have any sleeping pills?"

"We have Ambien," he replied.

"All right, then take her home, give her some sleeping pills and put her to bed. If she's not any better in the morning, either take her to her doctor or bring her back here to the hospital. I'll go and get someone to help you get her to the car."

"I can manage her." Xavier moved to pick her up.

"You can't carry her." The doctor nodded at his shoulder. "You'll pull your stitches out. I'll go grab a wheelchair."

While he waited, Xavier perched on the edge of the bed and pulled Annabelle back into his arms. They were close to catching Ricky Preston. He could feel it. Ricky teaming up with Isabella Everette was going to be his downfall. He was distracted, he had other priorities, someone else to focus on. Sooner or later he'd slip up, and then they'd get him.

* * * * *

12:12 A.M.

"Maybe we should go and see Paige," Sofia said to Ryan.

"No, Elias was taking her home and putting her to bed; she needs rest right now, you can call her in the morning," Ryan replied, rinsing out their mugs and setting them in the dishwasher.

"Are you sure she's okay?" she asked anxiously.

He crouched in front of her. "Paige is going to be fine. She has a bump on the head and a few stitches but no concussion, and her wrist is bruised and swollen but not broken. Her doctors want her to take it easy for a few days, but if I know Paige, she'll be at work in the morning."

"What about her stalker situation? Have Jack and Rose made any progress?" Ryan had told her about the guy who Paige had arrested whose friends were now harassing Paige.

"Not yet, but we'll find who's stalking Paige just like we'll find who's stalking you," Ryan assured her.

"I'm worried about her." Sofia reached for Ryan's hands and clutched them tightly. "What she went through as a kid and now having to go through it again."

"It's going to be okay, honey; it really is." Ryan kissed her forehead. "You and Paige are tough; we'll get you both through this. Now up to bed, you're wiped out; you shouldn't have waited up for me to get home."

"Yeah, okay," she agreed, she was wiped out. Jack had come by and hung out with her, or babysat her, she supposed might be a more accurate description. He had told her several times to go get some rest, that he'd stay until Ryan got home, but after Ryan's call explaining his evening, she had needed to see for herself that he was okay before she'd be able to close her eyes and go to sleep.

"Honey?" Ryan squeezed her hands.

Realizing that she'd zoned out, she focused her gaze on him, and suddenly it hit her that she could have lost him tonight. With her parents, grandfather, and brothers all gone, Ryan was the only family she had now. What would she do if something happened to him? Tugging her hands free from his, she threw her arms around his neck and let herself fall against him—trying to convince herself that he was okay.

"Sofia, I'm fine; I really am." Ryan seemingly read her mind. "Now you, off to bed." He picked her up, carried her through to the hall and set her on her feet at the bottom of the stairs. "I'm just going to check down here and then I'll be up."

Leaving Ryan to check and re-check every lock on every door and every window, Sofia started the long trek up the stairs. Her leg was aching, but a little less than it had the day before. Bit by bit it was getting better. Using the wall for support, since her cane was still downstairs, she made her way to the bedroom. Too tired to change into her pajamas, she dropped onto the bed on top of the covers.

Ryan appeared in the doorway. "I'll be glad once that security system's installed."

"Yeah, me too." Sofia was glad she'd let Jack stay with her tonight, she didn't want a repeat of last night's events, but she didn't want to have to have someone here to babysit her every night. "I wish I knew who he was." It would make things so much easier if she knew who was stalking her so Ryan could simply go and arrest him.

"Me too." Ryan sat beside her on the bed, her pajamas in hand.

"I'm too tired to change," she told him, letting her eyes fall closed.

"Then just rest." He hooked an arm around her shoulders and sat her up, her eyes opened as he tugged her arms through the sleeves of her sweatshirt and pulled it over her head, replacing it with her fuzzy pink pajama top.

"You don't have to dress me." She reached for her pajama bottoms.

"Shh," he admonished, giving her a quick kiss. "I want to."

Laying her back down, he tugged off her sweatpants and put on the fuzzy pink ones that matched the top. Then he removed his own clothes, threw on the sweatpants he slept in and climbed into bed beside her, pulling the blankets up to cover them both.

She snuggled against Ryan's side, resting her head on his shoulder. "Night," she murmured.

"Night," he whispered back, kissing the top of her head, and switching off the lamp on the table beside the bed.

Closing her eyes, Sofia tried to turn her mind off and let sleep trickle in. But exhausted as she was she couldn't seem to clear the jumbled thoughts that clambered through her head. Ryan could have been killed today. And if he had, she would have been completely without a family. Sure Ryan's family loved her, but without him to tether her to them, soon they too would slip from her life.

Of course, she knew that Ryan had a dangerous job, but this was the first time that it had been thrown so blatantly in her face. It was a genuine possibility that he could be killed, any day at any time. If they were going to spend the rest of their lives together, then she was going to have to get used to that. Could she? Could she handle the uncertainty that went with his job?

Determinedly, she attempted to push all such thoughts away. All she wanted was to shut down for a few hours and forget about all their troubles. Try as she might, though, sleep remained tantalizingly out of reach.

After what felt like hours, she opened her eyes. The room was dark, and thin moonlight shone through the window. Ryan was quiet and still beside her, his chest rising and falling evenly beneath her hand which rested on it.

Not wanting to disturb him and glad he was getting some much-needed sleep, Sofia gave up on sleep for herself and moved to climb out from under the covers to head downstairs and make herself a hot drink, when a hand clamped around her wrist. She stifled a scream when she realized it was only Ryan—apparently he wasn't asleep after all.

"Where are you going?" he asked, his voice tinted with sleep. Maybe he had been asleep and her moving had woken him.

"Downstairs to get a drink; you stay here," she told him. He needed his rest, and she wanted him sharp and on his game so that the chances of anything happening to him at work were as low as possible. If he were tired and distracted with worry about her, then he was opening himself up to all sorts of dangers.

"Can't sleep?" He reached over and switched the light back on, both of them blinked at the sudden brightness.

She shook her head. "You should, though; you need to sleep."

"So do you." He tugged on her so she would lay back down at his side, then wrapped his arm around her shoulders. "What's bothering you?"

She shook her head again. Sofia could feel tears welling up in her eyes and she didn't want to cry in front of Ryan. Even though pretty much every guy on the planet felt uncomfortable around a crying woman, she had cried all over Ryan so much the last few months that she didn't want to upset him by doing it again. Especially after the night he'd had.

"Baby, are you crying?" he asked gently, stroking her hair back from her face so he could see her better.

"No," she whispered, trying in vain to control her tears even as she could feel them spilling out onto Ryan's bare chest.

"Yes, you are. What's up, honey? Talk to me. Please."

"You could have died tonight," she cried.

"No, baby, that's not true." Ryan was rubbing small circles on her back, attempting to console her.

"Paige had a gun pointed at her head, and that other guy, Detective Montague, got shot," she countered.

"I told you that Paige is okay," Ryan reminded her.

"I know, but what if that man had shot her? What if Isabella hadn't been there?"

"Ahh," Ryan said as though he'd just solved his own mystery. "You're upset about Isabella."

Ryan had told her about Isabella when he'd gotten home, but Sofia had been refusing to think about her sister. To know that Ryan had been close enough to Isabella to see her and talk to her, to know that he had almost managed to convince her to turn herself in, only for Isabella to disappear again was too much right now.

"We're going to get her, soon," Ryan assured her. "We're close now. She loves you and doesn't want to hurt you; she might turn herself in all on her own."

"You really think so?" Sofia looked up imploringly at Ryan through tear-filled eyes.

"Yes, I really think so. I know you're worried about her..."

"She's with a murderer," she interrupted. "I know that sounds like a stupid thing to worry about given that Isabella is one, too, but I'm worried about her. What if he hurts her?"

"I don't think she's in any danger." Ryan sounded confident.

"Did she say anything about the baby?" Sofia was extremely

concerned about her baby aunt who had been abducted by Isabella. Her sister was in no state to be raising a child. What if she hurt the baby? Maybe even unintentionally in one of her fits of rage.

"No, she didn't, but her neighbor at her old house used to babysit sometimes and said that the baby was doing great and is a real sweetie. And some of her colleagues said she was a devoted mother. She named the baby Sophie," he told her.

"She named her after me?" Sofia was touched.

"She really loves you." Ryan hugged her tighter. "I know she shows it in an odd way sometimes, but she loves you more than she loves anyone else on the planet."

She choked on a sob. Hearing about her sister was worse than not knowing where she was and what she was doing. This was making her miss Isabella more and more. And yet, still she wanted to know everything that Ryan had seen and heard. "Did she look okay?"

"She looked fine." Ryan was brushing away tears from her cheeks even as more were falling.

"And what did you say to her?"

"I told her that you missed her and that you were worried about her. I said you wanted to see her and I told her about your stalker and that seeing her would really help you right now," Ryan explained.

"And...and what did she say?" Sofia asked hesitantly.

"I asked her if she wanted to see you and she said she did. I really think she'd have turned herself in if Ricky Preston hadn't grabbed her."

"What if he hurts her, Ryan?" she whimpered. Sofia didn't think she could cope if another member of her family was killed.

"I don't think he will, baby." Ryan tightened his grip on her. "I still think there's a good chance that once she thinks about it she'll realize that she can't run forever and that it'll be better for her, and for you, to just end it now. Even if she doesn't turn herself in, her changing her MO and working with this Ricky Preston changes things. Her focus is divided now. She'll start making mistakes. And that means we'll catch her. I know this has been hell for you, but you just need to hang in there a little longer and it'll all be over."

She laid her head back down on Ryan's shoulder, trying to convince herself that what Ryan said was true.

* * * * *

12:22 A.M.

Could what Ryan said be true?

Isabella hardly dared to hope that it was.

He had said that Sofia missed her and that her sister was worried about her. Isabella had been sure that Sofia was so angry with her for what she'd done to their family that she would never want to see her again. She also thought that Sofia was still scared of her. The last time they'd been together, it had been a disaster. Sofia could have died in that fall. Isabella had had to convince herself that her sister wanted nothing to do with her so that she could accept that the only relationship they would have in the future was for Isabella to watch Sofia from afar.

But Ryan said that Sofia wanted to see her.

Maybe despite her sister's anger and fear, she still wanted the two of them to be sisters. Maybe Sofia wanted things to go back to the way they'd been before. Isabella wasn't sure that it ever could, but more than anything, she wanted to try.

She was lonely on her own with only baby Sophie for company. Of course, she loved her baby sister, and wanted to raise the child as her own, but what kind of role model was she for a little girl? Obviously not a good one considering the murders she had committed in the past and the fact that she had no intention of stopping killing any time soon. Sofia would be a much better mother to Sophie than Isabella could ever hope to be.

Isabella was wondering whether she should do as Ryan told her. Maybe she should just end it all and turn herself in. She didn't want Sofia to be sad. She didn't want to cause her sister stress and worry, especially considering that Sofia's stalker had apparently returned. Isabella remembered how terrified her sister had been over her stalker. Her sister needed her family right now. Maybe she should do it. She could right now. She could go and get Sophie from the sitter's and go straight to Sofia's. She could see her sister again, face to face, after five months of missing her, in just a couple of hours.

"I take it you know that guy," Ricky spoke, breaking the oppressive silence in the car.

They had been driving in circles ever since he had dragged her into the car. When he'd flung her in and then jumped in after her, he had been concerned that someone would follow them so had told her that they were going to drive for a while before heading for his place. Then they had lapsed into silence, and neither had spoken a word until now.

"He's my sister's boyfriend," she replied.

"He's a cop," Ricky added.

"Mmm hmm," she nodded. "He and my sister met last August; he and his partner were the ones who worked the murders. My sister and Ryan decided they liked each other and now they're dating."

"He has a vested interest in catching you, then," Ricky observed.

"I guess he does," Isabella agreed. She knew that Ryan would stop at nothing to arrest her. Even though neither she nor Sofia liked any member of their family, Sofia was upset that they were all dead. And if Sofia was upset, then Ryan was upset. Isabella was under no illusion that her sister wanted her to go free. She knew that even though Sofia might miss her and want to see her again, she still believed that Isabella deserved to be punished for her crimes.

"He also has a vested interest in not killing you," Ricky mused.

She turned to study Ricky's profile. "So next time, you plan to use me as a human shield like you used Paige?"

It had been a shock to see Paige standing by the car out in front of her home. Of course, it had been a shock when someone came knocking on her door and Ricky had flown into a panic when he realized who it was. Apparently Detective Montague and Ricky had history. After Ricky had shot the man, he had dragged her toward the door. But then they'd spied a car pulling to a stop on the street in front of the house. So, they had hidden in the hall closet as two people came barging inside. While the others had been preoccupied in the kitchen, she and Ricky had slipped unnoticed from the house.

They had been about to climb into the car when Paige came outside, cradling one hand. At the sight of her sister's boyfriend's partner, Isabella had gasped and been frozen in place. Ricky had demanded she tell him who the woman was, and once he realized that she was a cop, he had freaked. He'd put his gun to Paige's head and told her he'd kill her in a heartbeat if she didn't do exactly what he told her.

Isabella hadn't liked seeing a gun pointed at Paige, and she didn't like the idea that Ricky would do the same to her to save himself.

"Your sister's friend is fine," Ricky told her. "At worst, I gave her a mild concussion. You asked me not to shoot her and I didn't. You should be grateful. If you hadn't asked, she'd be dead right now. Your Detective Xander may not want you dead, but let me assure you that Xavier Montague wants me dead more than he wants to breathe."

Ricky obviously loved killing, and for him to have spared Paige simply because she asked him to was oddly moving.

He took his eyes off the road to glance at her. "You were

going to turn yourself in," he stated. "What your sister's boyfriend said was getting to you. If I hadn't stepped in, then you would have let him arrest you."

"I thought my sister didn't want anything to do with me anymore," she explained. "I hurt her. Not just by what I did, but Ryan was on to me, and he told Sofia, she came looking for proof that I was innocent and I had to stop her. I knocked her out, but she was already sick before that. It was a mistake, I scared her, and then she fell down some stairs. I thought she hated me. When Ryan said she missed me, that she wanted to see me, it made me want to do whatever I had to just to see her again. I love her."

"So are you going to do it?" Ricky demanded, a hint of anger and reproach tinting his voice and making it hard.

"I don't know," she answered honestly. "I love Sofia, but I have to think of Sophie. If I turn myself in, I've got to give her up. Even though I know Sofia would be a better mother to her, I love her, too, and I'm not sure I could stand not being a part of her life."

"You have a kid?" Ricky sounded shocked.

"No, she's my sister—and my aunt. But I killed our mother and her father—my grandfather. And my father and her brothers, she only has me and Sofia left."

"You have one messed up family," Ricky chuckled.

"Who's Annabelle? You said that you miss her and that you think about her a lot. Is she a relative? Is she your ex?" The stab of jealousy surprised her.

That sent Ricky into peals of laughter. "Annabelle was my neighbor," he replied once he'd calmed down. "She thought we were friends—she didn't have any others—so I was the one stuck listening to her whining. Day after day she'd sit in my living room and I would pretend to care about what she was saying. Have you ever hated someone so much that everything they do annoys the hell out of you? Well, that's how I felt about Annabelle. She was so stuck up that all I could think about whenever I was around her was how much fun it would be to knock her down a peg."

"Did you rape Annabelle?" she asked seriously, already knowing the answer but hoping she was wrong.

"Would it bother you if I did?" he asked mildly.

"Yes. I was sexually assaulted by some kids at my school," she shivered involuntarily at the memory. "You're a rapist," she stated.

"I am," he agreed.

"Are you going to rape me?" She wondered what she would do if he attempted it. Would she kill him? Probably not. Although she would kill anyone else who tried it in a heartbeat. Would she try to stop him? Isabella was shocked to discover that she honestly couldn't say that she would. She *wanted* this man to touch her. She wanted more than that. She wanted him to sleep with her.

"Honey, there's no need for me to rape you; you're going to willingly give yourself to me," he drawled confidently, pulling to a stop outside a large house, surrounded by an even larger garden.

A warm tingling feeling started in her stomach. Nervous and excited, Isabella allowed Ricky to take her hand and pull her from the car and through the garden. Once inside, he didn't even ask. Before she could process what was happening, they were in the bedroom and Ricky was removing her clothes.

There was a moment where Isabella was anxious about what Ricky would think of her naked body. But the glint in his eyes and the hungry groan that emanated from his mouth were enough to assuage her fears.

As Ricky pushed her down onto the bed and climbed on top of her, he paused to whisper in her ear, "Say the word and I'll kill those kids who hurt you."

Disturbingly, at least Isabella supposed she should be disturbed by it, Ricky's offer to get revenge on the kids who had assaulted her was touching. She couldn't turn herself in. Not now. Not when she'd just been given the man of her dreams.

She could have it all.

Isabella was sure of it.

Maybe she could give Sophie to Sofia, and then figure out a way to keep both in her life.

She'd make it work.

She had to.

All her dreams had just come true and she couldn't give that up.

* * * * *

7:54 A.M.

They all looked tired.

That was the first thing Ryan thought as he walked into the conference room. The room was already mostly full, now that the two cases—Isabella's and Ricky Preston's—had joined together, the number of people working the cases had doubled. Belinda was there, and so was Stephanie and Frankie. He also saw Diane Jolly, who worked crime scene with Stephanie. Ryan had worked with her a few times but didn't know her all that well. Ryan knew they were still waiting for the medical examiner who had been dealing with the Ricky Preston case, Billy Newton. He had worked with Billy plenty of times and admired how the father of seven, which included three sets of twins, managed to make family time a priority.

They were also waiting on Paige and Xavier Montague. Ryan wondered whether perhaps the two were going to follow their doctors' advice and take it easy the next few days. He highly doubted it.

Just as Belinda was about to start their morning meeting, Xavier bundled through the door, moving smoothly without a hint of the gunshot wound in his shoulder. Ryan had spent several hours talking with the other detective last night and already liked him. Xavier was calm and confident and had admitted that he was precariously balancing his work and home life now, as his girlfriend Annabelle struggled to cope with the traumatic events that had brought her and Xavier together.

Ryan had suggested that Annabelle spend some time with Sofia. He had a feeling that Sofia would be able to help Annabelle learn to deal with what she'd been through. It would also make sure Annabelle was safe. His and Sofia's house was going to be bustling with people all day as the crew installing the security system would be there working.

"All right," Belinda announced, "let's assume Paige is either staying home today or running late . . ."

"Let's not," Paige offered a tired smile as she entered the room and dropped into the nearest chair.

"How's your head?" Stephanie frowned slightly at Paige, her face clearly saying she thought Paige belonged at home in bed—a feeling Ryan echoed.

"Sore, but I'm fine," Paige replied firmly.

"And your wrist?" Xavier asked uncomfortably. He obviously still felt bad about accidently hurting her.

"It's all right," Paige assured him. "How's your shoulder?"

"It's all right." He grinned, "Didn't your doctor tell you to rest?"

"Didn't your doctor tell you the same thing?" she grinned back.

"Yep, but I had no intention of listening to her. I'm surprised your husband let you out the door this morning. Last night he looked like he was ready to lock you up," Xavier said.

Rolling her eyes, she stated, "Yeah we kind of disagreed on that."

"Did you sleep last night?" Ryan asked Paige. Right now he was more concerned about her stalker than the bump to her head.

"Yes, Ryan," she replied.

"I mean, did you sleep *well?*" He knew Paige would know what he meant without him mentioning the nightmares. He was sure she wouldn't want the others to know about that.

"Yes, Ryan," she replied again.

"And you ate breakfast?" he continued his assessment.

"Yes, Ryan," this time she rolled her eyes at him.

"And no more issues?" He hoped that whoever was stalking Paige had backed off. Jack and Rose were still looking into it, but so far, without any luck. His partner wasn't going to like it, but they were going to have to fill Belinda in on what was going on.

"No, Ryan. Now can we please focus on work? We do have two killers to find," Paige was all but glaring at him.

"Just wanted to make sure you're okay," Ryan said mildly, not taking his partner's frustration personally. He knew if their positions were reversed, Paige would be asking him the exact same questions he was asking her.

"Well, I'm fine and you're not my mother," Paige grumbled.

"All right, we've established Paige is doing okay despite the fact she looks like garbage," Belinda shot a smile at Paige who rolled her eyes again. "So how about Detective Montague gives us a brief rundown of Ricky Preston's case and then we can give him a quick rundown of Isabella's."

"Eight months ago," Xavier began, "the Englewood family was killed in their sleep, all except twenty-three-year-old Annabelle, who we originally assumed had committed the murders, since she was the only survivor and had only relatively minor injuries. Only forensics hinted otherwise."

"We didn't find the murder weapon on the premises," Diane Jolly took over the narrative. "There was no blood on her other than her own. No clothes that had been recently washed. She had blood on her feet but it had been painted on; we found horse hairs mixed with the blood."

"Then over the next few days, three more families were killed—the Jenners, Ranklings, and the Littletons—all with one person left alive," Xavier continued. "We had a few suspects but it turned out to be the Englewoods' next-door neighbor, who had been the one to call nine-one-one when he claimed he saw someone with a knife in the house. We eventually realized it was impossible for him to have seen what he claimed and realized he was our killer. By then he'd kidnapped Annabelle and used her as a distraction because he had one last family to kill. We got there in time to save Annabelle, and Barney and Vanessa Adams, but Ricky Preston disappeared."

"What led you to think that these recent newlywed killings were Ricky Preston's work?" Belinda asked.

"Ricky Preston showed an inordinate interest in blood, and the Landers and Mendleson crime scenes seemed reminiscent of Ricky's previous ones," Xavier explained.

"Then we lucked out and got a fingerprint at the Mendleson house," Diane added.

"He's still leaving one family member behind," Xavier continued. "He picks couples from the hotel where he works, stalks them, then goes into their houses at night and waits until the couple falls asleep. Then he drugs them and ties them up; then once they're awake, he kills one of them with an axe."

"What's he use to drug them?" Ryan asked, wondering whether that could be the link between Ricky and Isabella.

"Sodium thiopental," Diane replied.

"Isabella, too," Ryan took that as confirmation of how the two had connected. "She stole them from the hospital where she's been working."

"I thought Isabella Everette killed her family. She seemed like a mission oriented killer; who's she killing now?" Xavier asked.

"She killed a Roman Hitacheel. He was a friend of the family and we think she may have killed him because he cheated on his wife. We think that may be her new mission. We were hoping to get ahead of her by asking her sister to give us the names of any other family friends who were cheating on their wives. Sofia gave us quite a long list. We have people checking them out and warning them to be careful. Isabella impersonated Roman Hitacheel's mistress to convince him to meet her, so she may continue to employ that tactic," Ryan explained.

"So let's say that Ricky meets Isabella buying the sodium thiopental," Xavier began, "but why are the two of them still together? Isabella is seventeen and Ricky is in his mid-forties. I can't see what the two of them would have in common."

Ryan shrugged, "As far as I know Isabella has never even dated, but maybe meeting another murderer intrigued her."

A knock sounded at the door and a moment later a curly head popped in. "Excuse me," Detective Tilton announced, "but you asked us to check out an Arthur Bentley."

Ryan nodded. Arthur Bentley was one of the men on Sofia's list of possible men Isabella may go after.

"His wife's caregiver tried to report him missing when he disappeared in the middle of the night—the night before last. He left his disabled wife home alone. The caregiver said it wasn't unusual for him to do that, but that he always turned up the following night. When he didn't return last night, she got worried. Mr. Bentley also owns an apartment so we sent officers to check it out. Even though he hasn't been missing forty-eight hours we thought it best to check it out given you're concerned he could be in danger. They found him about ten minutes ago."

He sighed—another victim of Isabella's. "Okay, we'll head straight over there. Xavier, you coming? Ricky was with Isabella last night; he may have been involved in Arthur Bentley's death."

"Yeah, I'm coming," Xavier stood, wincing slightly as he jostled his shoulder.

"Let me know how it goes," Belinda told them.

"We will," Ryan agreed. "Steph, Frankie, you two coming, as well?"

"Yep," Stephanie nodded. "Diane, you in?"

"I'm in," Diane confirmed.

They all filed from the room, he and Paige pausing at their

desks on their way. Ryan saw the note at the same moment his partner did. "Is that what I think it is?" he asked her as she picked it up.

Paige didn't need to answer. Her shaking hands and the haunted gleam in her brown eyes confirmed, without having to speak a word, that it was another message from the person stalking her.

* * * * *

8:36 A.M.

Xavier was actually feeling positive this morning.

Ricky Preston was back within his grasp. Sofia Everette seemed like she might be able to help Annabelle. And he had managed to get a good night's sleep. Every so often too many nights without proper sleep caught up with him, and he finally just crashed.

Thankfully, Annabelle, too, had slept well last night. He'd given her a sleeping pill as soon as he'd gotten her home and into bed. Then she'd fallen asleep in his arms; he'd drifted off shortly after. This morning she had seemed calmer, more together, although withdrawn. When he'd suggested to her that she spend the day with someone who might understand what she was going through she had raised a skeptical eyebrow but hadn't resisted. Xavier was hoping that Sofia would know what to say to Annabelle to help her.

Xavier was enjoying working with Ryan Xander, and Paige Hood, too. He was even considering transferring to work out of this precinct after this case was finished. Without Rose, work just hadn't felt like work. This was the first time he had felt like his old self since Rose went on maternity leave.

He parked his car behind Ryan's in front of a block of apartments—one of which belonged to Arthur Bentley. "Hey," he greeted them as they all climbed out into the chilly winter morning.

"Hey," Ryan replied.

Paige looked distracted and didn't say a word. It didn't take a genius to figure out that something was going on with her—something besides the injuries she'd received last night. Ryan had been asking her questions earlier this morning in some sort of code that she apparently understood. Xavier hadn't needed to understand the specifics; the concern for his partner had been evident in Ryan's face. And something that had been left on her desk had obviously upset her. Xavier hoped that they'd tell him what was going on if they needed help.

"Looks like Stephanie and Diane beat us here," Ryan gestured to the crime scene van already parked nearby.

"I'm not sure forensics are going to turn out to be too helpful in Ricky's case," Xavier told them. "Ricky would rather die than go to jail. And he's more than willing to take out anyone around him. He won't go down without a fight, and he'll take out as many people as he can along the way. When we find him, you need to be prepared for that. He's more likely to try and kill me than you two, because he knows killing me will devastate Annabelle. But if he thinks he can get some mileage for pain from her out of killing either or both of you, then he'll gladly do it. I'm surprised he didn't shoot Paige last night. That would have been a better distraction than just hurting her." He glanced at Paige, but she had fallen behind them and seemed lost in her own thoughts. "Is she okay?" he asked Ryan quietly.

He followed Xavier's gaze, his brows furrowing in concern. "No, she's not."

"Anything I can help with?"

Ryan looked back to Xavier, "Someone's been harassing her, sending her threatening messages. I have people looking into it."

"Should she be out in the field? She seems a little..." He paused wanting to be tactful, finally settling on, "...preoccupied. I don't want her to get hurt."

"Paige is a good cop; I know she seems preoccupied now, but she'll pull it together," Ryan sounded only mildly irritated, and a little unsure. "And if she doesn't, I'll make sure she stays at her desk," he added with a sigh. "I won't let her get herself—or anyone else—killed."

"What are we chitchatting about?" Paige suddenly appeared before them. From the looks on their faces, it was apparently obvious. "About me," she groaned. "Did you tell him?" she demanded, glaring at Ryan.

"I told him someone's stalking you." Ryan seemed unfazed by his partner's annoyance.

"Great, so now he can worry about me, too. Don't we have enough to worry about?" With a glare that now included them both, she turned and stalked toward the apartment building, disappearing inside Arthur Bentley's apartment.

"She'll get over it," Ryan announced as they followed her. "We just told our boss before we came here, and my brother and his partner are looking into it, so it's not like it's some kind of secret. Besides, you're working with us now, so you need to know."

"Hey, guys," Frankie joined them. "You been in yet?"

"Nope, although Paige is in there," Ryan replied. "Diane and Stephanie, too."

"Any idea what the cause of death is?" the medical examiner asked.

"No," Ryan answered Frankie.

"Then let's go check it out," Frankie paused at the door to slip booties over her shoes.

Doing the same, he and Ryan followed her into the apartment. Paige met them, her face grim. "It's pretty bad," she told them.

The smell of blood, which had been strong from the second they entered the apartment, was almost overwhelming as they walked into the bedroom. The scene before them was so reminiscent of Ricky's previous crime scenes that Xavier could practically feel his presence in the room.

Once more the room was bright red with blood.

The floor, walls and ceiling were covered with it. Two sets of footprints tracked around the room. The man on the bed looked like every drop of blood that had been inside him was now all over him.

"Looks like they cleaned up in the bathroom," Diane popped her head through a door on the adjacent wall. "They did a pretty poor job, though. They obviously weren't worried about us finding it; there's blood in the shower and all over the floor. Seems like they just cleaned themselves off and then left."

"I got fingerprints, too," Stephanie added. "I already sent a set back to the lab so we can confirm that they're Isabella and Ricky's."

While the prints would give confirmation, Xavier already knew that the two had committed this murder, seemingly together. They were a team now. He still couldn't comprehend what would have drawn them together. He could buy that it was the drugs that had led them to first meet, but what had made them start killing together?

"Ricky kills with an axe, right?" Paige asked. "That certainly looks like he used an axe," she gestured at the dismembered arms and legs that lay discarded on the carpet beside the bed.

"Looks like it," Frankie agreed.

"So they combined methods," Xavier mused. "Isabella drowned Roman Hitacheel in his own blood, right?"

"Mmhmm," Ryan nodded. "She drew it, like when you donate blood."

"That wouldn't have been enough blood for Ricky," Xavier explained. "He's obsessed with the sight of blood."

"So he used his axe to remove Arthur Bentley's limbs and that's how they got the blood to drown him," Frankie pointed to Arthur's blood splattered face, and the dried pools around his head.

"It's official," Stephanie announced. "Your two killers are now working as a team. Fingerprints confirm that both Isabella Everette and Ricky Preston were here in this room."

* * * * *

10:14 A.M.

"Hi there. Sorry about all the people; we're having a security system installed," a pretty redhead smiled at her.

"No problem," Annabelle attempted a smile back. She was standing on the doorstep of a house she had never been to before. She still wasn't sure why Xavier had insisted—all but ordered, really—that she come and spend the day with this woman. Sofia Everette was a few years older than her. They were about the same height, only Sofia was thinner. She had silvery-gray eyes, and golden red wavy hair. According to Xavier, Sofia might be able to help her.

Only Annabelle didn't want help.

And she didn't want to be here.

She wanted to be at home, in her pajamas, curled up in bed, pretending that her life wasn't her life.

Ever since yesterday she had been feeling even worse. Starting from when Kate had received a mysterious phone call and been extremely evasive about who it was from. Instinctively, she had known that something was wrong with Xavier. Then when she hadn't heard from him, her anxiety levels had started to steadily rise. Eventually, she had all but begged Kate to tell her what was going on.

Once she found out that Xavier had been shot, she had completely flipped out. She had felt like her whole life was about to come crashing down around her. The need to see Xavier had been overwhelming. Kate had assured her—many times—that Xavier was perfectly fine, that it was only a flesh wound, but she hadn't been able to believe it until she could see it with her own eyes.

Seeing him hadn't made her feel any better, though.

Even though she could see him, standing right there in front of her. He hadn't been wearing his shirt so she'd been able to see the small white square bandage on his shoulder.

After that, all she'd been able to do was cry.

Her guilt had been crushing.

"Annabelle?" Sofia was gazing at her with concern. Then she smiled confidently, "Come on in; it's cold, and I have a feeling we have lots in common."

Annabelle allowed Sofia to take her arm and lead her into the house. It wasn't until they started walking that she realized that Sofia was limping. She absently wondered what had happened to her. She was more focused on why Xavier, and now Sofia, was saying that she had something in common with this woman. Xavier had been vague about it this morning, just given her the address and told her to stop by. Annabelle wasn't even sure how Xavier had met this Sofia.

"You want some tea or coffee?" Sofia asked.

She shrugged disinterestedly, she wasn't thirsty or hungry. Nor did she like tea or coffee. When she wanted a hot drink she usually chose hot chocolate.

"Hot chocolate, maybe," Sofia persisted. "That's my favorite, especially on a cold day like this."

"Yeah, okay," she agreed.

"You didn't eat breakfast today, did you?" Sofia bustled about the kitchen. "How about some oatmeal? My favorite in winter."

Oatmeal was a favorite of Annabelle's, too. "Yeah, okay," she agreed again, hovering in the kitchen, unsure whether she should offer to help or not.

"Let's sit." Sofia carried two bowls to the table. Annabelle sat while Sofia retrieved two mugs and then joined her. "Why don't you tell me about yourself? Ryan didn't tell me anything other than he met your boyfriend at a crime scene last night. Apparently, our guys talked and thought we might be able to help each other."

That surprised her. She'd thought she was here to be counseled by Sofia. Perhaps they did have some things in common—besides liking the same foods. Sofia had known without having to ask not to give her too much oatmeal; Annabelle didn't have much of an appetite these days. She didn't, however, want to talk about herself. She had always hated that. Even more so now.

Sofia shot Annabelle an understanding smile, "What if I go first?" Sofia offered. "I'm guessing since our guys wanted us to meet, that you've been through something traumatic recently like I have. I lost my entire family five months ago. Well, technically, that's not true," she amended. "I have two young half-sisters who live in Europe. It was my sister who killed them, and she's still out there—killing."

"I lost my family, too," Annabelle admitted softly.

"I suspected," Sofia reached across the table and placed a hand on hers. "They were murdered?" she asked gently.

She nodded. "The police thought I did it at first."

"Ouch," Sofia said sympathetically. "Were they killed by someone you knew?"

"Our neighbor." She was debating whether to open up to Sofia. Annabelle wanted someone she could talk to—someone other than Xavier and her therapist. Whenever she went to her sessions, she was always very aware of the fact that her psychiatrist was only listening because it was her job. She wasn't invested in Annabelle or her life. And Xavier was *too* invested. Sometimes she didn't want to talk to him because she didn't want to worry him. But a friend, one who truly understood, would give her the best of both worlds.

"Annabelle?" Sofia prodded.

She finally looked up to meet Sofia's gaze. "I thought he was my friend. I didn't—don't—have a lot of friends. Any, really. And

I thought Ricky was. I talked to him, opened up to him—I thought he really cared about me. But he was just playing me. All the time I was telling him private things, he was sitting there planning how he was going to kill my family," the words came tumbling out in a rush.

"I know exactly how you feel," Sofia sounded sincere. "My sister was the only member of our family that I was close to; I felt so betrayed by what she did. And I felt so stupid. How could I not have seen who she really was?"

Annabelle was relieved that she was finally talking to someone who got it. "Ricky took what I told him and used it against me. He knew I wasn't very self-confident, that I felt like no one loved me, so he kidnapped me and used me as a ploy to distract the police so he could kill another family." She hesitated. "I blame myself for him still being free."

Sofia smiled grimly. "I blame myself for Isabella being free, too. Ryan told me that they suspected her of poisoning me and killing our family. I didn't believe him. I went looking for her and she found me, knocked me out. I got away from her, but she found me and I panicked, fell down some stairs. Ryan found me passed out, but Isabella got away. If I hadn't gone off on my own looking for her, then Ryan might have found her and arrested her before she had a chance to escape and kill more people."

"I've felt so alone," Annabelle said forlornly, wishing she had met Sofia months ago. "I...I've even thought about...about..." She couldn't make herself say the word.

"About suicide?" Sofia supplied.

She nodded. Embarrassed, she averted her eyes.

"Have you told Xavier? And your therapist?"

"Yes," she answered in a small voice.

"Then that sounds completely normal for someone who's been through something so traumatic. You know you need help, and you've asked for it."

"Have you thought about...?"

"I've thought about giving up," Sofia confessed. "Sometimes everything is just so hard. I had a lot of injuries to recover from," she indicated her leg, "a bad break in my leg and some other things. It was tough. Some days I just wanted to lie in bed and never get up again. But then I think of all the people who love me and are here to help me and it gives me the strength to get through another day. Do you have a good support group?"

"I have Xavier. I don't really like being around a lot of people," she explained.

"Well, now you have me and Ryan, too," Sofia patted her hand again.

"Sometimes I feel so angry." She was emboldened by Sofia's frankness to be frank herself. "Angry at Ricky for using me, angry at him for killing my family and leaving me alive, angry at Xavier for saving me, angry at myself for not being stronger."

"I'm furious with Isabella," Sofia told her. "She sprung some major things on me about our family and I never got a chance to confront them. I learned that the man I thought was my father, who paid women to bear his children, was actually my grandfather. That the woman who pretended to the world to be my mother but wasn't, was. And that one of my brothers was my father, and that he raped his stepmother and that's how I was conceived, then raped and murdered over thirty young girls. I'm so angry at all of them, but I never got a chance to confront them."

"I wish that I'd confronted my parents about what happened to me when I was little," Annabelle explained. "Something happened to me when I was four, only I don't really remember. All I know is that I was taken somewhere, and when I came home again I had scars on my back and my parents had changed. They were cold and distant; I thought they didn't love me anymore."

"Maybe they felt guilty," Sofia suggested. "Maybe they blamed themselves for whatever happened to you and that was why they couldn't connect with you properly anymore."

Xavier had told her the same thing. "Maybe," she agreed. "But now I'll never know. I was too cowardly to ask them about it, and now it's too late. My parents are dead and my chance to confront them is gone forever."

"Are you sure you really want to know?" Sofia asked seriously. "Are you sure you really want to know what happened to you? Once you do, you can never take it back."

Annabelle opened her mouth to state that of course she wanted to know what had happened to her, but then snapped it shut without a word. Sofia was right. And Annabelle had thought that hundreds of times before. Sometimes she wanted to know more than she wanted to take her next breath, and sometimes she didn't want to know so much that the thought of remembering made her feel physically ill.

"I always wanted to know who my biological mother was," Sofia continued. "I wanted to more than anything because I thought I'd have this wonderful fairytale reunion and she'd be the mother to me that I always longed for. I used to wonder if my mom was some young girl, taken advantage of by a wealthy, powerful man. I used to hope that she missed me and regretted giving me up. That maybe she had even fought for me."

Sofia paused as though to gather herself, and Annabelle had the feeling that what was coming next wasn't pleasant.

"Before my sister disappeared, she had me tied up—our brother, too—well, I thought that until I found out that he was actually our father. Isabella told me that Logan had raped his stepmother," Sofia's voice went faraway. "That the woman I had grown up hating because she refused to act as a mother to us really was my mother. I felt so guilty for hating her. Once I knew that her husband's son had raped her and that she had been forced to have me, I realized how hard it must have been for her. Having to live with me and see me every day. I was a constant reminder of what had happened to her. No wonder she hated me. Now I wish I didn't know. I wish Isabella had never told me. I wish that I still thought that Gloria was just my stepmother, and Logan was my brother, and my grandfather was my father. But I can't go back. I can't unlearn it. Now I know the truth and I have to deal with it."

"I'm sorry," Annabelle murmured, shocked by Sofia's horrific story. "It must feel awful to know you were conceived that way."

"Yeah," Sofia agreed in a small voice, her eyes shining brightly with unshed tears. "Ryan wants me to talk about it, but I don't like to. Knowing that I'm a product of rape makes me feel like I shouldn't exist. Ryan doesn't get that. He has a fabulous family; he doesn't know what it's like to grow up with a dysfunctional one."

Another thing she and Sofia had in common. While her family didn't sound like it came close to Sofia's on the dysfunction scale, they had certainly had their problems. Many problems. Annabelle was so glad that Xavier had suggested she come and meet Sofia. She loved him for recognizing what she needed and finding a way to get it for her. She had needed a friend like Sofia her whole life, but especially these last eight months.

"I'm really glad we met," Annabelle offered up a shy smile.

"Me too," Sofia smiled back, brushing the back of her hand over her eyes. "Now that we got all the deep stuff out of the way, why don't you tell me about yourself? Everything. I want to hear it all. What you like, what you don't like, what you do for fun."

With the confidence of knowing that her friendship with Sofia was already cemented, and excited by the prospect of having her first real friend, Annabelle complied.

* * * * *

6:48 P.M.

"Mmm," Ricky stretched and gave a contended sigh. He was feeling good. Better than good. He was feeling fabulous.

Teaching Isabella the art of sex had been fun. So much fun

that they hadn't yet made it out of bed. Well, that wasn't quite true. They had spent a little time in the shower.

To be honest, Ricky had never enjoyed sex so much.

With the possible exception of Annabelle.

Before Isabella, sex had just been sex. Okay, sometimes it had been rape, but to him rape was just sex. Aside from that, he'd had plenty of women in his time. By the time the woman realized he was only interested in them for their body, he had usually lost interest in them anyway. And there was always a long line of women at bars and nightclubs who were more than willing to sleep with someone on the first date.

Sex with Isabella was something more, though. Maybe it was because she was the first woman he had ever felt something for. Something real and genuine.

Oh, no, he groaned inwardly. Was he falling in love with her?

That would certainly complicate his life.

He was a wanted felon.

Detective Xavier Montague would never give up on looking for him. The man would hunt him down, and nothing but death would stop him.

He had no intention of stopping killing.

Was Isabella going to be okay with that?

Sure, she was a wanted felon, too. But she was raising a kid. And had a sister who she clearly still loved. Plus, she had been about to turn herself in.

What if she wanted to do that again?

Would she turn him in, too?

Even if she didn't, could he let her go?

And what if she didn't end up turning herself in? Could the two of them have a life together? With this baby Isabella was raising?

Somehow Ricky had never pictured himself as a husband and father. Did he want to commit to Isabella? Did he want to play daddy to baby Sophie?

As much as he didn't intend to stop killing, he also couldn't promise Isabella that he would never rape another woman. It was who he was. If he saw a hot woman, and he wanted them, he took them. For him, it was that simple. But Isabella didn't see it that way.

A horrible thought occurred to him.

What if Isabella didn't want him?

Was she falling for him?

She was only seventeen. That should bother him, he supposed, since he'd just spent the day doing her over and over again. What could she know about committing to someone? What could she know about love? Ironic, he knew, since he himself knew nothing on the topic.

It didn't bother her that he was a killer; however, she didn't like that he was a rapist. He understood that, given what those kids had done to her. She had melted in his arms when he'd said he'd kill them for her. He had meant it, too. Ricky felt like he would do almost anything for her. Already he had let that cop live simply because Isabella had asked him to.

Ricky actually believed he was in love with her.

He didn't know what to make of that.

He didn't even know if he wanted to stay with her. He didn't know if he *could* stay with her. The thought of committing to her—given who he was and what he did—was terrifying.

But more terrifying still, was the thought that she might not want to stay with him.

He didn't know if he could let her go.

Finding himself extremely uncharacteristically panicky, Ricky lifted his arm, hoping that the movement would jar Isabella awake. She was curled against him, her head resting on his shoulder, red hair spilling all around it.

She did indeed wake. Blinking sleepily, she lifted her head, a smile lighting her face as she gazed up at him. And Ricky knew then and there that they were in this together. All he needed was to hear that Isabella was on the same page.

"What time is it?" Isabella's sleep-laden voice asked.

"Around seven," he replied. "Are you hungry?"

"Not for dinner," she said with a sly smile. For someone who had never willingly had sex before today, she was a quick learner. The way she traced her fingers up his bare chest almost had him forgetting why it was he'd woken her up.

"We need to talk," he caught her hand before it could totally distract him. Keeping hold of it, he propped the pillows up behind him and levered himself up so he was half sitting; the slight distance between them helped to make sure he was thinking with his mind and not something else.

"About what?" she looked at him with wary surprise.

"About this," he gestured between them. "About us."

"Are we an us?" her face had gone deadly serious.

"Do you want us to be?" Ricky had to tell himself to let out the breath he was subconsciously holding.

"Yes," she answered honestly. "I think I'm in love with you. All my life I dreamed about someone who would understand me, someone who I could connect with. I didn't think I'd ever meet anyone like that, and then there you were. I don't want to imagine my life without you."

For a long moment, he didn't say a word. Couldn't say a word. Isabella's words had touched him in a way he didn't think he could be touched. He hadn't thought he had it in him to love someone, and yet, the way Isabella made him feel was something he had never experienced before. After just two days he couldn't imagine his life without her. And yet there were things they needed to sort out before they could ride off into the sunset together.

"We're both killers," he reminded her. "We're both on the run. Do you think being together is going to make that better?"

"Yes," she nodded, seemingly confident in her answer. "We won't be alone. We'll have someone to watch our back. Besides,

Ryan and Paige know we're together now, and so does that cop who's after you. Together we're stronger than we'd be on our own."

"Okay, what about your baby? Is it best for her to be with us? I don't plan to stop killing…"

"I never asked you to," Isabella interrupted. "And I don't either. I don't even think I could stop if I wanted to. And no, maybe we aren't the best people to be raising a child. Sophie needs stability, and we can't offer her that. We may have to pack up and take off at a moment's notice; having her with us would make that difficult. Maybe I should give her to my sister."

"I think that might be for the best," Ricky agreed. The idea of caring for a screaming, crying infant did not appeal to him. "You can't turn yourself in," he warned her. "I won't let you."

For a moment, she stared up at him and he thought she was going to disagree, but then she smiled, and tugged her hand free from his grasp to brush it across his lips. "I don't have any plans to turn myself in," she assured him. "I couldn't give you up. I don't think I could live without you."

"What about if I rape another woman?" he asked frankly. "What about when I finally go after Annabelle? I intend to make her suffer before I kill her. Are you going to be able to handle that, or are you going to split?"

She considered his words. "I'm not going to split," she said at last. "But I can't promise I won't be angry. Or jealous. I don't want to see you with another woman. But I do promise that I won't ever run out on you."

"All right," he drew the word out, knowing what he wanted to say to her, but struggling to get the words out.

"So," Isabella smiled seductively, "did I pass?"

"Pass?" he repeated, her fingers resting just beside his mouth was making it hard for him to concentrate.

"My test," she elaborated. "Did I convince you that I really want to be with you? That we can make it work?"

"Yeah, you did." He opened his mouth and turned his head enough to draw her fingers into his mouth and suck on them.

"Good," she pulled her hand from his mouth and leaned up to kiss him.

"So, where do we go from here?"

"You mean physically? We can't go back to my house, and the police don't seem to know where you live, so we're probably safe here for a while."

He smiled. "No, not physically," he explained. "With us. I…" Taking a deep breath, he let the words tumble out, "I love you, too. Marry me?"

Her gray eyes grew wide with surprise, then her face broke into an enormous grin and she clambered on top of him. They were both still naked, and at the feel of her body on his, his instantly responded. Isabella's mouth met his as she lowered herself onto him.

Immediately he rolled her beneath him and for the next few minutes they were all sweaty bodies moving in tandem, moans and groans and breathless gasps. When at last he collapsed upon her, both spent, he realized that Isabella had never answered his question. Although the hot sex could be construed as an answer of sorts.

Ricky looked at her, lying beneath him, still breathing hard, and was about to repeat his proposal, when she caught him watching her and met his gaze with pure adoration in her eyes.

"Yes."

* * * * *

10:34 P.M.

Sofia snuggled deeper into Ryan's arms.

They were both curled up in bed. Ryan had finally managed to make it home at a reasonable time tonight, and they'd eaten dinner together, watched a movie, and then climbed into bed. Ryan had fallen asleep almost immediately, but Sofia had been too wound up to drift off.

She had enjoyed her time with Annabelle Englewood today, but it had been draining. Annabelle was a few years younger than her and severely lacking in self-confidence. Sofia had known almost as soon as she opened the door, that she was going to have to drive the conversation. Left to herself, Annabelle probably would have sat there silently all day.

Once they'd gotten over the hump of sharing the similar traumatic experiences they had both recently endured, things had gotten easier. Sofia had shared her story mainly because Ryan had told her that Xavier had told him that Annabelle was in desperate need of a friend in whom she could confide. And she certainly was. She had been wary at first, but once Sofia had convinced her that they had a lot in common, she had slowly started to open up.

Annabelle had been honest and told her that she had never had a real friend, and Sofia could see why. Annabelle was shy, always aiming to please, timid, and she seemed to have no idea that she was beautiful. She had delicate features—silky brown hair and amazing near-white eyes. But Annabelle didn't seem to see it that way. She was embarrassed about her eyes and thought she was rather plain looking. She was also terrified to let anyone get close to her in case she got emotionally invested and then they turned cold. Like her parents had done.

Sofia was fairly certain, though, that with some gentle encouragement and support, Annabelle would soon come out of her shell. She was, however, concerned about the other woman's mental state. Sofia knew that she herself had been a mess the last few months, but she had never seriously considered suicide. Annabelle, on the other hand, had seriously considered it and Sofia was sure that she was still actively thinking about it. At least Xavier was aware of it. Sofia had made sure to get him alone so she could confirm it, and he seemed extremely supportive of

Annabelle. He obviously loved her a lot. Hopefully that would be enough to get her through this difficult time.

Recounting what she had personally been through to a stranger had left her both physically exhausted and mentally wound up. She didn't like to talk about herself, Isabella, and their family. She only talked to Ryan about it because he was so insistent that he usually wore her down and into compliance. Although, she somewhat grudgingly admitted to herself, she usually felt better afterward. However, she had known that the only way she was going to be able to connect with Annabelle was to share. So she had. But now she was paying for it with a killer headache and her mind stuck in overdrive.

Even though she couldn't sleep, she was enjoying just lying here with Ryan's arms around her. Sofia loved being held. Her family had not been emotional or demonstrative and there had never been anyone around to just hug her. She'd missed that as a child, just the simple act of having someone wrap you up in their arms and hold you. Luckily, Ryan was an affectionate guy.

Clearing her mind, Sofia cuddled closer against Ryan's warm body and attempted to fall asleep. She was going to be a mess tomorrow if she didn't get at least a couple of hours' rest. Maneuvering her leg into a more comfortable position, she could feel herself just starting to drift off when something startled her back into full awareness.

Was that footsteps?

No, surely it couldn't be. She and Ryan were the only ones here. And her stalker couldn't be stupid enough to break in here while Ryan was home with her. Especially now that the security system was up and running. If someone had broken in, the alarm would have been tripped. As well as alerting the police, it would also have sent messages to both hers and Ryan's phones.

Carefully, she moved out of Ryan's arms to reach for her phone on the small table beside the bed. Picking it up, she saw no alert from the security system.

Lying back down, she tried to calm herself. She was probably just being paranoid—which made sense given that the last two nights her stalker *had* broken in here. But she had been alone those times, and now she wasn't. And so far, her stalker had not been stupid.

It was probably nothing, she assured herself.

But she couldn't quite convince herself of that.

Instead she lay stiff and still on her side of the bed. Attempting not to move, to barely even breathe, her ears strained to hear any sound. But it seemed the more she tried to listen, the more she couldn't hear a thing. The silence seemed deafening.

And then she heard it.

This time she was positive.

Footsteps.

"Ryan," she whispered urgently, tugging on his arm.

"Mmm?" he groaned groggily.

"Ryan, wake up," she pulled on his arm more firmly. "Ryan."

"Yeah?" his eyes opened, for a moment still sleep laden, and then he snapped to attention. "What's wrong? Are you okay?"

"I heard something," she replied.

He was instantly on alert, "Are you sure? The alarm didn't go off."

"I'm sure," a little tremble crept into her voice. She was scared. Again. And she was so sick of being scared in her own home.

Ryan climbed out of bed and threw on some sweatpants. "All right, you stay here. Hide. Get under the bed." He reached into the lockbox on the top shelf of the closet and pulled out both guns, thrusting his spare one at her. "Take this. Don't hesitate to use it if you have to. Now go, under the bed."

"Ryan, no," she protested. No way was she going to stay here alone while someone else was in their house.

"Sofia, this guy is after you, not me; no way are we offering you up on a silver platter for him. Now hide," Ryan commanded.

"No, I want to go with you; I'll be safer with you than by

myself," she countered, grabbing the shirt he had discarded before bed as it was the closest garment and slipping into it.

He muttered under his breath, "Stay behind me," he ordered.

Relieved, Sofia clutched the gun in one hand and then crossed to Ryan, standing as close to him as she could physically manage without climbing on his back. Together they moved out into the hall. Their bedroom was the farthest from the stairs, and Ryan had cleared the bathroom and two of the other bedrooms when the door to the last bedroom was flung violently open.

"Hey, stop," Ryan yelled, taking off like a shot after the figure that darted down the stairs. "Stay put," he tossed over his shoulder to her.

There was no way Sofia was staying here by herself. She had seen enough horror movies where the girl who stayed behind while her boyfriend chased the monster never made it out alive. Using the wall for leverage, she worked her way as quickly down the stairs as her bad leg would allow. The front door was open, and by the time she got to the porch Ryan was halfway down the street, and a car was careening around a corner, tires screeching.

Limping down the path and out onto the street, she stopped under a streetlight; the glow that bathed her made her feel marginally safer. How could this be happening again? After the security system had been installed, she hadn't expected him to try breaking in again. And yet he had. He had been in their home while the two of them had been in bed. What if she'd fallen straight asleep like Ryan had? What if she hadn't heard him? What would he have done to them? They would have been completely vulnerable to him. He could have killed them before they ever woke up. Or he could have taken Ryan out and then grabbed her.

When was he going to stop?

When was he going to leave her alone? Right now, it felt like this nightmare would never end.

What did he want from her? If she knew the answer to that, she would gladly give it to him if it meant he would just stay away from her.

"What are you doing out here? I told you to stay indoors. It's freezing," Ryan appeared before her, tone reprimanding.

"Did he get away?" she asked in a voice that was bordering on a whimper. Sofia already knew the answer, but she still asked the question.

"Yeah," his tone softened. "I'm sorry, honey. He was already in his car by the time I got outside. I followed him but I couldn't get a license plate number."

"Oh," was all she could manage.

"I'm sorry," Ryan said again. "Here, let me take that." His hands covered hers and she realized that she was clutching the gun he'd given her in a death grip, so he eased it out of her hands. "Darn," he muttered, "you're like ice."

"So are you," she murmured, resting her cheek against his bare chest; his smooth skin was also ice cold. Neither of them wore shoes, Ryan was topless, and she was wearing only his shirt. Getting properly dressed hadn't been on either of their minds when they realized an intruder was in their home. Sofia hadn't even realized she was cold until Ryan mentioned it, but now that he'd brought it to her attention, she found she was shivering uncontrollably.

"Yeah, but I'm fine and you're not; you're shaking," Ryan countered. "Let's get you inside."

Before she knew it, he had scooped her off her feet and was carrying her back toward the house. Once inside he closed and locked the door and reset the seemingly pointless security system while balancing her in his arms. Then he set her in the living room, wrapped her in a blanket and disappeared into the kitchen. He returned shortly with a mug of steaming hot chocolate.

"Drink this," he handed her the cup. "I'll call it in. Not that it'll do much good; he never leaves anything behind," he added in a sour voice.

Sofia took a sip of hot chocolate as Ryan paced the room, but the mug was too hot for her freezing hands, and they were shaking too much anyway that she was afraid of spilling the burning liquid all over herself. Instead she set the cup down and, clutching the blanket around her shoulders, went to stand by Ryan. She felt safer beside him. Sure, they thought the stalker had driven off in his car, but he could have backtracked. He could be watching them right now. He could break back in here. Sofia was going to stick like glue to Ryan.

"How did he get in?" she asked as he hung up. Try as she might, she couldn't stop her voice from wobbling.

"All the windows aren't wired into the system yet," Ryan explained. "He came in through a back one. He knew which ones to use, which means he was watching the house yesterday."

A violent shiver wracked through her body and her knees went a little weak. Pitching forward, she leaned against Ryan's strong chest, allowing him to hold her up.

"You're still shivering," he said it grimly. "Come here," he led her back to the couch, sat down and pulled her into his lap, then took her cold hands in his and began to rub them.

She rested her head on his shoulder, burying her face in the crook of his neck. "He won't stop," she whispered. "He won't stop until I'm dead or he kidnaps me or whatever it is he has planned for me."

"He's not going to get his hands on you," Ryan said fiercely. "Never, Sofia. I promise you, he will *never* get his hands on you."

Resting in Ryan's arms, Sofia tried really hard to believe him.

JANUARY 13TH

"I don't need a ring," Isabella assured Ricky.

She knew she was gazing up at him with open adoration. She was nearly woozy with a blinding, all-encompassing love for him. She loved everything about him—everything.

Well, she amended slightly, she loved everything about him except his apparent penchant for raping women. She was, however, prepared to overlook that. Besides, now that Ricky had her, there was no need for him to go seeking sex anywhere else.

A tiny glimmer of doubt about that ignited inside her.

Isabella wanted to believe that was true. She really did. Especially since she and Ricky had spent the most amazing day in bed together. She had thought that she would be shy, that she would feel awkward. Isabella knew she wasn't pretty, and that her body was nothing out of the ordinary, and she had thought that showing it to a man would make her feel uncomfortable and embarrassed. But it hadn't. It had been perfect. Ricky had been perfect.

This whole thing was perfect.

She couldn't believe that she was engaged—to someone just like her. Even before she had started killing, she had believed she was one of a kind. That she was alone in the universe. That there was no other half for her. And then, once she committed her first murder she had believed that she didn't deserve to find her soul mate—that she deserved to be miserable and alone.

Only now it was like all her dreams were coming true.

Isabella felt like Cinderella.

215

When Ricky had proposed to her, it had been the most magical moment of her entire life. She still couldn't believe she was engaged. She and Ricky were going to spend the rest of their lives together and it was going to be perfect. Everything from now on was going to be perfect.

"Isabella?"

Ricky's hands grasped her chin and shook. Blinking in surprise, she had let her mind wander. She grinned at him, "Did you say something?"

He frowned slightly, "You zoning out on me, babe?"

She giggled like a schoolgirl, which while technically she may be one as she was only seventeen. Isabella had always been much older than her years. "A little."

"I said, of course you get a ring; any ring you want," Ricky looked offended.

"I don't want you to spend too much money." Isabella had grown up wealthy but she didn't care about money at all. She had siphoned off enough into private bank accounts so that once she went on the run she had enough to get by, but beyond that it just wasn't important to her. She had had money, more money than she would ever need in her lifetime, and it hadn't made her—or anyone in her family—happy.

"Don't you worry about that," he shot her a cheeky grin then opened the door to the jewelry store for her.

Once inside Ricky slung an arm around her shoulders, and Isabella felt her heart go pitter-patter. Not for the first time, Isabella was glad that she looked years older than she was. Otherwise the sight of a guy in his mid-forties with a teenage girl would draw too much attention. As it was they looked nothing more than a happy engaged couple ring shopping.

"May I help you?" A middle-aged saleslady approached them, a firm smile in place. Her look of confidence gave the idea of them leaving without having made a purchase was simply out of the question.

"We're looking for engagement rings," Ricky shot the lady an engaging smile.

"Ahh," the lady's brown eyes lit up, no doubt thinking they were going to be an easy sell into buying something way more expensive than either they needed or had intended to buy. "Congratulations."

"Thank you," Ricky's eyes crinkled as his smiled deepened, and he reached for her hand.

"So any idea what you're looking for?" the lady asked.

"None at all; something sparkly, I guess," he added with a chuckle. "We were hoping you'd be able to make some suggestions; the jewelry you're wearing is beautiful and it complements you perfectly."

"Thank you," the lady gushed, her cheeks tinting slightly pink. "Right this way," she turned and began walking toward a counter on the far side of the small jewelry store.

Winking at her, Ricky hurried after the lady, engaging her in conversation and throwing compliments at her left, right, and center. Ricky was a charmer, Isabella thought to herself as she followed him. He had the lady completely snowed. Isabella could tell she was smitten by the sly glances she kept tossing at Ricky, and the way she attempted to surreptitiously gawk at his body. She didn't have a clue that the man she was going to try and sell the most expensive ring in the store to was a serial killer.

Unlike herself, Ricky was a people person. He knew what to say and how to say it to put people at ease and get them to like him. He complemented her perfectly. Her weaknesses were his strengths.

She stared dreamily at him as he pretended to listen intently as the saleslady described different diamond cuts and the pros and cons of the different colors of gold. She was so lucky. Ricky was charming and handsome and had an awesome body, and he was an absolute gentleman with her. Even in bed. Well, in bed he was also an animal; it seemed that he was insatiable with lust for her, but he was a gentleman, too.

In short, Ricky Preston was absolutely and completely perfect.

And he was hers.

One hundred percent hers.

"Yoo-hoo, honey," Ricky's hand waved in front of her face.

Isabella blinked in surprise and found both Ricky and the saleslady staring at her. They had obviously said something to her, but what it was she didn't have a clue.

"See what I have to put up with here with Ms. Dreamy?" Ricky chuckled to the saleslady, who chuckled back appreciatively. "I said," Ricky began with exaggerated patience, "which ring do you like the best?"

She glanced down at the selection set out before her. There were six rings, all of them were gorgeous, but Isabella couldn't care less which one ended up being hers. All she wanted was Ricky Preston. And she had him.

"They're all so pretty. I like them all; you choose," she shot Ricky what she knew was another look of open adoration. Isabella couldn't help it; she felt giddy and schoolgirlish around him. When she was with him, she wasn't completely in control of herself. The thought was scary and yet also oddly freeing. She had thought herself virtually incapable of love, but she'd proved that wrong since there was no doubt she loved Ricky Preston.

"Okeydokey," Ricky nodded then examined each ring individually—picking it up and turning it over, taking her hand and sliding it on, then examining it on her. "All right," he announced at last, "this is the one. It looks lovely on you. We'll take it."

"A wonderful choice," the saleslady nodded approvingly. "And it suits her. You're a lucky woman," the look she turned on Isabella smarted with jealousy. "Now, we offer a range of flexible payment plans depending on your finances."

"I don't think payment is going to be a problem," Ricky's smile changed from disarmingly sweet and charming to something a little more sinister.

"Oh?" the saleslady looked surprised, but recovered quickly. "Will you be paying in full? I'm sorry, I didn't mean to offend, just most people go with a payment plan."

"You didn't offend me," Ricky assured her. "It's just, I had something a little different in mind." Before anyone could react, he had a knife in his hand and he'd reached across the glass display cabinet and slit the saleslady's throat. The woman's eyes grew wide as it slowly dawned on her what had happened. Her hands rose to press to the gaping wound in her neck, attempting, albeit fruitlessly, to stem the flow of blood.

Ricky was already on the move. There was an elderly couple being attended by a young salesman a few feet away and a security guard by the door. Swinging the knife as he moved, Ricky plunged it into the old woman's chest, then grabbed the old man, using him as a human shield and angling him in between his body and the security guard.

"I'd think before you do anything stupid," Ricky warned the guard, who had drawn his weapon and was pointing it in Ricky's direction. "Isabella, get his gun," he directed her. Obediently, she went to retrieve the weapon which the guard reluctantly handed over. Once she had it, she returned to Ricky's side. "Now, down on the ground," Ricky ordered the guard, who hesitated. He jammed the knife deep enough into his human shield's throat to make blood flow. "Hesitate again and I'll kill him." This time the guard complied. "Keep the gun aimed at him," Ricky commanded her. In swift, efficient movements he sliced the knife through the old man's neck, then lunged over the counter to kill the shop's other employee. Without missing a beat, Ricky crossed the room and thrust the knife four times into the security guard's back. "Well, that was fun," he grinned at her.

Isabella had to admit she was in shock.

Not that she had just witnessed five murders. She couldn't care less about that. It was that Ricky had done it all so seamlessly. So smoothly. He was an expert. A real connoisseur of his craft.

When they'd walked in here, Isabella had had no idea that Ricky had been planning all of this—not that she would have objected if he'd shared his intentions. But he had obviously worked the whole thing out. He had moved seamlessly from victim to victim. And now all five people lay dead in pools of their own blood. Isabella had never been so impressed in her life.

"Surprised?" Ricky asked.

She nodded shakily, "You're so good. You planned it out so quickly and executed it without a hitch."

"I'm a pro," he whispered huskily in her ear, "in more than killing." Then he pushed her up against the wall, his mouth hungrily devouring hers.

As he kissed her, everything else fled from her mind. All she could think of was Ricky. His kisses weren't enough. She wanted more of him. She wanted his hands on her, she badly wanted him inside her. She desperately wished they were back at home.

As if he were reading her mind, "We need to get out of here," Ricky announced as he abruptly pulled away. "I want you in bed—now."

"How are we getting out of here? We're covered in blood," she reminded him. Ricky had blood from both store employees, the elderly couple, and the security guard all over him. And since he'd just had his body pressed up against hers, she was now all bloody, too.

"No problem, car's right outside," he tapped a finger to the tip of her nose, then grabbed her hand and headed for the door. "Wait," he stopped abruptly, yanked the ring off her finger then knelt in front of her. "Isabella Everette, will you marry me?"

All she could do was nod and stare as he slipped the ring back onto her finger, then grab her hand again and yank her through the door. As Ricky pulled her out of the store and toward the car, all Isabella could do was giggle and go all weak-kneed over what Ricky would do to her once they got home.

* * * * *

10:49 A.M.

"Are we sure it was them?" Xavier already knew the answer to that by looking around the store.

It was Ricky Preston and Isabella Everette.

There was no doubt.

"Yeah," Diane paused and nodded. "They left fingerprints and we brought samples from both to compare. They match. It was definitely them."

"What were they doing here?" Xavier wondered aloud. They had been in their morning meeting when they'd received a call about a murder spree at a local jewelry store. Apparently, a witness had seen a couple matching Ricky and Isabella's descriptions leaving the shop. The whole drive over he had maintained that it seemed unlikely that either Ricky or Isabella would hit up a jewelry store, but now that they were here, the facts were evident.

"I think they were shopping for engagement rings," Paige announced. She was over by a glass counter on the side of the small shop farthest from the door. Paige was looking better this morning—calmer and more in control. Xavier knew that Ryan's brother and his partner hadn't made any progress into finding out who was stalking her, but despite that, Paige seemed to have somehow come to terms with it. At least for the moment. "There are five rings in their boxes on the counter here, plus an empty box. They look to me like engagement rings."

That was not the answer Xavier had been expecting.

Apparently, it wasn't the answer Ryan had been expecting either. "Engagement rings," he repeated grimly. "You think Isabella and Ricky are engaged? How am I going to break that one to Sofia?"

No one had an answer for him on that. Xavier felt guiltily pleased that he wasn't the one who would have to inform Sofia. She was going to be shocked and appalled to learn her sister was intending to marry a wanted killer.

On the plus side, though, if Ricky and Isabella were engaged, then that would probably make Annabelle feel better knowing some of his focus must now surely be shifted off her. But Xavier knew she would feel guilty about it anyway. Annabelle had taken to Sofia; in fact, she had asked if it would be okay to spend the day with her again today. He had met Sofia briefly last night when he'd picked Annabelle up, and after just those few minutes, he already considered her a friend. She was pretty and smart and funny and very sweet; just what Annabelle needed.

It had been a weight off his mind to see Annabelle enjoying herself—happy and at peace. Whatever Sofia had said to her had obviously made a difference. And Annabelle had even been comfortable enough to open up, to talk about what was going on inside her head. She had even confessed to Sofia that she had been contemplating suicide. Sofia had made sure to get him alone to make sure he was aware of that, and that, in his mind, had been what had cemented her place in his and Annabelle's lives. She was exactly the kind of friend that Annabelle needed.

"So they come here to buy an engagement ring and then kill everyone in the store?" Ryan's brow furrowed.

"They're devolving, losing control," Paige replied. "They were extremely organized, planning everything down to the tiniest detail, but this feels like it's the beginning of something bad, something different. It seems like they're no longer in control, no longer organized."

"I don't know," Xavier countered, scanning the scene. "This wasn't the same as before, but it's still pretty organized." He walked over to where Paige was standing, "It started here. They probably looked like a normal couple. She was just going to sell them a ring like she's done probably hundreds of times before.

Any defensive wounds, Frankie?"

The ME, who was kneeling over the security guard's body, paused and looked up. "Not that I could see, just a single wound to the neck. Sliced through the carotid artery, she would have been dead in minutes," Frankie replied.

"Then he got her by surprise," Xavier had already figured that.

"You think Ricky committed the murders, not Isabella, or not the two of them?" Ryan looked faintly relieved.

"I'm positive," Xavier nodded. "Isabella might not have even known what Ricky was planning when they came in here, but Ricky certainly did. He brought the knife with him."

Paige nodded her agreement. "You're right; he definitely came in intending to do this or he wouldn't have had a weapon with him. Once he took out the saleslady there were still four other people in here, including an armed guard. He had to have had a plan."

"He would have gone for the elderly couple," Xavier moved toward the other counter where the bodies of a man and woman in their eighties lay.

"Woman was killed first," Frankie supplied.

"Then he used the man as a human shield," Xavier continued. "That's how he disarmed the guard, threatened to kill the old man if he didn't relinquish his gun. Then once he had the guard under control. He killed the old man, and the salesman, then the guard on the way out."

"It does feel like they're devolving, though," Ryan considered. "They don't seem all that concerned with being caught. Before, both went to great lengths to take forensic countermeasures, but now they're leaving fingerprints and witnesses. They don't care anymore about getting caught. It's like the possibility hasn't even occurred to them. They seem to think they're invincible. That can't be a good thing. Random people at a jewelry store. What's next? I feel like this is the beginning of a spree. Who knows how many people are going to wind up dead before we get them."

Agreeing with that, Xavier had the same feeling. "At least if they're devolving, they'll get more and more careless and that's how we'll catch them."

Ryan sighed tiredly and rubbed a hand over his face. "Yeah, I just don't know how much more of this Sofia can take. She needs this to be over. She needs Isabella to be stopped."

"Yeah, Annabelle, too," Xavier agreed grimly. "It kills her that Ricky's still out there." He deliberately shook away his dull mood. They were closer than ever to catching Ricky; for now, that had to be enough. "The witness who called it in still here?"

"I think so," Paige nodded. "You want to talk to her?"

"Yeah. I was thinking maybe she could tell us what condition they were in when they left here, could help us figure out where they might go next," Xavier explained.

"You really think it'll make a difference?" Ryan looked defeated. And tired. Xavier had learned that Paige wasn't the only one with a stalker; apparently, someone was stalking Sofia, as well. And last night that person had broken into Ryan and Sofia's home for the third night in a row. The toll it was taking was evident on Ryan's face and in his demeanor.

"Can't hurt," Xavier replied mildly.

"I guess," Ryan agreed reluctantly. "You guys go ahead; I'm going to call home and check on Sofia. And Annabelle," he added before Xavier had a chance to ask.

"Thanks." He and Paige headed back outside where a nervous woman in her early thirties was pacing up and down the sidewalk. She froze when she saw them heading straight for her. "Hi, I'm Detective Montague, and this is Detective Hood," he made the introductions once they reached her. "Ms. Lipton, right?" The woman nodded. "We'd like to ask you a couple of questions."

"More questions?" The woman looked positively horrified by the prospect.

"Just a couple," Paige assured her.

"I already told the other officers everything I know," she

protested desperately.

"I know; I just wanted to ask a few more things," Xavier soothed.

"All right," she sighed miserably.

"Can you tell me exactly what you saw?" Xavier asked.

"Well," she begun hesitantly, "I was going to go shopping for an anniversary gift for my parents. They're renewing their vows for their fortieth wedding anniversary and I was getting them new rings. Their rings were stolen in a carjacking about a month ago, and . . ."

The woman was rambling. Hoping to refocus her on what they needed to know, Xavier asked, "And what did you see when you arrived?"

"Oh, uh, I saw a couple go running out the front door. They almost ran into me," she looked shocked, like she still couldn't believe this was all happening.

"Did you get a good look at them?"

She nodded.

"And?" he prompted.

"And the guy was tall and dark-haired; the woman was tall, too—a redhead," she summarized. "They were covered in blood. They went running to a car that was parked just out front of the jewelry store and took off."

"How did they look?"

"Look?" Ms. Lipton repeated, confused.

"Happy, sad, excited, surprised, shocked," Xavier prompted.

"Uh," she considered this for a moment. "Excited, I guess and, I don't know," she shrugged, "they looked like they were anxious to be alone."

"Why did you think that?"

"He was holding her hand, pulling her along with him, and she was staring up at him all puppy-dog like," she explained.

So, the two were all wrapped up in their little love affair. It seemed like that had overridden both their previous plans. If they were going to find them it wasn't going to be through newlyweds who'd honeymooned at the hotel where Ricky worked, or rich guys who were cheating on their wives and were friends with the Everette family.

"Okay, Ms. Lipton, thanks for your time," he was ready to move on. Ryan was right; this did feel like a spree. Ricky and Isabella weren't going to stop killing any time soon. The only way to stop them was to find them.

"That's all you wanted to know?" Ms. Lipton looked and sounded relieved. "I can go now?"

"Yes. Again, thanks for your help." As he watched the woman hurry away, Xavier started planning their next move. Ricky Preston was *not* getting away again.

* * * * *

1:24 P.M.

He watched her stare at her hand, her meal lay untouched in front of her.

Ricky was thrilled that he had made her so happy with the ring.

It had been fun. At the jewelry store. It was odd, though; he hadn't been even a little afraid that Isabella wouldn't be pleased with what he'd planned on doing. He hadn't told her beforehand; he'd wanted it to be a surprise. And she had indeed been surprised. Impressed, too.

Not to mention turned on.

They had gone straight back to his place where they had spent the last few hours in bed. And if her near insatiable hunger for him was anything to go by, she was as turned on by killing as he was.

It had been her first time being involved in killing someone she hadn't deemed deserving, but it hadn't seemed to bother her. She hadn't killed anyone, but she hadn't protested his actions, and she had followed his orders and helped. Which made him excited about their future. The things they could achieve together—once Isabella accepted that murder was murder, and in some way, everyone was deserving of it—were limitless, provided she even needed to give herself a reason. They would be unstoppable.

"Hey," he reached across the table and hooked a finger under Isabella's chin, tilting her face up so she was now looking at him and not the stolen engagement ring.

"Hey," she said back, a smile spreading over her face.

"You're not eating," he pointed out. After spending the rest of the morning in bed, they had decided to go out for a romantic lunch. Isabella had chosen a small Italian restaurant; there were only three other couples in the room and a few workers. They'd ordered and received their meals, but all Isabella had done so far was stare at her ring as though it may disappear any second.

"We're really engaged," she marveled dreamily. "I never thought that would happen to me."

He didn't bother to point out to her that at seventeen she was hardly an old maid. "Well, happen it did," he grinned. "And I guarantee you'll never forget the proposal."

Isabella chuckled. "That's true," she agreed. "I wish we were alone," she cast a glance at the other diners. "It could be really romantic here. We could close the blinds, turn the fairy lights on, play some music."

"We *could* be alone," he raised a suggestive eyebrow, wondering whether Isabella was ready to take the first step from pre-meditated murder to spur of the moment.

Both her eyebrows raised in surprise as comprehension dawned, but there was no horror or fear, only interest and a glimmer of excitement. "I have my gun on me," she said at last.

"You carry?" he couldn't quite hide his astonishment.

"Always," she replied. "And I am a perfect shot. There are seven people in here, plus another two out the back in the kitchen," she considered. "I could take out these seven, but the other two could get away once they hear the shots."

"I'll get everyone in here; you take care of the rest," he announced. Without hesitation, she nodded. Ricky stood, then bent to kiss Isabella, before heading for the bathroom. On the way, he pretended to stumble, careening into one of the couples and sending their table, meal and all, crashing to the floor. "Oh, I'm *so* sorry," he pasted on a look of horrified embarrassment.

"Uh, that's okay," the startled young woman assured him.

The middle-aged waiter came rushing over, "Is everything okay here?"

"I'm afraid I tripped," Ricky said earnestly.

"No one's hurt?" the waiter asked.

"I'm fine," Ricky replied.

"So are we," the young man at the table indicated himself and his girlfriend.

"I'm so sorry," Ricky said again. "I've made such a mess."

"Don't worry about it," the waiter assured him. "So long as no one's hurt we can get this cleaned up in a jiffy and get new meals for you guys." He turned to call over his shoulder at the kitchen, "Uncle Antonio, Aunt Natalia? Could you two come out here for a moment?"

A moment later a couple in their late sixties emerged from the kitchen, heading straight for them. "What happened?" the old man asked.

"I'm afraid we had a little accident," the waiter explained.

Pop, pop, pop, pop, pop, pop, pop, pop, pop.

In quick succession and with perfect accuracy, each person in the restaurant fell to the floor. A bright red dot in the center of each of their heads.

"Never go for a heart shot when you can make a head shot," Isabella came up behind him and slipped her arms around his waist.

"When you said you were a perfect shot, you weren't kidding," Ricky was mightily impressed. Having Isabella with him was going to be beneficial, not just personally but practically, too. Her shooting ability was bound to come in handy sooner or later.

She just grinned, then went quickly to the front door, locked it and turned the closed sign so it was facing out, then moved to each of the four windows and closed the blinds. While she did that, Ricky located the switch to turn on the fairy lights that strung across the ceiling and turned on some music.

"Dance with me?" He took her hand and led her to the middle of the room.

Isabella came into his arms, hers sliding around his neck, as she settled herself against his chest. Together they swayed to the music. Ricky had never liked dancing before. But now, with Isabella in his arms, it was heavenly.

"Make love to me, Ricky," Isabella whispered in his ear.

"Here?" his gaze travelled the room, taking in the nine bodies slumped in crumpled heaps on the carpet. Their frozen eyes staring sightlessly, little red puddles around their heads.

"Today is the beginning of a whole new world for us," she whispered; her gray eyes were dark with longing. "I want you. I *need* you."

That was all he needed to hear. Lowering her to the floor, he began to undress her, and she him. This time their lovemaking was slower, more focused—not the wild and hot sex they'd had before. This time it was about more than just simply sex. This time it meant something. It was a genuine joining—both body and soul—of two individuals. They were no longer two, but one.

Afterward, as they lay there together, their naked bodies entwined, there were so many thoughts rushing through his head. They had to get baby Sophie and drop her off at Isabella's sister's house. They had to find a place to get married. And someone to marry them. They had to move. With Xavier Montague around, he wasn't safe here. Before that had been fine. Tormenting Annabelle had been his number one priority, but now he had something—someone—else to focus on. He had to kill

Annabelle. Then they would move. He would need a new job. A new identity. Isabella would, too.

Deliberately, he stopped himself.

Planning was what the old Ricky would have done. But now he was going to go with the flow. Do whatever felt right in the moment.

He was a whole new Ricky Preston with a whole new outlook on life.

* * * * *

3:09 P.M.

Paige was tired.

Too many nights without sleep were catching up with her.

She hated those nightmares. Over the last almost twenty years, they had robbed her of so many night's sleep. She supposed she should be used to them by now. Over time they had faded. She could go months without the dream, then suddenly it would be back, ripping her from sleep as the events of that awful night played out once again in her dreams.

It made her uncomfortable to have Ryan know what had happened. Not so much the part about how someone had stalked her mother and then broken into their home and attacked them. It was that he knew how she had fallen apart afterward.

Sure, she had only been a kid, but still, the facts were that she had had a complete breakdown, and now that Ryan knew he would always be expecting it to happen again. Just like Elias was.

Of course, she had told Elias what had happened to her once it became clear to both that they were serious about each other and they saw a future for themselves together. And he had told her many times before that just because she had had a breakdown as a teenager didn't mean he thought less of her. But obviously, he had been lying. As soon as he knew that someone was harassing her, the first thing he had worried about was that she would fall apart again.

Still she was glad that they had talked last night and she had moved past feeling angry with him. When Ryan had dropped her off at home last night, he had come in, made sure she was okay, and despite her protestations that she was fine on her own, he'd stayed with her till Elias arrived. Then he had insisted that they talk things through.

At first, Paige hadn't been interested. Her emotions were still too raw, and she was still too hurt that Elias saw her as weak. But Ryan had persisted, telling her that she'd feel better if she sorted things out with her husband. Reluctantly, she had agreed, knowing that he was right. So, she and Elias had talked for hours last night, and her husband had managed to convince her that even though he worried about her, he knew she was strong

Stifling a yawn, Paige hurried toward her car.

She couldn't wait for this day to be over.

Hopefully, after several nights of practically no sleep she would be exhausted enough to crash tonight.

She wished desperately that they would find whoever kept threatening her. She knew Rose and Jack were looking into it, and they would keep looking until they found answers, but she wanted it over now. She wasn't going to be able to completely relax until the person was caught and the threats stopped.

The blow came without warning.

One second she was on her feet walking toward her car in the underground parking lot of the police station, and the next there was an agonizing burst of pain in her back and she dropped to the concrete floor.

She was winded for a moment, then the pain faded as she fought to catch her breath.

A pair of shoes appeared in her line of sight. Paige thought they were black, but her vision had gone fuzzy as she struggled to draw a breath.

Groggily, she thought that she should reach for her gun, but as she moved her hand, something struck her back again, and all she could do was gasp and collapse against the concrete.

A figure loomed over her. "Stay away from him," a menacing voice whispered.

Stay away from him? Was this her stalker?

"I saw you with him last night," the voice continued.

With him last night? The only people she had been around last night were Ryan and then her husband. "From wh...who?" she wheezed.

"From Ryan," the voice replied. "He doesn't belong to you."

Ryan? Why was someone concerned about her spending time with Ryan? They were friends, they worked together, there was no way to avoid him. And then it clicked. This was Sofia's stalker. Whoever had been harassing Sofia had obviously decided that she was a threat to her via Ryan and intended to try and take her out. But why did they care about her and Ryan working together? They were friends—good friends—but nothing more. Maybe the stalker thought she and Ryan were involved?

"I'm married," she managed to force out. Her chest was still heaving as she tried to draw a decent breath.

"I know. I know everything about you. And I won't let you hurt Sofia. Stay away from Ryan."

She rolled onto her back and attempted to calm her spinning head enough to focus on the man's identity. They didn't know who was stalking Sofia, but if she could get a description of him, then maybe they could figure it out. "Ryan and I...just friends...not involved..." she tried to explain.

"Liar," the shadowy figure hissed and raised something above his head.

Paige just managed to raise an arm to block the blow before it struck her head. Her arm exploded in pain, and she knew instantly that the bones in her arm had shattered. Before she could do more than moan in agony, another blow got her head. The world began to spin and tilt and twirl around her. Desperately, she tried not to black out. If she didn't stay awake, she had no chance of surviving this.

It finally occurred to her damaged brain to call for help. She was in the parking lot at work—someone had to be around, someone had to hear her. She opened her mouth to scream, but another blow got her in the chest and stole her breath again. It was all she could do to curl herself into the fetal position and attempt to protect her vital organs as best as she could.

Blows began to rain down on her in earnest now—striking her head, her arms, her body. She lost count of how many there were. All she knew was pain. So much pain.

Paige knew she was about to die and wished that she could tell her husband just one more time that she loved him.

"Hey!"

The voice came out of nowhere, and the man beating her suddenly disappeared.

Relief temporarily overwhelmed the pain and her broken and battered body collapsed back against the ground.

"Paige?" The horrified exclamation was uttered as someone dropped down beside her. "Paige, can you hear me?" It was Ryan and his fingers pressed against her neck. His touch seemed to reignite the burning pain that radiated the entire length of her body and she groaned. "Paige? Are you with me? Open your eyes, now," he commanded.

It took every bit of effort she possessed, but she managed to force her eyelids open. Her vision was fuzzy, but she could see enough to see Ryan hovering anxiously at her side.

"Hi there," his voice was forced calm, and he pasted on a strained smile. "He's gone. I'm here now, you're safe. Just hang in there; help's on the way."

She had to tell Ryan who attacked her. She had to warn him that Sofia's stalker had escalated. That he was dangerous now. Violently dangerous. The only problem was everything was hazy;

she was disoriented and struggling to stay awake.

Ryan's voice was rumbling above her, but she was in too much pain and too groggy to make out what he was saying.

Summoning her reserves of strength, she managed to lift her hand and grasp the leg of Ryan's pants, tugging on them until he looked down at her. He set his phone down and gently disengaged her hand from his pants, giving it a squeeze before setting it down. "Try not to move," he cautioned her. "I don't know how badly you're hurt. Help's going to be here soon; just hold on."

They both knew she was hurt badly. How badly, she wasn't sure, but her entire body burned, her head swam, and breathing was difficult, so she was guessing she was in bad shape. Already she was fighting to remain conscious, but before she passed out, she had to tell Ryan about the stalker.

Gathering her strength again, she managed to murmur, "Stalker."

"Is that who attacked you?" Ryan leaned down closer so he could hear her weak voice.

She nodded, then against her will her eyes fluttered closed.

"Paige? Come on, Paige, you stay with me," he ordered.

She forced her eyes back open. "Sofia," was all she could manage.

"What about Sofia?" Ryan sounded confused.

"Sofia's stalker," her breathing was getting more and more labored.

"Sofia's stalker attacked you?" Ryan asked. She nodded. "Was it Sofia's stalker who's been stalking you?"

Another nod. "Thinks we're cheating." Her eyelids drooped closed again.

"What?" Ryan sounded shocked, then apparently noticed she was drifting off because he gripped her shoulder, "Paige? No, no, no, no, no, come on, Paige, don't do that, you have to stay awake. Paige, don't go to sleep."

But it was too late—everything faded away into nothingness.

Footsteps pounding toward her was the next thing she was aware of.

"What happened?" Ryan's brother Jack demanded.

"Someone attacked her," Ryan replied. His voice was close by, so he must still be next to her.

"Is she conscious?" Rose's voice was also close.

"She was; she passed out," Ryan answered.

"Paige, honey, it's Rose. If you can hear me, I need you to open your eyes. Can you do that for me?"

Somehow she managed it. Ryan, Rose, and Jack were all hovering over her. She was covered in something soft and warm; a glance down confirmed it was Ryan's jacket.

"I thought Mark was coming," Ryan was starting to sound panicked.

"He was right behind us," Jack replied. "Ambulance should be here soon, too."

Paige didn't hear Ryan's response. She must have lost consciousness again because the next thing she knew there were voices floating above her. The voices were disjointed, nothing more than snippets here and there.

"Low blood pressure...internal bleeding...shock..."

The words swirled together until she couldn't decipher any of them and then faded altogether. When she opened her eyes again, Ryan's other brother Mark was leaning over her. Mark was a trauma surgeon and he was already assessing her condition.

"Hey, Paige," he smiled reassuringly at her when he saw she was awake. "We're going to get you to the hospital soon; just try to relax."

"I can't breathe," she gasped, she was breathing way too fast. Even though every part of her body ached, her stomach swirled with nausea, and her head swam. It was the fact that she was having trouble breathing that was scaring her the most.

"Yeah, I can see that," Mark replied, his voice was calm and that helped to calm her. "I think a broken rib may have punctured your lung. I'm going to have to put a needle in your chest, okay? It should make it easier for you to breathe."

Paige hated needles, but right now she was too weak to protest. She was too weak to do much of anything. The pain was so overwhelming that it was beginning to override everything else. Now she just wanted to sleep.

"Jack, can you hold her still?" Mark asked.

She winced reflexively as Jack's hands pressed down on her shoulders. "Sorry, Paige," Jack murmured apologetically but didn't loosen his grip.

"Okay, Paige, this is going to hurt," Mark cautioned. "I can't do anything about that; I don't have anything on me to give you. I'd wait for the paramedics, but you need this now."

Her head was beginning to pound so badly that she didn't think she was going to be conscious long enough to have to worry about Mark plunging a needle into her chest. There was one more thing she needed to do before she let herself fade away. "Ryan?"

"Yeah, I'm here," his face appeared above her.

"Elias?" she didn't have the energy to form the entire sentence and was counting on Ryan to know what she needed.

"Don't worry, honey, I'll call him for you and have him meet us at the hospital," he assured her.

Mark said something to her, but Paige didn't hear what it was. In fact, she didn't hear anything at all. Her hearing faded along with her vision, and with it the pain, as she slipped into unconsciousness.

* * * * *

5:26 P.M.

Ryan paced restlessly across the surgical waiting room.
He was out of his mind with worry over Paige.

As soon as he had dropped down beside her in the parking garage he had known her condition was serious. She had been weak and woozy, but lucid. Hopefully, her head injuries weren't too bad. The fact that she had been having difficulties breathing had been what had scared him the most.

In a panic, he'd called for an ambulance, and then his brother Jack. He'd lucked out because Mark had been coming to meet Jack at the precinct for some reason he could no longer recall. His younger brother was a doctor—a trauma surgeon—and had begun treating Paige immediately. Once Mark had inserted the needle into her chest, her breathing had improved, but she hadn't regained consciousness.

Mark had said Paige was lucky he had turned up when he had. If he hadn't, if Paige had sustained just a few more blows, then she might have already been dead by the time he got to her. At first, he hadn't known that it was Paige who was being attacked. All he'd seen was a man standing over a prone body and swinging a baseball bat. It wasn't until he had fallen to his knees beside the body that he had realized it was his partner.

At first Paige's eyes had been closed, her head and face covered in blood, and he hadn't even been sure she was still alive. As he'd pressed his fingers to her neck to check for her pulse, she had begun to whimper, and then at his command, she opened her eyes. His temporary relief at seeing her conscious quickly evaporated when she told him that the person who had attacked her was the person who had been stalking her, and that that person was Sofia's stalker.

The knowledge that Sofia's stalker had taken the leap to violence was terrifying. Obviously, the stalker was a threat to Paige, because he somehow believed that he and Paige were having an affair. It was also possible that the stalker would become a physical threat to Sofia, as well. Apparently, the stalker had appointed himself Sofia's protector. He wanted something from Sofia; when she didn't give it to him, he could flip quickly from protector to assailant.

Ryan was also worried about how Sofia was going to react when she found out that her stalker had nearly killed Paige. She was going to blame herself. She would think that if only she hadn't been friends with Paige, or if only she and he weren't involved, or if only she'd been able to identify her stalker, then Paige wouldn't have gotten hurt. But they couldn't play that game. Sofia had nothing to feel guilty about; it wasn't her fault. In fact, if it was anyone's fault it was his…

"Hey," Xavier suddenly appeared before him. "How is she?"

Ryan tiredly scrubbed his hands over his face. "She's in surgery."

"How bad are her injuries?"

"Pretty bad. She has multiple skull fractures, broken arm, broken ribs, pneumothorax, and internal bleeding in her abdomen, plus bruises over pretty much her entire body," Ryan listed.

Xavier winced. "What's her prognosis?"

"They don't know," Ryan replied. "She never woke up again, so they won't know if there's brain damage until she does, but she was awake and talking to me at the scene, so that's a good sign. They weren't sure where she was bleeding from, but they were hopeful that they'd be able to locate the source and fix it in surgery. Mark probably saved her life by starting treatment immediately. He's with her now."

Xavier absorbed the information, then was quiet for a moment. "We're all praying that she'll pull through. Here," Xavier handed him a bag. "Jack sent you some clean clothes."

Ryan glanced down at his sweater, which was smeared with Paige's blood. "Thanks," he took the bag. It was just like his big brother to think of something so practical as clean clothes. He couldn't walk around for the rest of the day covered in his partner's blood, but the idea of changing hadn't yet occurred to him.

"You're welcome."

"Please tell me that they found something to tell us who this guy is?" Jack and Rose had remained at the parking garage to run the scene, but Rose had wanted to travel in the ambulance with Paige to the hospital. The paramedics had refused to take all of them, and there was no way Ryan was leaving his partner, so he and Mark had gone with Paige, and Rose had reluctantly stayed behind—on the condition that he kept her updated on Paige's condition.

"Sorry; so far they have nothing," Xavier apologetically replied.

"Nothing?" Ryan repeated incredulously. "He dropped the bat when I yelled and he ran off."

"No fingerprints; he wore gloves," Xavier explained.

"There are security cameras," he pointed out.

"And he knew it," Xavier said. "He kept his face covered the entire time. Jack and Rose checked the footage, but we never get a look at him. I'm sorry, maybe Paige can give you a description when she wakes up. Or maybe this new information, that he thinks you and Paige are having an affair, will help Sofia figure out who he is," Xavier suggested.

Ryan vigorously shook his head, "Sofia doesn't know yet. I'm worried about how she's going to take it; she and Paige have become close. I asked Jack and Rose to hold off on questioning her until I can be there, and I can't leave here until I know that Paige is going to be okay. I'd appreciate it if you don't tell Annabelle, either. I don't want Sofia to find out accidentally."

"Of course," Xavier nodded understandingly. "We have news..."

"Ryan."

They both turned as someone called his name. Elias was rushing toward them, his face a mask of panic.

"How is she?" Elias asked as he reached them.

"She's still in surgery, she's in serious condition," he explained gently.

"How serious?" Elias was looking dazed, like he couldn't completely comprehend that this was happening.

"Very," Ryan replied.

"How could this happen?" Elias murmured, his gaze riveted to the blood on Ryan's sweater. "She was at work. I thought she'd be safe there. It's a police station," he added, seemingly more to himself than to them.

"It's my fault," Ryan said quietly.

Puzzled, Elias asked, "How is it your fault?"

"Paige is my partner and my best friend. I knew she wasn't sleeping, I knew she was distracted, I knew someone was stalking her. I should never have left her alone. I'm sorry." Guilt had been eating him alive ever since Paige had told him that it was her stalker who'd attacked her.

"Ryan," Elias' eyes cleared and he now looked deadly serious. "I don't blame you and you know Paige wouldn't, either. She didn't want you hovering over her. You said the guy surprised her, and that he had a baseball bat. He went there to hurt her. There was nothing any of us could do to stop it from happening. Right now, all I care about is Paige and making sure she gets through this," his voice began to crack.

"We're going to find who did this to her," Ryan fiercely promised.

Nodding distractedly, Elias' eyes glazed back over with shock. "Do they know how long she'll be in surgery? I want to see her."

"They weren't sure; they didn't know the extent of the damage," Ryan explained. He knew exactly what Elias was going through. He'd been there himself after Isabella caused Sofia to fall down a flight of stairs and she was left fighting for her life. Sofia had survived. Now they had to believe that Paige would, too.

"Ryan, I know you want to be here for Paige, but there isn't anything you can do for her right now. Isabella and Ricky have killed again," Xavier told him.

That caught his attention and momentarily overrode his guilt.

"Where and how many?"

Xavier led him a few steps away from Elias and lowered his voice. "Nine people at an Italian restaurant."

"How did they kill them?"

"They were all shot in the head," Xavier replied.

"Then this one was done by Isabella. She's a perfect shot," he explained. Sofia was not going to like that.

"They had sex there, after they committed the murders," Xavier told him awkwardly.

"They really are a couple," he said dully. Again, Sofia was not going to like that. She didn't even know about their supposed engagement yet, let alone that her sister was now killing with her lover. "That's how we're going to find them, something related to them as a couple."

"I agree," Xavier nodded. "They're engaged. Next logical step would be marriage. I doubt they'll use a justice of the peace, they could threaten a minister," he suggested.

"Or they could use a justice of the peace and fake identities," Ryan countered.

"We should check out both—and hotels and honeymoon suites—Ricky has a thing for them. I know you're worried about Paige. I am too, but we need to go to the restaurant, view the scene, and then start planning where we think they'll go next." Xavier kept his voice gentle.

Ryan was torn between wanting to stay here and wait for news on Paige and doing what he knew his partner would want him to do—go and find Ricky and Isabella. Reluctantly he headed to Elias, only because he knew Xavier was right. "Hey," he announced. Elias turned slowly to stare at him. "I have to go. We have a crime scene we need to check out."

"Okay," Elias still looked out of it.

"Call me the second you know anything about Paige," Ryan told him.

"I will," Elias promised.

He hated that he had to walk out of the hospital before he knew that his partner was going to live, but he was more determined than ever to find Isabella and the stalker.

* * * * *

7:35 P.M.

Isabella was curled up in Ricky's bed flipping through wedding magazines.

She had been on such a high after lunch at the restaurant that she'd asked Ricky to stop at a drug store on the way back home and picked some up.

She was still riding that high.

Who would have thought that killing nine innocent people could be so exhilarating?

Certainly not her.

She had always believed that if she was killing people who deserved it, then it was okay. But those people in the restaurant hadn't done anything that warranted murdering them. And yet, she felt no remorse. Maybe her father had been correct. Maybe she was just like him. He had killed girls who had never done a thing to deserve the horror and torment he dumped on them, and here she was, seemingly following in his footsteps.

How many more people would she kill who didn't deserve it?

If Ricky had his way, then she guessed an awful lot.

Could she be okay with that?

Before today, she wouldn't have been sure. Even after watching him kill those people in the jewelry store, she wasn't completely convinced. Sure, he had impressed her, but she hadn't known up until the moment she fired her gun that she could kill in cold blood.

Ricky had opened a whole new world to her.

A world she could never have experienced without him.

And now, thanks to him, she was engaged and planning a wedding.

Her wedding.

When they bought the wedding magazines, Ricky had promised her that she could have whatever wedding she wanted. Dress, flowers, church, justice of the peace, honeymoon. Whatever she dreamed of, he would do for her. So she had set about studying the magazines in earnest. She had never believed that she would ever have cause to look through one. At least not for herself. Maybe she could have imagined looking through them with Sofia as they planned her sister's wedding. Now, though, she was in full dreaming mode as she poured over every page, picturing herself as the beaming bride.

There were so many choices.

Did she want to go with a big white dress?

Could a murderer get married in a church or was a justice of the peace more appropriate?

She loved flowers, but she didn't have a favorite, so should she just pick whatever was traditional or go without?

Did she want to have a honeymoon? She and Ricky had barely been out of bed since they met, so did they need one?

They wouldn't have a reception because they wouldn't have any guests. Maybe she'd like them to have a special meal afterward—just the two of them.

Then they had to pick a date. Did she care what season they got married in? She didn't have a favorite, so she guessed not. So then what date to pick? Sooner rather than later was probably best.

The problem was that what she wanted most she probably couldn't have.

For her wedding, what would make her most happy would be to have her sister there celebrating with her.

Only Sofia wouldn't want to celebrate.

She wouldn't approve of Ricky Preston.

Still, Isabella wanted Sofia to be there.

Rolling off the bed, she retrieved her handbag and fished out her wallet. Inside was a picture of her and Sofia, taken shortly before Isabella had started with her plan to kill off their family.

She and her sister were sitting side by side on a swing out on the grounds of their family's estate. The sun was shining, making the natural gold highlights in Sofia's red hair shimmer like real gold. Their arms were around each other's shoulders and they were both smiling at the camera.

Was there a way to make it happen?

To get her sister to her wedding?

"Who's that?" a voice rumbled in her ear.

Jumping, she hadn't heard Ricky enter the room. He moved quietly. She bet that helped him when he was committing a murder. "My sister, Sofia."

"*That's* your sister?" Ricky's blue eyes opened wide.

"Yes," she confirmed, confused.

"She's beautiful." Ricky hadn't shifted his gaze from the picture.

A stab of jealousy shafted through her. She was used to people seeing her sister as the pretty one and herself as the plain one. She'd thought Ricky was different, though. She thought he loved her. "She is," Isabella agreed stiffly.

He seemed to read her mind and chuckled. "I still love you, but your sister is hot. I'm talking drop-dead-gorgeous hot."

Jealousy turned to suspicion. "She's my sister," she reminded him.

"I know."

The way he said it made her skin prickle. Ricky was a rapist. She didn't want him anywhere near her sister. "I've been reading the wedding magazines and thinking about our wedding," she announced, hoping to distract him.

"Oh, yeah?" He said the words, but his eyes were still glued to Sofia's picture.

"Ricky, you're not listening to me." She had to remind herself not to stamp her foot. She had a feeling tantrums would not help her get her way with Ricky Preston.

"Sure I am." He finally lifted his gaze to meet hers. "You pick a date?"

"No, but I was thinking as soon as possible. What about tomorrow?" she suggested.

He shrugged, a little disinterestedly. "Sure, whatever you want."

Isabella finally lost her temper. "Would you please stop staring at my sister?"

"Can't help it. I told you, she's hot. She turns me on." He didn't sound the least bit repentant.

A glance at his crotch proved that to be true. "You aren't thinking of raping her, are you?" Isabella hoped she sounded as outraged as she felt.

"Not just thinking about it; I'm planning on doing it. We can grab her before we leave town, take her with us. That's what you want, right? That way you can be with your sister. And we can keep the baby with us. Your sister can look after the kid, and you get to keep your family." He grinned at her, seemingly pleased with his plan.

"You are not grabbing my sister so you can keep her close by and rape her whenever you feel like it. I forbid it." She eyed him angrily.

"Tough," he shrugged again.

"'Tough'?" she repeated, astounded.

"Hey, you knew who I was from the beginning," he reminded her. "I see someone I want, I get them. I got you, didn't I?" he goaded.

"You didn't *get me*," she protested, outraged. "I'm not just here for your amusement, you know."

"Oh, no?" he teased, grabbing her and dragging her up against him, rubbing his bulging crotch against her. "I turn you on, don't

I?"

"No," she huffed, knowing it was a lie, but she was too angry with him right now to be honest with him.

"Liar," he laughed, kissing her roughly, then throwing her down on the bed.

"Get off me." She wriggled beneath him as he lay on top of her. Sex with Ricky was the last thing she wanted right now.

"No way. You want me; you know you do. So, your sister turns me on; so what? I'm not in love with her. When I do her, it'll just be sex. Nothing more. What we have goes way beyond that."

With that his mouth greedily took hers, and his hands began to roam her body. Unfortunately, they had been together so many times now that he knew exactly what to do to her to get her body responding almost against her will. Isabella fought it at first. How could she willingly have sex with a man who had told her outright that he intended to abduct and rape her sister? And yet, even as protestations flooded her mind, her body was hungrily melding with Ricky's, seeking more and more of him.

With a moan of pleasure, she surrendered and gave up her mind and body to Ricky.

* * * * *

10:46 P.M.

Sofia had that awful feeling in the pit of her stomach.

The kind of feeling that usually precipitated bad news.

Maybe she was just being paranoid because things hadn't been going so well lately—with her stalker breaking in here three nights in a row and someone stalking Paige, and Isabella seemingly teaming up with another killer. It was a lot to add to her already-full plate.

Then again, maybe she *wasn't* just being paranoid.

Ryan hadn't called. He had sent a text a few hours ago to say he was held up at work and wouldn't be home till late. That was odd. He usually called her when he was going to be late. It was like he hadn't wanted to talk to her. Her imagination was working overtime conjuring up reasons why that could be.

It was also odd that he hadn't sent Jack or Rose to come and stay with her. She knew he was worried about her here alone, and yet in his text he had merely said to lock the doors, set the alarm, and not to open the door for anyone.

He knew something.

She was sure he did.

Something he didn't want her to know just yet.

"Are you okay?" Annabelle came up beside her.

"I don't know," Sofia answered honestly. She was standing in the kitchen, staring out at the dark, cold night. She shifted her gaze to meet Annabelle's in their reflections in the window. "Have you heard from Xavier?"

"Only the text earlier to say that he was held up at work and would be here late to pick me up," Annabelle replied. "Why?"

Unable to suppress a shiver, Sofia said, "I have a bad feeling. I can't explain it."

"Did you try calling Ryan?"

"Yes, but he won't pick up. I keep getting his voicemail; he's avoiding me," she answered.

"Want me to try calling Xavier?" Annabelle offered. "He and Ryan are probably together."

"If they're together and Ryan's avoiding me, then he probably won't let Xavier talk to you. That's why I haven't bothered trying Paige," she explained.

Annabelle was quiet for a moment before proposing, "Why don't you go lie down for a while, and I'll answer your phone if Ryan calls you."

"Thanks." Sofia was touched by Annabelle's offer, but knew there was no way she was going to be able to close her eyes until she knew what Ryan was trying to hide from her. "But I wouldn't be able to sleep."

"At least take some painkillers, then," Annabelle suggested. "You look like you can barely stand up. Your leg must be aching, and I haven't seen you take anything for it all day."

Annabelle was right. Her leg was aching and she hadn't taken anything for it today. "Yeah, okay," she agreed. If Ryan had bad news, then she didn't want to be distracted by pain.

"Good." Annabelle's reflection smiled at her. "I'll get you something to eat, too." Then she moved off in search of food before Sofia could protest.

While Annabelle bustled about the kitchen, Sofia turned her attention back to the dark night. There was a clear sky, although they'd had a little snow earlier in the day. The moon hung like a huge white ball in the black sky, millions of stars sprinkled around it. Usually the night sky calmed her, made her feel better and more peaceful, but tonight it didn't seem to be working.

Something caught her eye.

Movement.

Behind the bushes.

A shadow.

A moving shadow.

Someone was out there.

Enough was enough. She was putting an end to this here and now. She grabbed the gun from the table where she'd left it—Ryan had told her not to get it out, but she couldn't just sit around unarmed and vulnerable. Disregarding the fact that she was dressed only in sweatpants, an oversize sweatshirt and fuzzy socks, she threw open the back door and darted out.

Startled, Annabelle called after her, "What are you doing?"

Ignoring her for the moment, Sofia headed straight for where she'd seen someone hiding. She stopped short when she saw a figure behind a tree. "Hey," she yelled. "I have a gun; come out where I can see you."

She anxiously waited to see if the person was going to comply. She was desperate to know who had been stalking her and at the same time, she was terrified. It could be anyone. Maybe even someone she knew and trusted.

Slowly, the figure began to move. As they stepped out from behind the tree, they were hit by a beam of light from the moon, their face illuminated.

Sofia gasped, "Isabella?"

Her sister said nothing, just stood and stared at her.

"It was you?" Sofia stared back in astonishment. Surely it couldn't have been her sister who had been stalking her for over a year? There wouldn't have been any need for Isabella to stalk her before. Maybe now that she was on the run from the police, but not a year ago. Isabella was crazy, though, so she didn't have to make sense.

Isabella continued to just stand there.

"Isabella!" Sofia was becoming exasperated, but she didn't feel like her sister was a threat to her, so she lowered her gun. "Why have you been stalking me?"

Isabella blinked. "Stalking you? I haven't been stalking you," Isabella protested. "I've come by a couple of times to see you, but I'm not your stalker."

"Then what are you doing in my backyard, in the middle of the night?" she demanded.

"I had to see you one last time," Isabella replied softly.

"One last time? Are you going to run? Please don't, Isabella," she pleaded. "Let me call Ryan, turn yourself in, I won't walk away from you. I miss you; I don't want you to disappear. Please, Isabella, Ryan told me that you've been hanging around with some guy—a killer. Isabella, that's crazy. He's no good for you, and you can't let him around the baby. Ryan said you named her Sophie. After me?"

Isabella nodded.

"Isabella, please, please come inside with me. Let's call Ryan, end this now. If you turn yourself in, they might be able to offer you a deal. You could go to a psychiatric hospital; clearly, you need help. What those kids at your school did, and then finding out about what Logan was doing, it messed you up. But I can get you the help you need if you'll just trust me." Sofia could see her sister was wavering. "Please, Isabella," she pushed, "please let me help you."

"Actually, Isabella already has someone to help her."

The voice spoke in her ear, and before she knew what was happening, an arm had wrapped around her chest, pinning her arms at her side, and a hand clamped over her mouth. Sofia struggled wildly, but it was no use. The man holding her was bigger and stronger than she was. She still had the gun in her hand and attempted to maneuver it so she could fire it, but the man holding her simply shifted her slightly so he could grip her wrist and twist the gun out of her hand. Was this the killer Ryan had told her about? Ricky Preston? Her frantic eyes turned to Isabella. Surely her sister would help her. Isabella loved her; she wouldn't let this monster hurt her. Would she?

But Isabella was just standing there—not moving to help her at all. Sofia wanted to beg her sister to tell this man to let her go, but with his hand still over her mouth she was unable to.

She frantically fought to get free. Sofia knew she was fighting for her life. This man wouldn't let her go, and it seemed she couldn't count on her sister for help. She should have stayed inside. Called the police. Now her only hope was Annabelle. The other woman hadn't followed her out, but surely she would realize something was wrong when Sofia didn't come right back.

"It's okay, Sofia." Isabella had come up beside her and brushed her hair back off her face with a gentle hand. "I'm so glad you miss me; I've been missing you, too. Now we can be together, you and me and Sophie and Ricky."

Sofia frantically shook her head, straining to speak past Ricky's hand, knowing it was pointless but having to try. They were going to kidnap her, take her with them, wherever they were planning on running to. She wanted baby Sophie, but not like this. She didn't want to live as a prisoner.

"We have to go before her cop boyfriend comes home," Ricky announced, lifting her higher so her feet came off the ground.

"It'll be okay, Sofia," Isabella promised.

Only Sofia knew that it wouldn't be okay. If they got her out of her backyard, then she'd never come back. Ryan would look for her but there were too many places where Isabella and Ricky could take her and hide her away. He would never find her.

"Sofia?" Annabelle called.

Ricky froze, and turned so they were facing the house where Annabelle was standing a few steps from the open backdoor. "Well, I'll be darned," Ricky drawled. "Annabelle Englewood. Of all the coincidences, of all the luck," he chuckled.

Annabelle stood frozen in place as she registered Ricky's voice. Sofia wanted to scream at her to run. Lock herself inside and call the police. But all she could do was squirm in a fruitlessly desperate bid to get free.

"Come here, Annabelle," Ricky ordered. When she hesitated and didn't immediately comply, Ricky stepped closer so Annabelle could see him, and see Sofia in his arms. "Come, or I'll kill her— slowly and painfully," he threatened.

Sofia had no doubt that was true. And apparently, Annabelle didn't either, because she whimpered and hurried toward them.

"Good girl," Ricky mocked. "This way." He gestured Annabelle in front of him and herded her toward the front of the house. "You didn't tell me your sister was friends with Annabelle," he commented to Isabella.

"I didn't know," Isabella replied. "They mustn't have been friends for very long."

"Then this was an amazing stroke of luck." Ricky stopped at the trunk of a car. "You get your sister and I get Annabelle. There are zip ties in the backseat," he told Isabella. "Grab me four."

Isabella did as she was told and retrieved the zip ties. "Try anything stupid and I'll kill your friend," Ricky warned Annabelle, then gestured at Isabella to put the zip ties on Annabelle. Once Annabelle was secured with the ties around her wrists—fastened behind her back—and ankles, Ricky turned his attention to her. She considered screaming for help when he removed his hand from her mouth, but she was worried about what Ricky would do to her and Annabelle if she tried it, so she kept quiet. In less than a minute, Sofia found herself bound and thrown in the trunk of Ricky's car with Annabelle beside her, making the already-small space unbearably cramped. "Just in case you think of screaming," Ricky smiled at them as he put a piece of tape over both of their mouths.

The thunk of the trunk closing seemed to echo inside Sofia's head with an air of finality that she found deeply disturbing and terrifying.

* * * * *

11:29 P.M.

Ryan was quiet as they walked through the hospital halls, heading for the ICU to check on Paige. Really, Xavier corrected himself, Ryan had been quiet ever since they'd left the hospital earlier.

After they'd left, they had gone straight to the restaurant where Ricky and Isabella had played out the next chapter in their sick, demented game of love. Ryan had been focused and observant, but quieter than he had been the last few days.

Once they wrapped up there, they had met Jack and Rose back at the station, where the two had briefed them on the little they had recovered from the parking garage where Paige was attacked. What they had discovered amounted to nothing—nothing that would help them find out who had nearly killed Paige. Nothing that helped them figure out who was obsessed enough with Sofia to almost beat someone to death because they believed that person was cheating with Sofia's boyfriend.

What they needed to do was talk to Sofia. Xavier sympathized with both her and Ryan. She was no doubt going to blame herself, and the fact that Paige was still in a serious condition was only going to make it worse. Her surgery had gone well, but they still didn't know if Paige was going to make it. They had found and repaired the sources of her internal bleeding, but she still hadn't regained consciousness, and until she did, they wouldn't know the extent of her head injuries and whether there would be permanent damage.

Xavier also got why Ryan didn't want Sofia told until he could be there to support her. It would be a blow to Sofia, and she was still fragile following her sister's murderous spree five months ago. However, facts were facts, and they needed to see if this new information would help Sofia figure out who was stalking her.

So as soon as they checked in on Paige they were going to go and talk to Sofia. And not just about her stalker. They also needed to question her about her sister. If getting married was now Ricky and Isabella's focus, then, hopefully, they could use that to get a step ahead of them. Sofia might know things about what Isabella would want in a wedding. Maybe she could point them in the right direction, like where Isabella would want the ceremony, and where she might buy a dress; these things could be crucial in finding them before the pair could commit another murder.

Reaching the intensive care unit, a nurse directed them to Paige's bed. Ryan went completely still at the sight of his unconscious partner. Paige's head was heavily bandaged, and her face beneath was bruised and swollen. She had a tube down her throat to help her breathe, and one arm was in a cast. Elias clutched her other hand as he sat in a chair at her bedside, his gaze riveted to her face as though he could will her into waking up if he tried hard enough.

"Hey," Xavier said softly, and Elias' eyes bounced their way. "How's she doing?"

He exhaled slowly before replying, "She's stable for now, which is good, but they're listing her condition as serious. I just wish she'd wake up," his voice trembled.

"It's only been a few hours; give her time," Xavier comforted. After Ricky had almost killed Annabelle, she had been unconscious for almost a day before she finally came around.

"Is there anything we can do for you?" Ryan finally ripped his blue eyes from Paige's face to look at her husband.

"I'm fine," Elias answered absently.

"Really," Ryan insisted, "we can get you something to eat. Or if you want to go to the bathroom, or even home to get a few hours' sleep, I can sit with her."

"No, I'm fine, really. I want to be here when she wakes up. And you should go home to Sofia. Paige told me about her stalker, breaking in three nights in a row. You should be home with her, make sure she's safe."

"I will." Ryan looked torn. "I just wanted to make sure Paige was okay; the stalker is still out there."

"Belinda put an officer on her," Elias gestured to a young man standing by the ICU door. "If the stalker tries to come back and finish what he started, he won't be getting to her. She's safe, Ryan; go home and take care of Sofia. I'll call you the second Paige wakes up or if there are any changes in her condition. I promise."

"Okay," Ryan somewhat reluctantly agreed. "Call if you need anything."

After another assurance from Elias that he would if he needed anything, Ryan allowed himself to be led out of the hospital. Xavier drove, heading for Ryan's house. On the way, he ran through what they needed to question Sofia about. It was a struggle to keep Ryan focused. It was like, after seeing his partner, the thin grip on control he'd had left, had been shattered.

Ryan needed to get it together before they told Sofia what had happened. She was going to be upset enough as it was, and feel guilty, and if Ryan was this distraught and guilty himself, Sofia would only feed off that. Xavier contemplated calling Ryan's brother, Jack, and his partner, and asking them to come straight to the house. Ryan had convinced them that he would be able to get more information out of Sofia than they would, but Xavier was beginning to doubt that. Jack seemed to have a calm and unflappable air about him, and Xavier suspected he was an expert at drawing out information from traumatized victims.

Pulling into Ryan's driveway, he surreptitiously typed on his cell phone, sending a text to Jack, whose number he had gotten earlier today, asking him and Rose to meet them at Ryan and Sofia's house.

He needn't have bothered trying to hide what he was doing. Ryan just sat there, staring into space, lost in thought. "We're here," Xavier finally announced when it became clear that Ryan had not noticed that the car had stopped moving.

"Oh," Ryan blinked, then turned dismal eyes his way. "I'm not sure I'm ready to tell Sofia about Paige; she's going to be so upset."

"I know, but you know we have to. We'll tell her about Paige, ask her about her stalker, and then about Isabella," Xavier reminded him as they both climbed from the car.

In a daze, Ryan walked to the front door and fumbled with his key. He fumbled so much that Xavier had to clench his hands together to keep from easing the key from Ryan's shaking hands and unlocking the door himself. Once they were inside, Ryan seemed to deflate even more. The prospect of telling Sofia what had happened to Paige was clearly crushing him.

"Sofia? Annabelle?" Xavier called out.

There was no response, but there was a light on in the kitchen at the back of the house, so they headed that way.

"Sofia? Annabelle?" Ryan called louder.

There was still no reply.

It was late; maybe the girls had decided to take a nap while they waited. Sofia was still dealing with medical issues, and Annabelle's sleep was so erratic that it seemed a likely possibility.

However, they both froze as they entered the kitchen.

It was empty.

The back door was open.

Ryan gasped, his already pale face growing even whiter. "They're gone."

"We don't know that," Xavier contradicted, clawing at denial.

"Their purses are here and their cell phones," Ryan gestured at the counter. "The stalker must have come here after he attacked Paige. He must have grabbed her, taken her away," Ryan was almost in a panic.

"We don't know it was the stalker," Xavier countered. "It could be Ricky and Isabella. If it was Sofia's stalker, why would he take Annabelle?"

"Who knows?" Ryan exploded. "Why would he try to kill Paige? He's crazy and he has them."

"The cameras," Xavier remembered suddenly. "You had cameras installed, right? As part of your new security system. We can check them, then we'll know who took them."

"Yeah, okay," Ryan agreed shakily, then took a deep breath and visibly pulled himself together. "I'm sorry. It's just first Paige, and now Sofia…but we need to remain calm if we're going to find them."

As Ryan rushed off to check the video footage, Xavier let his own panic overwhelm him for a moment.

Just a moment.

That was all he allowed himself.

Then he deliberately calmed down. Ryan was right. They needed to remain calm if they were going to find Annabelle and Sofia.

It was just that Xavier doubted that either he or Ryan could manage to hold it together for very long.

JANUARY 14TH

Ricky couldn't believe his luck.

Honestly, he had to be the luckiest guy in the world.

He had Isabella, he had her sister, and now he had Annabelle.

What an utter fluke that Annabelle and Sofia were friends. When he'd gone with Isabella to Sofia's house to grab her, he had never even dreamed of encountering Annabelle, too.

It had taken a little convincing to get Isabella to go along with taking Sofia. She didn't like the idea of him raping her sister. That didn't faze him. She'd get over it or get used to it. Whichever, it didn't matter to him. The idea of being able to keep the baby, and have her sister with her had appealed to Isabella so much that she was prepared to go along with pretty much anything.

And as if having Sofia to play with wasn't good enough, he now had Annabelle, too. Twice as much fun. He could now torture Annabelle to his heart's content without having to worry about her pesky detective boyfriend getting in the way.

Thoughts of Sofia and Annabelle were too much.

He was getting excited.

He abruptly pulled the car over to the side of the road. Isabella glanced at him in surprise.

"What are you doing?" she demanded.

"What does it look like?" he snarked back.

"It looks like you're pulling over." Isabella glared at him. "I thought we wanted to reach the cabin before daybreak; we shouldn't be making any stops."

"This can't wait until we get there," he informed her. He had rented them a small cabin in the woods—remote—the perfect place to hide away two abducted women. They were going to get Sofia and Annabelle settled, then they would go and collect the baby.

"Are you going to do what I think you're going to do?" she queried frostily.

"Yep," he agreed cheerfully.

"With my sister or the other one?"

"What do you think?" he flung open the door and climbed out into the chilly night.

"No." She jumped out and ran to the trunk, blocking him from opening it. "Don't touch my sister."

Ricky was starting to get annoyed. "I'll do whatever I want to do with whoever I want to do it with."

"Not right now. At least give her time to adjust to her new life," she challenged. "I thought it was Annabelle you really wanted anyway. Just please, leave my sister alone."

He resisted the urge to roll his eyes; Isabella could be surprisingly sentimental at times. Instead, he went with charming and understanding. "Fine, whatever you want; I won't touch her—for now."

She narrowed her eyebrows at him. "Thank you. I have to make a phone call, check on Sophie."

"Reception is spotty this deep in the woods. You may have to walk back to that gas station we passed about ten minutes ago," he cautioned.

"Fine." She was already pulling out her phone.

"You want me to drive you back?" he offered, hoping she would say no.

"No, I think I need some air," she huffed, turning her back on him and stalking off.

Ricky waited a full five minutes to make sure Isabella was gone before popping the trunk. Both Annabelle and Sofia stared fearfully up at him. He grinned, his irritation at Isabella fading as he fed off the girls' terror.

"How're my girls?" he reached out to stroke their hair; both women shrunk away from him.

"Annabelle, as much fun as we've had together in the past, I think I'm going to have to give your friend a turn first." He patted Annabelle's head, then hoisted Sofia up out of the trunk and over his shoulder. He had to hand it to her, she put up quite a fight, wiggling and squirming in a desperate bid to get away from him. Of course, it was totally pointless.

"Catch you later, Annabelle." He smiled as he closed the trunk. He set Sofia on top of it and pinned her down with one arm. With his other hand, he pulled out his knife and cut the plastic tie from around her ankles. Having her legs unrestrained meant running the risk that she could run, but he didn't want to have to carry her, and besides he'd seen her walking with a limp earlier. She was clearly injured.

After giving her a minute to let circulation restore to her feet, he lifted her up again then set her down on the ground. "This way," he said cheerfully, grabbing her bound wrists and dragging her along with him. Even as he pulled her along she continued to try and fight him, doing her darnedest to get free and yelling at him through the tape on her mouth. Her struggles only served to further excite him.

Ricky wanted to get her deep enough into the woods that anyone passing by and seeing the car wouldn't find them should they come looking. And if when Isabella returned to the car before they were back, she wouldn't be able to locate them until he was finished.

He was moving so briskly that Sofia couldn't keep her footing. In fact, she slipped and stumbled so many times that he gave up trying to get her to walk. Instead he hooked an arm through hers, which were still pulled behind her back, and simply dragged her.

When he felt like they had gone far enough, Ricky dumped Sofia on the snowy ground. As soon as she realized he was no longer holding onto her, she attempted to shuffle away from him as fast as she could manage. Ricky watched her for a moment before going to her. He pinned her to the ground as he straddled her stomach, a knee on either side of her hips. Beneath him she thrashed frantically. She knew what he was about to do and it terrified her.

"The first time'll be the worst," he consoled her, for some reason feeling vaguely sorry for what he was going to do to her. Maybe it was because she was Isabella's sister and he truly loved Isabella.

Oblivious to the cold, he tugged down his pants and then Sofia's and started to enter her.

* * * * *

1:34 A.M.

How could she have let him talk her into this?

How could he have convinced her that this was a good idea?

How stupid was she?

Isabella couldn't believe she had agreed to let Ricky abduct her sister and hold her prisoner. She'd been selfish. She'd known that Ricky wouldn't keep his hands off Sofia indefinitely, and yet she'd gone along with it anyway. Just so she could have her sister close by, she was going to let her fiancé rape her.

What was wrong with her?

She was putting an end to it now.

She had to make it better. Get her sister someplace safe—away from Ricky.

There was only one thing she could do.

She had never intended to call and check on Sophie. She knew the baby was fine and well taken care of.

"Hello," the voice on the other end of the phone all but snapped at her.

"Hello, Ryan," she said softly.

"Isabella?"

"Yes, it's me," she confirmed.

"Where is she? Where's Sofia? We know you took her. You and Ricky. We have cameras all around the house, we saw it all. Where are you?" Ryan demanded.

"I'm sorry," was all she could whisper, tears welling up in her eyes. "I'm so sorry, Ryan."

"What's happened?" Ryan sounded panicked now. "Did something happen to Sofia? Did you hurt her? Did Ricky Preston?"

"She's okay," she assured him. "But Ricky, he wants to keep her; Annabelle, too. I don't want him to hurt her."

"Then tell me where you are and I'll come get her," Ryan had deliberately gentled his voice. "Look, I know that no matter what, you love Sofia, so let me come and get her, you too. Isabella, we can sort something out, I promise."

"Okay," she murmured, feeling somewhat relieved. She had been naïve to think she could run forever. Maybe going with Ryan and Sofia and letting them sort something out was the best idea. Relenting, she gave Ryan the address.

"I'm going to be there soon," he reassured her. "I'm on my way."

"Ryan, hurry," then she hung up. She had to get back. Ricky had agreed to leave Sofia alone for the moment, but that wouldn't last.

She hadn't had to go all the way back to the gas station to get a signal, so it took her only a couple of minutes to reach the car. Immediately, she knew something was wrong. She couldn't see Ricky anywhere.

Popping the trunk, Isabella already knew what she was going to find inside.

Annabelle's terrified white eyes stared back at her.

Ricky had Sofia.

Ricky had her sister, and he was going to rape her.

Isabella couldn't let that happen.

She ripped the tape off Annabelle's mouth. "Did he say where he was going?" she demanded.

Annabelle said nothing, just trembled uncontrollably.

She didn't have time for this, grabbing the woman's shoulders, she shook her violently. "Answer me," she shrieked. "Did Ricky say where he was taking my sister?"

Tears spilled silently down her cheeks. Annabelle shook her head.

"Did he say that he was going to hurt her?"

Crying now, Annabelle nodded.

Darting to the front of the car, she flung open the door and rummaged through the glove compartment until she found a knife. Returning to the trunk, Annabelle's eyes grew wide at the sight of the knife. She whimpered and shrank farther back into the trunk.

Isabella didn't have time to reassure the woman, so she simply grabbed her, dragged her closer and cut the plastic tie binding her wrists behind her back. Then she tossed the knife at her. "You'll have to cut your own ankles free; I don't have time. I have to find Ricky and Sofia. I called Ryan, and he'll be here soon. Find someplace to hide in case Ricky comes back, and wait for Ryan."

Then she turned and ran, searching the ground as she went, looking for signs of disturbance. Catching a trail, she followed it, running faster and faster. Ricky had her sister, was probably raping her this very second.

Her chest was beginning to burn and her legs felt heavy, but she didn't stop. Couldn't stop. Sofia was counting on her. She had to make things right.

Just when she thought she couldn't run another step, she saw them.

Sofia was pinned to the ground and half naked.

Ricky Preston was on top of her. His pants were pulled down, too.

Isabella saw red.

* * * * *

1:59 A.M.

"You know I'm driving as fast as I can," Xavier commented mildly.

Ryan cast him a confused glance.

Xavier glanced off the road and at the floor on the passenger side. Ryan followed his gaze and saw that he had his gas pedal foot pressed to the floor.

"Sorry," he apologized. He had been even more on edge since Isabella's phone call. She had sounded sincerely concerned about Sofia and convinced that Ricky Preston was going to hurt her. Ryan prayed that they would get there before Ricky had a chance to do anything to her.

Returning home to find the house empty and Sofia gone was his worst nightmare. He had nearly lost it completely. If it hadn't been for Xavier, he probably would have. Even though Annabelle had been missing, too, Xavier had somehow managed to keep his wits about him. Suggesting they review the camera footage had given Ryan something to do, and it made him feel more in control of the situation and better able to remain calm.

Because calm was all that was going to help them find the girls.

Well strike that. Even once they confirmed it was Isabella and Ricky who had taken Sofia and Annabelle, that hadn't helped them find them. They were already looking for the murderous pair, and they already had no real leads as to where to look. What was going to help them find the girls was a stroke of luck—Isabella's phone call. She had given them the address of a cabin where Ricky was heading to hide out for a while, and they were currently speeding as fast they could on the icy roads to get there.

Ryan had to keep himself focused on the case so he didn't lose his mind. "The kidnapping was Ricky's idea," he said.

Xavier looked surprised. "But it's Isabella's sister they took. They probably didn't even know Annabelle would be there. Why are you so sure that Ricky was the instigator in the abduction?"

"Because Isabella would never intentionally hurt Sofia," he explained.

"I thought she poisoned Sofia."

"Only to keep her distracted so she could follow through on her plan to kill their family. And when she made an attempt on Sofia's life, it was a fake. She deliberately went with the heart shot because she knew Sofia was wearing a vest. Isabella has had more than enough opportunities to kill Sofia if she wanted, and she never has."

"Isabella said she was sorry, though. Why do you think she was apologizing on the phone if Ricky was the one who wanted to kidnap Sofia?"

"Ricky probably latched onto Sofia through Isabella," he reasoned. "It wouldn't have been hard for him to manipulate her. She loves Sofia; she doesn't really want to leave her."

Xavier nodded. "Sofia is beautiful, just the kind of woman to capture Ricky's attention." He paused, then began uncomfortably, "Look, I'm sorry I have to say this, I don't want to raise the possibility because I could be wrong, but I want you to be prepared."

Ryan's gut tightened. "Tell me what?"

"Sofia is pretty and Ricky likes pretty women. He probably took her because he wants to rape her," Xavier finished in a rush.

His gut tightened some more. Ryan had already thought of that, but hearing someone else say it seemed to make that possibility more real.

"He already raped Annabelle," Xavier continued softly. "Twice."

"I'm sorry to hear that." Ryan hoped Sofia was not about to

suffer a similar fate.

"It must have been rough." Xavier shot him a quick glance then returned his eyes to the road. "Falling for a woman in a case you were working."

"I already knew Sofia before the case," he explained. "Well I didn't really *know* her, but I had seen her around and I had a major crush on her. I thought I had hidden it pretty well; apparently, everyone knew. Including Sofia. She had seen me around, too."

"If you had a crush on her, why didn't you go talk to her?" Xavier looked intrigued.

"She was beautiful and rich and totally out of my league. And then I thought she was involved with someone. It wasn't until we spent some time together because of her family's case that I realized she wasn't dating anyone, and that we both liked each other. Things haven't gone smoothly for you and Annabelle?" he was just as interested to find out Xavier and Annabelle's back-story as Xavier apparently was to find out about his and Sofia's.

"No, they definitely haven't," Xavier replied. "It didn't help that at first we thought it was Annabelle who had killed her family. Then she found out something about my ex-wife, which made her doubt me. I got mad at her for digging into my past, which gave Ricky Preston an opportunity to get his hands on her. She already didn't trust people. Then with Ricky taking advantage of her, and me telling her that, although I'm not in love with my ex, I'll always love her made it worse. She still doesn't completely trust me and sometimes I wonder if she ever will. I just think if we'd met under different circumstances things would be different."

"She seems to have connected with Sofia, maybe that'll help her," Ryan encouraged, glad he had suggested introducing the two. Although if he hadn't, Annabelle wouldn't have been abducted tonight.

"I'm hoping so," Xavier agreed. "She really needs a real friend.

Someone she can trust, someone who she can confide in, someone who she doesn't have a reason to doubt."

"Sofia's a loyal friend," he assured Xavier. "She wouldn't do anything to give Annabelle cause to doubt her."

"She might not have to," Xavier said grimly. "If Annabelle perceives that something that happens to Sofia is her fault, that'll be all it takes. She'll shut down. Withdraw again. She's very sensitive about how people see her. She has no self-confidence at all. I really hope that things work out between Annabelle and Sofia because I think Sofia is exactly what Belle needs, but I don't want Sofia to feel badly if it doesn't."

"Sofia won't give up, that's not who she is. And I don't think you're going to give up on Annabelle, either. I think that's what she needs to see. That she has people in her life who aren't going anywhere. Eventually she'll start to believe it and to trust those in her life."

"I hope so." Xavier looked like he wasn't quite convinced.

"None of this matters anyway if we can't find them." Ryan could feel his panic swelling again. Ricky had had Sofia for over three hours now. More than enough time for him to have hurt her or killed her and buried her body.

"We'll find them," Xavier said confidently.

Ryan wished he was as confident of that. Isabella's voice telling him to hurry kept echoing in his head. If they didn't find them soon, then he didn't think they were going to find them at all.

* * * * *

1:59 A.M.

She was in shock.

Sofia knew she was.

Knew it because she had stopped fighting back.

She'd fought as hard as she could. From the moment he first

grabbed her, she had done everything within her limited ability to get away. Even in the trunk of the car, she had tried so hard to get out of the plastic zip ties that she'd made her wrists bleed. Now they ached horribly with every little movement. The trunk had been terribly cramped and her leg had begun to ache because she couldn't stretch it out.

As Ricky had pushed her along with him through the woods, she'd still done her best to escape. But the pace he'd set had been too much; her injured leg couldn't cope and had given out on her so many times that Ricky had gotten fed up with her and started to drag her. That had been worse. Unable to protect herself, branches had scraped her face and arms and legs, tearing through her clothing. Her feet, clad only in socks, had thudded into rocks and tree trunks, and were now so painful she wasn't even sure she could walk on them.

Still, the pain hadn't won out. The second that Ricky dropped her on the snowy ground, she had sprung into action. Sprung might not be the best word. Her battered and bruised and bound body wouldn't allow her to spring, but it hadn't prevented her from shuffling backward.

Of course, that, too, was pointless.

Ricky had merely watched her with interest and then when he was ready, he pinned her to the ground. As he'd straddled her, she had gone berserk. She'd thrashed desperately, like a trapped animal, ignoring the pain in her wrists and leg.

Again, it had done no good.

He was on top of her and she could feel him pressed against her stomach. Through the tape on her mouth, she tried to beg him not to. Tried to beg him to leave her alone.

But when his hands took hold of the waistband of her sweatpants, she froze.

It was like she lost the ability to move.

She didn't even notice the icy air against her bare flesh.

As awful as what Ricky Preston was about to do to her,

Isabella's betrayal was worse.

How could her sister let this happen?

No, not just *let,* but actively encourage.

Isabella had known that Ricky was going to do this and she had led him straight to her. Her sister had been selfish. Once again, Isabella had been so caught up in what she wanted that she had completely disregarded the consequences of her actions to others. Her sister had basically agreed to let Ricky keep her as a prisoner, a sex slave, just so they would be together. What kind of sister did that?

Even Isabella's betrayal couldn't occupy her mind enough to distract her from what was happening to her.

Ricky was just forcing himself inside her when a scream split through the night and something launched at them.

Too shocked to move, Sofia just lay on the ground, panting.

"I told you to keep your hands off my sister," Isabella screeched.

"And I told you that I do whatever I want," Ricky returned.

Isabella was a big girl, bigger and stronger than Sofia, but she was still no match for Ricky. He swung his fist at her and connected with her face. The blow caused Isabella to lose her grip on Ricky.

Her wild gaze darted from Ricky to Isabella, who lay bleeding in the snow, and Sofia suddenly regained control of her body. Frantically, she tried to move. But with her arms behind her and her pants around her knees she didn't get very far.

Ricky moved quickly. Before Isabella had a chance to recover, Ricky had positioned himself behind Sofia, using her as a human shield. Sofia would have tried to break free but Ricky held a knife to her throat.

Isabella moved too, brushing at the blood gushing from a wound on her cheek; she pulled out a gun and pointed it at them.

"You can't get the shot," Ricky taunted.

"Let her go," Isabella replied calmly.

Relief rushed through Sofia. Isabella couldn't go through with it. She couldn't let Ricky hurt her. Isabella had saved her from being raped and she could save her from Ricky. Her sister was a perfect shot, even with Ricky using her as a human shield Isabella should be able to get an angle.

"Try anything and I'll kill her," Ricky said in such a serious voice that Sofia couldn't help but shiver.

In fact, she couldn't seem to stop shivering. The cold was getting to her. She wasn't properly dressed to be outdoors on a winter's night. If she didn't get somewhere warm soon, she was going to become hypothermic.

"You won't," Isabella protested, although she didn't sound quite convinced.

"Oh, I will," Ricky assured her.

"You'd kill my sister? You said you loved me. If you really did, you couldn't kill my sister," Isabella countered.

"I don't want to kill her, but I most certainly will if you leave me no choice. It's not too late," Ricky sounded a little desperate now. "We can still do what we planned. We can take your sister back to the car and drive to the cabin. We can keep her alive, Annabelle, too. We can be a family. We can get married just like we wanted. And Sophie—you and your sister can raise her. You get what you want, a husband, a family, your sister, and I get what I want, Annabelle. It's not too late," he repeated beseechingly.

For a moment, it looked like Isabella was going to cave in, do what Ricky wanted. Sofia tensed, trying to still the tremors racking her body enough so she could focus. Between Ricky and Isabella, her chances of getting away were slim, but she wasn't going down without a fight. She wasn't going to willingly surrender and let them lock her away in some remote cabin for the rest of her life so Ricky could rape her whenever he pleased.

"I'm sorry, Ricky." Isabella looked genuinely remorseful. "It's already too late. Earlier I didn't call to check on Sophie. I called Ryan. I asked him to come and get Sofia. I couldn't go through with it. I'm sorry."

"Then I have nothing to lose," Ricky said.

What happened next became all hazy and jumbled in her memory.

Ricky plunged the knife into her stomach.

Sofia was immediately engulfed in white-hot burning pain. Warm, sticky blood gushed from her wound. As she looked down, her gray sweatshirt slowly turned red, the stain growing bigger and bigger.

Immediately light-headed, all Sofia could do was slump down against the cold earth. She knew she was completely helpless now, at the mercy of Ricky and Isabella, but there was nothing she could do about it. Her head was swirling so badly she had to clench her eyes closed in a desperate bid to control it and remain conscious.

Above her there was a loud bang.

It sounded like a gunshot, but she was too dizzy to put much effort into figuring out what was going on.

Something beside her went thunk. The sound seemed to reverberate through the dirt and into her head.

There was another bang.

Another gunshot?

Then footsteps.

Maybe someone shouted her name?

Then nothing.

* * * * *

2:10 A.M.

She had just shot someone.

Annabelle couldn't believe she'd done it. But she hadn't had a choice.

Back at the car, when Isabella Everette had come at her with

270

the knife she had been convinced that she was about to die. However, the younger woman had simply sawed through the bindings then tossed her the knife.

It hadn't taken Annabelle long to free her ankles, but it took a moment before circulation was restored enough for her to walk. She hadn't had to debate what to do next. She wasn't going to hide and wait for Ryan, and presumably Xavier, to come and find her. Ricky Preston had Sofia, and he was planning on raping her. Isabella had taken off after them, supposedly concerned for her sister's safety, but Annabelle couldn't be sure she truly was. Isabella was just as responsible for abducting them, restraining them, and tossing them in the trunk as Ricky was.

So, Annabelle knew she had to go after them.

She couldn't go unarmed, though.

Rifling through the car, she had come across a gun. Annabelle had never shot a gun in her life. Never even touched one. But that didn't matter now. All that mattered was finding Sofia so they could both go home.

Praying that Xavier and Ryan weren't far away, she had headed off in the same direction as Isabella. She had wandered through the woods for a while before finally stumbling upon them.

When she found them, Sofia had been lying on the ground. She wasn't moving. And Annabelle could see, even from where she was, that the front of Sofia's clothing was drenched in blood.

While her gaze had been riveted on Sofia's white face, a gunshot had gone off. On instinct, she had reacted. Shooting at the only person left standing. Hitting Isabella Everette.

The woman had dropped instantly.

A small red dot on her back.

Remaining where she was for a moment, when Isabella didn't move, just lay where she'd fallen, face down in the snow, Annabelle ran to Sofia's side.

"Sofia?" she called as she crouched beside her still form, pulling the tape off Sofia's mouth.

For the longest moment Sofia just lay there, unresponsive, then her eyelids began to flutter, then opened, blinking as if trying to focus. "Annabelle?"

She sighed in relief. "Yeah, its me."

"What happened?" Sofia's voice was weak, barely more than a whisper.

"You don't remember?" Annabelle didn't know a lot about first aid but she thought that was a bad sign, maybe Sofia had hit her head.

She scrunched up her face. "Ricky stabbed me, then there was a bang. No, two bangs. Gunshots? Isabella and Ricky, they're both dead?" she asked, she was shivering violently, her teeth chattering.

"Yeah, I'm sorry." Annabelle knew that Sofia loved her sister, and no matter what, she was going to be devastated that she was dead. How would she react when she found out that she was the one who had done it? That was something to worry about later. Right now, she had to tend to Sofia until Xavier and Ryan found them. On the plus side, Ricky Preston was dead. Isabella had shot him. Now he could never hurt her again. The sense of relief was overwhelming.

"I need to see her." Sofia made a feeble attempt at moving, but was hampered by her injury and her binds.

"I think you better stay still; you're bleeding pretty badly," Annabelle cautioned.

"Bleeding?" Sofia repeated.

"From the knife wound," Annabelle reminded her, pulling out the knife Isabella had given her earlier. "Let me cut you free, then I'll find something to use on your wound." Trying to be gentle, she eased Sofia, who moaned with pain, onto her side so she could cut the plastic tie, releasing Sofia's bloody wrists.

Turning her so she lay on her back once again, Annabelle searched for something to use to stop the bleeding. She was wearing only jeans and a hoodie, but Isabella had on a scarf.

Attempting not to look directly at Isabella's lifeless eyes, she quickly yanked off the scarf and pressed it to Sofia's wound. "I'm going to tie this around your waist," she informed Sofia as she tugged it underneath her and tied it as tightly as she could.

Reluctantly, Annabelle brought up the next pressing issue, attempting to make her voice gentle. "Sofia? Your pants are pulled down; did Ricky rape you?" Having to ask someone else, that brought home how awful it must have been for Xavier to have to tell her about what Ricky had done to her.

Tears welled up in her eyes. "He started to, but Isabella stopped him," she whispered.

"Okay," she brushed softly at Sofia's red hair, "let's pull your pants back up, you're already so cold." Trying to be as careful as she could, Annabelle got Sofia's pants sorted.

Now she had to figure out what to do next. They could wait here for Xavier and Ryan to find them, but who knew how long that would be? Even if they found the car, they'd still have to search the woods for them. It could take them hours to locate where they were. Sofia was bleeding, and already hypothermic, they couldn't stay put. They were going to have to try and make it back to the car. The car would provide warmth, and if Ricky had left the keys, then Annabelle could drive and meet the guys partway. Walking for the car was risky, too. Annabelle wasn't entirely sure of the way back, and Sofia was injured and she wasn't wearing any shoes. Still, it seemed like the only viable option.

"Sofia?"

Slowly, her gray eyes opened. "Yeah?"

"Do you think you can walk? I know you're hurt, but you're too cold, you can't stay out here any longer. We have to get you someplace warm. We need to get back to the car; do you think you can make it?"

"Yeah, I can make it," Sofia said bravely, although in her eyes was doubt.

"I'll help you, we'll go as slowly as you need to," Annabelle assured her. Sofia's body temperature should start to rise if they kept moving. She slipped an arm around Sofia's shoulders and she helped her to slowly rise. Sofia whimpered in pain, but didn't complain. Keeping an arm around her waist to keep her upright, Annabelle gave her a moment to get herself together before they started moving.

Their progress was painstakingly slow. Sofia was weak, both from blood loss and hypothermia. Her bad leg was obviously making things more difficult for her, and her feet seemed to be bothering her, too. Annabelle considered giving Sofia her shoes, but realized that wasn't going to work. One of them had to be able to walk properly, and since Sofia was already half-unconscious on her feet it was going to have to be her.

Annabelle wasn't used to having people rely on her like that. Sure, her parents had relied on her to run the home and care for her little sister, but that wasn't the same. No one's life was at stake. This was different. This was all up to her. The responsibility was overwhelming, but also invigorating. It felt good to be needed. It also felt good to know that she could do it. She could get Sofia to the car and warm her up. In fact, with Ricky Preston dead, there wasn't anything she couldn't do now.

Sofia stumbled again, but Annabelle managed to keep her on her feet, although she was now carrying most of Sofia's weight. "You doing okay? Do you need to take a break?"

"I'm okay, just dizzy," Sofia gasped through her chattering teeth.

"All right, a little farther then we'll rest for a bit," Annabelle assured her. They couldn't afford to rest for too long. The quicker they got Sofia someplace warm the better, but she also couldn't push her so hard that she passed out. If Sofia lost consciousness, there was no way Annabelle could get her back to the car.

They made it another five minutes or so before Sofia all but collapsed. Annabelle lowered her to the ground and propped her up against a tree. Sofia rested her head back against the trunk and closed her eyes. Her skin was pale—too pale—a bluish tint on her lips. Her skin felt like ice. She was still shivering, but her shivers were starting to fade. Annabelle knew that wasn't a good sign. As long as her body was shivering, it was trying to create heat. Once it stopped, they were in trouble.

A couple of minutes later Annabelle roused Sofia, helped her to her feet again, and off they set. This time they made it only a few minutes before Sofia sagged against her, and Annabelle was forced to lower her back down to the ground.

"I'm sorry," Sofia murmured, eyes already closed.

"It's fine," Annabelle assured her. "You're doing great."

However, Annabelle knew her assurances weren't founded in fact. They weren't doing great. They weren't making enough progress. Sofia was never going to make it to the car. Eventually she wasn't going to be able to stand up. And that eventually wasn't too far off.

What should Annabelle do then?

Should she leave Sofia and try and find the car herself then lead the guys back to her? Could she even do that? She wasn't an outdoorsy person. She wasn't even sure they were going in the right direction. If she left Sofia, could she find the car alone? And if she did, would she be able to find her way back?

Should she try carrying, or even dragging Sofia along with her? That might make her wound worse. It was still bleeding, and Annabelle didn't know enough about medicine to know how bad it was, but she thought that dragging Sofia probably wasn't the best idea.

Their only option seemed to be to keep moving as best as they could for as long as they could.

"Come on, let's try a little more," Annabelle encouraged, pulling Sofia up alongside her.

"Okay," Sofia groggily agreed.

As they set off again, Annabelle began praying that the guys would arrive soon. If it was up to her, she didn't think she could get either of them out of these woods and to safety.

* * * * *

2:52 A.M.

"Look, there's a car," Ryan gestured at a white sedan a few hundred yards ahead of them.

"Yeah, I see it." Xavier sped up.

Moments later, they were pulling to a stop behind the car. Ryan jumped from the car, gun in hand and was approaching the car before Xavier had even turned the engine off.

The white sedan appeared to be empty. The front passenger door was open, as was the trunk. Xavier came up beside him as he examined the trunk. Inside were three plastic zip ties and smudges of blood.

"They were here," Ryan announced, scanning the woods around them.

"You think they got away?" Xavier asked, picking up the ties and examining them.

"Not unless someone let them," he replied. Bound and locked in the trunk, there was no way the girls had gotten away of their own volition.

"Isabella?"

"That would be my guess," he confirmed. Isabella had had a change of heart; she wasn't going to let Ricky hurt the girls, so it was completely plausible that she had helped them escape.

"Then where are they?" Xavier asked. "She knew we were coming, why wouldn't she be here waiting for us? It's cold out and neither Annabelle nor Sofia were dressed for a winter night, why would she leave the car?"

"Maybe she didn't have a choice," he mused. "She couldn't have called me in front of Ricky. She would have had to leave him alone with the girls to make the call. Maybe when she got back he'd already taken them, or at least one of them," his heart clenched as he thought of what Sofia might be going through as they stood here wondering.

"Yeah, maybe," Xavier agreed. "Which way are we going?"

Examining the woods close to the car, if Ricky had taken one or both girls, he could have hurt them. If they picked the wrong direction, it could be too late to save them by the time they eventually located them. It was dark and determining where the woods had been recently disturbed was difficult. Finally, he stopped in front of a spot where the branches looked broken.

"This way," he announced.

Xavier didn't argue, just drew his gun and followed him into the woods. They walked in silence, both aware that either Ricky or Isabella or both were out here somewhere and that both were still a potential threat.

They had been walking for approximately fifteen minutes when he heard footsteps. A glance at Xavier confirmed that he'd heard them, too. They both froze, listening carefully to gauge which direction the sounds were coming from.

Apparently, whoever it was had already heard them because a tentative voice called out, "Xavier? Ryan?"

Relieved, they both hurried forward, where they found Annabelle with an arm around Sofia's waist. Sofia's arm was slung over Annabelle's shoulder and she leaned heavily against her. Although she was clearly injured, her clothes were ripped, and even from a distance he could see she was shaking, she was still the most beautiful sight he'd ever seen.

"Sofia," Ryan rushed for her. "I got her," he told Annabelle as he extracted Sofia from her grip and swung her up into his arms. "I got you, honey," he told Sofia as he cradled her.

Dazed silver eyes looked up at him as her head drooped against his shoulder. "Ryan?"

"I'm here, cupcake, I'm here," he assured her, pressing a kiss to her forehead. Beside him, Xavier had wrapped his arms around

Annabelle, who was clinging to him.

"Where are Ricky and Isabella?" Xavier asked, he was the only one of them still alert.

"Dead," Annabelle replied. "They're both dead."

Relief rocked through him. Isabella could never hurt Sofia again. Nor could she hurt anyone else. However, he also knew that Sofia was going to be devastated. "Does she know?" he asked Annabelle.

"Yes, but she's been out of it since I found her, so she might not remember," she answered.

In his arms Sofia was shivering uncontrollably, her teeth chattering together. She was as cold as ice, her thin sweater and pants were no match for the freezing night, and she wasn't wearing any shoes. There were rips in her clothes and a blood-soaked scarf was wrapped around her stomach. Balancing her from arm to arm, Ryan managed to get his coat off and wrap it around Sofia.

"What happened?" he asked Annabelle.

"Ricky hurt her; stabbed her, I think," she replied. She was shaking, too, burrowed against Xavier's chest.

For a moment, it felt like his heart stopped. "Did he rape her?"

"She said he started, but Isabella stopped him. But he'd pulled her pants down, so he did something," Annabelle added uncomfortably.

Started? What exactly did that mean? Did it mean that he had penetrated her, but never finished the act? Did it mean that he had never done more than remove her clothing? A glance at Sofia indicated he wasn't going to get any answers to his questions for a while; she was barely conscious. Right now, his priority was her physical condition—the most pressing, the cause of her bleeding. He was about to set her down on the ground to examine her wound when Xavier stopped him.

"Don't put her down." Xavier released Annabelle and stepped closer. "She's cold enough as it is. I'll check her out."

As carefully as he could, Xavier unwound the scarf, tossed it aside, then lifted the hem of her sweatshirt. Sofia moaned in pain and buried her face against his neck.

"Sorry, honey," Xavier apologized. "I'm being as gentle as I can, but I need to look at this."

"How bad is it?" Ryan asked fearfully. They were miles from anywhere, and it had already been a while since she was stabbed. If the wound was too bad, she could bleed out before they got her the medical attention she needed.

"It's deep, but not too deep," Xavier assured him. "Her low body temperature is probably helping keep blood loss at a minimum."

Adrenalin was masking his own cold. "Here, you hold her; I'll take my shirt off so we can bandage her wound," Ryan went to pass Sofia to Xavier, but once more the other man stopped him.

"No, she needs your body heat," Xavier reminded him. Shrugging out of his coat, he didn't bother undoing the buttons, just simply pulled his shirt over his head, then put his jacket back on. "Sorry, Sofia," Xavier apologized once more. "This is going to hurt, but I need to make it as tight as I can because your wound is still bleeding."

Sofia whimpered softly, snuggling closer, as Xavier pressed his shirt against her wound and then tied it tightly around her middle. She was still shivering, which was a good thing because it indicated her body was still attempting to generate heat, but she was cold. Too cold. No doubt already hypothermic. They needed to get her back to the car immediately.

"All right, let's go," Ryan announced as soon as Xavier was finished attending to Sofia's injury. "Sofia's hypothermic; you probably are, too." He cast a glance at a shivering Annabelle. "You aren't dressed much warmer than she is. We need to get you both someplace warm."

"I'm fine," Annabelle assured them through chattering teeth.

"No, you're not," Xavier pulled her to him. "Did Ricky do

anything to you?"

Annabelle shook her head and rested against him.

"Good." Xavier kissed the top of her head. "Let's move. Can you walk?" he asked Annabelle.

"Yes," Annabelle said tiredly.

They hadn't been walking more than a couple of minutes when they heard the crunch of footsteps. Freezing, he and Xavier exchanged glances. Someone was out here. And it wasn't Jack, Rose, and backup; they were on their way, but they would have heard sirens and seen flashlights if it was them.

"Are you sure Isabella and Ricky are both dead?" Xavier whispered to Annabelle.

Her white eyes grew wide and she shook her head. "Isabella looked dead, but I never looked at Ricky. He wasn't moving and Sofia was bleeding. I was more focused on her."

"Then he could be out there." Xavier looked panicked now.

"And he's armed," Annabelle looked ready for a full-blown panic attack. "There were two guns. I have the one I found in the car, but Isabella had one, too."

"Get Sofia to the car," Xavier had his own gun back out.

"No, he could double back; go around us and get her," Ryan countered, no way was he leaving a barely conscious Sofia at Ricky Preston's mercy. "I'll hide her someplace. It's dark and he's probably injured, he won't be searching under trees and bushes if he's looking for her. Annabelle should hide, too; then we'll take care of Ricky. Backup should be here soon," he added.

Xavier nodded. "All right."

Leaving Xavier to help find a place for Annabelle to hide, he quickly carried Sofia to a small group of bushes and set her down on the ground. Brushing away as much of the snow as he could, he placed her under the bushes. "Hey," he held Sofia's face between his hands and waited till her heavy eyes blinked open. "I need you to stay here, stay still, and don't make a sound." Sofia gave a groggy nod and Ryan wondered whether his words had even registered. He didn't have time to find out. He pressed a quick kiss to her lips, and then he covered her with branches.

Praying that they found and disabled Ricky Preston quickly, without his body heat, and lying on the cold earth, Sofia was going to succumb to hypothermia much quicker.

Joining Xavier, they began to search the woods. Moving as quickly and as quietly as they could. They had been searching for a good ten minutes without finding a thing. Ryan was ready to give up and suggest that all they had heard was an animal of some sort, when they saw a body lying face down on the ground about twenty yards ahead of them.

A glance at Xavier confirmed that he had seen it, too. With Xavier covering him, Ryan knelt beside the body and pressed his fingers to its neck. Even before he did, he knew what the outcome would be. The body was ice cold, and as he has suspected there was no pulse. Isabella was dead.

"I'm sorry," Xavier murmured quietly. "I know Sofia will be devastated."

Ryan nodded and reached out a hand to close Isabella's eyes.

"Ricky's not here," Xavier continued. "But I see blood."

Following Xavier's gaze, he scanned the surrounding area. "I don't see the gun. Annabelle said she had one; Ricky could have it."

"We have to get back to the girls."

Ryan was about to say that he agreed when he was suddenly hit by a jolt of electricity and collapsed.

* * * * *

3:47 A.M.

They'd been gone too long.

Annabelle was starting to panic.

Scratch that, she was *way* past panic.

She hadn't wanted Xavier to leave her alone. She had wanted him to stay glued to her side. She was cold and tired and scared and she just wanted to go home, climb into bed and curl up in Xavier's arms.

It was probably nothing, anyway.

Ricky Preston was dead.

He had to be.

She couldn't deal with him again.

Why didn't Xavier and Ryan come back?

Maybe she should go and check on Sofia. She hadn't wanted to leave her alone. Sofia was so out of it that if Ricky were still alive and he got to her, she wouldn't be able to do anything to fend him off. Annabelle had wanted to hide with her, but Xavier had insisted they were safer apart. There wasn't a place big enough for them to hide together and remain unseen.

The boys should be here by now.

Even if he wasn't dead, Ricky had to be injured. Isabella had shot him. How long could it realistically take for two able-bodied police officers to locate one wounded man?

That was it.

She was not staying here another second.

She was going to completely lose it if she stayed here alone, crouched under a bush.

Slowly, Annabelle inched her way out while cautiously glancing all around. She didn't see anyone—Xavier, Ryan, or Ricky. More than anything, she wanted to call for Xavier. She wanted him to come and scoop her up and hold her in his arms and make her feel safe. She needed him.

She was unsure what to do next. Should she go and check on Sofia or look for Xavier?

"Hello, Annabelle."

The voice sent shivers up her spine.

It couldn't be. She had been so sure that it was over.

It couldn't be and yet it was.

"Bet you thought I was dead," Ricky teased.

Maybe she was hallucinating—overtired and overstressed and creating her own worst nightmare to torture herself. She deserved to be tortured, she supposed; she had killed a person tonight. Yes, she convinced herself, Ricky was nothing more than a figment of her overwrought imagination.

To persuade herself, she turned around, expecting to see nothing more than a forest full of trees.

But there he was.

Illuminated by the moon's light.

Standing there grinning at her.

Blood covered his coat, but he didn't seem to be bothered by it.

Without even realizing what she was doing, Annabelle was screaming, "Xavier," at the top of her lungs.

"He's not coming," Ricky chuckled.

"Did you kill him?" her voice trembled terribly. She wished she could be brave, that she could stand up to Ricky, find a way to end his reign of terror, but she couldn't. She wasn't strong enough.

"Nope, but he's a little tied up at the moment." Ricky laughed at his own joke.

She let out a relieved breath knowing Ricky hadn't killed Xavier. He could still come and save her. She needed him so badly. She was so used to him taking care of her that she didn't think she could do this on her own. In fact, she knew she couldn't. She was too weak.

"He's not going to come running in to save you this time," Ricky told her.

Of course, he would, Annabelle wanted to yell at him. Xavier always came running to her rescue. Instead of yelling at Ricky, she did what she always did, kept her thoughts to herself and got ready to run.

"I wouldn't do that if I were you," Ricky commented mildly.

"Run, I mean," he added. "I have a gun."

He held it up and it glinted in the moonlight. His comment started the wheels turning in her head. She had a gun, too. It was in the pocket of her hoodie. Without thinking she wrapped a hand around the gun and pulled it out, aiming it at Ricky's head. "Me too," she told him.

Instead of being scared, Ricky merely burst into peals of hysterical laughter. "You're going to shoot me?" He laughed so hard tears were streaming down his cheeks. "You? Annabelle Englewood? The woman who is too scared to actually have a life is going to take one?"

"I killed Isabella," she countered.

"Well, yeah, I guess you did," Ricky drawled. "I wonder how your new friend Sofia will react when she finds out you killed her sister?"

Not for the first time, Annabelle regretted trusting Ricky so much that she had opened up to him. He knew everything about her—all her fears and worries and internal struggles—and he never passed up an opportunity to use it against her.

"Look," he began matter-of-factly, "we both know you aren't going to kill me. And we both know that you're never going to be rid of me. For the rest of your life I am going to be there, haunting you. Everything you do is going to be tainted by me. You'll never be free of me. You may as well give up. Let me have you. I own you, anyway. You can show me where the detectives stashed your friend and the three of us can go away together. Give me the gun." He took a step toward her, hand out ready to receive it.

"No." Her hands trembled, but she didn't lower her weapon.

"Come on, Annabelle," he sounded exasperated now. "You don't have the guts to kill me. You don't have the guts to do anything. You're weak, pathetic, useless. You're nothing but a scared little girl. You may as well give up now. You're already ruined. You're never going to achieve…"

The bang caught her by surprise.

It shouldn't have. She was the one who had pulled the trigger.

Still, the noise was deafening and Ricky suddenly dropping to the ground for some reason seemed incongruous with her firing the gun.

Footsteps sounded and two people appeared before her.

She swung around to face them, gun aimed in their direction.

"Whoa." A tall blond guy, who looked vaguely familiar, held up his hands. "It's okay, we're police officers. You're Annabelle, right? I'm Jack, Ryan's brother."

That made sense, he looked just like Ryan, but her heart was pounding painfully in her chest and she was breathing too shallow and quick. Her head was spinning, making logical thought difficult.

He took a tentative step toward her. "It's all right, it's over. He's dead." Jack cast a glance at the woman who was kneeling beside Ricky's body. She nodded at him in confirmation. "That's Rose; she's my partner. Ryan called us after Isabella called him."

Rose stood. She was tall and had long red hair pulled back in a loose ponytail. "Give me the gun, Annabelle," she said gently.

Annabelle couldn't lower her arms, but she didn't protest when Rose carefully placed her hands on top of hers and twisted the gun from her grip.

"Annabelle?" Rose's hand rested lightly on her shoulder. "Where are the others?"

"We need to get Sofia." Her common sense was slowly returning. "She's hurt; Ricky stabbed her. She's hypothermic, too."

"Where is she?" Jack asked.

"Over here." She started jogging toward Sofia, Jack and Rose at her heels. "Ryan hid her over here so Ricky couldn't find her. Under there," Annabelle gestured at the bushes.

Dropping to his knees, Jack shoved the branches aside, then hooked an arm around Sofia's shoulders and dragged her out.

Fingertips pressed to her neck, Jack muttered under his breath as he yanked off his jacket and wrapped it around Sofia's still form.

"Is she...is she dead?" Annabelle fearfully trembled.

"Jack?" Rose sounded just as fearful.

"No, she's not dead," Jack assured them. "But she's not in good shape. Ambulance will be here soon, though," he added upon seeing the looks on their faces.

"Do you know where Ryan and Xavier might be?" Rose asked.

She shook her head. "No, they went looking for Ricky. He must have found them, done something to them because he said Xavier couldn't help me because he was tied up."

They exchanged glances. "How long were they gone before Ricky found you?" Rose asked.

"I don't know. It felt like forever, but maybe only ten minutes," she guessed.

"Then they can't be too far away." Jack picked up Sofia and stood. "We'll look for ten, fifteen minutes, and if we don't find them we'll take you two back to the car and then keep looking."

With Jack carrying Sofia, they set out. Annabelle found herself relieved when Rose slipped an arm around her waist. She hadn't realized just how exhausted she was, but with the adrenalin draining from her system she was shaky now. She just wanted to find Xavier and Ryan and go home.

She got her wish a couple of minutes later.

Xavier and Ryan were tied to a tree, tape over their mouths, but both began fighting their bindings when they saw them. Ryan was staring at Sofia hanging limply in his brother's arms, his blue eyes frantic.

"She's alive," Jack answered Ryan's unasked question. "She's unconscious and she needs immediate medical attention, but she's alive."

Rose released her and rushed toward the guys. Annabelle dropped to her knees at Xavier's side and leaned against him. Still bound, he couldn't hold her, but he rested his head on hers.

"Are you guys okay?" Rose asked as she pulled the tape off their mouths.

"Fine, he got us with a stun gun," Ryan replied.

"Ricky?" Xavier was searching her face anxiously.

"He's dead," she whispered, pressing closer against him, needing him more than she ever had before. "I killed him." Annabelle wasn't sure how she felt about that. Part of her felt stronger. She wasn't weak and pathetic anymore. She'd been scared, but she'd done what she had to do. This time she hadn't just sat back and waited for someone to rescue her. She had saved herself. And yet despite all that, the knowledge that she had killed two people tonight left her feeling shaky and disconnected.

"Are you all right?" Xavier quietly asked her.

"I don't know," she answered honestly. "I just want to go home."

"Me too." Xavier gently kissed the top of her head.

The second Rose, who had been sawing through the ropes with a knife, had them free, Ryan jumped to his feet and took Sofia from his brother's arms.

Xavier stood, too, bringing Annabelle up with him and holding her tightly against his chest. She could feel him trembling and knew just how scared he had been, tied up and unable to get to her, knowing that Ricky was out there somewhere.

"Okay, let's get the four of you to the hospital," Jack announced. "And no arguments," he added before all of them, bar Sofia, could protest that they were fine. "You are all getting checked out."

The prospect of traipsing through the woods one more time was an exhausting one. Annabelle consoled herself with the fact that warmth and home were waiting for her. She was cold now and dead tired. It turned out she didn't have to walk another step. Xavier put an arm around her shoulders and his other under her knees and lifted her up.

"I can walk," she objected, even as she snuggled closer.

"Shh, just rest," was all Xavier said as he began walking with her.

And that was exactly what Annabelle did. She laid her head on Xavier's shoulder, closed her eyes, and was asleep before they made it back to the car.

* * * * *

5:03 P.M.

She was warm.

That was the first thing that occurred to Sofia as she slowly swam back to consciousness.

She wasn't sure where she was. The last thing she remembered was Ryan laying her down on the cold ground and telling her to stay still and quiet. But she didn't think she was still in the woods. Wherever she was now, it was too warm. And the woods had been so cold. Her body had been shaking so violently that her muscles had started to ache. It had been all she could think about. The cold had even overridden the pain in her stomach.

Voices were speaking quietly above her.

"Hey, how's she doing?"

"Better. Her core temperature is almost back to normal."

"How did her surgery go?"

"It went well. They were able to repair the damage. She lost a fair bit of blood, but thankfully, the cold helped her out on that one."

Were they talking about her? Was she in the hospital?

"How are you doing?"

Sofia thought that was Ryan's voice. Knowing he was here with her made her feel better.

"I'm doing okay," someone replied. Annabelle, maybe?

"Hospital released you?" Ryan asked.

"Yeah, a while ago. I pretty much warmed up in the car before we even got here. I spent some time with my therapist," Annabelle responded.

"That's good. You have a lot to sort out, but at least it's over for you now. You saved Sofia's life last night; thank you," Ryan's voice wavered with emotion.

"I just hope she's not angry with me." Annabelle's voice was also heavy with emotion.

Why would she be angry with Annabelle? Sofia wondered. She wanted to open her eyes and ask, but she didn't seem to have the energy.

"She won't be," Ryan assured her.

Sofia would have echoed that sentiment if she could have.

"Any word on Paige?" Xavier asked.

Paige? Sofia felt a slice of panic shoot through her. What had happened to Paige?

"She's still stable," Ryan answered. "I checked in on her a while ago."

"Did you sort it out?" Xavier asked.

"Jack and Rose are taking care of it." She could hear a smile in Ryan's voice now.

"She's going to be so surprised." Xavier, too, sounded happy. "We're going to go home, let Annabelle get some rest, but call if you need anything, or if there's any change with Sofia or Paige…"

The voices got quieter for a moment. And then Sofia felt Ryan's presence right beside her. She wanted to wake up properly. To find out what was going on. Pulling herself together, she managed to blink open her heavy eyes. She found herself in a hospital bed, wrapped in a warm blanket, attached to machinery, with Ryan in a chair at her side. He had his eyes closed, his head resting against the back of the chair, and he held her hand.

Sofia tried to call out to him, but her throat was too dry to produce a sound. Instead, she managed to lightly squeeze the hand that held hers.

Immediately, Ryan sat up, a smile lighting his face when he saw her awake. "Hi there, beautiful."

He moved to perch on the side of her bed, his weight made the mattress move slightly which made her stomach ache, but Sofia didn't mind. She was just happy to be alive and safe. "Hi," she managed to croak.

"Here." He held a straw to her lips, and she took a sip. The cold water felt so good sliding down her parched throat.

There were so many things she wanted to ask him, but she started with the most important. "Isabella?"

"I'm so sorry, cupcake, she's dead," his grip on her hand tightened. "I'm so sorry."

Tears welled up in her eyes. "She saved me."

"Shh, I know she did." Ryan brushed at the tears trickling from the corners of her eyes.

"Ricky was going to rape me, but Isabella stopped him. Then he threatened to kill me, but she wouldn't let him. She saved me, Ryan." She was crying in earnest now. It made her stomach hurt worse, but she couldn't seem to stop.

"I know, baby, I know; she loved you," Ryan tried to console her.

"She couldn't go through with it. She was going to let him have me, but she couldn't; she couldn't do it." Sofia had the feeling she was rambling incoherently.

However, Ryan seemed to understand her. "I know, sweetheart; she called me, asked me to come and get you."

The more she cried, the worse the pain became. "I hurt," she whimpered through her tears.

"I know, cupcake." Ryan looked so helpless; she knew he hated it when she was hurting and he couldn't fix it for her. "Ricky stabbed you, do you remember?"

She managed a nod as she struggled to control her crying.

"You were in pretty bad shape by the time Xavier and I got to you and Annabelle." He was stroking her hair with one hand, hoping to help calm her, while his other hand still held hers. "By the time Jack and Rose arrived, you were completely unresponsive. You gave us quite a scare. Once we got you to the car we wrapped you up in blankets, with hot water bottles, and the heater blasting. Then the paramedics arrived and used heating blankets, but for a while they couldn't get your temperature to start going up."

"Sorry I scared you," she sniffed.

Ryan smiled and kissed her softly on the lips. "I'm just glad you're okay now. Although you're going to be in the hospital for a few days at least," he told her apologetically. He knew how she felt about the hospital after her last long stint.

"I don't care. I'm just glad I'm safe now. Why would Annabelle think I'd be angry with her?" she asked.

"She's the one who shot Isabella," Ryan told her gently.

"She killed my sister?"

Ryan nodded, "I'm sorry."

Digesting this news, Isabella had been willing to save her, but would she have turned herself in? There were no guarantees on that. Last time, after Sofia had fallen down the stairs, Isabella had made sure Ryan came and rescued her, but hadn't stuck around. She could easily have done the same thing this time. As much as it pained her to admit it, her sister was never going to stop killing.

"Sofia?" Ryan was peering at her in concern.

"I understand. She did the right thing; I don't want her to feel bad about it." She tried to smile at him but feared it came out fairly wobbly. "What happened to Paige?"

His brow furrowed in confusion. "Were you awake earlier? When Xavier and Annabelle were here?"

"Half awake," she replied, aware he was stalling. "What happened to Paige?"

"We can talk about it later; you should rest now," was all Ryan would say.

His non-answer only made her anxiety grow. "Ryan? I need to know. Did something happen to her? Is she okay? You said she was stable. Is she here in the hospital?"

"Paige was attacked," he reluctantly told her.

"Is that why you wouldn't answer my calls the other night?"

"I'm sorry." Ryan looked a mixture of devastated and guilty. "Maybe if I'd talked to you, let you know what had happened, then Ricky and Isabella wouldn't have had a chance to get their hands on you and Annabelle."

She shook her head. "Life doesn't work that way, you know that. Was is it her stalker?" she asked.

"Yes," Ryan nodded.

He was holding something back. "Do you know who it is?"

"Yes and no."

She was too tired to figure out why he was being so vague. "What aren't you telling me?"

He sighed. "I don't think you need to know this right now. I was going to wait until you were stronger, but since you know about Paige, I may as well tell you. Paige was attacked by your stalker."

Shocked, Sofia could only gasp in response. Her stalker had attacked Paige? Paige was in the hospital because of her. It was her fault. If she had only managed to figure out who it was who was stalking her, then this wouldn't have happened. If she had been a better aim and managed to shoot the stalker the other night, then this wouldn't have happened. If Ryan hadn't had to make sure she was okay, then he could have caught the stalker the night they were together when he broke in. This was all because of her. Paige was her friend, and she had been hurt. How could she ever forgive herself for letting this happen?

"Sofia?" Ryan stopped stroking her hair and took her chin in his hand, giving it a little shake.

"Is she okay? Is Paige okay?" she demanded.

"She was hurt pretty badly; she's in the ICU," Ryan replied.

"I want to see her." Sofia tried to wiggle free from Ryan's grip so she could throw back the covers and climb out of bed.

He held her in place. "You're not going anywhere. You're still weak, you need to rest. You can see Paige later," he promised.

"Is she going to be okay?" She was chewing on her lip to keep from bursting into another round of crying.

"She was bleeding internally, but the doctors were able to find and fix everything. But she suffered some serious head injuries, and they won't know the extent of the damage until she wakes up."

"She hasn't woken up yet?" She could practically feel her pulse and blood pressure spike in alarm as her guilt grew.

"No," Ryan cast a concerned glance at the monitors beside her bed. "But when I found her at the scene, she was conscious and lucid. Those are good signs, Sofia." Ryan leaned closer. "We just have to trust and pray that she'll be all right. And don't even think about blaming yourself," he added. "It is not your fault."

She didn't agree but was too worn out to argue.

"Hey," Ryan brushed his knuckles across her cheek. "I have a surprise for you. Something that is guaranteed to cheer you up."

"Maybe later; I'm tired. Maybe I should just go back to sleep."

"You're going to want to see this, I promise." Ryan smiled at her, kissed her again, then stood, "I'll be right back."

Once Ryan was gone, she closed her eyes and rested wearily against her pillows. She was tired and in pain and all she wanted was to sleep. She was feeling so guilty. Guilty about Isabella. Her sister was—had been, she corrected herself—sick. She'd needed help and Sofia hadn't even noticed. If she had only realized just how sick her sister was, then all of this could have been avoided. She was feeling guilty about Paige, too. Her friends shouldn't get hurt because of her. What if the stalker didn't stop there? He could go after anyone she loved. When Ryan came back, she would ask him why her stalker would attack Paige.

"I have someone here who wants to meet you," Ryan announced as he came back through the doors.

When Sofia saw who was with him, everything else flew from

her mind. "Is that who I think it is?" she asked, a smile spreading across her lips despite herself.

"Yep," Ryan grinned. "Sofia, meet Sophie." He carried the baby over to her.

"She's so beautiful," she gushed, running her fingers across the baby's silky soft head. "Can I hold her?"

"Sure." Ryan balanced the baby in one arm and helped her sit up a little more with his other, then he placed Sophie in her outstretched arms.

Cradling the tiny little girl, tears began to trickle down her cheeks again. Only this time they were happy tears. "How did you find her?" she asked Ryan.

"Isabella texted me the address after she called to ask me to come and get you; she asked me to give her to you." Ryan sat back down on the edge of her bed. "As soon as we all got to the hospital, Jack and Rose went to pick her up."

She was almost afraid to ask in case the answer was no, but she asked anyway. "Can I keep her?"

"Yeah, you can. Brooke's parents don't want her, and you're her only living relative on her father's side. Stephanie has already taken a DNA sample to confirm she is Brooke and Logan's baby, but CPS is happy for you to keep the baby now. We'll call your lawyer, get the adoption papers drawn up, and then she is officially yours forever." Ryan took her hand and one of Sophie's little ones.

"Officially ours," she corrected. "You're going to raise her with me, right?"

"Honey, you couldn't keep me away from the two of you if you tried," Ryan assured her. Reaching into his pocket, he produced a small black velvet box, opening it to reveal a sparkling diamond ring. "Sofia, will you marry me?"

For a moment, all she could do was stare. "Are you sure? Is now the right time? Maybe we should wait till things settle down. Maybe we should wait until Sophie gets settled with us. Maybe we should wait…"

"Cupcake, I'm not waiting another second. I've already been waiting to ask you this since I found out you and Edmund were just friends," Ryan told her.

"Yes," she said, just as Sophie cooed and then giggled. "I think Sophie says yes, too," she laughed.

Sliding the ring onto her finger, Ryan kissed her and then pressed a kiss to the baby's head. "I love you."

"I love you, too." They gazed into each other's eyes until the door to her hospital room swung open and a doctor bustled in.

"Sorry to interrupt, Ms. Everette," he apologized. "I'm Dr. Daniels. You've been asleep since you came in so we haven't met yet, but I've been treating you since you came here after your surgery."

"Hi." She shot the doctor a distracted smile; she knew he was just doing his job, but she just wanted to be with her family right now. *Family*. That word had never sounded so wonderful. She and Ryan and Sophie—they were a family now.

"Sorry, Mr. Xander, but she needs her rest." Dr. Daniels shot Ryan a pointed look.

"Yeah, you should take Sophie home." Sofia didn't want either of them to leave her, but she was tired, and Sophie should go home, have dinner and a bath and go to bed. "Oh, we don't have any baby things," she suddenly realized.

"I'm not going anywhere," Ryan assured her. "Mark said he'll look after Sophie at his house until you get out of here. And he and Helen dropped their extra baby stuff off at your house already. They still had the extra crib and change table from the twins. They were just sitting in their garage so they offered to set them up in our guest room. I said yes; I hope you don't mind."

"I don't mind at all," she told him.

"There's the twins old baby clothes, too, plus some of the toys and bottles and things that Tony doesn't use anymore. Trust me, we have more baby things than we are ever going to need," Ryan grinned.

"Will Mark bring her back tomorrow?" she asked anxiously, already unwilling to be away from the baby for too long.

"You bet he will," Ryan promised. "I'll let Dr. Daniels check you out and go give Sophie to Mark, and then I'll be back."

Sofia didn't pay attention to Dr. Daniels as he checked her vitals and the wound on her stomach. She was so happy and had everything she'd ever wanted—a man who loved her, a baby to raise, a family of her own. A family different than the one she grew up in. A family full of love.

Content, she closed her eyes and drifted off to sleep.

* * * * *

6:00 P.M.

Closing the door behind him, Dr. Bruce Daniels sighed in relief.

She didn't know.

She hadn't recognized him.

If he had his way, Sofia would never know that it was he who was looking out for her. He didn't need the recognition. That wasn't why he was doing this. He just wanted to make sure that Sofia remained safe and happy. She deserved happiness. That family of hers was a nightmare. He was glad that Isabella had eliminated them. If she hadn't, he might have been tempted to do it himself.

He wouldn't let anyone hurt her.

Although she had helped Sofia by killing off their family, he was glad Isabella was dead. She caused Sofia pain and he couldn't allow that.

And now Sofia had a family of her own.

Ryan and the baby.

So long as Ryan didn't hurt Sofia, then he was happy for them to remain a couple.

Sofia's happiness was paramount.

She was all he had.

She was the center of his world, and he would do whatever was necessary to make sure she remained happy.

It had been a mistake earlier to beat up the other woman. Detective Paige Hood. He had been distracted and Sofia had been abducted, nearly killed.

He wouldn't make that mistake again.

Still, he had probably scared Paige away from Ryan. If the woman kept her hands on her own husband and off Sofia's man, then he would leave her alone. But if she ever tried to get her claws into Ryan again, he would eliminate her.

He couldn't make any more visits to Sofia's house either.

It was too risky.

He would have to watch her from a distance.

Maybe he could consider buying one of the houses on her block.

That way he would always be close by for whenever she needed him.

No matter what, he would keep watch over Sofia.

He was her guardian angel and he wasn't going anywhere.

Jane has loved reading and writing since she can remember. She writes dark and disturbing crime/mystery/suspense with some romance thrown in because, well, who doesn't love romance?! She has several series including the complete Detective Parker Bell series, the Count to Ten series, the Christmas Romantic Suspense series, and the Flashes of Fate series of novelettes.

When she's not writing Jane loves to read, bake, go to the beach, ski, horse ride, and watch Disney movies. She has a black belt in Taekwondo, a 200+ collection of teddy bears, and her favorite color is pink. She has the world's two most sweet and pretty Dalmatians, Ivory and Pearl. Oh, and she also enjoys spending time with family and friends!

For more information please visit any of the following –

Amazon – http://www.amazon.com/author/janeblythe
BookBub – https://www.bookbub.com/authors/jane-blythe
Email – mailto:janeblytheauthor@gmail.com
Facebook – http://www.facebook.com/janeblytheauthor
Goodreads – http://www.goodreads.com/author/show/6574160.Jane_Blythe
Instagram – http://www.instagram.com/jane_blythe_author
Reader Group – http://www.facebook.com/groups/janeskillersweethearts
Twitter – http://www.twitter.com/jblytheauthor
Website – http://www.janeblythe.com.au

sic enim dilexit Deus mundum ut Filium suum unigenitum daret ut omnis qui credit in eum habeat vitam aeternam

CPSIA information can be obtained
at www.ICGtesting.com
Printed in the USA
BVHW031018060423
661876BV00003B/23